Incident at Forest Glen

A novel by
Andy Johnson

Copyright © 2012 Andy Johnson
All rights reserved.

ISBN: 1-4783-8949-4
ISBN-13: 9781478389491

Beholding the bright
countenance of truth
in the quiet and still
air of delightful studies

John Milton

Chapter 1
Mermaid of the Glen

What incidentally becomes of the great majority who quietly take up the burden of womanhood and motherhood with such training as they can get? Should there not be some place where the girl who seeks training of any kind, may without hindrance or "entrance conditions" other than her ability to grasp the subject, find what she desires? Year by year the colleges lay heavier burdens upon the preparatory schools, and the danger is, that, losing all individuality, they will become mere adjuncts of the college system, slaves of a prescribed routine, drudges of the educational household, where so many pages are to be conned, so many books to be finished. Their pupils may not taste the sweets of the garden of knowledge; they may only dig among the bitter roots. And so digging, who can blame them if they lay down their tools and refuse to believe in the glorious college fruits to come? We are not so handicapped at the National Park Seminary for Women. We are free to develop the whole being by whatever courses, whatever means, we find most effective.

"Our Educational View"
The National Park Seminary for Young Women
Forest Glen, Maryland 1921

An early December front moving slowly across the Alleghenies stalls and drapes a heavy gray pall of clouds over the National Park Seminary. Cold rain falls incessantly and strips the trees of most of their remaining autumn color. Wet leaves blanket the manicured lawns and fill the fountain basins and roof gutters with impressionistic splashes of shimmering orange, red and yellow. Shrubs and perennials, carefully tended in majestic beds and a multitude of stone vases and urns, are lashed by the storm, their stems bowed and roots exposed.

When the saturated soil can take no more, low-lying ponds fed by rivulets of rain appear across the sprawling grounds. Water inundates the winding paths connecting the Seminary's buildings and cascades over the numerous retaining walls that give the expansive, sylvan campus its artificial contours.

By the deluge's second day, a continual rush of water flows down the steep ravine running along the school's northern boundary to the brook that bisects the lush glen routinely enjoyed by students. A serpentine stone staircase linking the lawn in front of Vincent Hall to the glen below carries the rain like a mining sluice to the banks of the engorged stream. The accumulated flotsam of downed branches, leaves and uprooted plantings unable to withstand the cascading torrent are swept away into the rising Rock Creek.

Thick mist veils the Seminary in a gauzy film and turns the sodden landscape into a dull canvas of drab buildings and abandoned walkways. The dense, protective forest of oak and cedar and walnut that encircles the isolated school ripples and sways as the storm's fury intensifies. At night, when all inside is still, girls unable to sleep lie in their darkened beds, covers pulled tight, and listen to the far-off cry of the wind rushing through the strained boughs, an unnerving sound, like that of a wailing banshee inhabiting the forest, that fuels their nocturnal fears.

While the protracted rain dampens the seasonal spirit of the students, the daily regimentation of school activities continues on. After breakfast, dutifully served at seven o'clock in the ornate dining room, small groups of young women depart their dormitories in the half-light of daybreak under phalanxes of umbrellas and head off to their Latin instruction and history lectures and music recitals. Following their morning studies, students race through the punishing sheets of cold rain and seek sanctuary in the school chapel before the luncheon period begins and, once inside and quieted, pray dutifully while raindrops roll off their cheeks and arms and legs and form puddles on the roughly-hewn, slate floor.

Afternoon time devoted for walking the grounds and other forms of outdoor recreation is necessarily cancelled until the storm releases its hold.

Girls instead decamp to their dormitory rooms and hang wet stockings across radiators or huddle at their sorority clubhouses around fires fed from dwindling stocks of dry timber. No matter how many burning hearths are stoked, however, a musty, unshakeable chill permeates the rooms and hallways of National Park Seminary and summons tiny bumps on the pale flesh of its inhabitants.

A growing restlessness spreads throughout the captive student body. The downpour pounds the roofs and eaves, and tattles against the window panes, the relentless sound maddening to those inside forced to wait out the tempest. Impatient girls deprived of their lush playground pace about their rooms, occasionally stopping to wipe away the persistent condensation that blurs the smooth, cold panes. In the evening, silhouetted figures in night gowns appear at lighted windows throughout the campus wondering and waiting for when their imprisonment will end.

Water everywhere. Water gushing from the down spouts. Water seeping through door jambs. Water trickling from stained, bubbled ceilings. Rain drops plinking against chimney flues. Mildewed towels overlapping crowded rods. Pervasive, indelible dampness. In the girls' clothes. In their shoes. In their hair. Thinly coating the service stemware on the dining room tables. Moisture absorbed in the very wallpaper lining the hallways and rooms of the students' redoubt.

Water everywhere. Inescapable and cursed. It turns the equestrian paddock into a soupy quagmire. It fills the storage basement beneath the servants' quarters. It penetrates the sky light caulking above the library reading room and trickles into a catch-bucket, bringing the sound of an exotic waterfall to the usually hushed and staid surroundings. Polished floors and hallways are coated with a powdery brown grit from muddied shoes and boots. And while an army of maids hurry about the dormitories and parlors and classrooms feverishly sweeping up the fine residue of dirt, they are powerless to rid the school of the insidious reminder of the siege the Seminary students are forced to endure.

Throughout this confinement the plaintive call of a solitary and unseen crow pierces the diaphanous, moisture-laden air and echoes throughout the grounds, unanswered and lonely. The boisterous bird, with its glistening ebony wings and stout beak, has settled in among the battered woods and stands sentry over the deserted fields and gardens during the interminable rain, patrolling about the rooftops and alighting on the heads of statuary dotting the dreary and forsaken landscape, looking to scavenge a meal.

In the predawn hours of the storm's fourth day, the turbulent, muddy Rock Creek rises and crests its banks. The fast-moving water quickly covers the saturated ground with the rapacity of a soulless viper.

An abandoned stone and timber home upstream of Forest Glen, built by the owner of a nearby dilapidated grist mill, is the first enveloped by the flood, the spreading waters lapping at the bowed and splintered porch and quickly swamping the smokehouse cellar. The water rolls on past the encircled homestead, diverging from the path of the creek, as if with conscious independence, and slithers across the grove before melting into the thick underbrush.

Minutes after the creek banks are breached, the son of a local orchard owner is stirred from his sleep by a faint pounding sound outside his bedroom window. A shrill, panicked noise follows and snaps the stout boy out of his somnolent state and he staggers from his bed. He navigates his way across the living room in the dark and rushes out the front door shoeless into the heavy rain, astonished to see the black water overrunning rows and rows of apple trees. In the open air, the arrhythmic blows that woke the boy are clearer and coming from beyond a nearby hill. He squints off into the distance and sees that the renegade water is flowing toward the family barn. He makes out little else in the pelting downpour other than the vapor of his own breath and runs off toward the frantic hammering.

The rush of chilled rain over his exposed feet and ankles makes it difficult for the boy to secure his footing and when he reaches the sloping ground he catches his toe on a submerged stone, slips and tumbles out of control down the hill toward the barn.

The disoriented boy's descent is violently halted at the bottom by the wide trunk of a red oak. The stinging blow catches him flush on the cheek and chest and sends him immediately to the edge of unconsciousness. He hugs the tree instinctively like a fighter sent to the canvas grabs hold of his vanquisher's legs, staggers to his feet, and unsteadily steps toward the commotion.

At the bottom of the hill, the water is knee-high and moving with tremendous force against his wobbly legs. He reaches out and blindly locates a fence post and pauses for a moment to get his bearings. His night clothes are soaked and muddied and cling to his shivering body. Inside his heaving, aching chest, his heart pounds so fiercely he can feel the veins in his temples throb.

The intrepid boy presses on through the torrent and slips past the barn door breached by the force of the onslaught. He hears the snorting of the alarmed mare in the abyss as she thrashes about in the rising water, kicking franticly against the confining walls of her stall. With great dexterity the frightened young man secures his footing and lurches forward, unlocks the stable gate, grabs the panicked animal's mane and guides her outside just as the entire barn starts to bend and shift under pressure from the powerful flood.

Moments later, from a nearby patch of elevated ground, the wide-eyed horse and her panting savior stand alone and watch helplessly as the barn sways, creaks, buckles and then collapses in a horrible explosion of structural sinew twisted and torn from bone.

The emerging aurora on the horizon, shielded by the storm clouds, turns the black skyline a faint gray and the stunned, shivering boy looks back across the ghostly expanse of his family's land and the dark water that covers it, unsure what to do. He calls out to wake his parents but his voice falters and is swallowed up in the rainfall. All he can do is wait, his grip of the mare's stringy mane unyielding as the blood from his shattered nose streams down across his lips and mingles with the mud at his feet.

Less than a mile downstream from the orchard, a maintenance worker flips an electrical switch inside a cinder block building hidden along the backside of the National Park Seminary campus and a necklace of pole lanterns bordering the walkways and bridges sputter and come to life, casting cones of illumination on the multitude of dormant buildings populating the cold, dormant land.

Senior House, one of the Seminary's five dormitories, occupies the privileged location nearest Vincent Hall, the school's imposing main building. For first-time students and visitors approaching the Seminary on the foot bridge spanning the glen, Senior House rises up before them framed by a gap in the trees, their initial glimpse up-close of the eclectic architecture for which the unorthodox educational institution is widely known.

Residence there is restricted to only those of the graduating class deemed by the class regents to have demonstrated exemplary maturity during their time at the school. Selection is by written invitation and is more than honorific. The rooms at Senior House are more spacious than those at the other dormitories and are decorated with the finest European antiques and ornate fixtures bought by school officials during overseas trips. On each of the dormitory's floors, hallway corridors connect the rooms to a central parlor where the students meet and socialize after hours beyond the observance of the faculty and without restriction of curfew. In the view of the school's administration, the young women of Senior House have earned such privilege and confidence, and in all the years the policy has been in effect, the trust placed in the leaders of the graduating class has never been violated.

The three-story structure with its central turret and peaked roofs decorated with layers of wooden shingles in turn of the century style stands out prominently among the nearby school buildings. Rectangular blocks of red sandstone cut from the nearby Seneca quarry form the house's above-ground foundation and first floor. The dormitory's brick façade is offset by white picket porch railings that give each resident access to a series of communal balconies overlooking the grounds and the deep ravine beyond.

Along the front of the building, atop a series of half-moon stone arches, is a wide, gable-roofed veranda which provides a larger outside assembly area. Guests invited to join the women of Senior House for socials on the veranda typically bypass the dormitory's front entrance and proceed along the campus walkway around to the side of the building where a steep, flared stairway leads to wicker chairs and settees and decorative flower vases. Along the way, students pass a distinctive plum-leaf English Oak planted by the senior class of 1915 to commemorate the century of peace between the United States and Great Britain following the War of 1812.

Above Senior House's foundation arches is a living tapestry of climbing ivy that spreads overtop the stairway railing and upward along the porch supports to the upper floors. This tightly-woven blanket of stems and leaves is actually a composite of individual vines acquired over time from hallowed lands and venerated sites by past senior classes and ceremonially transplanted prior to graduation. Ivy plants from Gettysburg, Stratford upon Avon, Walden Pond, and elsewhere form what became known as the Wall of Eternity, symbolizing not only the lasting spiritual bond between student and school but the permanence of the classical teachings constituting the marrow of Forest Glen's philosophy.

At a distance, the Wall of Eternity is a suspended wave of the deepest green, frozen in time as it crashes against and embraces Senior House. Only by pushing aside the dense overlapping leaves, however, can one observe through closer inspection the hidden subterfuge wrought by the pliable root tendrils gripping and insinuating themselves into the building's mortar.

Josephine Barnes is first in Senior House to wake. The lashing sound of the rainfall against her window roused her repeatedly throughout the night and made sleep fitful. Slipping out of the sheet linen, she stands and reaches to the ceiling, unfurling her lithe form in an elongating stretch, fingers spread, toes pushing off the rug. She feels a not unpleasant tightness along her calves and neck as she reaches higher, her curled blond hair tossed back between her shoulder blades. A deep inhalation and she feels the vertebrae along the small of her back click in succession like tumblers of a lock.

She loosely wraps a coat around her and opens the balcony door. Her senses stir. From her vantage point on the top floor of the dormitory, she makes out in the early light the vague outline of the swollen creek and the splash and churn of the water. The fury of what she hears but can barely discern fills her with a sudden rush of exhilaration. A sweet aroma of wet earth lingers in the air around her. Wind swirls about the balcony and a fine spray of rain clings to her cheeks and eye lashes.

It is Monday, she remembers, the day of no classes, set aside for the students to indulge in cultural pursuits, such as visiting the city art exhibits and museums, and other expeditionary activities. A feeling of conspiracy grows inside Josephine as she looks over the glistening landscape, rich and primordial, unmarred by the presence of others. Even the steady rain cannot diminish the sublime scene of luminous browns and greens laid out before her. She is mesmerized by the throaty rumble emanating from the mysterious depths of the glen.

"How beautiful," she whispers to herself. "How so very beautiful."

A forceful gust pushes open her unbuttoned coat and her night gown ripples in the wind. Josephine closes her eyes and draws a slow breath and feels the gust of air circle and play with her unfastened hair. Momentarily losing her balance, she grips the metal rail and feels a bracing shock of cold travel up the length of her arms. The balcony door is thrown open and strikes against the bedroom wall as the trees bend and groan.

"We must not let the moment go to waste."

Acting on impulse, Josephine leaves her room and moves silently down the dim hallway, leans her ear against the door to room 3B, and listens.

Quiet. Dead still.

A turn of the knob. Unlocked.

With the fluid precision of a stalking cat, she springs through the doorway and pounces on the unwitting prey lying on the bed across the room.

Beneath the tightly-drawn covers, Margaret Cleary grunts under the weight of her classmate. A whimpering "No" is all she manages in defense of the abrupt attack.

"Yes," Josephine responds in a defiantly cheerful tone, smiling broadly as she watches her quarry burrow defensively under a gold wool blanket with red fringe.

"While you sleep, my dear, we are imperiled," she continues, in mockseriousness. "Our beloved school is under threat. The instructors at National Park have trained you to be prepared and know how to respond in such an emergency as this. This is no time to cower, my dear Margaret. Get up, will you?" she exhorts as she playfully smacks at the protruding shoulder hidden beneath the bedding.

"Why are you being so dramatic? Why so early? Have you lost your mind?" a muffled voice responds weakly.

"Question my sincerity, will you."

Josephine presses her fingers into Margaret's rib cage until the covered form under her bucks and squirms.

"I do not arrive under trivial circumstances, my dear. I am not coming with news about a missing hair brush or a wardrobe crisis or the latest boyfriend drama. The glen has flooded!"

"Not a huge surprise, is it now, after…what…a miserable week of nothing but rain. Go back to your room, Josephine, and leave me be—before I get really angry at you."

"Exactly my point! When again will we see such a natural disaster and be able to witness the full force and fury of nature?"

"What time is it, for God's sake?"

"Who knows and who cares!"

"Seriously, get off, will you? You are not the delicate creature you imagine yourself to be. You're crushing me sitting on me like this."

"Nothing but pathetic protests of a spoiled girl with a weak disposition. Come to the window and you will see what I am saying. We are talking a flood of diluvian scale. Animals paired off, marching for higher ground. It's a Biblical happening, and you want to sleep?" Josephine pleads, twirling the hair on the back of Margaret's head playfully. "Let's get some of the others and go to the glen and look at the creek. No classes today."

"And no reason to rise," Margaret complains into her pillow. "The creek will be there later. Leave me."

"Slug."

Josephine grips Margaret around the waist, wrapping her inside the sheet and blanket, and rolls her over until she is face-up on the bed. In the ensuing struggle, both girls fall off the mattress and onto the wooden floor with a loud thud.

"I'll get the others," Josephine says mischievously on the way to door, escaping from the coil of cloth and flailing limbs before Margaret can strike back.

Margaret emerges from the twisted covers to hear her friend's receding footsteps down the hallway. Keeping her bed linen cocoon intact, she shuffles to the vanity and glimpses herself in the mirror, her hair unkempt and in no condition to be seen publicly.

"Something has to be done about that girl," she mumbles to her reflection. "But let's deal with you first, my love."

Josephine next knocks on Leah Hathaway's door two rooms down the hallway and waits. The door opens gradually and Leah answers sleepy-eyed, looking perplexed by the early morning visit.

"Are you putting me on? What time is it?" she complains, after hearing Josephine's plan.

On cue, Margaret cries out from her room:

"Six o'clock. You woke me up at six o'clock on a Monday!"

Josephine smiles at Leah.

"Even our elegant giraffe is coming along."

"I don't know. I'm tired and I have chorus practice today. I shouldn't be out in this weather. It's not good for my voice."

Leah leans against the half-opened door and her eye lids start to droop.

"Back in your room in twenty minutes, I promise," Josephine cajoles.

"All right," she says with an expression of resignation, "but—"

The lock directly across the hallway clicks and the door opens quickly, startling both girls. Josephine turns around to see the concerned face of May King emerge from the darkened doorway.

"What's the matter? Is someone ill? Oh, Josephine, it's you. I heard the knocking and thought something might be wrong. Is there? Is there a problem?"

"Josephine, come here and start the parlor fireplace," Margaret bellows down the hall. "It's the least you can do for waking me."

"Quiet Margaret," Josephine admonishes in a hushed voice.

"No one is ill," Leah assures May. "Josephine says the glen has flooded from all the rain and she wants us to go see it. And now Margaret is acting like she wants the whole house to wake just to share in her misery."

"Oh," May murmurs as she glances down the hallway, her rounded cheeks a light pink. "At least everyone is all right."

Josephine considers May's deflated expression. She hadn't thought of including her, but she sees in her face a trace of disappointment and feels that she now has no choice.

Their relationship is cordial, but not close. In their first days at the Seminary, Josephine quickly recognized May's self-doubt in the way she carried herself and interacted with the other girls. From the beginning she struggled to fit in and wore her unease about being accepted by her classmates prominently. And while this cloak of uncertainty initially engendered sympathy among those around her, the way May unfailingly clung to it eventually soured the goodwill into a palpable but unspoken loathing among students and instructors alike who see her demeanor as little more than a ploy for attention and pity. As a result, May occupies a different place in the school's social hierarchy than Josephine and the others—a girl on the outside, looking to get in.

"I'll return in five minutes," Josephine says to both with a reassuring look before heading back to her room to dress.

The four girls leave Senior House in the diffuse light, closely bunched, dressed in lush wool coats and finely sewn gloves, hoisting umbrellas over their heads. The chilled air is filled with the sounds of overflowing gutters and raindrops strafing the rooftops. Scattered window lights and smoke rising from the Vincent Hall kitchen chimney are the only evidence of other human activity as they set off for the glen.

Margaret moves forward and links arms with Josephine at the head of the group, their umbrellas bumping together as they walk, forcing Leah and May to pair up on the pathway behind them.

"Wonderful tonic for cabin fever, my dear. Let's not make a habit of it. And why exactly is May part of this group? Nice girl and all, but sort of peculiar. You know how she is during studies. Her incessant questioning in class makes me want to launch across the room and bury my pen in her neck sometimes."

Josephine squeezes Margaret's arm tightly until her friend gives out a yelp.

"Honestly Margaret, lower your voice. I wonder why anyone puts up with you."

"Because I am the only one who sees things for what they are and speaks honestly. You admire that in me because it's something you don't do. You are too worried about propriety and people's feelings. Face it, you are simply too nice for your own good. You need to unleash the brutally blunt Josephine from within. You may find it liberating."

"While emulation would no doubt be flattering to you, there can be only one maven of style and deportment at this school, and she wears a size eleven shoe," Josephine fires back with a smile.

"Wicked, wicked girl. You are learning."

"After all, aren't you the one always complaining about the drudgery of our existence here? If I recall correctly, just the other night you strutted into the parlor and announced melodramatically to everyone within earshot that you were going to 'perish from ennui' before heading back to your room and burying your nose in one of your dusty novels."

"Spoken like a true proletariat unaccustomed to the finer quality of continental literature."

Margaret leans her head to the side and momentarily rests her ear against the smooth felt of her friend's hat.

"If I catch cold out here, I know who will be nursing me back to health."

The group passes the darkened Odeon, the performance theater where the school's music classes also are held. During weekly recitals, orchestral sounds and lilting voices seep from the building's eyebrow windows and carry across the lawn, providing an ethereal accompaniment to nearby activities. When the sun is high, and the flower beds are in bloom and fragrant, girls dot the lush grass in languid repose, their hearts slowed by the narcotic notes drifting over them. In the early light of the wet winter morning, however, the hall is moribund. Its curved portico entrance, supported by massive columns, is cold and funereal in the steady rain.

Leah looks at the shadowy recesses beyond the ivory colored pillars and thinks of the chorus practice awaiting her later in the day. While she enjoys singing, and has since a young age, the hours of vocal training and repetitious practice over the past three years have ground her passion down to a fine powder of benign indifference and produced the self-realization that she is not to be the professional singer of acclaim her father and mother want her to be.

It looks like a prison, a dreary prison, she thinks to herself, as the girls walk by the Odeon. She secretly despises everything about the place—the musty smell of the wooden stage boards; the cold drafts that whistle through the rafters during the short days of winter; and, above all, her teacher's exacting glare and the way she incessantly taps her pointer against the stage during rehearsal. Leah smiles sadly, surprised by the level of contempt she suddenly feels toward the performance hall and the hours of compulsory practice she is forced to submit to.

Directly ahead of the group is Honeysuckle Bridge, the iron-trussed arch connecting the school with the Forest Glen train station. The bridge's name comes from the fast-growing vines that spread upward along its supporting beams in late spring and release their sweet, intoxicating smell under the blaze of the midday sun. The drop from the bridge to the waters of Rock Creek below is precipitous and alluring to students who congregate there during afternoon strolls and lean over the edge and draw in the wild ambrosia as they contemplate the lush expanse of the glen beneath them.

In the wintry morning, the bridge is cold and abandoned. Beads of rain coat the hand railings and bring out the luster in the span's black exoskeleton. As seen from the pathway, the crossing takes on a more ominous appearance against the hazy, gray backdrop, like that of a portal to a hidden and mystical realm, a place of storybook fantasy where the unreal exists in the isolated outskirts of imagination.

May raises her voice to be heard above the staccato of the falling rain, almost completely concealed under her umbrella.

"We should have brought along Virginia Shelton from the second floor. She's the editor of the yearly and could have written about this. I mean, if the glen is flooding, that is something to remember when we look back on our last year, right?"

"She can take my spot," Margaret retorts sotto voce.

"Perhaps even taken a photograph of the four of us."

"To be used as evidence that we've lost our faculties."

"I don't know Virginia well, but aren't you friendly with her, Margaret?"

"We use to be," Margaret responds over her shoulder.

"What happened? What came between the two of you?"

"I grew tired of her incessant questions," she deadpans, waiting for the pinch from Josephine that predictably follows.

Using her free hand, Leah pulls the scarf around her throat tighter while struggling to keep her umbrella straight as the group continues on. She imagines the cold air reaching the unprotected, exposed flesh of her throat and involuntarily swallows, feeling a tight, though not painful, sensation.

"Listen. You can hear the sound of the water from down the hill. It's growing louder. Are we going to look from the bridge?"

"What fun would that be?" Josephine answers Leah sarcastically. "Plus, Margaret insists on a full inspection up-close. Isn't that right, my dear?"

"Don't push it," her friend grumbles.

Josephine leads the others down the walk to a circle ringed with knee-high boxwoods. At the roundabout, the path to the foot bridge splits away and leads down a sloping hill to the creek and the Grotto, a stone amphitheater used by the school drama department for open-air productions. In season, the Grotto is a popular gathering place for students who seek relief from the heat under the shade-giving spread of dogwoods and magnolia trees and enjoy the cool feel of the curved granite sitting wall.

Beyond the amphitheater, across a diminutive crowned bridge and nestled in an azalea-lined hollow, is a natural spring which unfailingly produces a stream of water so clear and bracing as if it were magically transported from the Arctic. An Italian builder of some local notoriety constructed a mortar and brick niche arching over the spring, creating a dank enclosure for those who came, on bent knee, to cup the sparkling waters in their hands. Over the years, miniature stalactites formed on the underside of the springhouse from the moisture and absence of sunlight. Incoming freshmen to the Seminary are warned to avoid the Grotto waters during the daytime so as to not disturb the aggressive bats that allegedly sleep there and are known to swoop down on the heads of unsuspecting girls who come to drink from the fountain. The prankish tale serves to keep the spot reserved for returning students for the first few days of the fall semester when the colors along the glen turn and the rhythmic drone of camouflaged insects fill the air.

May slips on a slick step and quickly grabs onto Margaret's coat to steady herself. Unnerved by the near fall, she pleads weakly from underneath her umbrella that they might want to turn back, but her entreaty goes unheeded.

As the four girls carefully descend the treacherous stairs leading to the creek, they feel the temperature drop and a brisk breeze, channeled by the contours of the glen, angles the rainfall and stings their faces.

"Would you look at that? The Grotto is completely submerged!" May cries out, pointing to where the stone path abruptly disappears into the turbulent, fast-moving creek. "I've never seen anything like this before. It's like everything has been swept away."

"Not swept away. Underwater," Leah says before stepping away from the group and walking to the water's edge.

"What did I tell you, Margaret? It was worth getting up for," Josephine cheerily needles her friend under their overlapping umbrellas.

The rampaging, unbridled stream races along the overgrown banks of the hillside. Where the ground dips and turns out, eddies have formed, filled with accumulated leaves and branches and other detritus. Leah picks a fallen pine cone off of the ground and tosses it in the undulating water and watches in playful wonderment as it rapidly floats downstream and disappears from sight into the rainy mist.

Their progress halted, the four survey the dramatically altered landscape, marveling at the destructive power of the force roiling and swelling before them. Josephine moves forward, bends down and snags a long, narrow tree limb as it floats past, careful to keep her leather boots out of the water, and then steps back.

"Josephine, for goodness sake, get away from there," Margaret snaps disapprovingly, concealed almost entirely by her coat and pulled down hat, the vapor of her breath traveling along the underside of her umbrella. "If you fall in you'll be long gone before one of us even has the presence of mind to drop her umbrella. Leah, May, escort her back away from there. She has no sense. And she is clumsy. It wouldn't be the first time I've seen her tumble over without provocation."

Margaret's alarming orders heighten May's anxiousness. Mere feet away, the creek convulses chaotically. The water is swift and raucous, splashing along the grass and stone in front of them. All of the sudden she feels disoriented by the motion of the violent torrent. The fury of the untamed creek is unnerving and she instinctively steps away from the edge. It's not right to be here, she thinks nervously.

A phantasmal image flashes in her mind like a crack of lightning: a fleeting glimpse of the murky water, not just seething and raging, but launching toward them! She watches helplessly, frozen by fear, as the swift current reaches up at Josephine's feet with aberrant design and ensnares the unsuspecting girl.

May's body stiffens and jerks back, and she shakes off the chill that reverberates along the length of her spine like a dog throwing off water after a bath.

"This isn't safe. I think we should go back now. Also, it's cold down here. Really cold. Let's go back and warm up. Josephine, what do you say? Let's go back, please."

Josephine scans the water.

"I can't believe it. I can't believe we didn't notice it before. Where's the old girl? Where's the Mermaid? She's gone. Imagine that."

"You're right. I didn't notice," Leah says, moving over to Josephine's vantage point along the bank. "I hope it's not damaged. That would be a tragedy. Do you think it's washed away someplace downstream?"

Many years ago, National Park Seminary commissioned the construction of a fountain statue of a mermaid beyond the Grotto, anchored to a grouping of large rocks in the creek, as homage to Hans Christian Anderson's beloved storybook creation. When functioning properly, as is rarely the case, water spurts from her upraised arm and falls upon the rocks with a slapping sound as she looks skyward, her gaze and form suspended in time.

"Gone. Back to the deep sea, it seems. Another perfectly sad fairy tale ending shattered." Margaret offers scornfully. "What a dreary mess. May has a legitimate point for once. Unless we want to end up the same, shouldn't we head back and end this misguided journey?"

"I love that statue," Josephine says to no one in particular, ignoring Margaret's plea. "Do you think it's ruined? Could it have survived? I have fond memories of sitting down there."

She recalls only weeks before taking off her shoes and stockings and wading across the shallow water and finding a spot on the crowded rocks to read with others on one of the last warm days of autumn.

Margaret lets out a prolonged, eye-rolling sigh.

"I am sure it is down there someplace, dear. Nothing changes at the Seminary. You know that Dean Dawson and the administrators would never allow it. After all, let's not forget our proud academy's motto: *Cum Natura, Non Contra*—With Nature, Not Against."

Josephine and Leah take turns throwing pebbles at a half-submersed tree on the far bank as the rain continues to fall while the other two huddle against the elements. On the third round of throws, Josephine strikes the trunk just above the water line.

"I have an idea. Let's go see what has happened to the canoe shack," Leah excitedly offers to the group. "If the flood is this high here, I can only imagine what the storm has done upstream. But we should go back up the road and walk around. We can't go further this way. The path is cut off and it doesn't look safe following the creek."

"Here's a better idea. Let's go back inside instead," Margaret grumbles, stamping her feet to get warm. "Breakfast will be served soon. And it is cold and wet and miserable out here."

"Yes, let's go back," May chimes in, still spooked by the ferocity of the wild current. "The boathouse is almost certainly swamped too and we should let the dean or someone in the facilities office know about it. You agree, right, Margaret?"

Margaret reaches out and pulls May next to her, their umbrellas colliding, and looks earnestly into her eyes.

"They are canoes, May. They float. Stop worrying all the time about what we should be doing or not doing. And for goodness sake, running to the dean's office wild-eyed is a daft idea. From what I remember, those nasty old canoes needed a good cleaning to rid them of all the spiders and dead moths. Now stay here and keep me warm until Josephine gives us permission to sound the retreat call."

Josephine deflects her friend's taunt with a mock parry of her umbrella, steps off the path and walks carefully along the slick grass.

"You are sheltered and spoiled Margaret."

"Guilty—and unapologetic."

"Have you no humility as a witness to nature's fury?"

"None."

"The flood has removed from the glen all vestiges of the school. For a moment, we can look upon this awe-inspiring scene and imagine what it looked like before the school or any of this existed. Consider for a moment that we are standing on untouched wilderness, before the arrival of the Europeans, the forest untamed and unspoiled. The slate has been wiped clean. Where is your sense of wonder?"

"Snuffed out in this frigid wind which is making my teeth chatter and turning my lips blue."

"Imagine, Margaret, swarthy, savage Indians moving about the trees as they hunt. Early man in his natural element."

The Deerslayer is wretched prose. Now you want to romanticize it, my dear, in a repressed fantasy involving long, pointed arrows and buckskins. Are you fevered *and* uncouth?! The Seminary's faculty seemingly has failed you, as well as your parents, who are overpaying for your education."

May blushes at Margaret's remarks and pulls slightly away from her hold.

Josephine looks back at the two mismatched girls standing together on the lip of the grass.

"We have been captive to this miserable weather for nearly a week now. I can't take it anymore. Color has become pallor. Our rooms have become catacombs. Let's enjoy it for a few moments longer before heading back. We have the rest of the day to idle our time away. This—" she pauses and points back to the raging waters, "this will be gone soon."

The others dutifully comply and stare through the falling rain at their overtaken sanctuary, contemplating Josephine's words. In the swirling wind, the students' faces are covered by a thin layer of moisture, delicate beads forming on the length of their tresses. Dawn gradually energizes the cloud of mist hanging over the glen and brings sharper focus and clarity to the altered landscape.

A tree along the far bank suddenly fractures and May jumps at the loud, unexpected rupture.

"Oh my God," Josephine hears Leah exclaim behind her.

The severed trunk falls into the creek and floats a short distance before becoming lodged against a makeshift blockade of other toppled limbs accumulating along the hillside.

Despite the gentle infusion of light, the flood waters grow murkier and more opaque. Josephine feels a coldness creep inside the toe of her boot and looks down to see that the continually rising creek has found her.

She turns to rejoin the group and glimpses the outline of something upstream, a vague form at the surface, darker than the surrounding water, changing appearance as it is carried along by the overflowing creek. She gazes intently but struggles to make out the mysterious shape rapidly approaching their place at the water's edge.

As the shadowy, ill-defined object nears, it dips beneath the surface momentarily and then suddenly reappears, rolling over top of itself as it passes by the group, like chimney smoke pushed, kneaded and shaped by a winter gust, obscured in the raging tumult as quickly as it appeared, leaving Josephine unsure whether her eyes have played a trick on her in the muted light.

An involuntary shudder shakes her shoulders and her scalp tingles. As she stands transfixed by the chaotic scene, her umbrella lists toward the ground allowing the rain to fall freely against her. It is all she can do to suppress the physical revulsion rising up against the back of her throat as an inexplicable feeling of dread spreads like wildfire inside her.

Then, for an infinitesimal fraction of a second, nothing. All is suspended. The waters are still and silent, the sky bleached white. An almost imperceptible skip in time when she is caught between realms of consciousness.

"What was that in the water?" May asks, her voice wavering. "Did you see it? It looked like a rug or something."

"I saw it too," Leah echoes. "Josephine, did you get a better look? It was moving so fast. Could you tell what it was? You were the closest."

"What?"

"Did you see that, that—thing—in the water? What was it? It floated past you. You were standing closest to it. Did you see what it was?"

"I'm not sure."

"But you saw it, didn't you?"

Josephine feels a hand against her shoulder and turns to find Margaret next to her, her chestnut eyes showing concern.

"Are you all right, Josie?" she whispers. "You don't look well."

"Yes," she replies with a wan smile. "I'm fine. Why do you ask?"

"What did she say, Margaret? What did she say? What was it?"

"Enough of your cackling, May!"

It is Leah's stammering voice, not May's, that responds to Margaret's curt, over-the-shoulder command.

"Look! Margaret. Josephine. Turn around and look at the creek! Do you see it?"

The engorged stream is suddenly littered with objects being swept away by the rolling swells. A wooden fruit basket. A shattered section of fencing. An empty feed sack. More unidentifiable pieces of floating material, mostly small, rush past.

"Those are from someone's home, somewhere upstream," Leah calls out as a large piece of cloth resembling a bed sheet twists like a hooked worm and rides up and down the surface peaks of the turbulence.

The four girls watch despondently as more ruined belongings of an unknown family pass before them, struggling to fathom the personal devastation they are witnessing.

Margaret turns back to Josephine and nudges her gently, trying to force a reaction.

"Talk to me. Are you all right? What was it? What did you see in the water?" her voice low enough so as to not be heard by the other two.

"I don't know. I mean, I am not sure."

"Whatever it was, it did a number on you."

"How do you mean?" she asks Margaret with a confounded expression.

"You are white as powder."

The increasing sense of urgency, of being at a place where they should not be, of being complacent to the tragedy unfolding before them, grows inside May until she erupts.

"We need to tell someone, now! We shouldn't be here in the first place. Josephine, it is not for you or Margaret to decide. Something serious has happened, and we should not stand idly about like spectators at a steeplechase. We must leave and quickly report what is happening to the administration. They'll know what to do."

"Let's go back," Margaret whispers to her friend, as May continues to plead her case to Leah. "May's ranting, I'm cold, and you look paler than you usually do."

A knowing smile accompanies her playful insult, but it does not move Josephine who continues to survey the flooded glen.

May steps forward and grabs the shoulder of Josephine's coat.

"We are going now. I insist!"

Margaret turns around with a withering, protective stare that causes May to recoil.

"Get a hold of yourself, May King!"

Josephine drops her umbrella on the ground and picks up the tree branch she retrieved earlier. At the water's edge, she steadies herself on one leg and reaches out with the branch and attempts unsuccessfully to guide the stream of items to the shore before they pass. She eventually snags a small piece of fabric and hoists it onto the ground. The other three gather around to get a closer look.

Margaret bends down and uncoils the white cloth.

"How sad," she sighs, "It's a dress. It's a girl's dress."

Leah pushes past May and crouches next to Margaret and then smoothes the folds of the garment against the wet grass. The fabric is remarkably unmarred having emerged from the turbid flood and each of the front buttons is intact, looking as if it has been newly washed and ready to be dried.

"A young girl would fit in this, maybe five or six years of age," she says, pulling down gently at the collar and hem of the hand-sewn garment.

She stands up slowly and scans the glen in both directions.

"Does anyone see other clothes in the water?"

May's alarm overflows again.

"We need to go tell someone, this very minute! This is not right! We must do something and not just stand here. Can't you see?"

Leah studies the wild, agitated creek.

"I mean, everything we have seen float by so far comes from a house or farm—wood, old sacks, tin. This is different," she says, pointing down at the dress at her feet. "Let's say this came off a clothes line or something like that. Wouldn't there be other clothing in the water as well?"

"Clothes hung out to dry in the middle of a rain storm? That doesn't make sense," May sharply fires back at Leah.

"You're right, of course. What was I thinking? The administration office—"

"You are starting to sound like our dear canary May-belle," Margaret interrupts. "We should leave now and find a fire. My toes have gone numb. Who knows what's in the water or not in the water. It's none of our concern."

"What are you suggesting?" Josephine asks.

"I am suggesting we go inside and get dry so—"

"No, I am asking Leah. What do you mean about there not being other clothes in the water?"

"So if this didn't come off a clothes line, where did it come from?"

Leah draws a short breath and her eyes well up.

"Maybe this came off a person, I mean a girl. It's too horrible to think about but maybe the flood swept her away and the force of the current was so strong that it pulled the dress off."

Her voice quivers as the words leave her lips. Leah overcomes the surge of emotion and regains her voice.

"I don't want to believe this happened, but it's possible, right? I mean it could have happened. Look. You see the dress. The buttons are unfastened."

The four girls study the dark water as the sound of the violent churning reverberates in the glen, each of them chilled not just by the cold rain but by the seed of doubt planted by Leah. Was it possible that they were unwitting witnesses to a tragic drowning, the taking of someone so young and so innocent?

May turns and faces Josephine.

"We all saw something in the water, but you had the closest look Josephine. You were at the edge of the water. Remember? There was something in the creek before the dress and all the rest, just beneath the surface."

Josephine looks down at the ground and studies the wet tow of her boot.

"You heard what Leah said," May continues. "Is that what you saw in the water? Please tell me you didn't."

"I told you, I couldn't tell what it was. I mean, it didn't look like a person, if that's what you are intimating."

Margaret interjects forcefully.

"To be precise, May, *you* said it looked a rug, and that's probably what it was. Let's get a grip on ourselves girls. There is nothing else out there. And Leah, if I am not mistaken, you have concert practice today. I can only imagine Madame Kaspar's apoplectic fit if her star pupil came down with a cold days before the marquee performance."

Leah stares at the dress on the ground while May looks imploringly at Josephine.

"Josephine, agreed?" Margaret continues in a softened tone. "Shall we head back?"

Josephine looks up between the spread of tree limbs that shelters the Grotto and realizes the rain has suddenly ceased. The peaceful retreat she enjoyed so often in her years at the Seminary is gone, transformed into something indiscriminately cruel and foreboding.

She recalls how even in the grip of winter, when all in the glen is dormant and still, she would walk alone along the Grotto path and marvel at the solitary Mermaid, the quieted beauty, fascinated by the delicate fissures in the ice that encircled her. She remembers how the metallic statue would glimmer in the cross-hatched sun light streaming through the hushed forest, her eyes locked on the hillside obscuring Senior House and the other school buildings.

Josephine looks at the three girls as they await her decision.

"Let's go back."

She retrieves her umbrella off the ground, collapses it, and leads Margaret and May up the walk toward the Seminary in a somber processional line.

Leah lingers behind unnoticed, gazing down at the discarded dress on the matted grass at her feet.

The sentinel crow takes flight nearby and calls out twice before passing over Honeysuckle Bridge in the direction of the train station.

Leah impulsively picks up the dress and efficiently folds it, and then, making sure that she is not being watched, slips the white square of cotton inside her coat. She draws a sharp breath as the wet fabric touches her skin. Pinning the dress against her waist with one arm, she fastens her coat with the other. Just as she finishes and looks up, the others reach the top of the stone pathway and then disappear from sight. Suddenly alone in the glen, Leah is unnerved and races up the stairs to rejoin the group. With each level she ascends, the dampness of the confiscated dress bleeds along her arms, stomach, and the length of her torso.

Chapter 2
Hiawatha, Protector of the Mission

It may be trite to say that this is the age of organization. But the most frequent hindrance to the progress of woman's movements is her inability to work well in organization; to abide by the usages of parliamentary law; to preside judiciously; to speak well in discussion – forcefully, and to the point; to divorce opinion from personality and oppose it dispassionately; to carry triumph modestly, and bear defeat nobly; to meet opposition graciously; to give due weight to the arguments of others, and consideration to those whose opinions differ from her own; to appreciate and utilize the good in those personally uncongenial to her; to submit her will to the will of the majority and respect the decisions of the organized body. All these things are abundantly worth acquiring as a preparation for real life – and club life is the means of their acquisition and the arena for their practice. The club girl learns how to be a companionable woman. A companionable woman makes the best wife and mother. In the effort to maintain the high standards of her club, she gains her own highest development. To attain these objects, we have devised and developed a system of club life to which is peculiar and original with this school. Membership is voluntary but strongly encouraged and is adjudicated through a committee, composed of representatives of the Faculty and each club. Each one of the seven social clubs has its own separate house constructed in a distinctive architectural style as its place of assembly: Chiopi's Japanese Pagoda; Zeta's Swiss Chalet; Alpha's American Bungalow; Kappa's Dutch Windmill; Delta's English Gatehouse; Beta's Medieval Castle; and Theta's Spanish Mission.

Soon after the storm subsides, the leaden cloud cover moves off to the east and sunlight begins to slowly dry the campus rooftops and pathways. Students emerge from their dormitories to a crystalline morning as the rays of the low-slung sun shimmer in raindrops suspended from tree branches and reflect off countless puddles.

Word of the flood in the glen spreads quickly and soon groups of students assemble to go see the steadily receding waters. Even the school's headmaster, Dean Porter Dawson, is spied surveying the scene using binoculars from Vincent Hall's rooftop Belvedere tower.

The four women do not speak on the walk back to the school and separate when they arrive at Senior House, as if an invisible magnetic force repels each from the other upon entering the dormitory.

Margaret slips back into the comforting embrace of her bed sheets and sleeps until the commotion outside her door of hallmates coming and going makes further rest impossible. The activity of others in the house does not interest her and she spends the rest of the morning in her room reading. After a light afternoon lunch, she retreats back to the dormitory and eventually musters the discipline to pen long-overdue letters to her family in Fall River, Massachusetts. She writes an emotionless recitation of her studies and daily happenings at the school, occasionally sprinkling in references of trips into Washington to attend the theater and tour the national monuments. She has perfected the art of what she calls "dividend correspondence" to her parents—a detailed accounting of what the annual tuition of $850 is producing in the educational, cultural and social maturation of their daughter.

Her mother had last written of her plan, accompanied by Margaret's father and younger brother, to visit in mid-December and stay to the end of the semester, when they would return to Fall River together as a family. At one time, visiting relatives typically stayed in the city and commuted the short distance by rail or trolley to Forest Glen. Dean Dawson, however, found the separation unacceptable and convinced the school Board of Trustees to buy a parcel across the glen adjacent to the train station and construct a building of apartments to accommodate prospective students, their families, and distinguished visitors.

The newly-opened Glen Manor Hotel provides guests a fitting complement to the eclectic buildings of the Seminary. According to campus lore, Dean Dawson recreated in Glen Manor the storybook features of his grandparents's home in England. The driveway leading to the hotel passes through two stone towers connected by a wrought iron archway and topped with ornate vases. Vine arbors bordering both sides of the road create a natural tunnel during the height of the growing season from which visitors emerge and see an improbable Elizabethan country manor situated next to the glimmering silver rails of the Baltimore and Ohio line. The accommodations inside are modern and do not embrace the period décor of the building's exterior, and a center courtyard of neatly arranged perennials with boxwood borders provides patrons a private retreat buffered from the trains passing nearby routinely.

The two-story hotel contains ten rooms, each accessible by an exterior covered walkway. The view from the modestly-sized accommodations provides patrons of Glen Manor a panorama of the school across the wooded ravine. Immediately beyond the rail bed is the Forest Glen train station and platform which is connected to the insular campus by two routes. Those traveling by foot from the station proceed directly south along a pathway that leads to Honeysuckle Bridge. Traversing the glen across the narrow span provides a spectacular view of the hillside campus' natural allure and striking edifices. On the other side, the pedestrian path continues toward Senior House, passing the Odeon performance hall along the way, and eventually ends at a carriage circle in front of Vincent Hall. A massive, three-tiered, iron and marble fountain is situated inside the circle and is a dominating centerpiece at the main building's entrance. Water pumped through the fountain spews from the mouths of unbridled horses at the base and the putti that crowns the top. The fountain was purchased by the headmaster during his tour of Europe after the Great War and was shipped at great expense to the school, one of the latest and perhaps most garish additions to the hodge-podge, neo-classical design that pervades the Seminary grounds.

Just east of Honeysuckle Bridge, the waters of Rock Creek split and flow under a road, wide enough to accommodate horses and motorized vehicles alike, that also links the Seminary to the train station. The smaller Spring Branch meanders toward the railroad tracks and along the edge of the glen bordering the Italian Villa dormitory used to house underclass students. This main road continues a short distance past the Villa until it reaches a second bridge that spans the main waters of Rock Creek.

28 ANDY JOHNSON

Situated at the far side of the drive bridge is the fanciful English castle clubhouse of Pi Beta Nu, connected to the road by a drawbridge authentically decorated with inoperable chains and faux pulleys fastened to the castle's front. The Beta girls have bestowed upon themselves the honorific title of gatekeepers for the campus and carry out their duties with mock seriousness. Margaret knows many of the girls belonging to Beta and finds the way they perch atop the castle roof and crow and whinny at passing automobiles to be silly and downright embarrassing. Beyond the castle drawbridge, the road continues on past the Delta and Kappa clubhouses before skirting to the left of Vincent Hall and dividing into a number of utility driveways that serve the school chapel, library, gymnasium and other buildings on the south side of campus.

Margaret ends her letter to her parents with confirmation of the reservation she has made for them at Glen Manor Hotel. From her desk drawer she pulls a portrait photograph taken of her and studies it at arms length. She feels it flatters her, but disdains the prim smile the photographer insisted she wear. Her raven hair is pulled back and pinned up exposing the contours of a long and elegant neck, white as porcelain, set off against the dark neckline of her winter uniform. On the back of the portrait she writes of her love, and, after the inscription dries, slips it with the letter in the envelope and seals it. She will wait until later to mail it at the station, she decides, and places it upon other personal correspondence that has languished on her desk since the storm's arrival. Picking up a French novel, Margaret collapses into a high-backed chair content to spend the rest of the afternoon reading alone.

May, still shaken by the morning trip to the flooded glen and the lingering doubt about what she and the others may have witnessed, goes to see Miss Price, one of the school's English teachers and regent of the senior class. In her capacity as regent, Miss Price acts as counselor to eighty-two girls and helps prepare them for life after graduation, a duty given her relative youth and limited worldliness she labors at times to carry out.

Katharine Price arrived at the National Park Seminary two years ago after a short stint as principal in a defunct private school in Portland, Maine. Possessing a bright complexion, deep brown eyes, and an easy smile, she shares the youthful appearance of the girls she teaches. And yet her presence in the classroom is confident and commanding, with her lectures on nineteenth century English writers filled with dramatic readings and vocal characterizations that enrapt those enrolled in her courses. For an hour each morning, she transports her students into the vivid worlds of Dickens, Thackeray, the Bronte sisters, Kipling and other literary giants. She often tailors the setting to fit the literary theme under study. Comedy is enjoyed in the round on the Odeon stage. Melodrama is consumed on stone benches in the rose garden. Tales of gothic horror are read by candlelight in a cramped, windowless storage room deep inside the subterranean labyrinth of Vincent Hall.

Unmarried and attractive, she is the object of constant gossip among the students who imagine her daily interactions with male faculty members and administrators—married and single alike—as possible overtures bearing personal significance. This book, however, Katharine Price keeps closed to all. She has learned early in her professional endeavors of the dangers that come when matters of the heart are revealed within school walls.

Miss Price sits behind her desk and listens to May recount what happened at the glen earlier in the day. She knows May's type well: average intellect but outspoken in her views; a firm internal compass divining right and wrong; conscientious at times to the point of neurosis; short of stature, heavy, and a pedestrian countenance. Girls like May are essential contributors to the school's daily activities to be sure, but often excluded from the privileged inner circle of the student body. Miss Price is surprised to hear that May was part of a group that included Josephine Barnes and Margaret Cleary. She has not taught Leah Hathaway, but knows the other two well enough from the classroom, school functions, and daily observation to know that they occupy a rung of the social ladder well above May's.

"You took the correct action coming to see me, May," Miss Price offers reassuringly. "It's a grave matter to be sure. The information you have, though sketchy and circumstantial, to say the least, may be helpful to the authorities, if in fact there is someone missing. I will look into what has happened in the surrounding area and let you know what I find. Based alone on what you have told me though, I am skeptical. Perhaps that is simply what I want to believe—what we all want to believe."

May's brow pinches, her eyes dart to the office window. Miss Price can see that her consternation remains.

"Do the other girls share your worry?"

"It was Leah who first spoke about it—she was the first to suggest that someone might have drowned. And when she said it, I immediately thought about what was in the water a few seconds beforehand. And I became very scared, Miss Price."

"I understand. You explained that to me. And Josephine? She has a level head and good instincts. What does she think?

"I don't know," May replies softly, still avoiding eye contact with the regent. "I mean, I think, I think—," she stammers and then stops.

"What do you want to say? Don't be reserved, May. It is not your nature."

May's eyes quickly well with tears and her lower lip quivers, as she tries desperately to keep her emotions in check.

"Margaret thinks I am a ninny, I can tell you that much," she says, regaining her voice and wiping her sleeve across her eyes. "She's cruel, that one. Calling me names and constantly making fun at my expense."

Miss Price walks over and sits down next to May and places her arm around her shoulders to comfort her.

"That's unimportant, you know that May. You must have confidence in your convictions and in the way that you carry yourself and in how you conduct your affairs. We can't be despondent because how others may view us. The Seminary teaches us to steel ourselves against uninformed viewpoints and hurtful intentions. Let's put aside Margaret Cleary for the moment. I asked about Josephine and her reaction. What did she say was in the water?"

"Josephine…the water? She wasn't sure or wouldn't say. You understand, it was her idea in the first place to go to the glen. She practically cowed us into going. And when I said we should go back, she wouldn't hear of it."

"I see. Let me find out if there is a missing person report with the police and we can quickly put this whole matter and your mind to rest. You should be focusing on finishing the remainder of the year, and Christmas will be here before you know it. All right?"

May nods and goes to leave. At the door, she stops and looks pleadingly toward the teacher.

"I'm sorry to have disappointed you, Miss Price. I don't know what caused me to act this way. It's inexcusable. It's just that a peculiar feeling came over me when we walked back from the glen this morning and…and…

and I think the others felt it too. I know that doesn't sound rational. But it is how I honestly felt. Anyway, thank you so very much for listening."

"May, you have no reason to be hard on yourself. You took the responsible action—as usual."

After lunch Miss Price goes to Senior House to visit her troubled pupil only to find that she and a few girls from the Kappa sorority club have taken the trolley into the city to tour the elaborately decorated Christmas store windows and shop for dresses for the Seminary's end of semester gala. Pleased to know that May has pulled herself together after their meeting and joined the others, she walks down the third floor hallway and knocks on the door to Josephine's room. Not surprisingly, she too is out. Miss Price squats down and slides a note under the door and leaves to go see Dean Dawson.

Upon reaching senior status, students are assigned newly-enrolled girls to counsel and guide through their first year at Forest Glen. The academic philosophy of the National Park Seminary is to strengthen the intellect and character of young women, and the mentor-protégée program is integral in guiding the younger girls through the scholastic and social challenges of independent life away from the comforts of home, often for the first time. The Seminary is among the most expensive preparatory academies in the country and those who arrive as girls leave as women, perfected in all facets of the academic and cultural awareness. Whether they depart Forest Glen for college, the work place, married life, or simply return to the wealthy family homes from which they came, the training they receive in their years at National Park Seminary is to be an indelible part of their very being, including what Dean Dawson terms, "soul power"—the moral maturation that cannot be cultivated at the piano or the easel or taught at the mechanical drawing table or in the chemistry laboratory. What better way to chart this course than to let each girl have the personal attention and care of one more experienced; in short, give her an opportunity to see the young woman she is capable of becoming.

Jennie Milburn, a tall, thin, long-limbed girl who moves with an awkward bird-like stride, was assigned to Josephine at the beginning of the fall semester. The Milburns live in southern California, having moved there from New Jersey when Jennie was eight years of age. Her father's lucrative executive position at the United Artists studio catapulted her family into a stratum of celebrities and fame that filled her childhood with birthday toys from Mary Pickford and uproarious dinners with Charlie Chaplin, including one memorable evening in which the "Little Tramp" of the matinee screen nimbly scaled a tree to snatch and return Jennie's wayward cat from certain peril.

Jennie arrived at Forest Glen a disgruntled cast-off from the family's sparkling bungalow in the hills overlooking the San Fernando Valley. Her parents' decision to send her back east was received coldly, despite being spun into a positive weave of opportunity and enrichment and advancement, as if the considerable expense of her schooling was a sacrifice they were willing to bear in order to secure Jennie's future, a selfless gift to an unappreciative daughter unable to fathom the generosity of the act. Even at her tender age though, Jennie could see through the sales pitch they gave her on the family sofa that sad day. Her enrollment in the prestigious and exclusive academy was just another peg in her family's social ascent in the status-conscious world they now inhabited.

When Jennie's pleas to stay were rebuffed and the day came for her to travel to Forest Glen, the late summer siroccos blew down from the desert highlands with frightening ferocity. A blinding dust storm made the trip to the train station a laborious and at times harrowing journey, and by the time her father walked her to station platform to say goodbye, a thin layer of sand and grit coated their clothes and clung to their exposed skin. Though Jennie secretly hoped for a last-minute reprieve, she knew the melodrama of the movies was no more real than the blurred mirages on the brown, scrub-brush horizon she glimpsed from their home porch at sunset.

As she travelled back in time, watching the world reverse its course from her compartment window, Jennie's fingers unconsciously wandered to the part in her scalp and fingered the fine grains of desert sand infesting her head. Over and over she rolled the hard, nit-sized particles until the tender skin grew pink and sore, and the exiled girl had a painful counterweight that siphoned off the melancholy within.

As part of their mentoring relationship, Josephine and her charge have a standing commitment to attend the distinguished guest lectures held in Vincent Hall's Indian Room and then socialize afterward. Previous lecture topics in the series had been dreadfully dry and boring and had driven down attendance. They had endured Dr. Harvey W. Wiley holding forth on "Ethics of the Pure Food Law" and squirmed restlessly while Reverend Bernard

Vaughan delivered a soporific address on "Character and Need." Even Miss Janet E. Richards' commentary last month on the "The Present State of Woman's Suffrage" elicited a tepid response from the assembled students. Today's lecture, Josephine assures Jennie, promises to be more entertaining as the esteemed Professor Horace Parkington of the National Geographic Society is visiting to lecture on his travels to the temples and shrines of Greece, Constantinople and the Bosporus.

For over an hour the guest speaker leads the attentive assembly on a vicarious journey into the realms of the ancient world, of the perilous pursuit of buried artifacts and crumbling edifices comprising the mosaic of civilization in its infancy. Once he completes his remarks, Professor Parkington walks from behind the podium and leads the group down the hallway to the Reception Room adjacent to the building's front entrance where the fireplace burns fiercely. The room's plush leather parlor chairs and piano have been moved against the mirrored walls to make room for four tables, each cloaked with velvet cloth of the deepest violet.

"These rare antiquities have been brought to you based on a special arrangement between the Society and the National Park Seminary. The privilege you are being afforded to examine them up-close is rare indeed. I ask that when the table coverings are removed that you move in single formation past the collection. You may look at them and you may ask questions, but under no circumstance are you to touch any of the items on the tables. All of the rarities before you predate Jesus Christ's time on Earth. They have been acquired at considerable expense and trial and have been carefully transported halfway around the globe so as to preserve the integrity of their condition. We wouldn't want anything to happen to them in a girls' school parlor room, would we?"

The professor's last words linger on tightly curled lips as he surveys the faces in the room. Following his stern admonition, he motions to his assistants and the velvet covers are gently removed revealing the ancient treasures.

The girls walk past in hushed astonishment, bent at the waist, and marvel at the priceless relics, the fireplace flames reflecting in their widened eyes. Jennie grips Josephine's hand as their section of the line moves past the tables to choke the temptation building inside her to defy the professor's order. Josephine smiles at her friend's giddiness and is guided from table to table, pausing to inspect one antiquity after the next—amulets and amphorae, bowls and plates, coins and pendants.

At the next to last table, Josephine halts and studies a mysterious brown object, shaped like a sheathed ear of dried corn, unremarkable in appearance other than its notable difference from the delicately rendered pieces of art and culture that preceded it. It is neither polished nor painted, neither carved nor casted, but simple and common on the outside, belying any notion of value or rarity.

"So, what are we to make of this, you are asking yourself," the professor's voice carries over her shoulder.

Jennie's fingers slip out of Josephine's grasp as she moves to the final viewing table.

"None of the other girls have paid much attention to it. Most just glanced at it and moved on. Perhaps it is too puzzling, too challenging. An educated guess, Miss –"

"Barnes. Josephine Barnes."

The professor moves to her side and blocks the line's progress, forcing the remaining girls trailing behind to detour around them as the presenter and student study the curious item together.

Josephine bends over for a closer inspection and then straightens back.

"The relic is not what we see, but what is hidden inside. It is tightly wrapped in cloth—"

"Linen."

"—which has remained secure for quite a long period of time. There was purpose behind that. To protect or hide something."

"Something valuable, Miss Barnes?"

"No.

"Why not?"

"It is not ornate enough, unless the intention of its owner was to mask and mislead."

"A reasonable deduction, I suppose."

"But it is something important. Its shape is puzzling though."

"What if I told you we date this object anywhere from five hundred to a thousand years before Christ's birth? What would you say then?"

"Egyptian, perhaps?"

"Yes, very good."

Professor Parkington pulls a pair of white gloves from his coat sleeve and slips them on.

"Let's take a closer look; shall we?" he invites her, just before she feels the firm, surreptitious press of his covered palm against the small of her back.

The professor cradles the enigmatic treasure.

"Very light and delicate. Open your hand, fingers fully extended please, Miss Barnes."

He carefully rests the frayed brown linen onto her palm.

"You see, weightless, or nearly so."

Josephine is momentarily paralyzed by the ancient artifact unexpectedly in her possession.

"Let me entice you a bit further. You are holding the most fragile item in this priceless collection. By tightening your grip you would easily destroy it. Many of the other antiquities have been chipped or cracked or faded over time. Though protected inside this ordinary wrap, this one has lost something as well, something the others never had, something unique. Would you care to venture a guess what that might be, Miss Barnes?"

"I'm sorry Professor Parkington. I am stumped," Josephine says with a nervous smile, as she shakes her head.

"Its soul, Miss Barnes. It has lost its soul. *Falco tinnunculus.* An Egyptian kestrel falcon, mummified in the funerary ritual by its royal owner. Entombed so as to be transported to the afterlife. Look carefully at the narrow end and will notice a single talon emerging through a torn patch of the linen."

"Yes, I see. Very remarkable, professor. Thank you for this undeserved privilege."

"Not at all," the professor grins as his hands hesitate in retrieving the bird. "We only recently acquired this piece. The temptation is considerable, don't you think, to want to open the concealing wrap and look upon the treasure's features? One day, I shall, with obvious care of course so as to not damage it. The conditions must be properly set to avoid any disturbance of the fragile form inside."

"Yes, of course."

The professor's stare catches Josephine's eyes and lingers. She reflexively turns away, uncomfortable with the man's boldness.

"I see my friend has moved along. I should meet up with her now. The lecture was wonderful. Thank you again, Professor."

"I will make arrangements through the Seminary if you would like to assist in the recordation of the event when the time arrives," the scholar digs further, while gently laying the mummified creature back in its display case. "I can tell you have an analytic mind and well-suited to the applications of scientific theory. Or, if you decide to pass, I will extend the privilege to another girl at the school with a strong interest in the preservation of such wonders."

Josephine does not respond to the offer, preferring to politely smile as she leaves to catch up with Jennie at the final table.

Once the viewing is closed and Professor Parkington is properly thanked by the student sponsor, Josephine slips her arm into Jennie's and the two follow others at the lecture down the hallway to the Blue Bird, a soda fountain adjacent to the dining room.

The Blue Bird's origins trace back to the 1880s, prior to the school's existence, when Vincent Hall, in its original incarnation, was known as the Ye Forest Inne, a hotel built as a summer retreat to serve the Washington elite looking to escape the heat and the sanitary squalor of the city. Numerous improvements were made to the hotel when it was bought in 1894 by the school's founder and dean, John Vincent, and his wife, Maud. Considerable capital was invested by the Vincents to remodel the building and expand the land holdings to accommodate an aggressive construction plan. Long oak bars which previously dispensed gin, bourbon and rye were ripped out and sold at auction. Gambling halls were transformed into classrooms. The hotel's dining hall, renowned in the region for its fresh seafood delivered daily by rail from the city waterfront, was gutted and doubled in size. The kitchen was expanded and modernized to accommodate the large number of cooks and servers the school would soon employ. The flamboyant, gilded parlors and corridors covered with Persians rugs were largely untouched as was the Ye Forest Inne's exterior, constructed in the Queen Anne style popular in the day, with its encircling covered porch, jutting bay windows, and shingle-roof turrets. The Blue Bird too survived and became a beloved retreat dispensing confectionary creations to each student who walked through the ponderous double doors of Vincent Hall.

"Wasn't that a real treat? I mean it wasn't the Hope Diamond but to see all those old treasures up close was remarkable, wouldn't you say? It is like we had our very own British Museum for the day," Jennie says with great animation, leaning over her hazelnut ice cream served in a polished silver bowl. "It makes me want to travel to Greece and the Aegean badly. Father says the family will go to Europe one of these years, but I can't imagine ever traveling that far. It would be quite the adventure."

Josephine nods as she listens intently to the ebullient girl recount the lecture, repeatedly plunging her straw up and down into her glass. They are fortunate to have secured a table in the crowded room. Other late arrivals mingle in front of the entrance, searching for space to open.

"That is my dream, once I am married, to go with my husband and my family and travel the globe. Paris, Rome, Athens, the pyramids of Egypt, sail up the Nile, to see it all. It would take the good part of a year and cost a fortune, but time here at the Seminary is bound to improve a girl's chances of finding a man of means to make dreams come true, right? As they say, 'nothing attracts money like money.' Or maybe we will be able to fly in an airplane to these places before long."

"But there is more to it than that," Josephine counsels.

"Flying? I don't think I would have the nerve to get into one. An ocean liner would suit me just fine."

"I was speaking about what you said about finding a husband with money and why we are here. You make it sound like we are dolls on display in a storefront window."

"Don't get me wrong, I enjoy what the school has to offer, but it is designed for a purpose. I'm not alone in thinking this way. I hear the older girls talk."

"And you believe that purpose to be preparing us for marriage?"

"Not simply marriage. Marriage to a suitable match," she playfully corrects Josephine.

"A cynical view at such a tender age, don't you think?"

Jennie shrugs her shoulders.

"Not after listening to the other girls going on all the time about this guy and that guy? It's all many of them talk about."

"And beyond that? Surely Forest Glen provides you with some personal reward that is measured differently. There is a grander—to use your word—'design' at work here, don't you believe?"

"Is there? I am not so sure. I figured this place out within the first week of being dropped off at the train station. Most of the girls are sent here to find well-heeled husbands in the end. Whether they consciously know it or not, their parents do. For all the talk about the preparatory courses and academic fulfillment, the Seminary is a high-priced finishing school. Look around us. Everything about this place is unworldly, built as a fantasy world for a few hundred princesses to find their Prince Charmings. No one says it—at least not officially—because it sounds crass and demeaning. But it's true."

"Is that why your parents sent you here?"

Jennie pauses and idly scrapes her spoon around the edges of the serving dish.

"Honestly, I think that's exactly what they had in mind. For all their cheerful promises and enthusiasm over an elite education and what-not, I think this was the easiest way out for them."

"I don't understand. A way out of what?"

"Out of being responsible. Out of being involved. Out of being there for me. You know, the typical complaints of a whiny girl."

"You say that without a hint of bitterness. Do you really believe what you are saying? I have to assume that your parents love you very much and believe they are doing the best for you by bringing you to Forest Glen."

"Parents can be both loving and misguided, can't they? Or am I the one being naïve?"

Josephine is taken back by the girl's bluntness. It is out of character for Jennie to speak so seriously and with such unabashed conviction. Their previous conversations had been typically frivolous and mundane, focused mostly on studies or school events. This is a side of Jennie she has never seen before.

"And that is the role you willingly play, Jennie, that of a princess in waiting?"

"You make it sound so inconsequential. Is happiness not central to who we are? Why should we be ashamed or apologetic of this reality? The Seminary is a means to an end. That's all I am saying."

"You are fooling yourself, Jennie. Don't you see that our time here is meant to put us on a different path? Men of genuine substance will look at you and expect more than a girl whose sole goal in life is to marry well-off."

The expression on Jennie's face sours and she looks away. Josephine knows immediately that her rash words have unintentionally hurt the girl. From what Josephine has gleaned in previous talks, she does not have a boyfriend in California, and she has not attracted the attention of young men at school social events or group forays off campus since arriving at Forest Glen.

"What I mean to say is, why are we supposed to lead a passive existence? Why should we wait for someone to provide us happiness instead of seeking it out for ourselves? Surely it is more rewarding to accomplish something than it is to be handed it by others."

Jennie turns her gaze upward and skims her slender silver spoon across the top of the melting mound of ice cream.

"I understand your point, and I don't quibble with it," Josephine continues, "but don't you want to be in a place in your life where you aren't dependent on anyone, for anything? The only way that can happen is if we step out from the shadows of those who society expects will provide for us."

"How exactly does that come about, Josephine? We both sit here, girls of privilege, in a golden chrysalis, expected to emerge into a world we did not make and which we are ill-equipped to change."

"We don't need to change the world. We need to change what is in here," Josephine touches her temple and then slides her fingers to the neckline of her uniform, "and here. It is about being strong. Strong in word. Strong in belief. Confident. Unafraid of being alone. Challenging yourself. See those foreign wonders you want to see, but on your terms, not as adjunct luggage to the dreams of another."

She tenderly takes hold of the girl's free hand.

"Make the most of your time here."

"Be careful," Jennie answers after a long pause. "It wasn't that long ago that women were burned at the stake for speaking such heretical words aloud."

Josephine laughs and plays with the collapsing paper straw tip.

"Fortunately, we live in more enlightened times."

"It comes so easy for you," Jennie says with a look of admiration.

"What does?"

"Everything. I look at you and you always seem in control. Your life appears...I don't know...effortless."

"Hardly. I was just like you, Jennie, when I first came here. Everything was new and unfamiliar. It will take some time, and gradually the homesickness will go away. You'll see."

"Ah, the virtue of patience. Not my strong suit, I suppose," she says with an air of resignation, her angular face looking down as she traces the border of the cloth napkin on her lap.

"Jennie, one day soon you will meet a man and you will fall in love, and he will love you with equal conviction. I am sure of it. But he will not be the source of your happiness. He will not be the one who validates what is inside you."

Jennie smiles and swirls the spoon around the cup.

"Stirring words from a girl who has a handsome midshipman madly in love with her. He is coming to the Christmas ball, isn't he?"

Josephine nods.

"And hopefully with some of his friends in tow." Jennie pushes the half-eaten dish away. "I shouldn't eat anymore or I will lose my appetite for dinner."

A group of girls at the entrance stir as they eye the girls' table.

"Yes, Robert is a fine man and if he is part of my future it will be as a conspirator, not as a protector."

Jennie looks at the senior girl with a bemused expression.

"It's not hard to see why the men flock to you."

Inside the Odeon, Madame Marguerite Kaspar, the school's voice culture teacher, leads the Seminary chorus in an afternoon practice of the seasonal carols and religious hymns selected for Friday's Christmas concert. Madame Kaspar studied piano and voice in Frankfurt as a young woman before touring Europe with a French opera company. Her journey to the National Park Seminary was a circuitous one, following numerous teaching positions at prominent Washington schools catering to foreign students. At Forest Glen, she takes considerable pride in having American girls who arrive with no training or appreciation of music discover the tone, rhythm and harmony hidden inside them. Vocalization and elocution are prerequisite courses for all students at the school, and those who stand before Madame Kaspar hear her extol the beauty of the feminine voice and the obligation each student has to cultivate it.

"The possession of a singing voice is sacred," she preaches to each class of new girls. "If you ignore it, you ignore the gift of Providence."

The most advanced pupils are provided private instruction in opera oratorios and given the opportunity to join the school chorus. This year's group of thirty-two girls is exceptionally talented, the best, in Madame Kaspar's assessment, there has been in her eight years at the school. Weeks earlier, at the fall recital, their strong, melodic voices had filled the Odeon with soaring, harmonious perfection, the enraptured audience erupting in a thunderous ovation led by Dean Dawson and his wife standing in their private box overhanging the stage. The evening Christmas performance will be more intimate and solemn, with the amphitheater festooned with greenery and seasonal decorations and the stage lit solely by candles. She wants the faculty and students to leave the hall moved by the ethereal voices they hear, their hearts full and content. She wants the performance to be transcendent.

For two hours the chorus practices, their voices strained and their bodies exhausted by standing erect on the risers. Only the stage is illuminated in the cold and cavernous auditorium and Madame Kasper paces it during practice like a caged leopard, eyes down, ears attentive, hissing out commands, pawing at her students to maintain their posture, to elevate their chins, to draw from the diaphragms not their throats. Her wooden rod taps the floor in time, occasionally lashing out like the agitated tail of an impatient predator.

The last song of the Christmas program, Silent Night, will be sung in the original German and Leah and two other seniors have been chosen by Madame Kaspar to sing a stanza each as soloists. It is an honor of significant prestige, she tells the girls, to be selected to sing apart from the group.

"Stand alone poised and beautiful and with your voice make those who listen secretly want to be you," she prods the trio.

Leah, tired from rising early to journey to the creek, joins the other soloists in their positions in front and then Madame Kasper, when satisfied that all the choir members are set and attentive, raises her hand.

All movement is suspended. Darkness encircles the pale-lit stage. The vaulted rafters high above the stage are shadowy and quiet.

Madame Kasper's will yields and her hand draws downward in a steady motion, and all the girls' voices blend into a singular, jolting wall of flawless harmony. The soft, fluid hands that guide the chorus through a prelude to the ancient carol belie the teacher's rigid demeanor and exacting glare. The sound pours from the stage and flows over the rows of empty seats and fills the Odeon until a soprano crescendo rises and abruptly halts. Two silent measures and Madame Kaspar turns slightly toward the first soloist.

"Stille Nacht, heilige Nacht. Alles schlaft, einsam wacht."

Leah closes her eyes, listens to the girl's soothing voice, and waits her turn.

She has been fitful throughout the day ever since leaving the glen with May, Josephine and Margaret, helpless in shaking off the unsettling, icy chill that has seeped into her joints. The group returned to Senior House unable or simply unwilling to talk further about what they had seen in the raging creek. They left scared and confused as to what to do or what to say. Why hadn't we told someone, she questioned herself repeatedly after returning to the dormitory? What did we fear? We had done nothing wrong. We were only witnesses to...to what exactly? What had she and the others seen? In her room she replayed in her head over and over what took place, trying to recall some detail that had been overlooked, some shred of buried memory that would help explain the oppressive weight occupying her conscience.

"Holder Knabe im lockigen Haar. Schlaf in himmlischer Ruh! Schlaf in himmlischer Ruh!"

Eyes still shut, she feels a draft settle on her shoulders and recalls the sensation of morning mist in the glen on her skin. The tips of Leah's fingers tingle and twitch as her arms, heavy and lifeless, hang at her side caressing the cool fabric of her dress. Imperceptible to Madame Kaspar and the others on stage, she sways slightly to one side as a dulling sheet of fatigue is draped slowly over her head and body.

In her mind's eye, the wild, destructive stream reappears. She stares deeply into the swift current. Beneath the turbulence, smoky plumes undulate and recede and then re-form, drawing her hypnotically to the murky water. She takes one step closer and then another, propelled toward the chaos by the lure of discovery. Her weight sinks into the saturated grass as she nears the creek's edge forcing brown bubbles out along the edge of her boot soles. The air is thick with moisture and laced with the sweet aroma of putrescence. Out of the perilous current an embryonic shape begins to take form.

I can see it. Yes, I see it now.

An incongruous feeling of contentment comes over her as she steps into the numbing water. Her chest tightens as the cold robs her of breath. Just as the vision is about to come into focus, it again loses definition, its lines blurred in the churning miasma now encircling her waist.

No, don't leave! Not this close. Is this what you saw, Josephine? Do you see it too, May? Margaret?

The frigid morning air in the glen slips past Leah's coat collar and caresses the length of her exposed neck. As she wades further into the violent creek, the paralyzing chill grips her and she looks down just as her hands and wrists plunge into the consuming blackness.

Help me, she calls to the other girls as she moves deeper into the wild, bracing water. *Help me grab onto it.*

We can make it all right again.

Further into the accepting water Leah wades until she suddenly loses her footing and feels the firm ground under her boots drop away. Her body rises and floats above the receding creek bed. She is no longer guiding her progress toward the transforming shape in the water. She is being drawn to *It*.

An inexorable force reaches inside her chest and pulls her closer still toward the body forming in a telescopic tunnel of darkness. She struggles but is powerless to break away and feels the weight of her disconnected, overtaken body pulled deeper into the stream. A nauseating wave of abject fear courses through her veins and her eyes bulge as the deadly water laps against her shoulders and neck. Panic consumes her.

It can't end like this. Not like this.

Leah's harrowing descent is suddenly arrested by the strong grip of a hand from behind and she immediately thinks of Josephine. The counterweight halts the precipitous drag on Leah's body from beneath the ebony surface, and then begins to pull her back out of the sucking current.

Josephine, always reliable, always there for others.

An arm, tensile and swift, encircles Leah's waist and she feels a form press along the length of her back, the words of her faceless savior caressing her ear.

"Shepherds quake at the sight. Glories stream from heaven afar."

She feels her body lift unnaturally out of the raging stream until her feet dangle above the surface and the comforting embrace around her stomach constricts painfully. The powerful hold draws her away from the water's edge and up the stone path from which they came, as if in backwards flight, weightless and free. The trees along the glen sway wildly as if they were pliant saplings. The howl of the fierce gale swirls around her as her hair wildly lashes her face. As the creek recedes Leah sees May under her umbrella gazing forlornly into the water. Margaret is standing next to her, pale and expressionless. Before them, prostrate on the ground, dressed in a white gown of immaculate brilliance, is the sobbing body of the one she believed to be her savior—Josephine!

Horrified, Leah struggles against her captor in a futile attempt to reach out to them. Ribbons of cold flesh slip over her mouth and revulsion electrifies her body as she continues her silent ascent.

Light gives way to darkness.

Speak.

Speak. Now.

Speak now!

Leah convulses with a violent jolt. Her mouth opens and her chest heaves.

"Stille Nacht, heilige Nacht. Gottes Sohn, a wie lacht."

Her eyes open and through the tears she can see Madame Kaspar standing before her on the Odeon stage against the backdrop of empty seats.

"Lieb' aus deinem gottlichen Mund."

Leah feels the lyrics take flight as she sings, undistracted by the moist lines that streak her cheeks and neck.

"Christ, in deiner Geburt! Christ, in deiner Geburt!"

When the final notes of the last solo fill the hall and then dissipate, Leah gasps for breath and runs off the stage. After Madame Kaspar commends the chorus and dismisses them, she searches for her star pupil, eventually finding her in the half-lit recesses backstage.

"Leah, my dear," she reaches out comfortingly as she approaches. "Don't feel ashamed of the power of your voice. You have an extraordinary gift. Let it move you like it moves others who hear you. You are right to relinquish your soul to the emotion you feel. It is the beauty of the talent you possess. Only by giving yourself completely to your art can you reach the heights of accomplishment of which you are capable. It is an epiphany, my dear, a moment of religious revelation, when the connection between your voice and inner being becomes so pure. You are fortunate you are capable of experiencing such exaltation. Though it may be unnerving to you, do not fear it. Embrace it. Embrace it. This is who you are."

Leah nods as she continues struggling to regain her breath, refusing to face her instructor.

"When you feel more composed, join the others. Do not seek refuge in flight. This is a breakthrough, yes? I believe so. A breakthrough."

Madame Kaspar leaves the emotional girl and returns to the stage where her assistants are removing the chorus risers. She smiles contently as she walks, drawing her shawl tightly over her shoulders, feeling the melodic spirit well-up inside her.

Outside the Odeon, the sun is setting after its brief appearance and the temperature has fallen precipitously. The early winter air, raw and biting, descends through the Odeon's loose joints and rafters and settles over the spartan backstage.

Leah listens to the sound of Madame Kaspar's joyful humming recede behind her and stares down at her hands as they tremble uncontrollably.

For the first time since the storm enveloped Forest Glen, the sounds of girls talking and laughing are heard on the bridges and pathways, reverberating off the facades of dormitories and clubhouses, like frenzied cicadas emerging from a prolonged dormancy, trying to squeeze what enjoyment remains of their free day. By dusk, groups of students who had spent the day in the city begin arriving back to the station. Some return by train, while most others travel back on the Woodside and Forest Glen trolley, a feeder line that branches off the main streetcar tracks that run along Georgia Avenue and terminates at the post office building just south of the Baltimore & Ohio rail station. While locomotive service to the District is more comfortable and quicker, the trolley, with its large windows and breezy progress, is more frequent and less costly and provides students with a more intimate ride from which to experience the sounds, smells and sights of the city's uptown neighborhoods and downtown businesses.

More significantly, it was the streetcar that brought the overhead power lines to Forest Glen and, in turn, allowed the dean and the school board of trustees to electrify the entire National Park Seminary campus. Newly upgraded, the school was marketed throughout affluent communities around America as the nation's most prestigious and modern preparatory educational institution exclusively for young women. During the decade of prosperity that ensued, the Seminary enrollment swelled. When demand could no longer be accommodated, waitlists were instituted which further validated the school's marketing claims in the minds of the wealthy and the elite. Teachers were hired away from more established private schools along the East Coast to support the classroom expansion and separate quarters were built on the southern boundary of campus, near the riding stables, to house the growing number of cooks, maids, gardeners, and other workers who keep the school functioning on a daily basis.

Josephine returns to her room at Senior House after her social with Jennie Milburn to prepare for dinner and finds the envelope slipped under her door by Miss Price. The unexpected note is short and business-like:

Miss Barnes, please come and see me tomorrow morning during your scheduled gymnastics period. I have spoken to Mrs. Chesborough and obtained permission for your absence. I wish to speak with you about this morning's visit to the glen.

V/R, Miss K. Price

Josephine goes immediately to Margaret's room and finds her friend struggling to fasten the back closure of her evening dress.

"There you are. Perfect timing. I cannot get these buttons to save my life."

"Did Miss Price come to see you or leave you a note?" Josephine asks, deftly fastening the troublesome buttons.

Margaret adjusts her dress in front of the mirror and selects a strand of delicate pearls from the jewelry box and places them across her neck.

"No, why should she? Have I been accused of breaking some obscure house rule again? What do you think?" she asks glancing at the necklace.

Josephine hands her the note to read.

"I see, so you are the one who has run afoul of school canon this time. What exactly for, I have no clue. I was in my room the entire day, reading and catching up on the sleep you robbed me of. She would have passed by my door on her way to your room. I honestly think that woman does not like me. I've felt that from the first day I walked into her classroom. She picks favorites. And I think you are one of hers—at least until now," Margaret taunts her, passing back the note.

"Please be serious."

"Be serious about what? She wants to speak with you, nothing more, nothing less."

Margaret replaces the pearls and searches for a different necklace to go with serge wool dress. She catches Josephine's eyes in the mirror and sees the concern in her expression.

"Relax. Nothing happened at the glen. We went to look at the flood and Leah and May got spooked. That's all. I wouldn't be surprised if one of them went and said something to Miss Price. Wasn't that what May kept on saying we should do? Just go ask the skittish mouse and that will clear it all up."

Josephine ponders the advice.

"I am not sure about confronting May. She can misinterpret and over-react to the simplest of questions. It might be best if I find out first what Miss Price wants to talk about."

Margaret auditions a second necklace and Josephine nods.

"Perfect."

Margaret fastens it around her neck, smoothes the dress along the length of her body and over her hips and winks at herself in the mirror. Snatching her white gloves off the dresser, she playfully lashes Josephine across the backside.

"Go dress and I'll wait for you, but don't keep me waiting too long or I'll go without you and dine with the Sweets."

Both May and Leah are absent from dinner, which, for a Monday night, is not out of the ordinary. Girls traveling to the city, by rule with chaperones, often will make a full day of it and dine at the upscale restaurants in hotels along Pennsylvania Avenue, returning well after the dining room has closed.

But when neither of the girls comes to breakfast the following morning, Josephine's anxiety over the senior regent's note begins to grow. What exactly had Miss Price been told and by whom? She knows Margaret is right. Nothing happened to warrant her involvement and concern. And yet, the note's vagueness is troubling.

While Josephine sits and listens to her morning lectures her usual mental discipline and focus falters and her thoughts wander back to the scene at the glen. What had she seen moving past her in the water before the dress and the other items appeared? No matter how hard she tried, she could not conjure up any certainty or revelations about the troubling episode. Is it possible that her mind was tricking her, preventing her from understanding the truth of what she saw in the clouded water in those fleeting seconds?

Miss Price greets Josephine with a cordial smile and escorts her inside her tidy office. Sunlight streams through the window next to the teacher's desk and bathes the room in warmth. They sit in chairs next to a small oval table and Miss Price pours tea for both of them, not bothering to ask if Josephine wants some. Her demeanor is relaxed and friendly and Josephine feels the weight of self-doubt immediately rise from her shoulders.

"It's been awhile since we have talked alone, hasn't it?"

Josephine agrees and sips her tea.

"Soon you will be leaving all this," Miss Price mockingly motions to the view of sorority houses and dormitories outside her floor-to-ceiling window, lined up like islands in an archipelago of architectural whimsy.

"If you don't mind me prying, Josephine, what are your plans after graduation in the spring?"

"Honestly, I am not certain, Miss Price."

"You are among the brightest of your class. You will have options. Will you stay on in Washington to continue your studies or seek employment?

"Perhaps. I am not sure what I should do next. My parents ask me the same question and I struggle to answer them. I feel there is a...is a next step, a next chapter, something. It bothers me that I don't know what it is. I feel I should know."

"Don't fret. Among the girls in your class, your future is the least of my worries. How about marriage?"

"What about it?" Josephine replies snippily.

Miss Price's eyebrows arch in feigned surprise.

"Also a possibility, yes? A young woman with your pleasant disposition and feminine features surely is not wanting for attention."

"There is someone, yes."

"Good. All is well, then. I have fulfilled my advisor duties."

Miss Price blows across the steaming cup before drawing a sip.

"Speaking of your classmates, May King came to me yesterday quite agitated about your impromptu trip to see the flood. Did she tell you she came to see me?"

Josephine shakes her head.

"That's not surprising. By the time she left, I could tell she had second thoughts about coming to my office. In any case, she was quite upset, as I said. As I understand what happened, you went down to the glen with May, Margaret Cleary, and Leah Hathaway, and that at some point down by the Grotto you fished a dress out of the creek which alarmed Leah and May who thought it might have come off someone carried off in the flood. Is that pretty much what happened, in a nutshell?"

"Yes, I suppose."

"After May left my office, I went down to the spot where she said you were and looked around. I walked along the creek bed, upstream and downstream, as far as I could go before it became impassable. As you saw, the glen is littered with downed trees and branches and I could see the high water mark of sediment left by the flood along the banks. But I saw no evidence to confirm May's fears. I then phoned the county authorities and asked if anyone in the area had been reported missing or drowned. Thankfully, no one had."

"That is wonderful news, Miss Price. I could tell doubt was preying on May's mind when we walked back to the dormitory."

"It is wonderful news, Josephine. And May was quite relieved, if somewhat embarrassed, when I told her this morning what I had found out."

Miss Price sips her tea and then places it down on the table.

"I'm disappointed, however, that you didn't come to me or someone else in the administration about the incident. I would have expected you to."

Josephine is stung by the sudden pivot in the teacher's demeanor and stammers to respond to her admonishment.

"I am not sure why I am to be faulted—"

"Josephine, please," Miss Price interrupts, "surely you see your failing in the matter. There was a possibility that someone had drowned or was drowning while you and the others stood by. Just because it turns out that such a tragedy did not occur does not absolve you of the responsibility you had to act, to notify someone, so that it could be investigated further. You can't sit there now and tell me you don't understand this."

The accusation fills Josephine with shame and she can feel her cheeks burning as Miss Price's disapproving gaze locks on to her.

The regent is right, she concedes, too embarrassed to speak. She has been blind to her obvious failure to act when the moment called for it. The realization is painful to accept and makes her want to bolt the room as quickly as possible.

The teacher softens her tone upon seeing Josephine's physical reaction.

"May said she urged you at the glen to tell someone about the dress. Is this true? Did she request that of you? It's important that I hear from you the details of what transpired."

The rush of emotion makes it difficult for Josephine to process what she is being asked and she looks away distracted, settling her stare on an oil portrait of a dour man with a heavy moustache on the wall in front of her, the Bible clutched to his left breast, his right hand resting lightly on a globe.

Miss Price repeats her question, and Josephine regains her focus.

"Yes...I mean, no... May said '*we*' should notify the dean. I don't recall her saying that I should..." her voice trails off. Suddenly, she isn't sure what she remembers.

"May said that Leah agreed with her, and that Leah was actually the first to voice a concern about the danger of the flood. Is it accurate that both girls wanted to go notify someone in authority?"

"We all agreed that it wasn't necessary."

"Agreed or bullied into agreeing?"

Josephine holds her tongue. She recalls the way in which Margaret belittled May as she did almost all the girls when she became impatient.

"You are right, Miss Price, I should have reported what we found in the glen. I should have listened to May and come immediately to see you or someone else in the administration."

The words of contrition are spoken with sincerity and when she finishes she searches the eyes of her teacher for the absolution that will settle her conscience.

"But why didn't you, Josephine?"

"I don't know. It happened all so quickly and I suppose I wasn't thinking straight at the time."

"Were you frightened?"

Josephine laughs nervously at the question.

"No."

"May said that you saw something float by in the water before the dress was taken out. What was it that you saw?"

"Ask May, she saw it too."

"I am asking you. Is it possible that you were frightened by what you saw and that it alarmed you so much you couldn't bring yourself to tell anyone else? I am sincerely trying to help you deal with what happened there, Josephine, whether you believe so or not. But I'm having a hard time understanding why the girl at the top of her class, with your leadership skills and demonstrated maturity, would consider covering up a drowning—"

"No one drowned! You said so yourself, Miss Price," Josephine shoots back in exasperation, causing the regent to settle back in her chair.

"So we now know."

"And I did not cover anything up. Is that what May said, that I tried to keep secret what we found? Why would she make such a hurtful charge,

Miss Price? It was all rather innocent and I don't understand why she is now twisting the few minutes we spent at the glen into something deceitful. Why would May say such a thing? She knows better."

Miss Price does not respond to her student directly. She rests the tea cup and saucer on the table, pauses in thought, and leans closer to Josephine's chair.

"I am about to speak to you not as your regent or your teacher but as one woman speaking to another. As such, I expect what is spoken between us from this point on is kept in strict confidence. Do I have your word?"

Josephine nods her assent.

Miss Price continues, the sharpness of her earlier interrogation replaced by a hushed, more intimate tone.

"I know the school administration can be pedantic and preachy in its philosophy. I find it hard to accept at times myself. All the talk about taking young, impressionable minds and building them into modern Renaissance women can be tiresome. But it's the sort of thing parents want to hear. It's what sells them on sending their daughters off to a school halfway across the country and paying a considerable amount for the privilege—the notion that girls will be turned into women of distinction, their minds, their sensibilities, their deportment disciplined and made exemplary. The reality is, of course, something different. We teach our students about the importance of freeing the mind and encouraging self-expression but ignore the rigidity that underlies this entire place.

"When I look at you, it is not hard to see myself just a few years ago. I think we share a number of the same qualities, though you may not find the comparison a favorable one. I remember straining against the rules and expectations I was under at your age. May King and many of the other girls like her will leave here and struggle to find their way. They will have spent years at National Park Seminary and return to their homes, their lives largely unchanged and no better equipped to answer the question of how, moving ahead, they intend to leave their mark. They are too comfortably ensconced in the embrace of their family money and social status to think twice about why they are placed here on this Earth.

"It's the arrogance and complacency about this place that I disdain the most. You can see it in the faces of the girls, in the way they carry themselves, the sense of entitlement. I don't blame them as much as I pity them, for they cannot possibly understand how their privilege is robbing them of their individuality. Most of them waltz through National Park blithely unaware of the world beyond its borders, devoid of the intellectual curiosity that defines us."

Josephine has never been spoken to by a member of the faculty in such a frank manner and she struggles to decipher Miss Price's intention.

"When I asked you a moment ago to tell me what you saw in the glen, you deflected the question to what May said she saw. It was not only petulant of you to speak that way, it was a lazy, immature reaction. Never let May King or anyone else speak for you. Be responsible for your own views and actions and, when asked, speak with conviction. This may seem to be a tempest in a teapot to you, but it's a test of your character and your capability to deal with life when it is not tamed and tempered."

Josephine cringes at being lectured with her own words—the words spoken to Jennie just the day before at the ice cream parlor.

Miss Price rises and walks to her desk.

"I've made my point, and I have kept you long enough. I know it may seem a long way from now, but I hope when you leave our school next spring you will let me know your whereabouts and what you are doing. I hope we can continue our friendship."

The recognition of her hypocrisy sinks in and Josephine stares into her tea cup, chastised and repentant.

"Thank you, Miss Price for your counsel. I sincerely apologize for not coming to see you right away yesterday."

Josephine rises and opens the office door to leave.

"Josephine, before you go. There is something I forgot to ask."

"Yes, Miss Price."

"The dress. The dress you pulled from the creek. What became of it?"

"We...we left it there, on the grass, when we walked back to Senior House."

"The reason why I ask is that it wasn't there when I went to the glen. May explained to me that when you pulled out the dress it was laid on the ground a sufficient distance from the water so it is unlikely that it would have been washed away again."

Josephine conjures the image of the bright white dress lying against the glistening green grass. The details of its shape and simple design are vivid as if it rested now on the table in front of her.

"I suppose that's right, Miss Price. Perhaps another girl came to the glen after we left and took it."

"That's most likely what happened."

"Thank you for the tea, Miss Price."

Later that evening, following dinner and the requisite thirty minute allotment of dancing in the Vincent Hall grand ballroom, the girls of Theta Sigma Rho sorority assemble at the Spanish Mission to sing and recite poetry and gossip. Tuesday evenings are designated for weekly club meetings and the sorority houses dotting the secluded campus sparkle in the clear night. The mood inside the Spanish Mission is festive and frivolous as girls in their long evening dresses lounge on chairs bought from the desert plains of New Mexico and fantasize aloud about the parties and social engagements that await them when they return home at semester's end. The night has grown colder and the last of the girls from the rooftop garden patio move inside to find a spot on the sprawling hand-sewn wool Navajo rug, with its intricate pattern of red, green and brown diamonds, spread before the well-stoked fireplace.

The Theta clubhouse is one of the first built at the National Park Seminary and it occupies a location on the southern edge of campus, nestled against a wooded backdrop, near the school chapel and library. It is isolated from the newer sorority buildings of Beta, Delta and Kappa that line the interior drive running northward from the front entrance of Vincent Hall to the Villa dormitory and then across the glen to the train station. The Spanish Mission was constructed along a county road cutting east to west through the campus perimeter creating an artificial barrier between the outlying clubhouse and the school's main buildings.

Travelers heading east on the road from the Spanish Mission pass a row of distinctive structures on the left in quick succession: the Aloha dormitory connected to Recitation Hall by a statuary colonnade, the gymnasium, the greenhouse, and the equestrian stables. A side driveway runs behind the stables leading to auxiliary facilities, including the carpenter's shop and modest quarters for the colored men who work in the kitchen and tend to the grounds. A section of the woods across the road from the gymnasium was cleared three years before to accommodate an athletic field, where the annual field day is now held, and a riding ring. Lawn tennis courts were added soon after in an attempt to provide the girls of National Park, according to the Seminary's promotional brochure, the *"outdoor stimulus necessary to overcome all the distempers due to hot-house existence."*

In the opposite direction, the county road continues along the school's rear boundary and skirts past Chiopi's Japanese Pagoda and the Swiss Chalet of Zeta club before turning north. A separate walking path parallels this section of the road for a quarter mile before diverging and continuing toward the glen along a retaining wall that secures the rear foundations of Senior House and the Odeon.

Josephine sits in a wood slat lounge chair and listens to the cacophony of the other Theta girls around the fireplace in the adjacent room. She recounts in her mind the exchange with Miss Price, her lonely state of reflection occasionally interrupted by the greetings of her sorority sisters passing through. The smarting of the regent's words has not dissipated with time. Despite Miss Price's softened appeal at the end their meeting, Josephine carries a gnawing feeling of self-doubt since leaving the office.

But something in addition to Miss Price's reprimand preys on her mind. She ponders without resolution the very question broached with Jennie and, later, with the disapproving teacher, that being the course of her life, her future beyond the National Park Seminary campus. Of what value has her time at the school been if she continually struggles to navigate through her sea of emotional ambivalence?

Miss Price's words resurface: *When I look at you, it is not hard to see myself just a few years ago.*

Is this to be her path, the path followed by the judgmental administrator? The notion that she casually glimpsed her future during her meeting in the regent's office gives Josephine a palpable start. She has never thought of Miss Price in this way. Or perhaps she failed to see herself as others do. A reflection in an imperfect mirror. She pulls her legs off the floor and lays a blanket over her curled body to ward off the creeping chill.

Over a year has passed since she first met Robert and their relationship has progressed in that time despite the distance between the school and the Naval Academy in Annapolis and their intermittent contact. His future is a career in uniform, often away at sea. Hers is uncharted and adrift. It is understandable, she concedes, that some naturally gravitate to the conclusion that marriage between them is likely. But it is a topic that neither of

INCIDENT AT FOREST GLEN   55

them has broached, and a notion that others, such as Miss Price and Jennie, evidently contemplate more seriously than she. Why have I been so blind to what others presume?

Margaret enters the room in animated discussion with two underclass girls about where the Christmas tree, which the school has purchased and delivered to the door of each clubhouse, should be placed. One girl argues for the rooftop next to the mission bell and the other advocates for a location inside near the fireplace.

Margaret glances over at Josephine with a look of silent exasperation and intercedes.

"We will not to be the first sorority to burn its house to the ground, so the fireplace is out. Last year's tree was dropping needles before we even brought it inside. And while the roof has a certain allure, I can't see how we are going to be singing carols by candlelight in the dark. My vote is that we put it in front of the parlor window. There it can be seen by those passing outside and it won't clutter the room and get bumped into," she declares, leading the two girls in tow across the room to the large window that affords a generous view of the county road and the massive gymnasium beyond it.

In the foreground, twenty yards from the Spanish Mission, stands the resolute statue of Hiawatha, the bare-chested stone Indian wielding a bow who keeps vigilant watch over the girls of Theta house. So unnerving is his brutish presence and steely stare, Hiawatha is affectionately nicknamed "Peeping Tom," a moniker never mentioned in any school publication or map. Peeping Tom has become the club's adopted mascot and is decorated and dressed in women's clothes by tradition during the May Day celebration, the warrior feather jutting upward from his forehead topped whimsically with a straw boater.

As Margaret listens to the two girls continue to plead their cases for the tree's placement, she glances out the parlor window and marvels at the radiant beauty of the night. A full moon is on display and the trees cast faint shadows on the lawn and illuminate the white columns of the gymnasium's front portico. Frost twinkles on the granite pedestal beneath the swarthy, oversized watchman. Silhouetted clouds drift in a fathomless winter sky, playfully obscuring the nocturnal beams as they stray across the face of the moon.

In the ebb and flow of this muted half-light, Margaret catches the slight yet perceptible movement of something on the lawn, concealed in the shadows of the night alongside the figure of Hiawatha. She squints and focuses intently on the statue, but the brightness of the light inside the Spanish Mission makes it difficult to discern what in front of the clubhouse caught her attention. She stares out at the moonlit ground and waits to glimpse the intruder again, but all around the looming warrior is still. Perhaps it was the interior reflection against the window pane of one of the other girls moving about the room, Margaret wonders.

Then she notices it, an irregularity in the familiar shape. The outline along the left side of the statue's pedestal is different than the right side—curved, misshaped, not as crisply defined. She wasn't hallucinating after all. Someone or something is crouched behind Peeping Tom.

She watches unblinkingly while her club sisters drone on in debate.

"I see you," she whispers to herself. "I see you. And you know I see you."

A few seconds pass and Margaret realizes she is at a disadvantage, for whomever is out in the night looking in can see her and the other girls illuminated behind the bay window as if they were projected onto a theater screen.

"Enough. Enough, girls. Take it to the others around the hearth and put it to a show of hands," Margaret abruptly dismisses the two and then walks over to Josephine's chair.

She reaches down, tugs away the blanket, and takes a hold of Josephine's wrist.

"Let's go out front and get so more wood, my dear."

Ignoring her friend's protest, she leads Josephine past the boisterous group and to the door.

"What is it? What's the matter? Margaret, I don't have my coat!"

The frigid air splashes Josephine face and her muscles brace against the chill. Margaret refuses to release her wrist until she wrestles her away from the entry.

"Quiet!" she huffs.

As they stand on the covered porch, Margaret looks over Josephine's shoulder toward the statue, her eyes adjusting to the sudden darkness.

"I think someone is standing by Peeping Tom and has been there for awhile," she whispers.

Josephine turns to look.

"Are you sure? Who is it?"

"I don't know. But I most certainly saw something move out there when I was at the window with those two magpies."

The porch offers a different perspective than the parlor window and Margaret strains to find the distortion in shape she spotted before. The raw night air summons bumps along her arms and legs. Josephine moves away from Margaret and is about to step down off of the porch when she feels a hand grab her arm and pull her back.

"Wait. Where are you going? There might be a pervert or escaped convict hiding out there for all you know."

"Then why did you drag me out here? Is it your plan that we stand here and have a staring contest and freeze? There is only one way to find out what's going on. And you are coming with me," Josephine insists.

The two lock arms and move slowly across the moist lawn toward the steadfast sentry. Margaret glimpses back across her shoulder at the brightly lit parlor window and sees no one. If trouble awaits them ahead, there will be no witnesses to come to their aid.

Neither girl sees anything out of the ordinary as they approach and Margaret feels her anxiety dissipate with each step. As they near, Hiawatha's familiar carved lines and features come into view. Had Margaret spotted someone next to the statue, the person is now gone.

"What exactly—" Josephine begins before abruptly stopping. She is jerked back by the countervailing pull of Margaret's arm as her friend halts in her tracks.

A dark figure steps out from behind the imposing stone warrior and stands silently before them, its features cloaked by a hooded cape. Josephine squeezes down hard on Margaret's hand and arrests her friend's attempted flight. The ominous form moves forward and the two girls step back as one. Margaret feels a scream rise and lodge in her throat. With a quick thrust upward, the stranger removes the concealing hood.

"It's me. Leah. I didn't mean to frighten you."

Margaret's fear quickly turns to rage at the unexpected appearance of her classmate.

"What the—why in God's name are you skulking around here at night?" she lashes out. "How long were you hiding before I saw you from the window?"

"For a while. I am not sure how long. I am not sure of a lot these days. I came after nightfall."

"After nightfall! You've been here standing here that long, next to Peeping Tom, in the cold, by yourself, since nightfall! Are you out of your mind? You should see a doctor because you are not acting sensibly!"

"Calm down, Margaret. Stop yelling at me."

Josephine detects in Leah's expression a troubled and scared girl. Her cheeks are pale and her eyes rung with circles. The moonlight makes her seem much older than she is. Thin charcoal lines emanate from her mouth and eyes.

"Why, Leah? Why did you come here and spy on Margaret?"

"I am not here to spy. Is that what you think? I came to see you, both of you."

"But why not come inside the clubhouse, or wait until we returned to Senior House?"

Leah flashes a nervous smile and looks past her classmates and blinks back tears.

"I couldn't sleep last night and this morning before class I had this feeling come over me...a strange sensation that made my arms and legs feel light, almost numb...I don't know what I am saying exactly. I felt different; that's my point. I went from one class to the next and walked around campus like I was in a trance. I didn't speak and no one spoke to me. It was like I wasn't really here. Even when I speak now—I know it sounds crazy—but my voice sounds different, like it's not mine. None of this makes any sense, I know it. But it's what I am feeling. And it is starting to scare me. The way I am feeling. I am really scared—a lot. I don't know who to see or what I should tell them. The school nurse wouldn't understand how I feel. I can hardly explain it myself.

"So, I started to watch the two of you. I thought it might help me somehow. I watched you from a distance. In class. At dinner. Dancing. I wanted to see if you were....if you were... *affected* like I was. And then I became even more worried. I waited for you to look up and see me, to notice me, to notice me watching you. But you didn't. Not in class or at dinner. The whole day, it was as if I was invisible to the both of you. The recognition I was hoping for from the two of you never came."

Josephine glances over at Margaret and sees that her anger has been replaced by stunned silence, her mouth parted and her eyes wide.

"Why watch us?" she asks.

"I am not sure why I feel the way I do, but I *know* it has to do with what took place at the glen with the four of us."

Leah stares intently into Josephine's eyes, searching for the validation she desperately needs. Surely Josephine will find in her stumbling explanation an answer for what brought her to Theta house.

"Leah, you poor thing, I know what happened at the glen gave all of us something of a fright, but Miss Price looked into it and found out that no one drowned in the flood," Josephine says, unsettled by the plaintive eyes locked onto her. "We got scared and prematurely jumped to the wrong conclusion. You see, there is no reason to worry."

She releases Margaret's arm and steps closer and embraces her troubled classmate. A moment passes and then she feels Leah's arms reciprocate and pull her even closer.

"Leah, Leah," Josephine whispers in her ear, "you are clearly not well. Perhaps you have a fever. We need to have you see the nurse. It's this horrid weather and I fear our trip has made you ill. Walking around like this will only make it worse. You need rest."

The two separate and Leah takes Josephine's hand and gently presses it against her cheek and then her forehead. Not only is Leah not gripped by a fever, her skin is unnaturally cold to the touch.

"What did you see?" Margaret asks over Josephine's shoulder. "You said you watched us during the day without us knowing. What did you see?"

"You were no different Margaret. You went about your day as usual. You behaved as you always do. You socialized. You laughed. You danced. The same. Your elegant presence dominated every room you stepped into."

The sting of the girl's final words fails to penetrate the thickness of Margaret's self-awareness.

Leah looks back at Josephine and waits with anticipation.

Ask me about you, Josephine. I know you want to. Ask me what I saw.

"And what of May?" Josephine abruptly inquires, unnerved by the look in Leah's eyes. "Did you watch her too?"

"No, just the two of you."

"But why not? She was with us as well."

Leah simply shakes her head, unable or unwilling to voice her reasons, the imposing statue of Hiawatha behind her.

Margaret rubs her bare arms and exhales.

"This makes no sense. Let's go inside. It's frigid out here on the lawn. Leah, come inside with us and we can talk more there."

Her invitation is ignored as Leah keeps her eyes trained on Josephine.

"You know of what I speak, Josephine, don't you? Tell me you do. I can see it in your face. Relieve my tortured mind. At least give me that, will you?"

"Stop it Leah!" Margaret interjects, and for the second time Leah ignores her.

"You have changed too. I see it. You have been changed in some way by what happened. Tell me in confidence if you must," she implores, the emotion in her voice raw and urgent, the grip of her hand on Josephine's tightening.

Josephine shakes her head and watches the look of disappointment sweep over Leah's face.

"Go back to Senior House, Leah, and take a hot bath. It will warm you up and help you sleep tonight. We will come to check in on you in a bit. And then tomorrow morning we will help find what ails you. You have my word."

Leah releases her grip and steps back toward the pedestal where she had hidden. She reaches behind her and pulls the hood over her head as she recedes, never breaking eye contact with Josephine until she reaches a nearby poplar tree, turns, and melts away into the darkness.

Josephine and Margaret walk back to the Spanish Mission without speaking. Unprotected, their exposed bodies shiver in the wintry air. Margaret unexpectedly bypasses the entrance and proceeds to the backside of the woodpile where she blindly searches about until she locates a secreted flask. On the porch the two sit in their expensive evening dresses and share the bottle between them, their veins instantly warmed by its illicit contents.

In the distance, barely visible over the domed chancel of the chapel, a solitary window on the third floor of Senior House is illuminated. Inside, Leah lifts the mattress off her bed and removes her carefully hidden possession. She unfolds the white dress, still moist from the creek water, on the bed, caringly smoothes out the creases in the fabric, and looks upon it. After she undresses, she kneels beside the bed, bows her head, and quietly prays.

Chapter 3
Joan of Arc at Domremy

Too early specialization, the sacrifice of symmetrical training to the abnormal development of a special gift, is largely responsible for filling the world with half-educated women, unintelligent teachers, musicians, artists and readers. A wonderful gift, without intelligence to direct it, brings its owner neither fame, fortune nor happiness. The instrument is much; but without the ability to use it, it is simply a thing of brass. Let the mind, the directing power, be fully developed first; then perfect your instrument. Travel, training abroad or in the professional school, the stimulus of the artist's studio or of the city are all good in their way, at the right stage of development. But a girl must become a woman first, an artist incidentally. Make her a strong, fine, intelligent woman, give her time to reach her full mental stature—then her gift will make her thrice blessed.

On the walk back to Senior House, Josephine explains to Margaret her plan to fulfill her parting promise to Leah. If, for reasons that are perplexing to Josephine, their brief experience at the glen has left Leah emotionally distressed, then they must return. If Leah finds no comfort in Miss Price's assurance that her fears are unfounded, Josephine surmises that the physical act of searching out the answers of what happened will exorcize the doubts that trouble her conscience. Provided Leah is rested and cooperative, the three girls will leave early in the morning and follow the creek upstream on horseback until they find the overrun property damaged by the flood and the source of the dress and other personal items carried off in the swift water. Only then, Josephine believes, will Leah's agitated mental state be cured. Margaret is skeptical and loathes the idea of waking earlier than necessary once again, but after an initial protest, she relents. She too is unnerved by Leah's alarmed look and irrational claims.

Reaching the dormitory, they find Leah bathed and resting. The plan is explained and agreed to and while Margaret watches over Leah until she finally succumbs to exhaustion Josephine changes and walks alone to the equestrian stables to leave instructions for the three mounts they will need in the morning.

The girls awake before dawn and don the accepted Seminary riding attire: white blouse, buttoned at the neck, wool jacket and jodhpurs, calf-high leather boots, lambskin gloves, and black velveteen helmet. Josephine moves quietly down the still hallway and finds Margaret inside her room striking a familiar pose before the full-length oval mirror in her room, her long legs accentuated by the lift of the boots, the outline of her perfectly tailored form backlit by the Tiffany lamp on the writing desk. She winks in the mirror, smiles devilishly at Josephine, grabs her helmet, and walks out of the room without speaking a word.

Leah sits on her bed dressed and waiting for the gentle rap on her door. Feelings of embarrassment and shame fill her as she relives the episode outside Theta clubhouse the night before.

What must they think of me now, she wonders, after my peculiar behavior? She feels she is losing control of her faculties, bit by bit. First the emotional breakdown before Madame Kasper, and then the way she stalked her friends and confronted them with wild, incomprehensible claims. Even in the pale moonlight, she could see their disapproval. They will forever see her as *that* girl at school, you know, the one who...

Josephine quietly enters Leah's room smiling, her eyes showing concern, followed by Margaret.

"Feeling better?" she says softly. "You look much better. Our old Leah."

She sits on the bed and takes the troubled girl's hand.

"Do you still want to do this?"

"Yes, I do. I feel much better this morning."

Margaret paces around the room waiting for Leah to retrieve her riding gear and stops suddenly. Something is not right. Something is out of sorts. She inspects the room and steps over towards the closet.

"Why is your mirror turned toward the wall?"

The three leave Senior House in the dark unnoticed and walk to the equestrian stable in the bracing morning air. A hoar frost has descended overnight and covered the tree limbs and plants with translucent crystals and encrusted the lawn. They take the pathway that leads past the Beta and Chiopi clubhouses to the county road so as to avoid Vincent Hall and the notice of the cooks and servants arriving to prepare breakfast for the students. While there is nothing improper about their planned ride, Josephine prefers to keep their departure a secret in the hope of avoiding questions that might be difficult to answer. As they reach the three-tiered Chiopi Pagoda, its entranceway marked by a pair of four-hundred year old stone Japanese lanterns, a rattling car unexpectedly roars around the curve and briefly illuminates the girls with its headlights as it drives past.

Horseback riding is a staple of life at National Park for both utility and pleasure. Competitions are held year around at the equestrian ring and sometimes judged by Army officers stationed nearby in the city. After fire destroyed the original stable, the Vincents built a spacious replacement, connected to the main campus by a formal rose garden claimed by the school to be the largest and most exotic of its kind in the Washington area.

Eli Raymee, the school groom, is waiting in the tack room for the girls to arrive. He is the most tenured of the many colored men employed at the school. While others rent beds in a clapboard building behind the stables or commute daily from the city, Mr. Raymee resides alone in a small room on the lower level of the barn. Diminutive in stature and slight of build, the middle-aged groom lives among the horses he loves, his familiarity with the behavior and tendencies of each of his charges legendary. A friendly disposition and gentle nature endears him to the girls, some of whom, like Josephine, board their own horses at the school. A precocious but respectful boy also works at the stable cleaning out stalls and tending to the horses, but Mr. Raymee is always the one who brings out a student's horse before a ride and is there to help her dismount when she returns.

The horses inside the stalls stir and speak as the girls approach, the aroma of straw and manure heavy in the air. A lone light glows inside the tack room and Josephine knocks gently on the door before entering. The groom is seated holding a steaming cup of coffee in gnarled fingers with polish-stained nails, a leather tapestry of bridles and saddles hanging from hooks on the wall behind him. A slight wince of pain creases his face as he rises slowly to welcome his visitors.

"Good morning, Mr. Raymee," Josephine greets him cheerfully, the other two following behind. "You are very kind to help us so early."

"It is not only my job, Miss Barnes, it is my pleasure. I've been up and about for sometime now. They don't keep the same schedule as you and me," he says in a gravelly baritone, nodding toward the stalls.

"Mr. Raymee, do you know Miss Hathaway and Miss Cleary? They are the other riders joining me this morning."

"Of course. Good mornin' ladies," he replies with a toothy smile. "I have your horses saddled up and ready to go. I will bring Sable out front first, Miss Barnes, and then the other two, if that's all right."

The groom retrieves the eight-year old gray mare and steadies her while Josephine mounts. The horse's mane is combed and her coat well-brushed. Even before she slips her boots into the stirrups, Josephine knows they will need no adjustment. Mr. Raymee prides himself on knowing the strap length needed for each girl before she takes to the saddle and his knack for estimation is rarely in error. Josephine likes the way he handles Sable and how he engages the spirited mare in a one-sided conversation whenever he leads her to and from her stall.

In her years at the Seminary, Josephine has broken through the formality Mr. Raymee shows all the girls he serves and, in the process, achieved a level of familiarity with the man that few of her fellow students either seek or want. Gradually over time, he has grown comfortable and trusting enough around her to confide the salient details of his personal life. Mr. Raymee divulged little facts about his past now and then, like stray clues in a mystery, when they were alone and eventually his reticence waned, leaving an unspoken understanding between the two: around the other students and school workers their discourse was to be no more cordial than decorum allowed.

Josephine knows that Mr. Raymee's skill with horses developed at an early age on a tobacco farm in southern Maryland where he and his family worked and lived as tenants. He moved to Washington alone as a young man of fifteen where he secured a job working on the Potomac waterfront unloading and cleaning fish, crabs and oysters brought in from the bay daily to be sold from one of the many floating stands moored to the dock. He hated the work and the way the wretched, inescapable smell of the discarded viscera that lapped at the water line of the company barge penetrated his nostrils and permeated his skin, hair and clothes.

He eventually left the waterfront to take a loading dock job in the market district and soon after met Althea, the woman he would marry. Initially, Josephine was unable to elicit much about this chapter in the man's life. The protective barrier was too thick to penetrate. But in time and with careful perseverance three crucial facts emerged: they had a son; his wife died young and tragically by the hand of a jealous former boyfriend; and he, incapacitated by grief, succumbed to alcohol until he lost his job, apartment, and custody of his boy.

Once these painful revelations were made, Mr. Raymee never felt comfortable revisiting them around Josephine and she has respected his wish since. She wants to believe that his job at National Park Seminary provides him with both physical and emotional separation from the tragic events of his past, the stable a refuge that allows him to practice his first and inalterable love.

After Mr. Raymee returns with the mounts for Margaret and Leah, the girls proceed in a line along the county road, the sound of the horses' hooves striking the hardened ground echoing against the side façade of the empty gymnasium. The route along the road to the creek is a familiar one. Faint streaks of red light paint their path as the sun crests over the horizon and warms their backs.

Once past the rear of the Odeon, they reach the northwestern boundary of the school marked by an elegantly carved sign. Just beyond, a bridle path takes the group into a gradual descent down the old corduroy road through the woods. Josephine leads on Sable, followed by Margaret and then Leah on their rides. The nascent morning light is extinguished as they disappear into the dense forest. The frost-covered trail is slick and the deluge of the previous week has carved a furrow along the center of the path which slows the group's progress. As they ride down a series of switchbacks, guided blindly by their horses, the cutting chill grows heavier with moisture. Leah's horse slips on a mound of exposed rocks and quickly steadies itself, barely avoiding striking Margaret's mount from behind.

The trail levels off as they reach a small clearing and the three riders halt next to Indian Rock, the prominent and unmistakable triangular stone monolith on the banks of the swollen creek. The sides of the rock are smooth and steep and reach an asymmetrical peak fifteen feet above the ground. According to local legend, the pyramid-shaped rock served as a marker to Indians who traveled along this trail and was used to dry the fish and eel they caught from the unsilted creek. It is a favorite excursion destination for the Seminary girls, a place where they picnic and skip pebbles on the water as canoes from the upstream boathouse paddle by. Numerous students have left their mark on the protruding brown and gray stone, its surface scarred by initials crudely carved by the dulled edge of a penknife or a pointed rock.

The flood has receded but left behind standing water that encircles Indian Rock and saturates the trail. A number of small trees and broken limbs litter the dirt path paralleling the creek. It is difficult in the muted light to see how much further they can ride before the trail becomes impassable. Josephine dismounts and hands her reins and crop to Margaret, the breath of their mounts rising about her like steam from a cauldron.

"What are you doing?" Leah asks, watching Josephine navigate through the multitude of puddles.

"I want to climb up and see what I can."

Josephine cautiously steps up the base of Indian Rock and then bends over and grips its spine with her gloves as the incline steepens. Her boot slips halfway up and she struggles to regain her footing. Muscles in her forearms and shoulders ripple and strain until she finds a suitable toehold and uses her athletic prowess to push upward and grip the peak like she has done many times before. The cold, smooth surface presses against her chest as she steadies her position. From atop Indian Rock she surveys the damage upstream and can barely make out in the distance the concrete ramp of the school boathouse. Behind it, largely obscured by trees, is, to her surprise, the boathouse itself, still standing.

After shimming carefully back down the rock face, Josephine takes back the reins to Sable.

"The path is clear to the boathouse. Beyond that, it's anyone's guess."

Margaret rises out of her saddle and looks around.

"Are you sure? It looks like a quagmire in all directions."

Her boots caked in mud, Josephine sidles up to Margaret's bay.

"Don't loose your nerve on me—again."

Leah glances over at them talking, and Margaret relents.

"As far as the boathouse. After that, you risk an insurrection, understand?"

Situated on the stream bank sufficiently far enough from the water's edge, the modest, peak-roofed building has been spared. A metal winch at the end of the ramp used to take out canoes and pull them toward the shed where they are hoisted on racks is encased by a tangle of vines and sticks left by the ebbing flood. At the base of the winch, a glassy-eyed fish shimmers, lifeless and stiff.

Primitive in construction, the boathouse is not electrified and, except for when the afternoon light streams through a single, square window in the back wall, its interior is dark and foreboding. During the summer, the building is a cooling respite after canoeing in the sun, but offers no more comfort than an ordinary tool shed. Notwithstanding the shelter from the heat the boathouse provides, girls do not tarry inside. The dirt floor is uneven and pebble-filled, the air is stale, and the space is cramped because of the storage racks. Prolonged time within the building's walls produces a gradual feeling of being confined inside a cellar keep. When all the canoes are accounted for after an excursion on Rock Creek, it is the duty of the last student to close the sliding wooden entrance door and secure it with a latch.

The three riders dismount and tether their horses to a nearby tree and slog through the mud toward the boathouse. Margaret is the first to notice the metal latch dangling from the whitewashed entryway, bent and held on by a solitary, rusted nail. The door is slightly ajar, the opening too narrow for a person to fit through. Beyond the sliver of a gap, there is only blackness.

"Well, what do you make of this, Josephine? See the scrapes on the wood around the metal. The storm didn't break the latch."

"It looks like a rock or hammer was used to get inside," Leah observes.

"And based on my rudimentary sleuthing skills that rules out raccoons and other mischievous woodland creatures," Margaret says, tongue-in-cheek.

Leah looks around her, searching the trees bordering the creek.

"I don't like how this feels, Josephine. It might be a smart idea if we turn around."

Josephine examines the damaged latch and then peers through the opening.

"Don't worry. No one has been here this morning. See. The frost on the handle is undisturbed. It's safe to go inside. Leah, this might help explain the personal belongings we saw in the creek yesterday when it flooded. Don't you understand, this may be the answer we are seeking?"

"I don't know."

Leah's mount shakes her mane and paws the malleable trail. The horse's wide rib cage swells and then exhales loudly.

"It just doesn't feel right."

"I'm sorry," Margaret interjects, her tone agitated, "but I am not convinced at all by your assurances, Josephine. It's one thing to ride through this muck in the dark and cold, but our little reconnoitering journey wasn't meant to be an excuse to contract tetanus by exploring every dilapidated shack we came across. I forbid you from going inside. Really girl, have you no common sense?!"

"Quiet down. It's the boathouse, for goodness sake. We've been inside plenty of times. Why are you so contrary all the time, Margaret?"

"Perhaps we should think twice about this," Leah says in a timid voice.

"Why?"

"The handle."

"What about it?"

"You said that no one has touched it since the door was closed. What if the person closed it from the inside and is still in there?"

Josephine sees Leah's alarmed expression and knows that her anxiety will only grow more acute the longer the three stand before the pried open door. She needs to act decisively or the collective nerve of the group, fast eroding, will be lost.

"Then he has heard everything we have said since we arrived. Let's remove this advantage and make our acquaintances properly."

Josephine grips the handle and tugs it with both hands until the door lurches and begins to slide open. Above the high-pitched squeal of the door dragging along its rusted metal runner, she hears Margaret cry: "Josephine, don't!"

But she forces the balky door and doesn't stop pulling until it can slide no further and the handle slams loudly against the building jamb.

With the door opened, the girls immediately see that something is amiss.

The canoes are stored in two groups of six. Iron frames on both sides of the boathouse hold three overturned canoes on a lower tier and three on an upper tier. Only eleven of the twelve canoes are accounted for. One is missing from a lower rung.

A narrow interior walkway separates the two storage racks to allow access to retrieve and replace the boats. Along this bisecting space Josephine cautiously enters alone. Margaret grumbles to herself and follows her friend reluctantly.

Leah remains outside, paralyzed, nervously fingering her riding crop, her eyes transfixed on the scene before her. She has never been to boathouse other than during warm days of light-hearted recreation, and she is chilled by the striking contrast. In the shadows of the early winter morning, the smooth tan elongated forms, in their orderly arrangement, forgotten in their grim, dank chamber, look like an ancestral sarcophagus in ruins.

One of the horses groans and she can hear it pull against its restraint.

Don't let them leave you. Follow them. Follow them inside. You can't stay here alone.

An acrid smell of ash hangs heavily inside the rustic shed and causes Margaret to cough as she enters. Her mind flashes back to the memory of working, as a girl of no more than ten, in the smokehouse at her grandparents' farm and how the sweet, thick, curing vapor in the circular outbuilding stung and made her eyes water. A mouse dashes from a pile of open cans lying beneath the left boat rack and scurries across the dirt floor before disappearing into the corner recess. A whiff of pungent decay triggers a reflux in the back of Margaret's throat and she involuntarily gags in revulsion. She sees Josephine crouching down beyond the boats with her back to her. As she walks over, her hand over her mouth, a fine dust rises into the fetid air with each step. There on the ground, flush along the far wall, is the missing canoe.

"What is it?"

"Someone has been living here, inside the boathouse," Josephine says pointing at the small fire ring of rocks nearby.

"I know. Did you see all of the empty food tins on the ground over there?"

"Whoever was here was using the canoe as a makeshift bed. There looks to be a ragged blanket and other things left here."

Outside, Leah waits anxiously for the others to reemerge from the concealing, black interior of the building. The raw air has reddened her cheeks and penetrated her wool riding jacket robbing her of warmth. A scraggly fox bolts from the underbrush lining the trail and disappears deeper into the woods in a rustle of leaves. High overhead, bare tree limbs bend and creak gently in the breeze.

Leah takes a step backward, away from the boathouse, pauses, and then takes another, until she clips the edge of the apron with the heel of her riding boot, causing a loose piece of concrete to tumble into the turbulent water. A brooding sensation comes over her as she contemplates the emptiness where the missing boat should be.

I can't. I can't go in there.

Her lips tremble as she strains to speak.

"Josephine. Margaret. We must leave."

Josephine continues to rifle through the canoe as Margaret stands over her trying to make sense of the secreted cache before them. A kerosene lamp is produced and then what looks to be a leather satchel of some kind. The offensive odor continues to nauseate Margaret as she leans over to inspect the grimy stash of soiled items.

"Josephine, have you stopped to think the person who these belong to may not appreciate strangers rummaging through his possessions? We have our answer now, don't we? A squatter is living in the boathouse and the flood swept away some of his meager possessions."

"The water didn't reach inside the boathouse. You can see that for yourself."

"He probably kept some of his things outside. You are over-thinking this. Let's leave and go back to the Seminary. We've found what we set out to find. It isn't safe here."

Josephine stops her search, stands and moves away from the canoe. When she turns around, Margaret instantly recognizes her discovery as the pale light from the open entrance glints off the long, unsheathed blade of a hunting knife.

"Not the sort of thing you would expect a young girl to be playing with," Josephine whispers in the dark.

A whip-like crack punctures the silence and the tethered horses stir just beyond the wall of the cramped boathouse.

"Give me a hand and we can pull this outside," Josephine orders.

"Wait a second. Let's consider what we are doing. If we move the canoe, he will know someone has been here—"

"—And what then? He will know that he has been discovered and, if he is smart, our resident vagabond will leave before he is arrested for living on school property."

Margaret, recognizing the headstrong state of her friend, rolls her eyes, capitulates and grabs a looped rope handle and begins dragging the canoe along the dirt floor as Josephine pushes the other end. A discernable trace of flavored tobacco swirls about them as they make for the doorway.

"Leah, we are coming out," Margaret calls ahead, fighting to repress her revulsion.

The two clear the entrance lip and slide the canoe outside to find that Sable and Margaret's horse have broken loose and are drinking along the edge of Rock Creek, their reins dipping into the swirling current. There is no trace of Leah or of her horse. A thick, shattered branch is on the ground at the base of the tree where they had left the horses tied.

A train whistle blows in the distance and Sable's bowed head rises to attention, her ears perked and her prominent cobalt eyes searching. The lingering cold of the woods is slowly giving way to the broadening reach of the rising sun. She hears the birds trill in the tree canopy above her and thinks of the pesky sparrows that incessantly forage through the straw in her stall. Her nostrils flair and she catches a new scent intermingled with that of her owner. The other one walks toward her and she feels the grip of a firm hand slide under her bridle. Sable is led over to where her owner shakes out a soiled cloth along the ground, followed by a number of fur pelts. A sensory bolt tingles along the length of the horse's flat forehead and she gives a violent shake that dislodges the other's hold. The powerful gray mare noses one of the skins and recognizes the smell of the animals that burrow along the trails, and then she begins nibbling on a nearby patch of grass. As she pulls at the moist, matted blades, she tracks a noise in the distance, obscured in the tree line beyond the boathouse, barely discernable above the rising voices around her—the sound of another horse's slow, measured gait and labored breathing.

A droning locomotive lurches to a halt at the Forest Glen station platform and announces its arrival with a hissing exhalation. A diminutive man, wiry and impeccably tailored, bounds off the train and dons his hat, followed eagerly by a younger man toting a leather case and a box made of unfinished pine. As a few other passengers disembark, an attendant greets the two men and gestures to a waiting automobile parked by the station.

"Not necessary, young man. Please tell Dean Dawson that I thank him. We do appreciate his thoughtfulness, but we will walk to the school from here."

"Sir, the foot bridge is icy and many of the steps are steep and difficult to navigate. Speaking for the dean, I think he would feel more comfortable if you allowed me to drive you to Vincent Hall as arranged. I can have you there safely in little more than a minute or two."

"Sounds like a challenge, young man."

"No sir! I was just saying—"

"We'll see you on the other side."

The defiant man places his hand on the driver's shoulder and smiles, a playful glint in his eye.

"And don't worry, I will make sure to tell Dean Dawson that you practically tackled us trying to force us into the car."

"But sir," the driver weakly protests as Douglas Stratton, renowned New York City industrialist and builder, moves briskly over the rail crossing and down the connecting path toward Honeysuckle Bridge.

As his assistant follows, he turns and calls back with hollow reassurance.

"He likes to walk, always has, don't take it personally, my fine fellow."

Reaching the iron truss bridge, Mr. Stratton stops to admire two large stone lions, full-maned, in repose, resting atop pedestals that bookend the entry stairs like resolute guardians of the Seminary grounds.

"Did you know Charles that after Sam Tilden was cheated out of being president he left a fortune to create the New York City Public Library and that the same sculptor that carved our city's beloved Astor and Lennox is responsible for these inferior commissions?"

"What a fascinating insight, Mr. Stratton. I was not aware. I see your point about the workmanship though. They most certainly lack the grandeur of the originals and there is a roughness in the sculptor's hand. You can see it in the lines. All in all, extremely self-derivative."

"Self-*what?*"

Mr. Stratton chuckles at how his traveling companion is always trying too hard to impress him. The mortified assistant grins with embarrassment.

"I have always been struck by this view of the school, Charles. From here, you can take in the full panorama of the buildings and grounds. No

INCIDENT AT FOREST GLEN 73

matter how many trips I've made, it never fails to grab my attention. What do you think? It's your first glimpse of the exclusive National Park Seminary for Young Women. Be honest now. Just don't tell me what you think I want to hear."

The young man lowers the weighty box onto the ground and buttons his coat under his chin.

"The view is indeed impressive."

"Is that all? That's all you have to say?"

"Well, to be blunt, I find the school, like these lions, to be somewhat artificial, kind of a contrived playground. I mean not to offend, Mr. Stratton. Whimsy is fine, I suppose, but from what I see there is certain desperation to this place. It reminds me of an over-stuffed attic filled with treasures, both genuine and imagined."

"To the point, Charles. To the point, as usual. I only wish you were with me when my wife proposed the idea of our friends here, Cleo and Theo, as a gift to the Seminary when our daughter Claudia graduated."

He bends over and inspects a small iron plaque affixed to the pedestal of one of the lions.

"And what sort of uneducated buffoon spells Douglas with two's's? I mean it speaks to the overall shabbiness of the project, doesn't it?"

"Indeed, Mr. Stratton. Very sloppy."

Walking across the footbridge, Mr. Stratton and his assistant are exposed to buffeting gusts that sweep down the glen, and the titan of Gramercy Park pauses to steady himself along the wrought iron railing. The campus rises before them, visible behind denuded trees, glistening under the patina of the hoar frost. Students move quickly from Senior House to Vincent Hall for breakfast while a groundskeeper busies himself bundling tree branches downed by the storm.

He spies the car across the glen slowly pacing them along the drive bridge that runs by the Villa, the Castle and the other clubhouses on the way to the roundabout. Holding down his hat with his free hand, he calls for his aide to step forward.

"Charles, I want you to go ahead and meet the car at the circle. Have the driver inform Dean Dawson that I will be there momentarily."

Weighted down by the leather case and bulky pine container he is toting, Charles Carter shuffles across the bridge in an awkward trot, careful not to lose his footing, and then proceeds along the meandering pathway leading to the heart of the campus.

Now alone, the contemplative New Yorker lays both hands on the bridge railing and turns toward the glen, glancing first at the train station and then back at Vincent Hall atop the hillside. A rush of wind presses along the length of his wool coat and he feels the bridge move and give off an unnatural groan. He reaches inside his coat and fumbles around trying to reach something in his suit pocket until, frustrated, he bites the finger end of the cumbersome glove and removes it and restarts the search. A small rectangular box bound with thin blue ribbon is finally produced.

Of their five children, Mrs. Stratton had borne him three daughters, all of whom were sent to National Park Seminary for their education and personal development. Mr. Stratton's support to the institution was considerable during those years, and in the course of time he became a financial pillar to the school, a benefactor in high-standing with the Dawsons and the Seminary's Board of Trustees. Over three years have passed since he last visited Forest Glen. He stood on this very bridge then as the proud father of his beloved Claudia. The entire Stratton family had made the trip, save one. His eldest daughter, Elizabeth, having volunteered as an Army nurse, was at the mobilization center on Ellis Island, anxiously awaiting transport to France.

On this raw winter morning, he arrives at Forest Glen a different man, sober and resolute, on a mission cloaked in mystery and intrigue. Rather than escape the chill of the exposed bridge, he embraces it and finds perverse solace in the way it fuses with the private pain that occupies his core and pervades his emotional state.

How different Claudia's graduation day had been in '18. Bright and sun-washed. A floral malaise filled with intoxicating laughter. An impeccably choreographed extravagance of pomp and prestige. Wealth and power on prominent display. Speeches lauding their daughters' ascension into womanhood. Claudia, sweet dear Claudia, walking between her parents along the promenade in front of Vincent Hall, arm in arm, beaming under the adoring gaze of her teachers and classmates, to accept her diploma. The promise of youth everywhere, in the girls' eyes and in their smiles, in the heartfelt testimonials that filled the idyllic, cloudless commencement day.

He remembers Claudia boarding the train to leave Forest Glen that afternoon three years ago. He recalls how still she sits looking out the car window at the school on the distant rise, oblivious to the commotion of her family crammed into the private compartment. There she waits, as if in a protective cocoon, the delicate contours of her face, her deep brown eyes and rounded lips, reflected in the glass. The image is still vivid and fresh. He recollects how, sensing his stare, she turns and with a labored smile communicates to him how difficult it is for her to leave. It pains him to recall what happens next, when, face to face with his youngest daughter, the realization strikes him with thunderous force and unleashes a wave of melancholy that leaves a residue of bitterness on his heart.

Who is this woman sitting at the compartment window?

She is a stranger to him. He knows more about the lives, the inner workings, the daily frustrations, the fears and hopes, of those that work for him on Wall Street than he does his now-grown daughter, his own flesh and blood. His involvement in the formative years of her development into maturity has been tangential, increasingly restricted to financial and logistical matters that allowed the familial closeness that existed between them at an earlier age to wither over time. Detachment, in both proximity and emotion, grew in its place. As her brothers and sisters have left to chart their own way, Claudia remains, a trailing afterthought to an increasing preoccupied and indifferent mother and father. Neither the celebratory events of commencement nor the warm displays of affection throughout the day can mask the truth in his daughter's expression as she looks out the train window. She is about to leave the only true home and family she has known for years. Sadness blooms in her unblinking stare.

Did you feel abandoned, he wonders? Do you understand that sending you to Forest Glen was an act of love, testimony to the fact that we want the best for you, Claudia, like the your sisters before you received?

The regret he feels at that moment on the train wounds him deeply. The opportunity presents itself, a fleeting pause in time, sufficient for him to make amends. He begins to speak. His lips part to tell her of the pride he feels over the fine woman she has become, to perhaps offer some words of assurance, however clipped and sparing, that matters between them will be different from now on, better, closer. By doing so, he will make her see that he understands her and what she is feeling, that distance and time have not severed the bond the two of them once felt.

He speaks only to have the train whistle drown out his lost words.

Claudia suddenly rises and runs to the far window and waves to the remaining school teachers and staff standing on the platform. As the train departs, she gestures more wildly and soon the comforting voices drift away. The rocking of the car levels out as the locomotive accelerates while Douglas Stratton, dubbed by the Saturday Evening Post as a *"prominent piston of America's industrial engine,"* sits isolated, walled-off from the conversations swirling about him, silently wrestling with the growing shame that eats away his insides.

A shiver ripples down the length of his body, bringing the businessman out of his reflective state. He slides the slender box back inside his breast pocket and feels the numbing cold on his exposed fingers. He has absent-mindedly dropped his glove on the bridge's wooden planks and retrieves it before continuing on his journey. The span sways again under his step and he grips the lapels of his coat and pulls them tightly over his chest. Stepping off the bridge, he gingerly navigates the uphill contours of the icy path until it levels off in front of the Odeon. He can see Mr. Carter waiting for him just ahead at the moribund ornate fountain in front of the covered entrance to Vincent Hall.

Three students leaving Senior House stop and wait for him to pass.

"Sir, can we help you?" one offers to the struggling man.

"I suppose you don't see many old goats like me huffing up the hill early in the morning." Mr. Stratton's deprecating remark elicits polite laughter from the girls.

"If you are going to the main hall, we are headed that direction as well and could accompany you."

Mr. Stratton tips his hat and smiles at the girl.

"The three of you are timely samaritans. You are students in the senior class, I suppose?" he says nodding toward the dormitory, producing more admiring smiles.

"Yes, sir. Do you have a daughter at National Park?"

"No longer, but all of my daughters went here. Three of them in fact, three fine young women like you. My youngest graduated a few years ago. Perhaps you might remember her. Her name is Claudia. Claudia Stratton."

The short brunette speaks up through a bulky gray scarf.

"My goodness, yes, I knew Claudia. We met my first year. The sweetest girl you ever wanted to meet. A lovely smile and warm toward everyone around her. We were in the same clubhouse. All the freshman girls looked up to her back then. Tell her Dorothea Bridger says hello. She probably won't remember me; it's been a while."

"I'm sure she will," he reassures her.

Something behind the girls grabs his attention.

"If I could impose a moment more, the statue there looks familiar, the one over in front of your dormitory, of the girl kneeling on the ground. I know it. I have seen it before, but not here, I am sure of it. I would have remembered it. Is it new? Can you tell me about the statue?"

Mr. Stratton steps toward it to gain a closer look and searches his memory.

The crossed hands resting on the bent knees. The simple maid's dress, buttoned. The hair tied and covered. A shoeless girl, attentive yet serene. An indescribable presence captured in softened contours.

"It's Joan of Arc," the third girl answers. "The alumnae association donated it to the school a couple of years ago. They thought it would be inspirational I am told."

"Evidentially, we are lacking in statuary," the first girl jokes as she moves next to introspective stranger.

"Yes, of course," he mutters to himself, the sudden realization of the statue's significance brightening his eyes. "I recognize the likeness now. Why did I not remember?"

"I find her expression to be beguiling," the helpful student opines. "Her appearance is so unassuming, but you can see in her face that destiny awaits. She is undeniably beautiful."

"I should have recognized it," he continues on, still wearing a puzzled expression. "That's what the passing years will do to your memory. Not the sort of thing any of you young ladies have to worry about."

"Perhaps she reminds you of your daughter."

"What's that you say?"

"Your daughter, Claudia."

"Oh, of course."

"Sir, it is rather cold and I think it would be best if we walk with you over to Vincent Hall."

Mr. Stratton pauses to consider the revelation before turning to face the girl.

"I apologize for babbling on."

He spots his assistant up-ahead standing next to the impatient driver, who is hopping from side to side to fend off the cutting wind.

"I am meeting with your headmaster, Dean Dawson, and would like to speak to him about your thoughtfulness. May I ask your names? Let's see, Dorothea I've already been introduced to. And my other two helpers? First names only, otherwise I will remember nothing."

"Lucille, sir."

"And you, young lady?"

"Mary, sir."

"Dorothea, Lucille, Mary. My three angels. Very good. I feel like quite the imposition keeping all three of you from your breakfast. Lucille, would you be kind enough to walk me over to where the tow-headed driver by the fountain is doing a jig?"

Lucille smiles her acceptance and slips her arm through his as the other two girls hurry ahead. The wily businessman basks in the young girl's attention.

"Lucille, you seem to appreciate artistic expression."

"Very much so, sir."

"Since we have only a few remaining moments together, let me tell you about the most wondrous place on Earth."

From his diamond-lattice window, Dean Dawson watches Mr. Stratton and the student shuffle toward the veranda overhang, their arms intertwined and supporting each other. The fireplace rages in vain to vanquish the pervasive chill that has settled overnight in the lavishly decorated office. Around an oval mahogany table each of the four class regents sit and wait, passing the time in casual conversation, while the Prefect of Studies, Charlotte Martin, stands before the warming flame, engaged with George Geary, the school's bursar, in a more private discussion.

"I question the propriety of involving the instructors in matters of administration, George. Our duties are in the classroom, not the boardroom. The Vincents, weak as they may have been in certain areas of management, understood the importance of maintaining the division. Am I not correct? You must agree. But these days my time is increasingly in demand to address matters I am neither equipped nor interested in handling. We are not the trustees, after all."

"This is true, though I suppose the dean wants us here more as representatives of the National Park Seminary than as deciders of any particular matter. So let's not get carried away about our places."

"All the worse, I say. Trotted out as a greeter is a necessary evil when meeting with parents, but we are here to bow at the feet of a wealthy baron like obsequious toadies. It's unseemly."

"Really, Charlotte, lower your voice," the bursar admonishes, as he turns his back to wall off their conversation from the others seated in the room.

The agitated prefect moves closer until the fire light dances across her squat neck and sagging cheeks.

"We have both been here for many years, George, and you must acknowledge that it has been different—and not always for the better—under Dean Dawson than when the Vincents ran the operation."

"Times have changed. So must we."

"Then perhaps we can forgo the next European treasure hunt and replace the school's dysfunctional heating instead. That would be change I could support."

"Are you always so contrary early in the morning? The point is that Douglas Stratton was a valuable backer of the school when his girls attended. He has come to renew ties. Why? I do not know. But, as they say, a rising tide lifts all boats. If it means a few minutes out of your day spent in the dean's office, then it's time well spent. Let's hope the fire can take away your frosty edge before he gets here. It serves no purpose to greet our benefactor with a scowl."

"Mere window dressing. That's what we are. Mere window dressing. Douglas Stratton didn't care a damn about our curriculum or the pedigree of our staff when his daughters were here. And I will wager you he has no recollection of either of us. We will have to fumble through awkward introductions and forced niceties, and for what: to show that we are the dean's marionettes? It's not our business."

"I, for one, don't mind it, Charlotte. Suffer through it and you will be on your way shortly to cheerfully mother your brood of teachers."

"Well, I—"

"He has arrived," Dean Dawson announces abruptly as he steps away from the window. "Miss Price, may I speak to you for a moment?"

The senior regent leaves the others at the table and joins the dean next to his desk.

"I need you to do something for me immediately. Douglas Stratton was led here by one of the girls in your class, I believe. I spotted the two talking in front of Senior House and then walking over here just now. Go downstairs and find out who the girl is and then return. You can speak to her later on and find out what they discussed. And, Miss Price, if you see the driver when you are down in the reception room, please convey to him my extreme displeasure and tell him that I cannot wait to hear why he let a captain of industry worth twenty million dollars walk here from the train station in wintry conditions like these."

The dean warmly receives the Gotham tycoon and his aide and after he finishes introducing the assembled staff he beckons his guests to reserved seats at the table before the hearth. He is immediately struck by how much older Douglas Stratton looks since their last meeting. His salt and pepper hair is now a shock of white and thinner than before. His shoulders are more rounded and the thick, solid frame that once filled expertly tailored suits is lean and angular. The transformation is stark, and Dean Dawson wonders if illness has winnowed down the physically imposing man he remembered.

"You have done well, Porter. The school is quite the jewel and after a few years of being away, it still sparkles."

"You are kind, Douglas. As you know, our talented instructors and administrators are the one who polish our scholastic jewel, if you will. They are the ones who deserve to be acknowledged for their work."

"Of course. I have the pleasure of knowing some of you. As for the rest of you, I am privileged to make your acquaintance," Mr. Stratton offers with a pleasant demeanor, his eyes going around the table until they stop on the smiling prefect, who clandestinely nudges Mr. Geary under the table with her knee.

"You have traveled a great distance, Douglas, and we are pleased to host you as our guest. We have taken the liberty of reserving two rooms at Glen Manor for you and Mr. Carter, at our expense, of course, for as long of a stay as you like."

"Most kind, Porter. Most kind."

"I trust Mrs. Stratton is in good health. And what of your daughters? I am anxious to learn how they have put the gifts they received at the National

Park Seminary to good use since they left. I have read nothing about them in the alumnae quarterly."

A forced, unconvincing smile comes across Mr. Stratton's face. He scans the faces seated around the table and pauses before responding, unsure how to answer the headmaster's innocuous inquiry.

"Yes, I suppose our alumnae chapter dues have lagged," he finally answers, prompting uneven laughter in the room.

He motions to Mr. Carter, who walks over to Dean Dawson's chair and hoists the pine box he's been carrying since New York onto the table in front of the headmaster.

"What is this?"

"A gift. The first of two I brought with me this morning," the businessman replies.

"You don't waste time, do you, Porter?"

"There is nothing I abhor more. It is a lesson I have learned late in life."

With an air of anticipation, Dean Dawson unfastens two brass latches and opens the box lid to reveal six wine bottles, packed securely in a wooden yolk and surrounded with saw dust. The blood rushes from his face.

"Relax Porter. I bought a vineyard along the Hudson River a number of years ago. As an investment, it was a loser. It bled money every year. And now with Prohibition in place, I have been forced to shut it down—which was probably a merciful outcome, if you listen to my accountants. But, thanks to a nice loophole in the law, I am legally allowed to produce a couple hundred gallons of wine a year for 'home consumption,' as it were. Provided I don't sell it to you, these bottles of cabernet are yours to drink with a clear conscience and without fear of scandal or prosecution."

Dean Dawson stammers and searches for a gracious response, and is doubly stunned to hear Mrs. Martin break the prolonged silence.

"This might be the spark we need to launch a course in our Home Building and Management program on how to make grape juice and wine bricks as staples of the family dinner table."

Mr. Geary returns the sharp nudge beneath the table.

"Yes, indeed! Yes, indeed!" Mr. Stratton shouts out. "Though by the look on your face, Porter, I see that my gift may have been somewhat misguided. Perhaps I have unintentionally unleashed the specter of revenue agents descending on Forest Glen."

82   ANDY JOHNSON

"Your generosity is always appreciated and valued, Douglas. I am simply surprised, that's all. As I say often in business circles, National Park Seminary has no greater benefactor than you. It is a thoughtful gift indeed."

"You are an unconvincing liar," he replies with a coy smile. "Let me see if I can make it up to you."

The industrialist's assistant removes an envelope from inside his suit jacket and hands it to the dean.

"I don't like to beat around the bush, Porter. I prefer to get to the heart of the matter."

Mr. Stratton's directness flummoxes the dean and causes him to fidget in his chair.

"Am…am I being served a legal summons?" he laughs nervously.

"A summons! Hardly! Did you ever hear such richness, Charles? A summons! No, Porter, consider it an early Christmas gift."

"Brought from the North, sir," his sycophant adds with a self-satisfied smirk.

"Yes, I am an old man from the North delivering gifts this Christmas season! Very good, Charles."

Mr. Stratton lets out a boisterous laugh with as much gusto as his rail-thin body can muster. The bursar catches Dean Dawson's eye from across the table and offers an approving nod.

"I see, Douglas. Perhaps it would be best if we continue our conversation in private then. Let me make arrangements for breakfast."

Mr. Stratton does not reply, his gaze upon the dean unyielding.

From her seat at the table, Miss Price watches Dean Dawson finger the corners of the envelope, a single bead of nervous perspiration clinging to his left temple. A log pops loudly and sends a dying flare of embers against the fireplace screen. She expects to be ushered out of the room along with the others when, to her surprise, the flustered headmaster stops dawdling and slips his finger inside the offering.

Dean Dawson's expectations of the impromptu meeting called by Douglas Stratton are driven by the man's record of philanthropy in support of the Seminary. He assumed a personal visit meant the industrialist would bestow an endowment onto the school of some significance as he had previously done, perhaps the sponsorship of a new capital project or the dedication of a business course of study in his name, some sort of vanity project to further the Stratton name in a sphere not yet touched by his influence or his wealth. The dean consulted with the Board of Trustees preemptively to discuss the parameters under which such an endowment could be accepted. After all, the commissioning of decorative stone lions is one thing. The carefully crafted and tended image of the National Park Seminary, however, cannot be compromised by the well-meaning yet misguided wishes of a wealthy donor, no matter how generous.

The envelope is opened and the dean looks inside as an awkward silence comes over the room. The bead of perspiration Miss Price has been watching lingers on the protrusion of bone above the headmaster's jaw, and then quickly rolls down the length of his splotchy cheek.

Inside the white envelope Dean Dawson finds…nothing. It is empty.

For good measure and dramatic effect, he turns it upside down and shakes it.

"I am afraid you have bested me again, Douglas. I do believe I am the butt of a prank," he meekly offers before Mr. Stratton erupts in another fit of laughter.

Holding the envelope aloft, Dean Dawson has two simultaneous thoughts: first, he is in the presence of an eccentric lunatic; and second, would he be so branded if he gave into the mounting desire inside him to lurch across the table and throttle Stratton's minion until the reptilian grin he wears gives way to frantic gasps for air.

The elated business tycoon tamps down the cork on his outburst and regains his composure.

"You were right, Charles. I doubted you. But you proved me wrong."

With a self-satisfied expression, Mr. Carter nods in return, an air of smugness that almost launches the befuddled dean from his chair.

"I do apologize, Porter. You see we had something of a gentleman's wager on the trip here and I am afraid you were an unwitting pawn in it all. Young Mr. Carter here has an opinion on the matter of the acceptance of gifts as it applies to the different genders. His theory is that women, as a general rule, are attentive to the details of presentation. The writing on cards, the care of the wrapping, the color and the texture of the ribbons and the bows. Men, on the other hand, seek the prize within and ignore the human touch that fashioned its presentation. I, of course, had to defend against such a sweeping broadside against our sex from someone so green. Have I fairly summarized your position, Charles?"

"With succinct clarity and magnanimity, Mr. Stratton. Most kind."

Miss Price is transfixed by Dean Dawson's vacant expression and how his jaw slowly opens, in minute increments, while the guest continues with his explanation. Mouth agape and unblinking, the dean seems under the spell of the businessman's ramblings, incredulously still holding the envelope before him as if it were a mouse snatched from the kitchen pantry by the tail.

"The gift *is* the envelope."

The confused headmaster turns and looks down the table.

"What is it that you say, Miss Price?"

"I said, the gift is the envelope, Dean Dawson, not what is inside it. I believe that is Mr. Stratton's point."

"Game, set, and match, Charles! Miss Price has proven your case on both counts."

Dean Dawson glowers at the senior regent for her impertinence until Mr. Geary intercedes.

"The lighting in this room is dreadfully dim, Dean. But I believe that I notice some writing on the front of the envelope from Mr. Stratton. An easy oversight to make given the weak overhead light."

The dean flips the paper over. In a delicate, pale violet script, the overlooked words appear.

"For the National Park Seminary for Young Women, Forest Glen, Maryland, the amount of—"

Mr. Stratton watches Dean Dawson's perplexed look transform again as if he is strapped to an electrical chair at the moment of ultimate judgment.

"This cannot be," the stunned man musters.

All around the table move closer, eager to learn more.

"I mean...I mean, I am beyond words, Douglas."

"I am doing this in the names of my daughters, Claudia, Alice and Elizabeth. Mrs. Stratton and I want to do something bold to build upon the legacy of this school in their lives with the hope that other girls will continue to benefit for years to come under the expert tutelage offered by the Seminary."

"Yes. Yes. Of course," the dean replies giddily. "We are missionaries in pursuit of a common purpose. Together we will churn the soil of higher learning. What immense good can be done with such capital! I can hardly comprehend it. But can this be accurate? Surely, this is too..."

He rises from the table, his eyes locked onto the envelope pulled closely to his nose. Before the hearth, the paper glows scarlet red and the pen strokes, backlit by the flame, grow dark and vibrant, and unmistakably clear.

"In my thirty years working in the fields of academia, I have never heard of an endowment this size."

Over his shoulder he hears Mr. Stratton's sudden inhalation and laughter, a disarming outburst promptly echoed by his assistant's dutiful howl.

"Endowment? I think you misunderstand, Porter. I mean to buy your school."

The trail of tracks in the mud and dross left by the flood leads upstream from the boathouse and further away from the school property. Had Leah headed back to the Seminary stable, Josephine's consternation over her disappearance would have subsided. Perhaps Leah lost her nerve, she would have thought, and rode back alone. She had no reason, though, to continue farther on into the woods without them. As Margaret repeatedly curses the girl's name, Josephine knows they have no choice but to follow and find her and return together before their absence is detected and suspicion grows.

A downed tree diverts the passage paralleling the creek and Josephine, in the lead, is forced into a large patch of newly broken brush and then up a rise of dense trees where the hoof marks are partial and intermittent. Margaret's horse lags on the incline and she pushes up and out of the saddle and sends a swift kick to the gelding's ribs in a failed attempt to get it to pickup the pace. Steadied by the grip of her long, sinewy thighs she is in equipoise as she brings the crop against the recalcitrant stead's flank and anticipates the break forward.

Deeper into the woods they follow. Twice the tracks stop, retrace backward, and then set off in a different direction all together, as if Leah is lost and searching for something recognizable to lead her out of the labyrinth of thick vegetation. Just when it looks as if a clearing is reached, the woods close again and envelope Josephine and Margaret in a maze of uncharted turns and dead-ends. Tree limbs, punished by the passing storm, impede their progress while the thorns of withered wild rose hips snag the fabric of their jodhpurs and prick the flesh of their horses and leave slashes of crimson.

Within minutes, Josephine realizes her mistake. In their desperate attempt to find their classmate, they too have become lost. In the struggle to extract themselves, the horses begin to labor, the skin under the saddles glistening and slick with moisture, their nostril plumes more frequent.

At a place where the trees and ground vegetation thin out, Margaret moves her horse alongside Josephine and grabs Sable's reins.

"Hold on. Hold on a moment. Let's talk."

"What was she thinking?" Josephine frustratingly exclaims, not waiting for an answer. "Why did Leah panic and ride away? Doesn't she realize the trouble she's brought down on us if we don't return soon?"

"I don't think she panicked. She's been acting queer since the other day. We should leave her and worry about getting ourselves back to school. Should we try to go back the same way we came? I don't know if we can get to the road from here."

Josephine removes her velveteen helmet, wipes the sweat from her brow with her jacket sleeve, and lifts the bunched blond curls off the back of her warm neck.

"If you listened to me and cut that unruly mane and showed some fashion sense, you wouldn't be so bothered," Margaret teases as she dismounts.

Just ahead in a swale, a pool of rainwater reflects in blinding brilliance a solitary beam of morning sun piercing the walls of their prison.

"I swear that it is getting colder by the minute."

She drops the reins and her horse bows to nibble at its fetlock and then seeks out the quenching water.

Josephine rises out of the saddle and searches in every direction for a familiar sign while she steadies the panting Sable. In their pursuit of Leah, she hasn't had time to consider the significance of what they found in the boathouse. The forced door latch. The canoe. The collection of animal skins. The hunting knife.

"Is it possible that Leah didn't just decide to leave without telling us?"

"You saw her last night outside the clubhouse. She was hiding behind Tom and making no sense. Fever. Psychosis. I don't know which, but something is not right with the girl."

"Well, if she got spooked, why did she head this way, up a steep path and into a section of woods none of us have ever been? All she needed to do was call out to us inside the boathouse. And if she lost her nerve, she would have ridden back to the Seminary along a trail she has travelled time and again and knows well."

"But she didn't, did she? Our melodic bird flew away into this maddening thicket of brambles and brush. And now we are stuck too, covered in mud, with no idea as to which way is up or out."

Margaret removes her leather riding gloves and places them in the saddle bag. She then slowly squats down to the pool of rainwater, the tightness from her time in the saddle clawing down the back of her legs, and playfully pushes aside the gelding's head.

"Show some manners to a lady."

"Don't you see, that's my point? She had no reason to come this way."

"And…"

Margaret cups her hands and squints to shield her eyes from the flickering reflection on the surface of the standing water.

"What if the man living in the boathouse returned or was hiding and watching us when we went inside? He left those things behind in the canoe. He was coming back at some point, right? Maybe he heard us riding along the creek and went to hide."

"Maybe."

Margaret dips her palms into the shimmering silver light and draws the chilled water to her lips. Her throat muscles contract involuntarily as the drink is almost too cold to swallow.

"He could have taken Leah." Josephine's voice falters before the words leave her.

Margaret looks up from the pool, her lips wet.

"Let's not get hysterical, Jo. We were inside the boathouse for no more than a minute or two. Leah didn't call out or scream or make any noise—"

"But I remember a noise! I heard a loud sound when we were inside. It wasn't a voice, true, but I heard it. Just before we dragged the canoe outside. Remember?"

"What I remember is how I felt like ants were crawling all over my skin while I was in that filthy place."

Margaret draws two more quenching drinks from the pool of rainwater and then shakes her hands dry as she rises out of her crouch.

"Look, there was a single track of hoof prints; that's all. I saw no shoe prints in the mud along the way. If you had, you would have said something about it, I have no doubt."

"Two people could ride on Leah's horse. He could have abducted her. Don't just dismiss my concerns, Margaret. We can't ignore that Leah could be in danger."

"Then let's find our way to the road and get back to school. I am not going back the way we came. It was too rough. I say we follow the tracks the best we can, but if we see a way to the road, we take it. With or without her."

Using the rising sun as a guide, the two riders emerge from the dense, confining woods into a fallow pasture alight with the promise of the new day. On the edge of the clearing a large rectangular stone, hand-chiseled and weathered, rises prominently in a bed of scarlet leaf ivy. Bearing no inscription and unlike any stone in shape and color they have come across so far, the gray monument lists to one side, its carefully carved lines marred by a violent blow that has severed its upper right corner.

As they pass on their horses, Josephine, already rattled by Leah's disappearance, is momentarily captivated by the enigmatic shape—a forgotten marker, out of place and out of time. She glances back over her shoulder and twists in the saddle to take one last glimpse and notices how the faint contours of the fallow patch are slightly concave and narrow in front of the stone. At that singular moment, as if by the trick of the light and the elevated angle of her Josephine's perspective, a forgotten secret is tantalizingly revealed. And then, as suddenly as the moment unexpectedly presents itself, the peculiar alignment between light and shadow, past and present, all serendipitous and ephemeral, falls apart.

Josephine's look falls upon Margaret, who is riding behind her and scanning the pasture for sign of Leah. In her riding gear, her striking beauty and sophistication are accentuated. Whether on horseback or at formal dinner dances or in the classroom, she captivates her surroundings with an effortless grace that make her classmates want to emulate her confident stride, her impeccable fashion, and, above all, the way she can, with her alluring stare and her full, slightly parted lips lay a man to waste.

"What is it?" she snaps in a peeved voice at Josephine's prolonged stare. "Turn around and get us out of here."

"I'm sorry, Margaret. I am truly sorry to have dragged you into this," she says with heartfelt remorse.

"Don't worry. I am calculating your debt to me. If we miss breakfast, it will really cost you. But you *will* pay."

Josephine smiles and Margaret returns to surveying the field.

"You are a softy, you know. You may not want others to know that. You want them to believe you are some sort of Teutonic goddess. But I know better. I know the real Margaret Cleary."

"If you were only half as smart as you thought you were, my dear, then we would not be in this little mess in the first place and I could regain the feeling in my fingers and toes."

Something moves in a rough of pendulous tan grass and Sable snorts a warning. Josephine feels the horse's massive rib cage expand between her legs and the powerful back muscles twitch and tense as if trying to cast off a pesky fly. And then her mount takes a half-step backward.

The high grass parts as an unseen creature heads directly toward them. So unexpected and swift is the charge, neither girl has time to react. Retreat into the protection of the forest is not an option. They have no choice but to face the fierce attacker bolting across the field.

Margaret instinctively grips her riding crop and raises it high at the very instant a broad-chested mongrel bursts through the concealing growth and digs its front paws into the soil a few yards before the startled riders. Tattered ears flop above enraged eyes of black and frame a snub-nosed face and a well-defined and powerful jaw line. What the dog lacks in stature it more than compensates for with the pugnacious attitude of a badger. Its bared teeth, uneven and fractured over time by a steady diet of bones, nip the air in quick repetition as the low-slung, crouched sentinel of the field furiously scuffs the ground and bounces its chest along the grass in a frenzy of confrontation. The display is so captivating and alarming that neither girl notices the boy sprinting across the pasture toward them.

"Lucius! Lucius! Come here, boy! Heel, Lucius, heel!"

Breathlessly the boy flings himself to the ground and, from his knees, wraps his arms around the dog so violently its aggressive posture instantly turns to tuck-tailed submissiveness.

"He's only checking you out. He's not a bit mean. Only for show. What you see is only for show, I promise."

"It looks like he knows who the boss is," Josephine says to their surprise savior, looking down on the boy as he cradles a panting animal as large as himself. "Lucius, is that his name?"

"Yes, ma'am."

The black boy, slight of build, thin-limbed and angular, releases the suddenly compliant dog and brushes the knee patches of his overalls.

"He seems like a nice dog. Is he yours?"

"Yep. I train him and I take care of him."

"He won't bother our horses, will he, now that you are here?"

"Naw. Lucius's been 'round horses all of his life. They don't pay him any mind and he does the same."

"You *have* trained him well."

The boy smiles at the words of praise and self-consciously looks away, pulling his wool coat tight against his chest. A brown, loose fitting hand-me-down cap slides over his brow before he nudges it back. At the boy's feet, the now-docile dog playfully turns on his back and wriggles from side to side looking for a hand to scratch his exposed belly.

"I was messin' around the summer house over there with Lucius and didn't see you coming. He doesn't usually charge folks, you see. Then again, people usually don't come out the woods like you did."

"As trespassers, we seem to have forgotten our manners. I am Josephine and this is Margaret."

"Ma'am," he replies with a polite nod to both girls.

"And you are?"

"My name is Robert. I am ten. Lucius here is five. Known him most of my life, or so it seems."

"What a coincidence! A very close friend of mine is named Robert. Now I have two friends named Robert."

"I suppose, ma'am," he sheepishly answers. "Those are the finest horses I have ever seen. We have a horse but he's old and beat up. Nothin' like these two. You come from the big school, don't you—the girl school on the hill over that way?

"Yes, we do," Margaret speaks up, "and we are looking for our friend. Looks like us, also on a horse. We think she got lost looking for the road and came this way."

"Lost like you?"

"Yes, Robert. Lost like us," she replies, the despair dripping from her words.

"Naw. Just me and Lucius foolin' around out here. We can show you how to get to the road though. You are not far from it."

The boy, with his dog under foot, leads the riders across the frost-encrusted field to where a dilapidated cabin sits in a state of advanced decomposition. The vertical posts along the front have collapsed and brought the awning crashing onto the wooden porch leaving a concave barrier of shattered boards and shingles sealing off the entrance. Crumbling patches of chinking pockmark the cabins exterior and the cumulative force of decades worth of storms has left gaps in the seams bonding the hewn timbers offering narrow glimpses into the rough, dingy brown interior.

Shards of broken glass litter the ground around the foundation as if the twisted amputated limbs of the elm arching overhead had shaken loose everlasting green and brown petals in its final throes. The outline of a dismantled fireplace is visible along the length of the decrepit building's side wall, the remnants of its construction nowhere in sight. Nearby, a rust-colored pump protrudes from the hard soil, ensnared in a tightly wrapped web of poison ivy.

Robert separates from the horses and runs ahead to the cabin, the faithful Lucius, with his broad bounds, overtaking him before they disappear behind the sagging structure.

Josephine despairs that Leah has not been seen by the boy.

"We lost her trail somewhere along the way."

"We have no other choice but to do as we agreed. We find the road and go back. For all we know, she's probably there waiting for us, the skittish loon."

"Will you please be serious, Margaret, and stop with the name calling? I'm worried."

"It's how I cope. Let's just find the road and get out of here."

Their carefree guide reappears with a sack slung across his shoulder and urges the girls to follow him with a wave of his hand.

Josephine watches the boy lead through the field grass and the scene inexplicably conjures up memories of the school trolley trips into the city. As her hips rock rhythmically in the saddle and her exposed cheeks grow a deeper red from the chilling breeze, Josephine slips into thought, fatigued and numb by the ordeal. Watching the gangly boy, she recalls the feel and sound of those streetcar rides.

Images bubble up from her psyche.

How the car clatters through a tapestry of rolling farm land that shrinks and fragments with each journey, fractured by the voracious spread of new development along the route.

How the smartly constructed homes, freshly minted in neat rows, on lots staked out with pubescent maples and virginal white fences, quickly multiply and the sound of hammer blows and the pervasive aroma of freshly cut pine in the air greet the girls at the early stops.

How, as the trolley continues southbound into the District, this vanguard of creation, this outer ring of domestic Eden, an expanding horizon full of promise, abruptly gives way to a dystopian realm of overcrowding and squalor.

How, in the poorer sections, the children, in grimy, ill-fitting clothes, stop their play and stare at the passing streetcar, sometimes waving, more often not.

How the trolley, with its tether spitting electrical sparks overhead, does not make stops in these neighborhoods and the faces of the children like Robert stream past in a two-dimensional blur void of depth, lacking connection to those inside.

How from their lacquered wooden seats she and the other girls routinely travel through this netherworld, glimpse the impoverished state of existence outside their windows, and dutifully shake off the uncomfortable thoughts that settle upon their consciences by returning to reassuring conversations of the treasures awaiting them in the marble cathedrals at the end of the line.

Young Robert leads the horses through a copse of trees and carefully guides the group around a swampy morass of mud and standing water. Up ahead a thin man wrapped in a soiled blanket feeds green tree branches to a struggling fire spewing thick, white smoke as he bounces on his toes to keep warm. Chickens roam nearby pecking the bare ground in search of nonexistent morsels.

In the distance, an emaciated, swayback horse with a sallow coat and overgrown, tangled forelock stands motionless in a lake of gripping mire inside a split-rail corral, covered by a crudely built lean-to which offers meager shelter from the biting cold. The miserable hollow-eyed beast stares across the yard at a clapboard house situated on a rise of uneven ground. A sheet of burlap ripples in the doorway and the tar-papered roof sags. The gutter is separated and the attached rain spout dangles precariously above a belted pickle barrel. Along the side of the house, a makeshift chimney pipe, haphazardly forced through the exterior boards, belches a plume of smoke.

The solitary man steps away from the fire when he notices Robert and the girls approaching. His face is hardened with misery. Deep furrows crease his forehead and taut, ashen skin covers pronounced cheek bones. Reddened eyes, slightly hooded, follow Josephine as the young boy leads her across a thick patch of weeds.

"Is this your home, Robert?" she asks.

"Yep. That's my Uncle Zachary by the fire."

"I don't like this," Margaret whispers to her friend.

"I thought you were taking us to the county road, Robert. That's where we need to go. It's important we get to the road. Do you understand?"

"The road is past our house, just up the path there, on the other side. It's not far, like I said."

As they draw nearer to the flagging blaze, the wind shifts and blows the acrid smoke over the group. Josephine loses sight of the man in the obscuring gust and turns away to shield her eyes. After a few seconds they emerge from the blinding fumes. Robert's uncle has now positioned himself directly in their path. The lashing wind raises the trailing edge of the clutched blanket off the ground causing it to flap like a tattered flag.

Josephine steers Sable to the left to avoid the cloaked man but he springs to life and anticipates her move, quickly side-stepping away from the fire and placing his hand firmly against the startled horse's nose.

"Whoa there. What's the hurry?"

Josephine sees that under the blanket he is a tall man, in his twenties, with a short, cropped mustache and a prematurely receding hairline. Up close, his appearance is even more haunting and troubling. Vacant, lifeless eyes exude a sinister aura. A jagged scar, fresh and pink, runs along his jaw line. A short, unlit pipe, gnarled with chew marks, is held precariously in chattering teeth.

"Uncle, we met by the summer house—"

"Quiet Robert," he spits out harshly, "I've been looking for you boy. Out here freezing by myself. Go to the shed and get the kerosene can. This wood too wet to burn."

As Josephine watches the boy and his dog run off, a punishing blast of air whips across the yard and cuts through her riding coat. The gust pulls and then plasters the thick column of smoke from the fire to the ground and then shapes it into a funnel that briefly consumes the man, leaving only his bony hand gripping the harness visible. He makes no effort to escape the stinging fumes and waits for a shift in the wind before speaking directly to the lost riders.

"Searching for something?" he asks Josephine, stroking the skin between Sable's eyes with fingers horribly chapped and cracked.

"We took a wrong turn on our ride and ended up here. Robert was kindly showing us the way to get back to the county road."

"You took a lot of wrong turns, I'd say," he says with a smirk, revealing a set of misaligned and missing teeth. "What I am to make of the two of you girls riding across our property on the heels of the sunrise? Cold as hell and here the two of you show up. You know, you have no business being here. There are laws about such things."

"If you would please stand aside, we will leave and cause you no more trouble. It was not our intention to ride on your property. As I said, we became lost riding down by the creek and then Robert found us and led us here. He is showing us the way back."

The man stares intently into Josephine eyes as if to divine the truthfulness of her words, never losing touch with her horse.

"What did Robert tell you? The boy jabbers like a blue jay around folks he don't know."

"Nothing. Now would you please step aside?"

"The day hasn't come when Robert says *nothing.*"

As if on cue, the boy hurries back to the fire with the kerosene can and hands it to his uncle.

"Robert, your new friends look chilled to the bone. Why don't you steady their horses so they can come on down and warm themselves by the fire before they get on their way."

The boy obeys and takes hold of Sable's harness as the man walks away, splatters a trickle of kerosene on the smoldering pile, and watches the flame ignite in a fireball of incandescent orange.

"Don't do it," Margaret interjects too late as Josephine swings her leg over and pushes out of her remaining stirrup.

The man, hermit-like under the stitched, patchwork blanket, feeds the reinvigorated fire and waits for Josephine to join him.

With a flick of her crop and withering glare, Margaret chases the eager boy away from her horse.

Josephine crouches closer to the fire and can see the man's limbs, protruding under the thin wrap, shake and clench, his lean muscles unable to arrest the spasms.

"We were riding with a friend. Did you see her come this way? We are worried about her."

"How come you ain't worried about yourselves? You have no business here."

"Once we find her, we are going back to our school. I promise. There are people there waiting for us to return. Robert says the road is just beyond the house. That way."

"Showing up on private land can get a girl like you in a big mess real fast. You think you can ride our land like it is your playground or something, just because of who you are."

"Help us and then we will leave."

"Help you? Girl, you must have fallen and scrambled up your head or something. This ain't your world any longer. You left that place when you crossed through those woods. You don't tell me nothing. The rules here are different. Understand? *Understand!* My advice to you and your friend is that you get on out of here fast, real fast. Every minute that passes, my patience grows thin."

Agitated and unable to get warm, the man paces around the fire and Josephine watches out of the corner of her eye as he moves behind her. She stands and presses the matter further, undeterred by his menacing tone.

"Please. We'd appreciate any help you can give us in finding our friend."

"*Appreciate*, that's a funny word. The sort of word that can mean different things to different people, depending on their circumstances. What kinda *appreciation* exactly are you proposing?"

Robert moves away from the fire and cowers against Sable's glistening shoulder, catching his uncle's attention.

"That horse maybe. Would that be proper payment for what you've done and the trouble you are causing me? I tell you what, I'm a reasonable man. How about just the saddle? Looks pretty worn from what I can tell. You leave it behind in *appreciation* for you riding our land without permission. You won't miss it. Probably ain't even yours, so it's no skin off your nose."

Josephine stands up and faces the man glowering at her. She stares back at him and calls his bluff.

"That's not going to happen."

The man shrugs indifferently and then snaps a branch against his knee and tosses it on the resuscitated blaze.

"You're on your own, as far as I am concerned. I'm not here to clean up your mess. You've got me confused with someone else, missy. I'm not the type to wear an apron and gloves."

"Let's go," Margaret pleads from the saddle.

Josephine turns and walks over to Sable and takes the reins from Robert, aware that the ill-tempered man is watching her closely. She glances at the boy who immediately looks away, a hint of fear visible in his averted eyes and narrowed lips.

"Let's go," her friend repeats with more urgency.

She pauses and considers her next move. Her first impulse is to do as Margaret wants and ride away and find the road like they agreed to do. But she senses in the poor boy's conflicted expression a sign that the man knows more than he is letting on.

Dealing with life when it is not tamed and tempered.

That is what Miss Price told her the day before was the test of character.

She decides that riding away would be to abandon not only Leah but young, defenseless Robert in a time of need. She watches the contemptible figure leaning into the billowing gray column of smoke.

"Do you live here, Mr. Zachary? Do you live in that house over there?"

The hunched over form pivots and she sees the fury in his eyes directed at the boy, who quickly buries his face against the horse's neck. She lets the question hang over him and remounts. A sharp nudge of her boot and she steers Sable nearer the crackling wood pile and looks down on the shrouded shoulders of the miserable man.

"Whoever does own this land should know that there is someone living down by the creek, not far from here. And until our friend is found, that fact will be of chief interest to the police. The first place they will look will be those woods. And after they scour the woods, they will come looking here. You will not be able to dodge their questions like you have mine, I suspect. They will demand thoroughness and they have the means to compel it."

As the girls turn and ride toward the house, the meandering dirt path leading to the county road promised by Robert comes into view. The boy, with Lucius in tow, jogs alongside Sable to keep warm while Margaret repeatedly looks back, paranoid that Josephine's threatening words might have lit a fuse of rage in the man. They had told no one where they were going, and only Mr. Raymee knows they left the school campus and even he does not know where they headed or for what purpose. Their secretive journey has landed them in an isolated patch of land where a call for help will die off in the impenetrable surroundings, unheard and unanswered. A wave of light-headedness sweeps over Margaret and she is forced to grip the pommel to steady herself. An alarming thought sends an icy tingle down the length of her body: is the distance between them now enough? Can they reach the road if they have to—before being caught?

"Robert, come here now!"

The booming command halts them in their tracks.

Knowing from his uncle's tone that he will not be asked twice, the boy runs back to the fire. Lucius does not follow this time, choosing to hide in the protective shadow of strangers.

The girls watch but cannot hear what is said between the two by the fire. Robert tills the ground with the toe of his mud-encased shoe while his uncle stabs his finger emphatically in front of his face. Then, with a grand sweep of the blanket worthy of a caped magician at a traveling vaudeville show, his uncle turns back to tending the waning flame.

Robert quickly doubles back and stands before Josephine panting, hands resting on his knees. Lucius licks at the air from his mouth and wriggles excitedly between his master's legs. Regaining his breath, Robert recites the message he has been ordered to deliver.

"My uncle says you are trespassers and says the law would see it that way. He also told me to tell you that there is a horse tied to the tree behind our house and that he found it trespassing on our property before I found you in the pasture. He says the horse is his by right and that the law would see it that way too. But he wants you to take it with you because he doesn't want no trouble."

Robert pauses and struggles to remember the rest of what he was told.

"Is there more?" Josephine prompts.

The boy's face brightens and he suddenly points to something over her shoulder.

"Yes. My uncle says she's been staring at him every since he came outside and she ran off and hid behind the coop."

Both girls turn in their saddles and see Leah standing statue-like next to a primitive, weathered gray enclosure topped with an orange-rust, tin roof. She neither speaks nor waves, but her eyes are alert and moist, shimmering brown pools cupped by a pale blue palette.

"My uncle says you're to take her too when you take the horse."

Chapter 4
Minerva and Silva

We plan for the pleasure of our girls, believing that desire for pleasure is natural and should, within reason, be gratified. To isolate the large body of students from the warm cheeriness of hospitable homes, without supplying right opportunities to develop and gratify the social being, is neglectful and dangerous. Right, natural instincts, if repressed, are sure to develop into abnormal, unwholesome, clandestine habits. Youth hates monotony and punishes it with revolt. Remembering that it is the province of woman to interest herself no less heartily in the pursuit of others than in pursuits of her own, we desire that her range of sympathies be wide and her knowledge practical and varied. We have sought, wholly regardless of worn traditions, to direct our efforts to the needs of womanly life, to ask ourselves simply what preparation will best serve our girls when they are confronted by actual responsibilities. We conceive it to be our duty to stimulate ambition, arouse the love of study, and present ideals that lead to intelligent and noble womanhood.

Liberated from the grip of the storm, and with the weekend's leisure behind them, the girls of the Seminary greet the resumption of classes with renewed vigor and a spirit of cheerfulness absent the previous week. The routine ebb and flow of campus life returns as girls congregate in the dining room to be served breakfast, carefully navigating along the way the stone paths and steps turned icy and slick over night.

The downward slope of the semester is before them, and the scholastic load has receded with the approaching holiday break. Classroom study is increasingly curtailed in favor of musical recitals and dramatic expressions of the season. As the days grow shorter and the solstice approaches, a frenzy of engagements and formal celebrations takes over, like that of the bee colony frantically racing against the approaching killing frost. Afternoon teas, sponsored by each dormitory and steeped in formality and exclusivity, are the traditional launch of the winter social season at the Seminary, and are soon followed by twilight tree trimming parties and troupes of evening carolers, guided by candlelight, laying siege to one club after another until tribute is offered.

A phantasmagorical explosion of Christmas decorations over the weekend has transformed the school into a living Currier and Ives lithograph. Bells and ribbons hang in dormitory hallways and candles softly glow in windows at night. The multitude of sitting rooms and parlors in Vincent Hall are festooned with boughs of evergreen and adorned with silver and red trim, as the sweet, enticing aroma of ginger and spice seeps out of the kitchen and permeates the hallways.

From her solitary perch in the far corner of the dining room, May sips her tea while her breakfast, picked over and cold, sits neglected on a bonewhite china plate off to the side. She stares across the spacious room, with its high wooden ceiling stained in a molasses hue, hanging tapestries, and intricately carved triangular support posts, as her schoolmates sit in Chippendale reproductions and breakfast noisily, their plates brought and removed by colored women in starched white aprons and caps, using silverware cleaned and polished by colored men never seen during dining hours.

May watches in silent contempt as a freshman girl bounds from one table to another with uncouth ferocity, gesturing and laughing in frivolous conversation, mindlessly clutching a fork as she banters with others in her class. On the far wall, a colossal, ornate Dutch fireplace, with painted ceramic tiles above the mantel and trimmed with brass, bathes those seated at coveted tables nearby with waves of warmth.

When she first arrived at the National Park Seminary, she too sought out these privileged seats, privately desperate to feel the acceptance of her classmates, hoping to feel the bond of friendship grow naturally in the casual discourse of the day. Not anymore. How differently she felt then. So naïve. So foolish. She idolized many of them and ached when they refused to return her attention. She can almost see a shadow of her former self moving among these fresh faces. And what would she say to them now, if she dared? Rather, she wonders, what would she say to her younger self, if she could go back in time armed with the lessons of what lay ahead? Would it really matter?

Would anything change? How exactly would the benefit of perspective wipe away the familiar pain that marks her days at the Seminary? The subtle acts of exclusion she faces. The offers politely but consistently declined. The reciprocal invitations never tendered. The insidious creep of self-doubt she feels when she enters a room. How the vortex of conversation hovers about and then passes over her. The unflattering feel of her uniform as it bunches and squeezes during her daily gymnastics class. The way her evening dresses never fail to escape the thoughtful notice of the other girls. How, with the passing of each of a thousand days, she fades by degrees into the background of the school tableau, always present but rarely seen.

The garish freshman flicks her bangs off to the side, plops into the lap of another student and playfully shoves a roll into the girl's mouth as the table erupts. May seethes at the childish behavior and how the others around the irrepressible girl egg her on. She scans the room expecting someone to intervene but the conversations at the other tables continue uninterrupted. Servers move efficiently from table to table carrying plates and pitchers of milk and go about their duties undistracted by the disruptive group.

May picks up her knife and gently taps the base of her crystal water glass twice in the hope of sending a subtle corrective signal to the offending table but her admonishment is lost in the din of voices and soon the cavorting worsens until the two girls at the table are locked in a giddy embrace of tickling and laughter. As they wrestle in the chair, a stray elbow nearly clips a server carrying a stack of plates to the kitchen to be washed and May grows more incensed over the near catastrophe. She wants to stand up and march over to the table and pull the irresponsible child away by the wrist and explain to the surprised, slack-jawed imp how her embarrassing behavior is, in no uncertain terms, unacceptable and will not be tolerated, and how, from this moment forward, she is to conduct herself like a woman with manners.

But May remains bolted to her seat as an alternative vision of events plays out in her mind instead: how upon reaching the table of boisterous freshmen girls she loses her nerve and how, with the group noticing her uninvited intrusion, the laughter stops and their collective gaze falls upon her, and, on cue, the uncomfortable surge of anxiety courses through her veins that twists her stomach and silences her lips. The swelling rush of indignation recedes and she is left standing alone under the scrutiny of everyone in the room. And then the look she hates the most will appear on their faces, the one she loathes beyond comprehension—the silent amusement twinkling in their impudent eyes.

No, May has come to accept, reluctantly, her lowly place in the school strata. In the classroom, at the Kappa club, in the music room, on the dance floor, even in the dining room, hers is an ordinary life. In the solar system of the National Park Seminary, her orbit is a distant one. Beyond the warming reach of the flame she moves slowly along a lazy, predictable path. A cold, marginal existence few teachers or students are interested in knowing or willing to alter.

For a princely sum, the Seminary provides a privileged life of compulsory enfranchisement in which all students are embraced in a communal structure of instruction, activities and residence. But no where in the representations of the school administration or in the pages of the student application and reference forms will one find the promise to parents of their daughter's acceptance among her fellow students or the guaranty of her happiness while enrolled. The avowed mission of the National Park Seminary is to train and cultivate the whole personality of those in its care. Shielding a girl from the challenge of overcoming social shortcomings would be indulgent and limit the otherwise well-born and well-bred from realizing the great power of "doing."

The two demonstrative girls finally untangle and the provocateur continues her ebullient journey around the dining room, rising on her toes as she moves about in an improvised dance, confident and graceful. For a moment, May's derision yields and she is captivated by the girl's youthful spirit and the playful way her arms swing and her toes dip and rise with each step. With nimble fluidity she winds through those standing in front of her, carefully avoiding the tolerant servers as they continue to circle about the tables delivering and removing the morning's fare. May watches the spectacle incredulously, her contempt laced with a hint of admiration at the girl's audacity.

Foolish girl. Do you not know how the others look at you? Do you not care how silly you look, prancing about, bobbing up and down like a carousel pony?

The girl glides past the fireplace on her way out and then upon reaching the hallway arch she suddenly stops, pirouettes, and basks in the ovation from her classmates. With a coquettish smile, the freshman grabs her navy blue uniform scarf, draped along the front of her blouse in a v-shape, and flings it playfully over top of her head so the bow at the scarf's end crowns her straight, bobbed hair as if she was a common dishwasher, and then turns and leaves, her dramatic performance complete.

A violent burst of wind rattles the window panes behind May and she feels the cold air squeeze through the cracks in the putty and chill the flesh along her arms. The sensation brings to mind the rawness of the morning in the glen, and the unexpected parole in her social exile.

Why had Josephine invited her on the walk to the flooded creek? She did so knowing that Margaret, her closest friend, views May with disdain. Margaret Cleary. The way she glides across the room in that self-assured stride of hers, preening for all to see like a prized wolfhound. Always setting herself off from the other girls. Always thinking that's she better than the rest. She rules her corner of the school with a tongue sharp as a rapier and an effortless beauty displayed with regal indifference. She is everything I am not, May laments, tracing the knife in a figure eight through the congealed yellow yolk left on the plate.

She can't understand why Josephine is drawn to the girl as a friend, and so blithely succumbs to her needy, manipulative ways. What does she see in Margaret that forgives the girl's considerable flaws? Surely she is too perceptive not to see through Margaret's transparent egotism. Why does she indulge that arrogant, self-centered girl?

The gleaming silver knife now moves across the plate, side to side, carving thin lines in the viscous residue.

May remembers being immediately attracted to Josephine the first time they met years ago. Genuine. Direct. Caring. Soft blue eyes offering calming comfort as she listens to the troubles of others. She admired Josephine's innate ability to blend in, chameleon-like, with all whom she came in contact and how it allowed her to break the shackles that bind most other girls to one social caste or another. Her allure, in contrast to Margaret's, is more layered and complex, undeniable yet mysterious in its origin. It's not in the way she smiles or in the way she speaks. It's not in the way she dresses or in the way she wears her flaxen hair. It's not in the way she moves on the dance floor or in the way she sprints across the grass courts. It's not in the way her eyes survey a crowded room or in the way her fingers absent-mindedly twirl her curls in class. Hers is a consummate presence, an entity of comely charm and inner beauty greater than the sum of its parts. A disposition that is sweet, true and selfless.

Surely she sees in me a kindred spirit, May presumed as she got to know Josephine better over time, someone she would gravitate towards and turn to for advice in times of need. And yet, the friendship May had hoped for back then—the bond between two students of common values, of mutual aspirations, of shared confidences—never materialized. Josephine, though friendly to all, never offered the intimacies of true friendship May craved. She watched others like Margaret assume this role instead and fumed. But as much as she refused to admit it to herself, being rebuffed took a corrosive toll on May. The profound disappointment of her social shortcomings left a kernel of resentment inside the girl from Richmond that grew and hardened and calcified with the passing of each semester full of slights. By May's last year at Forest Glen, the weight of bitterness inside her was so ponderous it pressed against her heart like a malignant black tumor.

"Shall I take your plate, Miss?"

The polite voice snaps her back and she embarrassingly nods and places the knife down. Her server removes the plate, careful to avoid the messy yolk pushed over its edges.

May scans the room. Most of her class has come to breakfast and since left, off to their rooms to prepare for classes. Josephine hasn't, however. She usually dines with other girls from the third floor. They haven't spoken since the glen and May frets about the possible ramifications of her visit to Miss Price's office.

What had she done!? For once, she had been included. Wasn't this what she wanted, what she longed for? For reasons still unclear to her now, she was asked to join; she was brought into the fold. She walked shoulder to shoulder in the raw morning rain with Josephine and the others as a friend, not as an interloper—and the rest of the girls at the school knew it. That's how it works at the Seminary. No secrets remain buried for long. All confidences, no matter how private and closely held, eventually rise to the surface.

Why then had she gone running to Miss Price immediately after? She knew her mistake sitting in the regent's office when Miss Price started asking about what Josephine did at the glen. She went to see Miss Price out of concern that someone may have drowned; it was the proper action to take. And the regent had ended up twisting it into something else all together. Self-loathing burns inside May as she recounts their exchange and the indignity she felt as Miss Price lectured her on the virtues of strong character as tears steamed down her cheeks. The memory of how the teacher went on about Margaret—the one person above all she holds in derision—produces a sour taste of contempt. And how she apologized! Why? Why did she apologize? She had done nothing wrong. She was being the responsible one and doing what was right.

Most troubling of all is the realization that rushing off to see Miss Price surely poisoned any chance that Josephine's overture would be repeated in the future. Word of her visit to the regent has no doubt spread and May, already an outcast, will be branded a tattle. This Margaret will not forgive and Josephine cannot ignore.

Perhaps Leah understands. Surely she can count on Leah as an ally in this unwanted drama. She is the one, after all, who first rung the bell of alarm at the creek. She will understand, she will...she will...she will what? She will never vouch for May if it means taking sides against the other two.

May scrutinizes the faces of the girls across the room as they delicately raise their forks and sip from their glasses. She searches for any sign that they are witting of her betrayal. Is the occasional glance in her direction a knowing, meaningful one? Are the circles of frivolity and the whispered exchanges at her expense?

As May simmers in the juices of her paranoia and prepares to flee the room, she realizes that Josephine is not the only one absent. Both Margaret and Leah are missing as well. Taking a mental roll call of the girls from Senior House, she concludes all are accounted for, all that is except for the three girls.

Before she has time to consider the significance of this surprising revelation, the noise level in the dining room suddenly drops as Miss Price enters, as if May has magically conjured up her form through the power of her thoughts. She wears a stern expression, much different than her usual pleasant demeanor, and moves with clear purpose to a table in the middle of the room. May cannot hear what is spoken but after a few moments Lucille Wilhoit, a girl from the second floor, excuses herself and follows the regent under the stained glass archway and into the corridor, out of view of the others.

Beneath a delicate oil painting of a girl reading by candlelight, the teacher and student sit in a high-backed sofa from the Orient with protruding dragon heads cast of iron supporting the armrests. As directed by the dean, Miss Price asks about the girl's chance exchange with Douglas Stratton on the way to Vincent Hall. Surprised to hear that the regent knew of it, Lucille recounts their brief walk together, as small groups of girls begin to leave the dining room and walk along the corridor past them.

Her hallmates, Mary and Dorothea, sensing that Miss Price has pulled Lucille away from the table for reasons other than social, slip past unnoticed, until Lucille looks up and sees a smiling Dorothea shaking her head in mocking disapproval, walking arm in arm with Mary, who slowly and silently mouths the words, "You are in trouble."

"So, this was the first time you had met the man. And he told you about his daughters going to National Park?"

"He mentioned they had gone here in recent years, but didn't want to say much when I asked about them. He told us that he was late for a meeting with the dean."

"Us?"

"I was with Mary and Dorothea."

"Mary Ferguson?"

"Mary Collins. And Dorothea Bridger. We were on our way to breakfast when we saw the man and asked if he needed assistance. We just happened to be there. He called us his 'three angels.' He was sweet. It's all rather innocent. What is this about, Miss Price?"

"It's a small matter, Lucille, nothing to worry about. I won't keep you long. I know you have class shortly. So then, the three of you walked him to Vincent Hall?"

"No, just me. He only asked me to walk with him, and when we reached the front steps, we talked a bit longer and then we said goodbye."

"You passed the time during the walk in idle chat?"

"Actually, no. He was curiously friendly and at ease talking to me. Like he knew me all of my life."

"What in the world did this total stranger want to talk to you about?"

"The most wondrous place on Earth."

"Pardon?"

"Those were his exact words, *The most wondrous place on Earth.*"

Miss Price grows frustrated trying to draw out the details from the girl as the noise of the departing diners increases around them.

"And this place is?"

"The Louvre. You know, the art museum in Paris."

"Yes, yes, I know where it is. Please, Lucille, you are confusing me. I need your help, and I need you to be more direct. What specifically did he say to you?"

"I was confused in the beginning too, Miss Price, but then it made sense. The man was looking at the statue in front of Senior House—"

"The water carrier?"

"No, the other one."

"The garden ornament?"

Lucille shakes her head.

"Then which one? There are so many of the damn things, Lucille!"

The regent's harsh tone and intemperate words make Lucille rear back in her seat. She now realizes that it is not, as Miss Price said, *a small matter* after all.

"The one of Joan of Arc, sitting on the wall near the porch. You know the one. He said he saw the original at the Louvre, and told me how when he was there he felt as if he was among the greatest riches of mankind. He said he walked through the museum in a trance for days, grateful that he was lucky to have seen the beautiful creations on the walls and on the pedestals. Is he an art collector or museum director, Miss Price?"

"No. It's of no concern to you, Lucille. Anything else?"

"I haven't told you the strangest thing of all."

"Then get to it girl."

Lucille hurriedly searches the pocket of her school uniform until she finds what she is looking for. She slowly opens her fingers to reveal a metal lapel pin in the shape of a shield bearing a cross of red. Miss Price takes it from the girl's palm and scrutinizes it.

"When we reached the veranda, there were two men waiting for us. One I recognize from the school staff. The other, I had never seen before. He said—"

"Good morning, Miss Price," a voice suddenly interrupts, and the impatient teacher looks up to see May standing before them, the migratory push of students leaving the dining room crowding the corridor behind her. "Good morning to you too, Lucille."

"Yes, May, hello," the regent responds with a forced smile, quickly closing her fingers around the pin. "I trust you will have a pleasant day."

Miss Price's polite send-off fails and May remains standing with an anxious expression, her hands interlaced across her protruding waist.

"Is there something I can help you with, May?"

"I just wanted to tell you that everything is much better today."

"That's wonderful. I am glad to hear it."

The reply, transparently half-hearted, hangs awkwardly between teacher and student and Lucille notices how the girl's thumbs, positioned before her at eye level, rub against each other, over and over, red from the repeated friction and intense pressure.

"Looking back on it now," May continues, "I see that I was rash in coming to see you the other day, after, you know what. It was an unnecessary burden on your time."

"Perhaps we can speak about this more later, May."

"That won't be necessary Miss Price. I only wanted you to know that there is no reason for further concern, and if we could keep the matter between us, I would greatly appreciate it."

"Of course, May," she curtly replies, forgetting, in the rush to send May on her way, how she had called Josephine to her office the day after the flood.

The words are unconvincing and fail to douse the feeling of regret that rose inside the troubled student over breakfast. Disappointed over not having received the reassurance she seeks, May's eyes dart to Lucille, who has now turned her attention to the girls mingling about in the foyer as they don their coats and prepare to face the stinging lash of the blustery, early winter wind.

With nothing else to say, May repeats her greeting and leaves. Parting the group in the foyer, she grabs her coat and hat and bounds down the stairs, past a pair of grotesque gryphons guarding the front entrance to Vincent Hall. Instead of returning to Senior House she turns right at the carriage sweep and the silenced fountain and walks past the Alpha sorority house and towards the automobile bridge. Ahead of her, the walkway splits. To her right, on the south side of campus, a number of ancillary buildings supporting the school's daily operations, rarely visited by students, are situated along a paved drive that runs behind Vincent Hall and leads to a back entrance to the kitchen. Here, hidden from the view of most, is the infrastructure that makes National Park Seminary run. Workers use the drive to access the boiler house and store house, and then further on, a large rectangular conservatory where plants are grown year around. On the opposite side of the divide, a water tower and pump station house dedicated solely to the school are located near the gymnasium, an extravagantly designed Greek temple, with its massive portico and elephantine Corinthian columns, and rows of soaring half-Palladian windows running the full length of the building.

Students turning left at the juncture find a lengthy two-tiered pergola walkway connecting Vincent Hall to the Italian Villa dormitory that circumvents the automobile bridge. During inclement weather or when the sun is brutish and unrelenting, students walk under the pergola's shelter along herringbone-patterned brick, protected by a wooden canopy. Interspersed between the supporting columns, climbing roses have been planted and trained along a wrought iron railing on both sides of the elevated platform. In pleasant conditions, girls walk along this second tier, twelve feet off the ground, physically transported above the Seminary grounds onto a floral plain of blooming reds and pinks and yellows, their gait, in contrast to those walking below, slower, more languid, as if the creeping roses, with their unruly tendrils outstretched and overpoweringly fragrant, are lotus plants, and the manicured lawns and tended gardens they pass on both sides of the pergola are dreamscapes of their altered perspective.

Head down and tucked tightly into her coat, May crosses the driveway and eschews the steps leading to the protected level of the pergola sought by the other girls headed to the Villa, choosing instead to be alone, above grade and exposed to the harsh morning conditions.

The loitering crow sits perched atop the shingled roof of Kappa house, its ebony feathers dancing in the stiff wind that pushes the sails of the faux windmill slowly around, and watches the solitary figure below approach. The bird hops to the branch of a nearby tree as the creaking timbers lumber past, and tracks the sound of May's heals striking the wooden boards.

Rich, succulent, enticing smoke pours from the nearby chimneys. Hunger stirs in the bird's belly. The particular angle of the sun above the eastern horizon. The line of students leaving Vincent Hall. All signs. Pieced together intuitively. Predictably. Soon, the scavenger's next meal will arrive. It waits patiently for the rustling and clanging of pots and trash can lids behind the kitchen to seek out the regular offering. It knows not to arrive too soon and be spotted or its chances at pilfery will be compromised.

A solitary cry of protest and the crow takes flight, catches an updraft, and spies the girl from above as she continues her lonely journey through a gauntlet of woody vines, stripped of foliage and its thorns bared. With a dip of its wing the tracker corkscrews downward, picks up speed, and glides over a swollen stream before circling past the castle drawbridge and landing on a rooftop rampart of Beta house, where it bobs and caws repeatedly into the wind for no apparent reason.

May stops along the walkway and, shielding her eyes against the low-lying sun, searches for the boisterous bird. Beneath her, a huddle of girls, move hurriedly toward their dormitory, unseen from the upper deck but their voices and footsteps clearly audible.

Across a rolling field of generously spaced oaks, the pergola doglegs behind the castle. Beyond the walk, in the direction of the thick woodlands that constitute a natural buffer to the few homes bordering the southern boundary of the campus, there is a brackish lake populated with hardy lilies and cattails and covered with a thin, translucent layer of overnight ice. In the adjacent grove, the concrete statue of Silva, the demi-goddess of the forest and unfailing protector of those brave enough to swim in the opaque waters, looks over the stilled lake, its shore lined with decapitated seed stalks and dormant brown thickets.

Close by, in a triangular parcel bordered by the towering Villa dormitory and the pseudo medieval castle, Silva's near twin, Minerva, sits prominently at the epicenter of an elaborate formal garden clutching a caduceus against her robed chest with one arm and holding a lyre with the other.

The sisters oversee two contrasting domains, natural spheres separated by the pergola: one untamed and fallow, the other constructed out of meticulous beds and concentric pathways. Only the most attentive observer would notice that the gargantuan figures positioned across the divide are facing in opposite directions, their backs to each other, as if stubbornly estranged and their proud postures frozen in callous indifference. Their identical facial features, flawless and pristine at birth, show the wear of age and exposure. Along the left side of Silva's face, protected against the reach of the sun, remnants of green mold stain her cheek and neck and have insinuated themselves into the grooved folds of her tunic. A fouler blight desecrates the ivory luminance of her sister however. With each steam engine that idles at the Forest Glen station and with every freight train that passes by headed toward the District hauling a caravan of cars loaded down with brimming mounds of lustrous black coal, particles of decay are left behind and settle on Minerva's countenance, turning her a dingy gray until she is scrubbed clean by the Seminary maintenance crew before the start of the new school year.

Exposed and alone on the raised platform, May feels the frigid winds swirl about her. She often comes to the pergola in the winter when she wants separation from the other students. Here she can find solitary refuge along the desolate avenue, away from their lilting voices and their trifling games and their constant mindless chatter.

She glimpses something moving in the distance and spots a herd of a half-dozen deer emerge from the woods and move silently across the field, cautiously making for the lake, their dappled coats glistening and their delicate features crisply defined in the morning light. May steps closer and grips the pergola railing, captivated by the beauty of the scene, feeling excited that she and only she is privileged to witness the intimate moment.

The deer turn as a group and search about for danger, ears perked and twitching, brown eyes wide and bright, as their long, thin legs part the frost-covered grass.

More beautiful than any painting hanging on the walls of the Seminary, May thinks.

The lead deer stops at the water's edge, looks about once more, and then bows to drink. Others in the herd follow in succession.

May is transfixed. She feels as if she is there at the lake, standing next to the skittish herd. She can hear their breathing, smell their musky odor, close enough to discern the thin scars on their coats rendered over the years by bramble and antler. How she would like to walk among them, and be part of their world, even for a short time. How it must feel to be with others like her. To live as one. In harmony with your surroundings.

A jarring explosion bursts in her ears and violently punctures the silence, startling May and causing the deer to bolt. The lead doe jumps forward as others in the herd break for the trees. Momentarily disoriented, the startled beast heads onto the new ice and her forelegs slip and struggle for footing. The shimmering surface holds and the deer's front legs begin to straighten. Then suddenly, the thin ice shatters and the panicked animal plunges chest-deep into the murky water.

The sound of a car engine rattles and roars behind her heading across the bridge and then backfires a second time. May watches breathlessly while the deer thrashes about trying to extract herself from the soft, gripping mire of the lake. A wave of alarm sweeps over May as she witnesses the animal's struggle. Her muscles tense and her heart pounds as the disruptive car disappears over the glen and out of earshot.

The chest of the trapped deer rises and falls in quick succession. Her rapid breathing grows deep and labored, and her nostrils flare. She suddenly stops thrashing about and lets out a pitiful bellow. Seconds pass and the deer does not move, the outer ring of white in its frantic eyes visible from across the field. Shards of broken ice bob on the ripples sent off from the trembling animal. Captivated by the trapped beast's plight, May silently urges the animal to not give up, to fight against the suction of the lake mud.

The doe musters a mighty, desperate push and finally breaks free from the morass and tumbles clumsily onto its side, momentarily submerged, before regaining her footing in a shallower part of the lake and jumping onto the bank. May exhales as the frightened creature, covered completely on one side with thick mud, sprints into the woods to find the rest of the scattered herd.

So enthralled by the thrilling spectacle before her, she does not notice the crow, also chased off by the belching machine, leave its perch on the castle turret and glide down and land on the pergola walk, mere feet away. The pugnacious black herald dances and taunts May and blocks the narrow path toward the Villa.

As the bird's shrill squawking fills her ears, she feels a dull pain in her hand grow in intensity. How odd, she thinks calmly, as she releases her grip on a thick, woody rose cane and dispassionately looks over her thumb. A large thorn, curved like a viper's fang, is deeply embedded in the soft flesh, a single drop of blood slowly oozing from the piercing.

Once led by young Robert to county road, the three girls canter their horses to the stable in a race against time, frantic that their prolonged absence not be detected. Josephine and Margaret, fatigued by the misguided journey through the woods and the confrontation at the dilapidated farm, want answers from their wandering classmate. But there is no time to reconcile why Leah left them at the creek and how she came to be separated from her horse.

"We will meet in Leah's room during the afternoon break," Josephine decrees to the other two, as they hurriedly dismount at the stables, "and no one speaks of what happened out there until then."

When Leah, passive and expressionless, doesn't respond, Margaret goes over and stands directly in front of her face.

"Do you understand? I want to hear you say it."

"I understand," she answers in a submissive tone.

"I'd like to throttle you right now, after what you put us through."

"Margaret!"

"No, really Josephine," Margaret fires back at her friend, "she needs to hear it. We escaped a very bad situation back there and we have her to thank for what happened."

"Is that what you think—that I am responsible?"

Mr. Raymee's young assistant emerges from the stable, disheveled and scraping off the remaining fruit from an apple core. He whips the remnants at a barn cat peeking around the corner, sending the harassed animal retreating into the shadows of the building, and then jogs over to where the three girls wait.

"Look, I'm sorry. But it wasn't my fault. You don't understand. Give me a chance to explain."

"I can't believe you, Leah. You run off into the woods like a rabbit and force us to chase after you. And you stand there—"

"Not know, Margaret. Not here."

Josephine greets the dutiful helper and hands him the reins to her horse. He looks over the mud-splattered animals and sees that his morning work has only begun.

"Rough riding," he observes. "Must have left the road." Margaret glances at Josephine as the stable boy inspects the horses. "Big mess."

"You have no idea," Margaret unable to hold her sharp tongue, earning a disapproving stare from Josephine.

"Sorry about that. There was a lot of standing water along the road."

The boy takes the leads from the other two and secures his hold on the compliant mounts.

"Not a problem for me. They are the ones who don't like the cold water on a day like today."

Once back in Senior House, which is already empty with the start of classes, the three walk quietly down the silent hallway and go to their separate rooms without saying a word, leaving incriminating tracks of dirt on the carpet along the way.

Josephine changes out of her riding clothes and readies herself for class. As much as she tries, she cannot suppress the trembling that grips her limbs as she slips on her uniform. Nor can she dismiss from her mind the image of poor Leah standing before them, confused and helpless, at the homestead hidden in the woods. Margaret was right. The girl's actions were inexcusable and her behavior inexplicable. Josephine hurries about the room trying to focus on the task at hand. She can't think about what happened now. She quickly looks in the dressing mirror to make sure nothing is amiss. The chapel bell tolls calling students to their seats and the pure tone resonating through dormitory momentarily mesmerizes Josephine as she contemplates her reflection, suddenly feeling the physical effects of the botched excursion as the adrenaline begins to wear off.

Margaret hears a door closing in the corridor and tracks Josephine footsteps as she runs off to piano practice. Feeling no motivation to join her English recitation and in no frame of mind to endure the indignities of bowling at the gymnasium, Margaret writes off her morning classes and draws a hot bath. She will rejoin her classmates for the daily luncheon after chapel, she decides, once she feels civilized again.

Down the hall, Leah listens to the water pipes behind the wall hum as they feed Margaret's bathtub. She sits on the floor, still dressed in her riding attire, and leans her back against the radiator coils and rubs her arms desperate to chase away the chill, her legs pulled tightly against her chest.

The Christmas concert is in three days and Madame Kaspar will be expecting her and the rest of the girls to unfailingly attend the daily afternoon and evening practice sessions at the Odeon. The prospect of singing seems oddly foreign to her now. The strange events of the past day have deadened her interest in music and left her numb inside. She is no condition now to sing, maybe not even by Friday evening. Her throat is raw from spending the morning outside and a heavy cloak of exhaustion weighs down her limbs and siphons the energy from her body. Gradually the heat from the radiator reaches through her riding jacket and pleasurable warmth spreads across her shoulders and down her spine. Leah remains seated on the floor as the darkness encroaches. Her eyelids flutter and narrow. Her heels slowly slide along the floor boards until both legs rest straight on the ground, the toes of her tawny leather boots pointed slightly outward. Across the room, at eye level, is her bed. Too far, she decides. I will remain here, propped up like a broken mannequin. A faint smile appears, the first light-hearted moment she's felt since the incident at the creek.

What is wrong with me? I can't even muster the strength to walk over to the bed and lay down.

Comfortable and relaxed, she willfully gives herself over to sleep. The curtain draws down and she drifts away without resistance. For an exquisite moment, her psyche is no longer besieged. Gone are the persistent specters that torment her. At the burgeoning banks in the glen. Before the boathouse entrance. In the plume of dense smoke billowing from the fire.

On the verge of unconsciousness, her descent into sublime nothingness is abruptly arrested. Through glassy, bloodshot eyes she stares across the room at the sliver of black between the mattress and box-spring, an artificial horizon against the far wall beckoning her.

The white dress.

After leaving Dean Dawson's office, Mr. Stratton and his assistant are driven back to the Glen Manor Hotel where the capitalist places a number of business calls to New York. He meets with Mr. Carter over lunch in his room to discuss the timeline for the purchase of the school. Up to this point, he has been sparing in divulging the details of the tender to his traveling companion. Only the basics were discussed on the train ride down from New York, information sufficient enough to carry out their unorthodox presentation to the school administrator.

He sits in shirt sleeves in a wing-backed chair upholstered in plum cotton, his slight build swallowed by the furniture's deep recesses, and balances a cup and saucer on his lap, while his young assistant heartily devours a sandwich at the coffee table before him. Mr. Stratton watches the man's ravenous assault on the meal, alternately amused and disgusted by what he is witnessing. One bite after another until no more can be held in his assistant's bulging mouth. The roast beef is ground down by a prolonged gnashing of teeth and the considerable mass is forced down his throat with audible difficulty.

"I was wise to decline the dean's offer of breakfast, I think. Had they seen you eat like this, the whole deal would be scotched. You eat as if you are headed to the scaffold, Charles. I know we are in somewhat informal surroundings, but seriously, have you no comprehension of the loathsome manners you are displaying now?"

Mr. Carter draws a napkin to his mouth to conceal the carnage, more than slightly embarrassed by his employer's brutal commentary. While he labors to finish what he has consumed, he looks around the spacious suite in an attempt to avoid the old man's narrow, piercing eyes and judgmental scowl.

"I mean, let's be frank, good man. You eat like that in front of a woman and she will not want to have anything to do with you. Unless she's interested in having a dog about to feed table scraps."

The ridiculed aide feigns a smile, unable to speak and desperate to deflect the criticism, the accumulated bread and meat straining inside his cheeks as he works to suppress the tremor of choking rising up his throat.

"Oh, that's even worse, boy. Why wear an expensive tailored suit if you are to act like a circus clown?"

Mr. Stratton watches his assistant's face turn bright pink and mistakenly assumes shame has come over the man. A raised vein appears across the choking man's forehead and realizing that a point of no return has been reached he bolts from the divan clutching the napkin to his mouth to muffle the fit of uncontrollable coughing and makes for the nearby sink.

The tycoon is unrelenting, even with Mr. Carter defenseless and in retreat.

"Have some respect for yourself, boy. You must treat your body like a temple. Shoveling food in it like your feeding coal to a furnace is bad for your digestive track. It will cause problems down the road if you are not careful. Look at me. I am fit and wiry as a mongoose. My measurements are the same as when my father took me to buy my first suit at the age of seventeen."

His advice is drowned out by the sound of convulsive retching in the bathroom.

"Don't expect me to come to your rescue. You've done this to yourself. Let it be a learning experience."

When Mr. Carter reemerges, wiping his face with a wet hand towel, he finds his boss standing before the window, the embroidered curtain pulled back, looking at the school across the glen.

"That's a gold mine over there, Charles," he points emphatically out the window. "A treasure trove if I have ever seen one. A man of a certain status would be blind not to see it and a fool not to take advantage of it."

"Most certainly, Mr. Stratton. A prize for the taking. Are you confident the Board of Trustees will bite?"

The amused businessman shakes his head and laughs, and then steps away from the window and takes a cigar from a box underneath the table lamp.

"Charles, if memory serves me, you are twenty-five years of age, though a man occasionally prone to juvenile and uncouth behavior. On the positive side of the ledger, you are bright and you are industrious. You are a decent looking man. But at times you make me scratch my head."

He smells the tobacco wrap, clips the end, and places the cigar in his mouth.

"Girls. I am talking about hundreds of them. How clueless can you be? All from families of means. Each the product of the higher rungs of society. Each on the threshold of womanhood. Intelligent, articulate, classically-trained, well-read girls. Daughters of senators and daughters of cabinet secretaries. Daughters of old money and daughters of new money. Girls with blood lines leading back to the Mayflower, for Christ sake. Get it? And you know what else they have in common?"

Mr. Stratton strikes a match and draws it to the cigar. A mushroom-shaped cloud of pale white smoke rises to the ceiling.

"None of them are married. Even if a third of the students are betrothed—a generous estimate in my opinion—that means any single man, like yourself, who walks across that bridge enters a protected colony of around two hundred of the most attractive and eligible young women in all of America."

"Oh, I see."

"You don't see anything," his employer says brusquely, leaving an encircling trail of smoke as he walks about the room. "If you did, you would be thinking about how you would go about meeting some of them while we are holed up here, instead of gorging yourself. Look around you."

"My duty is to serve you and see that all necessary arrangements are made and that, in the end, our business proposition stands the greatest chance of success. That is my job and why you employ me. Pursuing matters of personal interest would not be appropriate, especially searching out the future Mrs. Charles Carter."

"True enough, Charles. By the rule as usual. But you must know that when a golden opportunity presents itself, you should take it, whenever it may come. And you might never pass this way again. Consider it free, fatherly advice. Over the years, I frequently felt the odd man out in a home overtaken with a wife and three daughters. So forgive me if I've been too blunt."

Mr. Carter is surprised by the counsel from the normally crusty man. Rarely in the two years of working for his employer has he heard such private reflections and never before has the topic of Charles's love life and marital prospects been broached. Uncomfortable with the unexpected turn in the conversation, he feels a need to redirect the focus back to the school's purchase and extract himself from further, unflattering scrutiny.

"I am confident your tender to purchase National Park will be accepted. I have a good feeling about it. I mean, did you see the expression on Dean Dawson's face when he saw your offer? I could barely control myself. If my hunch proves out, your business at Forest Glen is not done, but just beginning. Your name will be imprinted on one of the nation's flagship preparatory schools. As you told them this morning, you are prepared to take the institution and build an enduring legacy. Many decisions will need to be made. And if I am fortunate to accompany you back—." Mr. Carter pauses and shrugs, searching for the right words. "Well, let's say, there will be other opportunities."

"The future is unpredictable Charles, and life has a way of keeping those who wait on their heels."

Mr. Stratton lands back in the chair and rolls the glowing orange-tipped cigar between his thumb and fingers.

"I wouldn't be so casual if I were you. Consider the world we live in. Who knows what tomorrow holds? I certainly don't. I've seen men I admire and respect squander away fortunes on investments they knew were 'sure things.' They simply couldn't comprehend how they could be flush one day and then bankrupt the next."

"Risk cannot be avoided, only managed. I've heard you say so often, Mr. Stratton."

"Risk is one thing; fate is something else all together. Do you believe in fate, Charles? Have you considered the notion that we do not chart the course we travel; rather, it is set for us?"

"Honestly? Not in the least, sir. I find the way some rely on notions of chance and kismet to be a sign of personal weakness. If a man can't make the grade, he has no one to blame but himself. There are circumstances beyond one's control, to be sure. But in the end, we create the world we live in."

"So you see no evidence of a divine hand at play?"

Mr. Carter pauses to consider his employer's probing question.

Mr. Stratton turns around in his chair.

"Am I making you uncomfortable, Charles?"

"No, sir. I just thought we were speaking of shaping one's future—the idea of personal responsibility."

"We are. Let me see if can remember the line. *As flies to wanton boys are we to the gods. They kill us for their sport.* "

"I'm not sure I understand."

"Look around you boy. How can you *not* understand? Millions of men, women and children, young and fit like yourself, healthy one day, and then dead within weeks. The Spanish flu killed over three thousand in New York City in one week alone. You saw it like the rest of us. The morgues were overwhelmed before the quarantines could be put into place. Death came down swiftly like the blade of a scythe and wiped away entire towns. Photographs of mass graves being dug by steam shovel. People were hysterical and feared an apocalyptic plague was sweeping across the globe. All on the heels of Europe being turned into a damn abattoir. Year after year of senseless fighting. An entire generation of fine men, like yourself, decimated by war and pestilence."

His voice cracks with emotion and drops to a whisper.

"So many promising lives sacrificed. And for what?"

"Yes, sir, a horrible toll was exacted."

Mr. Stratton's words buffet the young man's ears and bruise his conscience. He had left his hometown of Sandusky, Ohio, to attend Columbia University and become an accountant on the eve of the great conflagration, and when America entered the war in 1917 he was in his last year of study, on the threshold of becoming the first member of the Carter family to earn a college degree. Some of his Sandusky classmates volunteered and many

120 ANDY JOHNSON

more were caught in the net of conscription. The long arm of the draft board never reached him in the city, however, and he was convinced at the time that it was the proper outcome, even as his parents wrote to him of how the docks and plant production lines were losing immigrant workers to the lottery by the droves. Soon after, newspaper clippings were included in the family letters from Sandusky. In the beginning, they were mostly enlistment announcements and unit deployments. Then came the reports of local soldiers being wounded and killed in action, occasionally sent along with memorial cards printed on thick stock, thoughtfully mailed with added postage by his mother.

No one questioned his choice not to serve, and his family continually praised his ascent in the world of finance. But when the American soldiers returned home, and the parades were held, the young man began to ask himself why so many others willfully served and he didn't. Even now, years later, the uncomfortable feeling of regret comes and goes intermittently. To this day, whenever he passes a man in uniform on the streets or on the train he unfailingly avoids eye contact and finds a reason to look elsewhere until the tormenting flare of inferiority and guilt subsides.

Around his employer, this sense of remorse is never far from the surface. And yet he has never marshaled the courage to confess his feelings or describe the purgatory he occupies when he is in the company of the stoic man. There are times when he wishes Mr. Stratton would just come out and say it point-blank, and ask him how it feels to have avoided the indiscriminate touch of deadly battle. Speak the taboo and relieve him of his private stigma once and for all. But there is no absolution, no forgiving words from the oracle of pain.

The industrialist rests the cigar in an ash tray and rubs his hands over his eyes and back along the thin remnants of his hair line. He leans back in the chair lost in thought.

How it must kill him to be here, Mr. Carter wonders, admiring the man's iron discipline.

Why the National Park Seminary of all places, the young assistant thought, when Mr. Stratton announced his decision to buy the school? Why Forest Glen? But no one at Stratton Enterprises, none of the dour executives and investment wizards under him, dared question the decision. Their perfunctory endorsements and silent assents masked a unified and unspoken belief that the decision was personal, not about business, and that protest was futile, for the headstrong executive will never be dissuaded in his pursuit. Even for someone so close to the financial throne, as it were, Mr. Carter feels he is in no position to speak up. What standing does he have in the man's eyes, after all, on matters outside the neatly tended columns of the business ledger? Still at a green age, Mr. Carter knows his proper place.

Adaption is the key to advancement, a credo he has put to profitable use during his brief tenure at the company. The oft-repeated words seem hollow and self-serving now as he stands looking upon the reflective tycoon, the troubled man's riches of no comfort. The familiar wave of shame makes it suddenly uncomfortable for him to be in the same room with his employer. The contrast is too stark to ignore. Fool as he might his friends and fellow workers, Mr. Carter can't deny in his heart that avoidance, not adaptation, got him to where he is today.

So many promising lives sacrificed. And for what?

Behind the dynamic persona of Douglas Stratton, and the empire he towers over, concealed in public by the witty, confident, strong-willed demeanor of a self-made millionaire, Mr. Carter sees what escapes the notice of others. He knows of the resolute shield behind the old man's twinkling eyes that holds back any signs of sentimentality, a private bulwark that keeps at bay the tide of grief that must darken his heart still.

Three years have passed since that black day. Three years of denial. Three years of enduring. Three years of keeping the demons locked away. Three years of exhaustive dedication to building a monetary juggernaut. Three years and the emotional wall, hard and steadfast inside the enigmatic man seated before him, remains unbreached.

"How long do we give Dean Dawson to answer?"

"He will need time to go to the board and seek their direction. Send a note to him this afternoon relaying that I will remain in Washington until Friday morning. If he needs additional time, he can have until Monday close of business. If necessary, I will have you stay behind, Charles, to work with the lawyers handling the execution of the purchase contract and the filing of the title and deed transfer documents. I am prepared to show Dawson and the board a few days deference, but I won't be prisoner in this peculiar boarding house he calls a hotel."

"And if they decline?"

Outside the window an electrified streetcar rumbles past on its return trip to Washington. Mr. Stratton grins with amusement at the question, a familiar smugness lacing the lines of his face, and his assistant correctly predicts the answer before it is spoken.

"They won't. I have done my homework, young Mr. Carter. I have it through confidential and reliable sources that the school trustees will view my offer favorably, notwithstanding any misgivings Dean Dawson or his wife or anyone in the school administration may have about the sale."

Admiration brims inside the aide. The man is always two steps ahead of the rest of us.

"I will own National Park Seminary lock, stock and barrel before the New Year."

Josephine passes the hours in class anxiously, her thoughts often drifting away to the events of the disastrous ride as her instructors hold forth on the study topic. No matter how hard she tries, she cannot chase away the image of the man at the fire and his malevolent stare and menacing words. And when she changes out of her uniform for gymnasium class, she notices streaks of dried mud along her wrists and forearms from when she and Margaret pushed the canoe out of the boathouse. In her rush to get to class, she hadn't seen the now obvious markings. Had others seen the incriminating evidence of their morning ride into the woods, she worries, as she watches the warm stream of brown water circle the sink in the changing room?

At the conclusion of her history studies, the final class before the luncheon break, Josephine is the first to leave the classroom. She walks briskly through Vincent Hall, politely deflecting an offer from a fellow classmate to go and listen to records in the music room and then another invitation to join some of the senior class officers in the dining room.

She is troubled but not surprised that Margaret never shows for classes. Leah's absence, however, is more worrisome given her peculiar behavior outside the Spanish Mission the night before and unexplained disappearance during the morning ride. She remembers the unnatural expression on Leah's face when she stepped from behind the chicken coop, the distant stare of an altered mind, looking directly into Josephine's eyes, as she wasn't even there.

When Josephine arrives at Senior House, she goes directly to Leah's room and is stunned to see Leah sitting on her bed, still dressed in her riding jacket and jodhpurs, and Margaret positioned behind her, stroking a brush gently through the girl's fine hair, as if they were loving sisters. Neither speaks when Josephine enters, and the grooming continues, a tender moment too comforting to interrupt. Head tilted slightly to the side, Leah is relaxed and exudes the contentment of a kitten being washed by its mother. Gone is the frighteningly gaunt visage when they found her hiding at the grim homestead. Color has returned to her complexion and her cheeks are a soft pink hue.

Margaret arches her eyebrows and smiles at Josephine, silently communicating her shared surprise at the incongruous scene. In their time together, Josephine has never witnessed her friend brush anyone's hair other than her own, which she does with relentless vigor to produce, as she often says, "the luster of satin." Even more uncharacteristic is the display of subservient intimacy.

Standoffish and prickly, Margaret keeps her classmates at arms length, unwilling to engage the sort of acts of kindness and generosity typical among the Seminary girls. Josephine, and Josephine alone, is the exception to the rule. From their early days at Forest Glen, she saw through the Margaret's gruff exterior and refused to be cowed by her alienating behavior. Through sheer persistence and force of will, Josephine overcame the girl's social clumsiness and Margaret came to respect her for it. She is perhaps Margaret's only true friend at the school, and on more than one occasion Josephine surmised it is because no other self-respecting girl would tolerate the continual streams of mockery and narcissism that poured out of her.

"Why don't you ever brush my hair?" Josephine says with a feigned look of disappointment.

"Why must you always ask the impossible of me? I have neither the strength nor the tools to tame that unruly mop of yours. I came to check on Leah and it seems she forgot to change after our little adventure. I found her in bed, sleeping in them. Boots and all."

"How do you feel Leah? You look much better now. You gave us a real scare out there."

Gradually Leah emerges from the stupor brought about by the rhythmic brush strokes and straightens up on the bed.

"Much better, though I suppose I will need my clothes cleaned and pressed," she replies with a slightly nervous laugh.

"And a bath, my dear. It did wonders for me. I felt beastly until I washed away all that grime off me."

"Yes, soon, but we need to talk first," Josephine interjects. "We need to talk about what happened this morning. And the quickest way to get to the bottom of this is for you tell us in your own words, Leah. You need to explain exactly what happened from when we went into the boathouse until we found you at the colored family's property."

Leah reaches for the blanket and wraps it around her shoulders as Margaret rises and sits in a rocking chair opposite the bed. Josephine slides a desk chair over next to her.

Leah avoids their stares and surveys the wall hangings in her room—the assorted museum lithographs, the felt National Park pennant pinned to the window curtains, the aged and tattered Alpha Epsilon Pi club banner made of green cotton cloth hanging above the vanity mirror, the cork board filled with portrait photographs, including the one of her family she likes so much, and—

"Leah. Do you hear me?"

Josephine's impatience brings her back to the subject she would do anything to avoid.

"You need to talk to us. We need to understand what happened. Why won't you talk to us about this morning?"

Margaret leans forward as the uncharacteristic voice of motherly calm.

"You see, we want to help you, my dear. We are all a bit jittery about what happened. It's natural to feel this way. If only you knew what we found in the canoe you—"

"What did you find?" Leah interrupts forcefully.

"No," Josephine insists, her anger over Leah's evasiveness boiling over. "We don't have much time. You tell us what happened to you first. We were in the boathouse for no more than a couple of minutes. And when we came out, you had left us. You and the horse, both gone. Nowhere in sight. Then we spent the next hour searching for you, not knowing where you went, and not knowing if you were hurt or what might have become of you. We were worried to death about you. We got lost following your tracks into the woods. And then we started worrying about ourselves and how we were going to get back to the school. Only out of sheer dumb luck did we find you. If we hadn't come across that helpful boy and his dog in the field there is no telling how long it would have taken to find the road. And if we hadn't crossed paths with that contemptible men at the fire—if he had enough smarts to just waive us on instead of stopping us and threatening us, if he simply let us go on our way—you might still be there. The school's horse stolen. Or worse."

The implication of Josephine's closing words is not lost on either girl. Margaret leans back in her chair. In the most direct and forceful terms, Josephine has laid it on the line for Leah hoping to shock her out of her daze.

"And just so you understand the gravity of the situation, Leah, I am this close to going to Miss Price and telling her everything that happened today. Unless you explain what happened at the boathouse, I see no other choice. And if I do, I fully expect that she will discipline the three of us."

"Why would you do that?" Leah asks with a quizzical, almost innocent, expression.

"How can you ask such a thing of me?"

"We are all in this together, that's what Josephine is saying."

The girl fidgets under the covers and her eyes dart about the floor as she turns Josephine's ultimatum over and over in her mind. She can feel them looking at her, their eyes on her, fixed and unwavering, waiting for her to speak. More than anything, she wishes they would leave so that she can be alone. She needs time to pull herself together for the afternoon chorus practice. She needs time to sort this out by herself. She can't go on like this. Concealed under the blanket, Leah slips her hands inside the lining of her riding blazer and presses down with her arms to steady the onset of nervous tremors.

Tell you what exactly? What do you want me to say?

Josephine stands, impatient with the girl's stalling, and breaks the prolonged silence.

"Fine then. We need to take you to the infirmary, Leah. We should have done so last night. It's up to you if you want to change clothes before we go."

Margaret follows Josephine and stops her at the hallway door where they talk privately.

"Don't you think we should discuss this before running to Miss Price? Nothing good will come of that. And since I am a part of this, I think my opinion matters."

"We have no choice."

"Weren't you the one just complaining about being called to her office after that ninny May King went squawking to her? How pleased do you think she will be when she hears about all of this? And she will get to the bottom of it; you can be sure about that."

"And why should we fear that, Margaret?"

"Because in a week the semester will be over, and I don't want Miss Price throwing the book at us for some idiotic infraction of school rules or an obscure honor code violation just before Christmas break. Once she sinks her teeth into this, she will be like a dog with a bone. And might I remind you, my family is travelling down next week and staying until the end of the semester. I have enough drama to deal with when my mother is around. You have no idea what having her daughter called on the carpet will do to her."

"Look at her, Margaret. She is not right. You said it yourself."

"Then send her to the infirmary. Get her some medicine for whatever is making her act so peculiar. Leah won't say anything to the nurses if she won't even speak to us. But don't involve Miss Price. I'm begging you. Only bad things will come of it if you do."

"Bad things are happening now. And you are too worried about yourself to realize it. For all we know, that man could have kidnapped Leah and molested her. We don't know how long she was there and what happened to her. All we have is the word of a man looking to take advantage of the situation. Leah was in danger. We were in danger. Don't you see how serious this has become?"

"I saw a scraggly, sickly-looking man with barely enough energy and wits to keep a fire burning."

"He lied to us, Margaret. He knew Leah was hiding on the property and he was ready to let us leave without her. And he stole her horse. These are truths that you cannot deny. Then you have to ask yourself, why would he do such a thing? Tell me what you think would have happened if we rode on past. I shudder to think of what may have taken place after we left."

"Leah never said he threatened or molested her. He said he came out and she was frightened and ran off and hid. That's plausible. And the horse may have run off at the same time she did. Leah was confused and frightened. Just like we were."

"There is an evil purpose to that man."

"Look, I am not saying there isn't something wrong with her. But let's find out first before we involve the administration. Whoever was holed up in that infested boathouse knows that he has been found out. He'll come back, see the canoe and his belongings on the ramp the way we left it, and high-tail it off the property thinking the police are not far behind. That problem just took care of itself. As for the uncle or whatever the boy called him, he knows he's in the crosshairs too. If he was intending to cause trouble, he won't now. He knew a circumstantial case could be made that would implicate him in a serious theft. He had just enough sense to recognize he was flirting with a police investigation. That's why he stopped us. He knew having the horse on the property would be incriminating. And his miserable world was about to get a whole lot worse. You made that abundantly clear to him in case he hadn't already figured it out."

"Sweeping it under the carpet, like it never happened, is not right. He's a dangerous person and if Leah won't tell us what happened, we need to find out somehow."

"Is this about the lecture Miss Price gave you in her office? Has she gotten under your skin about what happened at the glen? Don't let her convince you did something wrong. You didn't. May King is such a—"

"No," Josephine protests angrily. "It's not that."

"Then let me ask you a question, Josephine. Why didn't Leah speak up when we stopped at the fire? Why didn't she say something—a shout, a warning, anything—when she saw us ride away? If she thought she was in danger, she would have said something, right? But she didn't. Not a word. Not a peep. She watched us ride off toward the road and she didn't try to stop us. Why is that?"

"Maybe he threatened her and told her not to say anything or he'd hurt her."

"He wasn't exactly holding a knife to her pretty little throat. He had his back turned and she was twenty yards away from he was standing. She could have outrun him to the road, if she wanted."

"I don't know. Maybe he told her he'd hurt us too if she gave herself away."

"And at the last second, just as his extortion was about to succeed, just as we were leaving that God forsaken place, seconds from being out of sight, he stops us and motivated by a pang of guilt, I suppose, he tells us about

Leah and the horse. If he had said or done to Leah what you are intimating, he would have never let her leave that property with us."

Margaret's right, Josephine concedes to herself, mulling over what's been said. The man would have been signing his own arrest warrant had he harmed Leah and then let her leave with them. Instead, he was the one that turned over both Leah and her horse to them. He knew that she would tell them what happened when safely away from the property.

Margaret takes a hold of Josephine's hands and looks earnestly into her eyes, a slight smile trying to break through the cloud of apprehension encircling her perplexed friend.

"If you tell anyone what I am about to say, Josephine Barnes, I will deny it and spend the rest of my waking hours at National Park destroying your pristine and undeserved reputation. Understand?"

Josephine silently signals her acceptance.

"I've been on a knife's edge since Leah popped out from behind Tom after watching us half the night, and when we rode off into the woods in the dark this morning I had this horrible feeling inside me, like what we were about to do was all a terrible mistake. I didn't say anything then, but I felt we were going too far, that we were doing something that we would regret. And when we got to the storage shed and the jimmied door, I was this close to turning around and galloping back to the school, with or without the two of you. So in a weird way, I know what she is feeling—at least a bit. That's why I started to panic in the boathouse. I am not use to these type of adventures, and I felt alone and scared and completely vulnerable. The smell of stale tobacco and mouse shit was more than I could take and by the time we finally pushed that canoe out I could barely breathe. I am not exaggerating. I had to work to catch my breath. You were probably too busy looking around for Leah to notice. But for a few moments I was having a hard time functioning, like I was going to faint. In all the confusion that followed, the feeling passed. But it was real and I was frightened."

"Why didn't you say something?"

"Shush...let me finish. When the colored boy found us in the field, the feeling I had at the boathouse started to come back. It wasn't the dog and the way it came at us out of nowhere. I mean, that gave me a start, but it was something else about the place we were riding through. It bothered me, in the same way the boathouse did. And then I started to curse you for bring-

INCIDENT AT FOREST GLEN *129*

ing all this upon us. And I started hating Leah too for what she had done—whatever that was—because she was prolonging the nightmare. That's what it seemed like, a nightmare."

Margaret's revealing confessional cuts Josephine deeply. Never before has her usually implacable friend revealed her vulnerability like this. All the while, she is aware of the growing pressure of Margaret's grip on her own fingers.

"By the time we came upon the uncle, Zachary—that was his name, Zachary—I felt it even worse. He repulsed me and scared me like no person I have ever met before or any imaginary figment that has ever tormented my dreams. When you dismounted at the fire, I was deathly afraid for your safety. I both hated you and feared for you. All the king's horses and all the king's men could not have made me step out of that saddle. At that moment, when you confronted him, I truly was in awe of your courage."

"Sweet Margaret, it's all right."

"Yes, with every fiber of my being, I thought he was a dangerous, menacing man, and what I felt told me that we were in serious trouble. And I wondered if I let out a scream just then who would hear us, who would care? I was that scared, Josie. But when I saw Leah appear suddenly from behind the shed, the purest, most sobering thought came to me and wiped away all the other dark fears I had been feeling up to that point. And do you know what that single revelation was, the epiphany that brought clarity to my emotional trauma?"

Josephine shakes her head slowly, captivated by Margaret's story.

"It wasn't real. We were chasing phantoms. It was written on Leah's face. Her affliction, her madness, whatever you want to call it, was behind it all. She hasn't been the same since we were together at the glen and the way she and May fed off of each other's hysteria about the flood and the dress. You remember, the white dress."

Miss Price's pointed question about what happened to the dress flashes into Josephine's mind.

"It became clear to me then, when we found Leah standing there as if she just materialized out of thin air. If she doesn't go to glen, she doesn't show up at the clubhouse that night, and then all the rest of this doesn't happen. We have allowed ourselves to be swept up in Leah's delirium and we have imagined things that are not real. I think she might be having a nervous breakdown. We need to step back and understand this for what it is. Leah is the problem."

"*Leah is the problem!*" a high-pitched, mocking voice echoes across the room.

They turn and see that Leah's placid, withdrawn expression has changed to one of barely contained anger, her lips downturned and pursed.

"I told you. I warned you outside the Spanish Mission. And you didn't listen to me. Margaret, you made me out the fool. You said I didn't make sense when I told you that something happened to us there. You were so dismissive then. And now to hear you speak, and for you to blame *me*, that's rich. And you," Leah says accusatorily, turning to Josephine, "you are so earnest and head-strong and always trying to make everything fit neatly into its proper place. She is a hypocrite, but listening to you threaten me with your matronly, sanctimonious words just now is even more galling. All of your incessant questions! Do you really want to know what happened at the boathouse?"

Josephine is caught off-guard by the fierce edge in Leah's voice as she lashes out and pauses before answering.

"Yes," she sputters, shocked by the transformed girl's sharp barbs. "We simply want to help you. That's all."

"I do too. I want to know what happened there as well. Desperately. But I can't remember a thing."

"How do you mean?"

Leah runs her finger along the top edge of her leather boot and feels a small rip in the fabric of her riding breeches just large enough to push her fingernail through the opening.

"I recall being on my horse following you into the woods. It was dark. I also remember dismounting at the boathouse. And after that, nothing. My next memory is standing outside and that I am feeling very, very cold. And the two of you are walking toward me. I didn't know where I was or how I got there. I wasn't sure if I was really awake or whether I was dreaming. It was like my brain was surrounded by impenetrable fog."

"How is it possible that you don't remember how you got to the farm?"

Leah shakes her head.

"What is happening, Josephine? What is happening to us?" she pleads. "Please, I'm scared. You feel it too, don't you?"

"You need to rest, dear."

"I can't."

"Sleep will help you."

"It won't. It will only make it worse."

Leah balls up the bed sheet in her fist and twists it.

"I don't like it. Something's happened. Something's horribly wrong, and you won't admit it. And all you can do is blame me. *'Leah is the problem. Leah is the problem.'* Why won't you tell me the truth?"

Margaret leans in and reaches her hand out toward the troubled girl, who only glares at the offering.

"Look, I am sorry, Leah. I didn't mean my words to be hurtful."

"Come on, Leah. Let's put it behind us."

The agitated girl with the storm raging in her eyes looks back at Josephine. Her words, though direct and accusatory, are softly-spoken, barely above a whisper:

"You will see. In time, it is all you will see."

Margaret sighs and withdraws, not sure if she should embrace the distraught girl or slap her across the cheek to bring her to her senses.

"There is something else."

Leah slides off the bed and stands in the middle of the room under the chandelier light and pulls the hair from the left side back across her head revealing a reddish-brown mark along her temple and scalp line. The abrasion is fresh and raised.

Josephine reacts immediately to the sight of the bruise and raises her hand to her mouth.

"Oh no. That happened at the boathouse?"

Before she can answer, there is a soft knock at the door and Leah lets her hair fall back in place.

"Come in," she tells the visitor.

May is momentarily perplexed upon seeing Margaret and Josephine inside the room, unexpectedly coming face to face with all three absent girls for the first time since her meeting with Miss Price.

Why are the two of you here in Leah's room, she immediately wonders, as her conspiratorial suspicion deepens?

Margaret glances disdainfully at May before turning away, while Josephine can only stare, stunned by her inopportune arrival and searching for what to say.

"I came to see Leah," May says weakly and Josephine steps aside.

"May, what a nice surprise. How have you been?" Leah says cheerfully with a wide, toothy smile.

The other two exchange a glance of surprise over the latest shift in the girl's mercurial behavior.

"I'm fine, thank you. I was checking to see if you were all right. You weren't at breakfast or classes."

"I woke up with a migraine and just needed to rest for a bit. I'm fine now though."

May waits for Josephine and Margaret to speak up, but they remain silent, stunned by Leah's ability to pivot her emotions so dramatically and so convincingly.

"Well, I see you are about to go for a ride. Clearly you must be feeling better. That's a good sign. I won't keep you."

Leah pauses, having forgotten that she is still dressed in her riding clothes.

"I was, but I have changed my mind. The turn in the weather has made it too cold."

"*Post nubila, Phoebus.* After clouds comes the sun."

Leah laughs heartily at May's pun.

"Well, I did not mean to interrupt," the flustered girl says as she retreats to the door.

"You aren't interrupting, May. I have an idea. If you don't have plans with someone else, would you like to have dinner with me later? The two of us can catch up."

May halts, taken aback by the offer, and quickly glances at the two girls standing quietly off to the side.

"Yes, thank you. That would be nice. I'll knock at six."

Once May leaves, Leah walks to the dressing mirror facing the corner wall, reaches down and takes hold of the pedestal, and turns it back around. For the first time in over a day, she looks upon her reflection. Her fears are confirmed. The change she noticed then has progressed. It must be obvious to them too.

She turns her head slightly and inspects the mark.

"Some powder will do the trick at least until it turns purple."

She sees in the reflection Josephine appear over her shoulder with a distressed look on her face. Their eyes lock.

"You probably have a concussion, Leah. Perhaps you fell or maybe the branch we tied the horses to broke away and struck your head. We found the tree limb on the ground when we came out of the boathouse. That would explain why you can't remember what happened. Regardless, you must go to the infirmary and see the nurse."

Leah plays with her hair in the mirror, tossing strands from one side to another and trying different ways to conceal the mark.

"Didn't you hear what I told May? My migraine is gone now. I feel fine," she responds coolly. "I need to change now before I go to chorus practice."

"We need to continue our conversation. If we tell you what happened at the farm before we found you, it may help you recall what happened, or at least fill in some of the gaps in your memory. You also should know what we discovered inside the boathouse."

"I told you, I am fine. I don't have the time or interest to discuss it now. I must get to the Odeon on time or Madame Kaspar will be in a fouler mood than usual."

Leah locates Margaret in the mirror as she continues to style her hair.

"Margaret, can the two of you leave now?"

Outside, a wintry blast smacks against the front of the dormitory. The building's ceiling joists creak and moan and the buffeted window frames emit a high-pitched whistle that carries down the interior halls. The late afternoon sun dips toward a horizon layered in nursery pink and blue. The voices of returning students herald the end of another day of instruction and the sound of doors opening and closing fill the dormitory. Classrooms inside Vincent Hall fall dark and silent. Nearby, cooks begin preparing for the evening meal. Newly washed linen are draped across the dining room tables by the serving staff as stacks of plates bearing the NPS monogram are wheeled in on carts. In the cavernous ballroom in the rear of the main hall, tear-drop lights hanging from the soaring vaulted ceiling are switched on while a solitary man pushes a cloth broom across an expansive, flawlessly waxed dance floor, dwarfed inside a cathedral of suspended balconies and oak buttresses. At the Odeon, girls dutifully light row after row of candles on stage under the silent watch of Madame as her students file in and prepare for their rehearsal. The class regents, relieved of their teaching duties, wait in the anteroom of the dean's office, along with the Prefect of Studies and the school bursar, as Dean Dawson and his wife meet privately to discuss the shocking offer from the head of Stratton Enterprises. As twilight approaches, the ancient stone lamps of Nara in front of the Japanese Pagoda are brought to life and the soft glow returns to the sorority clubhouses. Silhouettes of sparrows and juncos and mourning doves streak across the violet sky in search of shelter for the evening. In the alley behind the kitchen, the crow rummages through discarded scraps at the bottom of a wood barrel, until it locates a slender bone bearing nubs of flesh and rubbery tendons with its powerful beak. Hopping out the barrel, the black bird pins its treasure to the dirt and methodically strips the remaining morsels until the white of the bone is revealed and shimmers in the ascending light of the desolate moon.

Chapter 5
Hebe, Cupbearer to the Olympians

Many educators have been unaccountably blind to the educational value of current events. The importance of studying the manners, customs and daily life of historic people is conceded; but the progress and development of the race in the grandest century of all are either discarded or treated as matters of minor importance. We believe that it is impossible to interest properly in the peoples of other times girls who do not understand or care for the people of their own time. No woman is broad until she regards herself as part of a greater whole, with which her life and sympathies are indissolubly bound. To form right estimates and opinions upon current questions, and to arouse and develop an interest in social problems, is no insignificant part of the work of an educator.

Dean Dawson quietly sits at the head of a long table in the private dining room adjacent to his office and stares at the National Park Seminary coat of arms suspended above the doorway. The shield is divided into four quadrants, diagonally situated, solid gold along one axis, a pattern of black and white diamond shapes along the other. Atop the shield sits disembodied wings, feathers spread and upturned, cradling an oil lantern with a flame burning from its spout. A crescent shaped scroll is draped along the bottom of the shield bearing the phrase, *scientia est lux lucis*, knowledge is enlightenment.

He remembers when he took over the Seminary from the Vincents and how he and his wife, wanting to place an immediate imprint on the school, spent hours one night around a table like the one he sits at now, littered with failed sketches, until they came up with an acceptable symbol that embodied their vision for the school. Their world seemed to unfurl with endless promise on that day. His dream of building an institution of renown and innovation was finally being fulfilled. He would transform what he saw as a second-rate finishing school, still bearing the trappings of the hotel and casino era preceding it, into an unparalleled school for young women, situated on the door step of the Nation's capital, expressly designed to cater to the needs of the elite.

Dean Dawson's vision was realized sooner than he ever thought possible. Through a broad advertising campaign and aggressive faculty recruitment, Seminary enrollment nearly doubled in the first three years under his stewardship, allowing the dean to seek out investors to recapitalize and expand the school facilities and infrastructure. The rapid growth in turn fueled the administration's ability to attract greater academic talent and siphon off the enrollment at other upscale private girls schools around the country. No longer just a local draw, the National Park Seminary for Young Women could claim that girls from every state had matriculated to the prestigious academy on the wooded hilltop. The names of Hershey, Wrigley, Heinz, and Stratton began to appear on the student enrollment and this representation of wealth only furthered the perception of the school's exclusivity and, therefore, desirability. Alumnae associations were established in states and cities throughout the land and functioned as unofficial recruitment centers and helped open the spigots of financial patronage. To celebrate the growing reach of the school's influence, a formal gala is held every spring at the Pension Building inaugural ballroom in Washington where alumnae, administrators, and patrons mingle with political power brokers and business heavyweights among Greek columns as wide as sequoias.

scientia est lux lucis.

Over and over he repeats the phrase.

He learned it as a young boy, seated in a stiff, tortuous chair at a crudely fashioned desk in a one-room prairie school house in the Dakota Territory. Young Porter Dawson, the eldest son of immigrant wheat farmers, would wait for the teacher to announce recess and as the other children rushed outside he would seek out the single shelf of books that constituted the primitive school library. There he would find worn adventure novels and ancient primers, historical biographies and abridged compilations of Swift and Defoe, many donated to the school, others retrieved from abandoned homesteads, and a few plucked from trash heaps. He would sit cross-legged on the classroom floor, thankful to be free of his seat, and read quietly, while

INCIDENT AT FOREST GLEN   *137*

indecipherable exclamations of delight, spoken in Norwegian and Swedish and German, streamed through the open window as boys and girls frolicked on the treeless expanse under a cornflower blue sky.

The Book of Latin Phrases.

He can still recall how the book looked and the feel of its weight in his hands. How the corners of the cover were black and worn. The fractured brown binding. The dirty white pages filled with tightly-spaced printing. The occasional notations in ink that would appear in the margins as he turned the pages.

He feels a rush of hidden delight as he remembers, fifty years on, how one day after he made sure that his teacher was occupied outside, and in no fear of being caught, he turned to the inside of the back cover, dipped his pen into the desk well, and with steady hand wrote, *Property of Porter A. Dawson.* Though the book was of no interest to his schoolmates, he surreptitiously laid claim to it, which, other than the clothes on his back, was the first possession he could call his own in his seven years of existence.

Some years later, during a particularly brutal winter on the prairie, he arrived at the school house with the other children from surrounding farms and noticed the library shelf was depleted and nearly bare. With the wood stack exhausted, their teacher was left with no choice but to cull the shelf of unneeded books to keep the stove fire burning. Throughout the day, as the flame waned, each student was called upon in turn to search their flip top desks for old scraps of paper and feed the stove. When his name was called, he brought forward an essay booklet he had saved out of pride and slid it through the vertical slits in the grate. As the pages of his vivid recounting of the Boston Tea Party ignited and burned brightly, he caught a fleeting glimpse of the charred brown binding of his Latin book in a bed of pulsating embers.

The dean surveys the table, where his senior administrators and faculty dine on golden-skin pheasant and venison steaks. The hastily scheduled dinner is a prelude to a discussion of Douglas Stratton's offer to purchase National Park Seminary. Earlier in the day, he placed a personal call to each of the school's Board of Trustees to inform them of the tender and preparations were made to convene the board in an emergency meeting Friday morning at the downtown offices of the Columbia National Bank, a few blocks from the White House. Had he his druthers, knowledge of the offer would be closely held and limited to a select few. But Mr. Stratton's unorthodox presentation in front of the assembled group has prevented that. Until the board meets, he decided, a lid needs to be kept tight on the proposal's existence so as to not prompt wild speculation about the school's future among students and, by extension, their parents. After the businessman's departure, Dean Dawson spoke in no uncertain terms that disclosure of what took place at the meeting would not be tolerated and that any person found to have violated the directive who be held accountable and summarily terminated.

"It is in your personal interest and the most importantly in the supreme interest of the school," he warned further, "that no one be told until the board has considered the offer and acted upon it, and only then, will the decision rest with the trustees on the question of if and when others are told."

The private dinner offers a chance to reemphasize this earlier decree while at the same time allowing the staff to blow off steam and speak freely in a confidential surrounding. Why risk the chance that hallway conversations will be overheard or that one of them will let slip in front of their spouse at home? Keep them sequestered like a jury, the dean decides, until the excitement, or anxiety, as it were, dissipates. It's the best chance you have to keep the whole affair from blowing up in your face.

Once the waiters remove the china plates in preparation for dessert, the headmaster nods to an assistant, a prearranged sign for him to leave the room and keep the serving staff from reentering. He rises from his chair and smoothes his vest and coat as the conversations trickle away. He looks earnestly at the faces around the table, his face beaming with grateful pride.

"When I took over National Park Seminary from John and Maud Vincent I possessed a blueprint for leading this marvelous school into profitability and prosperity. I arrived as an architect of sorts, with a plan in hand to elevate what was then a fine institution into the finest of its kind. Over these many years you have been my builders and we have dedicated ourselves to erecting a premier educational campus of singular distinction. In this wooded glen, shielded from the many distractions of modern existence, our collective work has fashioned a sanctuary which feeds the minds and bodies of girls who thirst for direction and hunger for purpose. And when they leave, their embryonic intellects and sensibilities have grown, matured, and strengthened into those possessed by a confident and capable young woman. In my tenure at National Park Seminary, we have tirelessly made it our mission to produce a generation of America's finest women, and we have succeeded in this mission beyond expectations. It has been a difficult journey, not without its tribulations and occasional missteps. But no one can deny that we have achieved much in a brief time. The only restraint we have labored under during these times is one of resources, the means to fully execute the vision of the blueprint I brought with me to Forest Glen so many years ago.

"We live in heady times, my friends. We stand at the precipice of realizing the dream I have held close to my heart for as long as I can remember. Sufficient resources may soon be at our disposal to carry out the unfinished work before us. Some might suggest it is divine providence. And while I am tempted to say my prayers have been answered, I believe the seeds of our recently delivered good fortune can be found in the secular realm. It was your exemplary work, and that of the teachers and administrators you supervise, that produced the goodwill and results which, in turn, brought Douglas Stratton to us this morning.

"The purpose of his visit to the National Park Seminary, once revealed, was a shock, to be sure. But perhaps it should not have been so unexpected. His offer to purchase this institution, in his own words, can be directly linked to the superlative education bestowed upon his three daughters in their stay with us. Douglas Stratton's affirmation is not the first such acknowledgment of our successful deeds. As you are aware, family endowments and donations have been a valued pipeline of support for our institution. And yet, Douglas Stratton's offer must be viewed for what it is: the most declarative expression to date that our work here is of tremendous value. Together, we are making a difference in the lives of girls from across our great Nation.

"So I ask that you join me in raising a glass for a toast. Tonight, around this table, we herald a new era in excellence at National Park Seminary, and we rededicate ourselves to completing the most virtuous journey that lies ahead of us."

Crystal glasses are raised around the table in unison, as overlapping calls of "here, here" fill the room. Dean Dawson thanks his supporters as he slowly descends into his velour arm chair. In the ensuing murmur of conversation, he spots Gladys Rowe, the junior regent, at the far end, her arm half-raised and hand open, waiting patiently to be recognized by the headmaster.

"Yes, Mrs. Rowe."

She remains seated and waits for the others around the table to quiet.

"Thank you, Dean Dawson. Your words are both comforting and inspiring. And I think I speak for all in commending your leadership in bringing us collectively to this point."

The dean nods his appreciation.

"Are you at liberty to speak to the question of continuity? Are we to expect that new ownership will not produce detrimental changes in the senior faculty that you so kindly lauded in your remarks?"

"Yes, Mrs. Rowe, of course. It is not only my desire but my expectation that the daily management and decisions of the National Park Seminary, including, most importantly, the continuance in place of my faculty assignments, will still rest with me. More to point, I will insist upon in it with the board."

Seated directly across from Mrs. Martin, the bursar shifts uncomfortably in his chair, the slight, almost imperceptible wrinkle in his brow not escaping the prefect's raptor-like attention.

"Mrs. Rowe, I believe Mr. Stratton understands the importance of continuity in furthering the legacy he so fervently seeks to perpetuate. We have in him, I believe, not only a financier but a true believer in the educational reform we seek to bring about. He has shown a great interest in what we are working to achieve. Perhaps this would be a perfect time for me to call upon Miss Price to relay a brief anecdote from this morning which I believe illustrates the commitment to the educational mission our prospective owner displays."

The senior regent is caught off-guard, not expecting to be called upon. Her discussion with Lucille Wilhoit outside the dining room after breakfast was not exactly how the dean described it to the group. The story she was able to pull out of the girl lacked any significance, in her mind, with the possible exception of the keepsake he left the girl without explanation—the lapel pin in the shape of a shield, bearing a cross.

"Yes, of course, Dean." Miss Price fiddles with the cloth napkin on her lap. "Before Mr. Stratton arrived at Vincent Hall, he took a moment to stop and talk with some of our girls as they were leaving Senior House. I am told he showed a keen interest about life on campus and their studies."

Mrs. Martin listens and readies her aim.

"He was particularly animated about the school and took the time to discuss the subject of fine art with one of the girls."

The Prefect of Studies watches Miss Price as she continues on and waits patiently for the right moment.

"The student was impressed by his passion for the subject and how he boasted of his daughters' graduation from National Park. As the dean alluded, he took a moment, on his own volition, to spend it with these students, and without pretense. They were unaware of who he was or why he was here."

Just as she finishes, Mrs. Martin hears the internal mechanisms of the corner clock awaken and prepare to sound the hour's arrival and she seizes the momentary break.

"And how exactly does a passing conversation with a group of students *'illustrate a commitment to the educational mission'* of this school, Miss Price?"

The words, though spoken directly to Miss Price, are meant unmistakably for the headmaster. The regent turns to the dean as the first of seven blows strikes the chimes waiting for him to step in, but it's Mrs. Rowe who responds.

"That is exactly my original point. Do we have sufficient insight into what selling the school to Stratton Enterprises would bring about? I realize this is all quite new and exciting and the details about the future are lacking, but how confident are we that he won't make dramatic changes at the school? What's to stop him from firing any one of us and bringing in others to take our place?"

"I am," Dean Dawson, finding his voice, forcefully replies. "I am, Mrs. Rowe. The board and I are in lockstep on matters related to the future of the school. How confident am I, you ask, that our mission will not be sidetracked due to interference? Supremely confident, Mrs. Rowe. Supremely confident."

Mrs. Martin immediately sees through the mask of certainty worn arrogantly by the dean.

"But no such agreement has been ironed out to this effect, at least not yet?" she adds, teasing out the loose thread a bit more.

"Of course not, Mrs. Martin," the perturbed man says dismissively, half-laughing at the impudence of the question. "We only received the offer this morning. You and the others were here."

"And to clarify further, headmaster, the particulars of the sale, including pedestrian matters such as continued employment, have not been broached, making any assurances premature, so as to be completely accurate."

The smile on Dean Dawson's face disappears.

"My assurances are not hollow, Mrs. Martin. They are based upon a deep understanding of the board's philosophy concerning the management of this institution, a familiarity, I would note, based on interaction neither you nor the other members of the faculty around this table have been privy to."

Mrs. Martin does not flinch in the face of the dean's withering retort. Her expression softens and her tone turns differential though.

"No doubt many of these points will be hammered out in the course of time."

Sensing the prefect is approaching a line best not crossed, Mr. Geary pushes his chair from the table and places his napkin before him.

"Such a sumptuous feast, Dean Dawson. We are in your gratitude. National Park Seminary is indeed blessed as the Christmas season approaches. And I think I speak for all of us when I say that we are as excited as you are to enter this new era of prosperity. I, for one, understand the complexity of such a sale and recognize that many days will be required before all the *t's* are crossed and all the *i's* are dotted. But I do not want your eloquent toast to go unanswered."

The bursar rises, glass in hand.

"To Dean Dawson, a man of guiding vision and prudent leadership. For the summits you have conquered and for the even greater heights you are about to scale."

The crystal goblet held aloft winks in the chandelier light and the headmaster bathes in the words of tribute from around the table that follow. Mrs. Martin reluctantly holds her glass high and smiles convincingly, not wanting to give the appearance of churlishness or ingratitude. Just then, the French doors swing open and the waiters, wearing white jackets and gloves, stream in with coffee and tea service and a tray bearing a towering chocolate and custard trifle, teetering precariously to one side.

In the sudden bustle and renewed celebration, Mrs. Martin looks across the table at Mr. Geary and inwardly admires at how deftly he parried her thrust. She senses he is aware of her stare but refuses to acknowledge it, pretending instead to listen to Mrs. Rowe and Mrs. Wingate, the freshman regent, discuss tomorrow's visit to the army hospital.

"Have it your way, George," she mumbles to herself, "we will talk later."

A swell of good cheer consumes the room as the discussion turns to the approaching end of the semester and the multi-layered dessert is spooned and served. The table candles, encircled by greenery, give off a festive glow that warms the complexions of the smiling and carefree faces.

Mrs. Martin watches the merriment with a condescending eye. She detects a shared naïveté among her colleagues, as if they are unwilling or unable to grasp that something is not right about the whole affair. First came Douglas Stratton's sudden appearance and grand gesture to buy the school, followed now by Dean Dawson's clumsy attempt to paper over the uncertainty that the sale of the Seminary would bring about. It doesn't add up. They don't see it. They don't wish to. A blithe spirit has blinded them. But she sees. She is not so easily fooled. Something about the timing and pace of events is curious to her. The prefect is convinced a crucial piece of information is missing.

She remembers occasional interactions with the Strattons years ago when they came to Forest Glen to visit their daughters. He, like a goodly number of the fathers she has dealt with, was twice removed from the happenings at the Seminary, beyond the desire to be assured that his sizeable investment in tuition and board was being wisely spent.

But he returns now a man reborn, an apostle of higher education? What need did this man of staggering wealth have for a girls' preparatory school? Why does a man, once so insulated from the upbringing and education of his daughters, seek to build a legacy in their names?

As the tiny beetle, overlooked in the concealing grass, with its thin fragile legs lightly touching the soil, is first warned of the tectonic shifts miles beneath the surface, she alone feels the distant rumblings, the prescient tremors, which portend a coming disaster.

Pressing the point further at this time without something tangible to validate her suspicion would be futile.

In the fullness of time, all will be revealed.

Leah and May arrive at dinner late and many of the tables have emptied as students head for the evening dance session or their clubhouses. A man stokes the fireplace and then tosses a heavy oak log into the brilliant molten orange flame as the wait staff hurriedly move about clearing plates and snatching up one napkin after another. Once the girls are seated, a middle-aged woman arrives immediately and their orders are taken with routine efficiency.

"You must be terribly excited about the concert on Friday. The program sounds wonderful. You are fortunate to possess such a talent. I do not know how you and the other girls can produce such an angelic sound. When I see the chorus perform I am always in awe. What I wouldn't do to have such a gift. My voice is so horrid."

The word 'horrid' lingers between them, like a cup of soured milk, unappetizing and untouched. Leah refuses to take the bait and indulge May's self-pity. She finds the way the cherub-faced girl is always fishing for soothing compliments to be pathetic. Looking at May, with her incessant neediness, she decides she cannot play by the rules of polite conversation any longer, not now, not the way she feels, not after all that happened in the woods. She feels strangely unchained, free to express herself honestly and without regard for the restraints of propriety.

"Honestly, May, I will be relieved once the concert is over with. I will be happy when Madame Kaspar's practices have ended and we are no longer required to perform like trained seals. I would like nothing better than to lie down to sleep tonight and when I wake have the semester be done with. Even better, I wish I was able to close my eyes and sleep to the day after graduation. If I were to have one Christmas wish fulfilled it would be that I could skip it all—everything! The endless parties, the contrived cheer, the ponderous sermons and incessant carols. Nothing makes me want to grind my teeth than the prolonged monotony of Christmastime here. I can only imagine God in heaven looking down upon this place, our little patch of cultivated earth. What would he think, May? What would he think about all of this?"

"My Lord, Leah, what has gotten into you?"

May is flabbergasted by the dark turn in Leah's attitude and looks about to see whether any one else has overheard her blasphemous words.

"Why are you so peevish? This is the best time of the school year. The concert on Friday and then the ball Saturday night. You've always enjoyed the week before winter break. This is not like you, not at all."

Leah sees the alarm in May's imploring eyes. But they are powerless to pierce the malignancy that has encased her heart since their trip to the glen.

"I wish I could make you understand, May."

"Understand what? Tell me."

Leah pauses in thought and then a sly smile creases her face.

"Imagine that you woke one morning and everything you believed in up to that point had changed. And for the first time in your life you felt that your past, everything you had grown to know and believe in, was no longer valid. A child's charade."

"I don't have a clue as to what you are getting at. You are acting...I don't know... peculiar."

"I thought I could talk with you openly, May. Are we not friends? Don't be so reactionary all the time. Play along. For once."

May bows her head slightly and accedes.

"All right. I am to imagine that everything is not real."

"Real, but changed. A complete shift in how you view the world about you and your place in it."

"I'm not following you."

"Imagine that which once had great significance to you is rendered useless, and all of the sudden there is meaning in what used to be meaningless."

"Leah, you are worrying me. I think you are taking your philosophy studies too seriously. I like the old Leah. This new brooding way of yours doesn't suit you."

"Why, because I possess the clarity to see the world around me for who it is, and because I am not pleased by what I see?"

"What do you see that does not please you? Really Leah! I don't understand the point of this at all."

Leah pushes away from the table and settles back into her chair. Before she can answer, two girls from the chorus spot her at the table and hurry over to join them. May is familiar with both.

Julia Tewes, a brunette of slight build, with wide eyes and a diminutive, up-turned nose, also resides in Senior House. May and Julia have shared many classes together at National Park over the years and their relationship is congenial but not warm, largely because of the envy May feels when she is around. Julia's prodigious musical talent seems unbounded. A virtuoso on the violin and an accomplished pianist, she separated herself from the rest of the class after arriving at Forest Glen and soon commanded private tutelage from the school's music staff. For her, chorus is a mere hobby, almost an afterthought, a casual decision made to occupy her time when not practicing her instruments. Her soprano voice, effortless and immaculate, immediately captured the attention of Madame and cemented the enmity of the other girls who had toiled for years to perfect their own voices, only to fall short of what they heard from the throat of the petite phenomenon.

With her is Mattie Bishop, the gregarious sophomore class president who moves about the campus as an indefatigable force, engaging with whomever she crosses paths with and leading others in one pursuit or another. In contrast to Julia, her features are dark and severe, and her unusually broad shoulders and tensile arms allow her to reign supreme on the grass courts and in the lanes of the gymnasium pool.

Both, in the objective assessment of May King, share an all-too-common malady with many of the girls at the school—a high regard for themselves.

Neither girl acknowledges May as they sit, their attention directed at Leah, who makes no effort to mask her look of annoyance at their uninvited appearance.

Mattie leans forward and grabs a hold of Leah's hand.

"Well, this is good sign. Aren't you supposed to be resting back at your room drinking tea and honey?" she asks with a devilish grin, "I thought you needed to rest and take care of your voice."

"I am feeling better now."

"You had everyone's jaws on the floor when you told the old tyrant you were leaving and stormed off the stage. I could tell by looking at you during practice that you were feeling out of sorts, but I never expected you to lose your temper like that."

"What happened, Leah?" May interjects. "You got into it with your chorus instructor? How come you have been keeping this from me?"

Leah turns away as Mattie continues the story.

"You see, Madame was in foul mood, worse than usual, and when a couple girls arrived to practice late, everyone knew it was going to be bad, especially with the concert two days away. She kept on stopping the practice and making us repeat the songs, and then she grew more and more frustrated and started singling out girls and forcing them to sing solo. And no matter how well they sang, it wasn't good enough for the crusty fascist. 'Again! Again!' she shouted over and over. Then, about an hour into the practice, in the middle of a song, she screams 'Halt!' at the top of her lungs, like a cat whose tail has been slammed in the door."

Julia laughs at Mattie's animated, blow-for-blow, retelling.

"So everyone stops and Madame storms toward us and points her stick right to the middle of the group, directly at poor Leah here, and yells, 'You are not singing! Why are you not singing?!' Every girl on stage turned to see who she was accusing. I was in the front row and when I looked back, Leah was just staring at the screaming harpy with this blank expression. I could not believe how composed you were."

"Which only made Madame Kaspar angrier," Julia chimes in.

"Yes, most girls would have lost their nerve and apologized or muttered an excuse; some probably would have cried—it's happened before. But not our dear Leah. Oh no."

At this point both girls are overcome by a giggling fit, unconcerned that Leah has withdrawn from the conversation and is looking away from the table as the dénouement approaches.

Mattie composes herself and leans over the table toward May and lowers her voice.

"So there is Madame, her herding staff pointing directly at Leah, waiting for an answer. A few seconds pass. Nothing. A few seconds more. Nothing. And then the girls standing on both sides of Leah start to instinctively move away from her as if she is about to be thrashed and they are fearful of stray blows. You should have seen Madame's face. It was all puckered and pulled tight. Her age spots seemed to grow darker, and her eyes were squinting and the purple veins along her neck were popping out."

"Eew!" Julia adds with a shudder.

"The end of her stick was shaking, inches away from Leah's face. And just when we expected Madame to explode with rage, our brave soul here tells her matter-of-factly that she is tired and that her throat aches and—"

"This is the best part!"

"And I quote Leah here, 'I would advise Madame to regain her composure and lower her cane from my face so that I may return to my room.' Just like that."

"Just like that!"

"And that is just what Madame does! Just as she was told. She lowers her poking stick. You could hear a pin drop in the hall. I think she was too shocked to know what to do. I don't believe a girl has ever spoken to her in such a tone before. And then Leah walks away, off the stage, up the aisle, and right out the door, without saying a word, and never looking back. It was priceless."

"Absolutely priceless."

"And Leah, do you hear what happened next, after you left? Did you? I suppose not. Madame Kaspar was as nice as could be for the rest of the practice session. No more yelling. No more criticism. No more pointing. We sang and she listened. She was a tamed tigress."

Puzzled by Leah's placid indifference, Julia draws close to her.

"Are you positive you are feeling well, Leah?"

Leah nods begrudgingly.

"I still feel a bit under the weather. Perhaps after I eat, I will be more myself. It's nice of the two of you to come over and ask."

May is surprised at how Leah's previous bluntness recedes around the two girls and gives way to an almost polite submissiveness, as if an unseen switch has been thrown transforming the testy, mercurial girl from across the hall into a demure model of courtesy.

"Yes, she who slays the dragon has earned her meal," Mattie says with an exuberant smile. "We are leaving for the ballroom. Come after you finish. Bettina invited some of the girls to her suite after dinner. She would want you to come too."

"I'll try. Thanks."

Over dinner, the conversation between the two flags after May tries and fails to elicit more details about Leah's confrontation with Madame Kasper. Perfunctory topics, such as the Saturday ball and Christmas shopping, are raised and quickly dispensed with. Each is reluctant to revisit Leah's bleak remarks before Julia and Mattie's arrival and an awkward formality descends on the table, until May decides to be direct about her festering concerns over the events following their trip to the flooded glen.

"You don't know it, but your offer to dine together was serendipitous. I came to your room because something was on my mind and I wanted to speak with you."

"What did you want to talk about?"

"Well, interestingly, it has to do with Josephine and Margaret, who just happened to be in your room when I knocked on your door this afternoon. I was more than a bit surprised to find them there."

"Why?"

"First, I need to know that I can speak freely with you, and that anything I may say, including any confidences I may relate about the two of them, is kept between us."

Leah acquiesces and places her fork on her plate, as May squirms uncomfortably in her chair.

"It's about the other day at the glen, the Grotto, you know."

"The storm? The flood?"

"Yes. I felt then that you and I had shared concerns about being there."

"About being there?"

"About what happened there."

Leah breathes deeply and locks onto May's round face across the table and studies the way her eyebrows arch as she speaks and crease the smooth porcelain skin of her forehead, and how the muscles above her plump cheeks twitch ever so slightly when she is nervous or flustered.

"What do you think happened there, May?"

"I was worried like you were Leah that someone might have drowned. Remember? The four of us talked about. And you and I agreed that something needed to be done. You remember, don't you?"

"Of course."

Leah's answer is prompt and reassuring. She wants May to view her as an ally so she will open up to her.

"Anyway, I told Miss Price about what happened after we returned to school. I regret it now, but I think the other two are mad with me for doing so, and I worry they've made it known to the rest of the girls that I am a snitch or something."

"Are you?"

"Leah, how can you ask such a thing!? I thought you of all people would see it my way."

"What did Miss Price say?"

"She said it was right of me to tell her. But I am starting to think she wasn't being sincere. Sometimes I feel she says things just so that I will feel better and go away and leave her alone. I think she views me with contempt for forcing her to deal with a matter she didn't want to be bothered with in the first place."

"So you are worried that all three—Margaret, Josephine and Miss Price—are upset with you? And that they are whispering to the others girls, calling you hysterical and weak, mocking you, as a form of retribution?"

"Yes, yes. But I knew you would understand. You were there. You saw what passed us by in the water."

"And the dress too? The white dress, remember? Josephine pulled it out of the flood."

"That's right, the dress."

"Tell me, May, how did you feel when you saw the dress?"

"We were all worried, whether the other two admit it or not. I made the right decision to go and see Miss Price when they wouldn't, didn't I?"

There on the white table linen, it appears in front of her, rising out of the smooth cotton. Leah admires its delicate stitching and pristine appearance. Its lines are simple; its beauty pure.

"Leah, tell me I did the right thing. Leah! Do you hear me?"

Leah looks up from the table and sees that May's attention is focused on her, undistracted.

"Of course you did. Josephine and Margaret are making you the scapegoat for their own duplicity. They refuse to acknowledge what you and I accept: that something happened at the glen."

"But Miss Price told me nothing happened. She told me that no one drowned in the flood."

"Miss Price is either a fool or a liar, just like Josephine and Margaret."

"I...I...I don't understand. She told me—"

"The three of them are trying to discredit you and intimidate you into believing that what you feel is not genuine. They are working together, don't you see? You went to Price, she then went to Josephine and Margaret, who then did what they and the others like them do so well—they talk in sweet, private, knowing voices with words that hurt and cut and destroy."

"Yes, but I am not sure that I follow what you are saying. Do you have proof of this? Has someone else confided in you?"

"Proof? What proof do you need to convince you of what you already believe? You know what they are capable of."

"I'm confused, Leah. What are you keeping from me?"

"What if I told that they have been watching you for last ten minutes?"

"Who?"

"Look over your shoulder, by the hallway."

May turns and spots Margaret and Josephine mingling by the dining hall entrance, standing next to a half-filled table.

"They've been looking over here continually while we've been talking."

"Why would they care about who I am dining with? I have hardly seen either one of them since Monday, that is until I knocked on your door this afternoon."

"I suspect they are worried that *we* are talking. They don't want you to know what I know."

"Which is...?"

"That they have been lying to you. That contrary to what Miss Price told you, something serious did happen. Like I said, they want you to be quiet and to go away."

"How can you possibly know this?"

"Because this morning, before sunrise, while you and the rest of the dormitory was asleep, the three of us rode to the creek and went upstream to the canoe shed and beyond. It was Josephine's idea and she didn't want you or anyone else to know about it. If you don't believe me, you can go see the stable groom and ask him. She wanted to search about the glen in hopes of finding clues about what she continues to deny she saw in the water. She can't have you know this, now can she?"

"I had no idea," May says weakly, stunned by the revelation.

"We didn't find anything, mind you. It was a monumental waste of time and riding around in the cold left me chilled to the bone."

"How can she be so manipulative?"

Leah leans closer to the betrayed girl and speaks in a hushed voice.

"Now it's your turn to give me your word, May. You must promise you will not confront Josephine about this or let anyone else know what I have just told you. It's not to your advantage, or mine, especially in light what took place between me and Madame Kaspar. Do I have your word?"

"Yes, of course." May replies, now understanding why the three were missing from breakfast and morning classes. "But why are you telling me this now?"

152   ANDY JOHNSON

Leah smiles and utters the words that she knows will put a padlock on her deceitful ruse:

"Because you are my friend, May, and I don't want to see you hurt any more than you already have."

Music streams like a siren's melody from a large credenza Victrola placed against one of the supporting brick pillars encircling the ballroom, enticing the girls inside Vincent Hall to the dance floor. The notes of the powerful phonograph fill the cavernous chamber as paired off girls in evening dresses glide across the sparkling, painstakingly polished wood.

Underneath the ballroom's second floor, a wide, horseshoe-shaped tract of carpeting wraps around the vaulted Gothic interior and offers wicker lounge chairs and plush sofas for those wishing to rest or socialize or only listen to the records. At each end of this ambulatory, chairs and tables situated around a fireplace provide refuge away from the bustle and sounds of the dance floor. Here, girls gather in a more intimate setting and look upon hand-painted scenes of the Italian countryside along the wall and fantasize of a pastoral world of undulating green hills and umbra homes under a lemon yellow sun.

Margaret and Josephine, arm in arm, join the parade of girls passing through the causeway connecting the Vincent Hall and the ballroom. Inside, long runs of garland, pinned by red ribbon bows, are draped across the front of the curved balcony railings suspended above the dance floor. Other seasonal decorations are hung throughout as work continues to transform the school's social cathedral into a winter wonderland for Saturday evening's ball. At one end of the floor, a temporary stage has been erected for the expected band. A wooden ring, fashioned from the wheel of an ox cart and adorned with silver and gold beads and pillar candles, hangs over the center of the dance floor, suspended, almost magically, from the clerestory ceiling by a thin black chain that is imperceptible against the dark overhead beams to the dancers on the floor. Only at sunset, when the angled light pours through the stained-glass dormers and the ballroom is filled with a wondrous kaleidoscope of colors and all objects within the atrium are bathed in beams of shifting hues, can the primitive chandelier's support be seen clearly.

A fox trot is played as the two girls enter and more couples take to the crowded floor. Josephine slides her arm out of Margaret's and searches out

INCIDENT AT FOREST GLEN *153*

two empty chairs in the ambulatory close enough to watch the dancers but sufficiently removed from the music so that they can continue their conversation.

"I am exhausted," Josephine sighs, as she settles into the chair. "I feel as if the entire day has been a blur, almost as if it wasn't real."

"If it wasn't so brutish outside, I would like nothing better right now than to slip outside for a cigarette. I feel an edge that I need to get rid of badly."

"You need to eat, my dear. You haven't had anything today. You are too thin as it is. You can't afford to lose any more weight. Plus, not eating puts you in a foul temper."

"And ruin my dream of modeling in Paris—not a chance!"

"Seriously, Margaret. We've been through a lot today."

"*Seriously*, Josephine. I have no appetite."

"Well, leave a note for your parents absolving me of any responsibility when they find your emaciated corpse."

"Pleasant," Margaret playfully rebukes her friend, as she turns her attention to the dance floor. "Some of the new girls are absolutely clueless out there."

Josephine also watches for awhile and thinks about Robert arriving on Saturday. It's been nearly two months since they last saw each other for a weekend lunch at a stuffy Washington restaurant. Afterward they strolled down the wide avenue lined with broad elms ablaze with red and yellow as automobiles jockeyed with horse-drawn carts.

She recalls the way he suddenly stopped walking and turned her towards him and drew her close and she felt his body press flush against hers. The sensory images flash rapidly before her, vivid and present, as if she is there again. A pervasive scent of coal and ash permeating the air. The stiff feel of his wool overcoat as she gripped his shoulder. His arm slowly tightening across the arch of her back. Brush strokes of color down his flushed cheeks. The penetrating silent stare into her eyes. And then the simultaneous, paradoxically intoxicating feel of his warm lips against hers as the tip of his nose, cold and smooth, grazed her cheek. They embraced, warming each other with their tenderness, suspended in time and oblivious to the world moving around them, content as never before, no words dare spoken or needed to explain the rush of emotions between them.

"Are you excited about meeting Robert's friend, Caleb, again?" she asks, trying to pull Margaret's attention away from the dance floor.

"Remind me, which one is Caleb?" she answers, pretending to not know the name of the friend Robert has arranged to bring as her escort for the ball.

The transparent act of feigned indifference prompts a mocking laugh from Josephine.

"Really?! You don't remember him? The boy you were quite thrilled to know a few weeks ago finds you beautiful and was beside himself at the chance of dating you. The one who practically begged Robert."

"He is not that contemptible little man, trollish, who we met after the concert at the D.A.R., the one with the poor complexion and the aroma of moth balls."

"No, and you know very well that's not him. The four of us met after the tour of the National Museum. The Senate clerk. Polite, quite polished, and well-read. The two of you talked literature as I recall as they walked us back to the train station."

Margaret shrugs.

"Sounds vaguely familiar."

"Vaguely familiar or not, he is coming Saturday. So you best drum up a bit more enthusiasm."

"Where would I be without my own personal social secretary?! Do you want to dance?"

"Not just now. Soon."

There is a break in the music as the record is changed and Josephine pulls her chair closer to Margaret's so that they are touching. A waltz begins and the dancers move across the mahogany floor in the synchronized motion of tiny dancers atop a music box, as if propelled by tightly-wound springs concealed beneath their feet.

"I want to thank you, Margaret, for what you said in Leah's room. Sometimes I get caught up in my own tempests and lose perspective. But you were right—a bit forceful perhaps—but you were right to push back like you did. After Miss Price took me to task, I was unsure of myself. I thought the ride this morning would help matters. But going with Leah to the creek this morning was a mistake, a mistake in many ways. You did not need to be forced into it either. I don't know what is wrong with Leah. But we can't get hysterical as she deals with whatever afflicts her. It was proper for us to be concerned, but we cannot bear this burden alone. Nor can we place ourselves in a compromising situation because of it. By threatening to go to Miss Price, I was doing just that. As far as I am concerned, Leah is on her own from this point forward. If she decides to speak of what happened this morning to Miss Price or anyone else, that is her decision and I will take responsibility and accept whatever consequences come about."

Margaret waits for her to finish, smirks, and lets out a deep sigh.

"Do you feel better now?"

She then leans over and kisses Josephine on the cheek.

"Just because you have appointed yourself my social secretary does not mean I am to be your confessor. Let's dance. And I lead."

Nearby, Leah leans against the wall support next to the Victrola watching the others dance as May peruses the record vault. Mattie and Julia rush over when they spot Leah. After a brief discussion, Mattie points up to the third floor where a dozen students live, at a significant premium to their annual tuition, in spacious, expensively decorated suites overlooking the ballroom, each with an adjoining room for a personal maid.

The private suites were incorporated into the design of the ballroom after repeated comments from the wealthiest parents whose favorable inclinations toward the school were colored by their misgivings about the boarding arrangements. Complaints about cramped dormitories and communal living quarters came from those accustomed to an opulent lifestyle and the amenities it provided. The wisdom of Dean Dawson's investment in the costly accommodations was immediately validated, as the expansive rooms were quickly snatched up by daughters from families who gladly (and without much thought) paid three times the supplemental boarding fee.

When the waiting list for the ballroom suites grew and families began offering reservation deposits years in advance of their daughters' matriculation to the school, the headmaster began to regret that he had not foreseen the demand and been more bold and extravagant in the designing the building. Ever since, whenever he enters the ballroom, he looks upward and imagines how much more grand—and lucrative—the building's design would be with a fourth or even fifth floor.

A slender girl in a chartreuse dress sidles up to May at the record vault and waits to be noticed. A few seconds pass as May thumbs through the paper sleeves and the girl reaches across and halts the search with a touch of her hand.

"I like this one. They played it last night. It's wonderful to dance to."

May, startled by the abrupt intrusion, turns and sees the fresh-faced, green-eyed girl, with a blanket of faint freckles across her nose and cheeks, smiling widely.

"I've never seen so many records before, have you? This school has everything doesn't it?"

"It's quite a collection," she answers the unfamiliar girl.

The girl's smile turns sheepish as she subtly knifes her legs back and forth under the chartreuse dress and sways her hips.

"I just can't get over this place. Very grand."

"You're one of the new girls, aren't you I? Is this your first semester here?"

"Yes. Does it show much?" she responds with a waver in her voice and looks slightly downward, a brown lock slipping from behind her ear and falling across her cheek.

"Nellie Danaher. And you are May King, am I right?"

"I apologize, but have we met before?"

"No, but I thought it would be helpful if I knew every girl's name when I came here in September, so I looked over the school directory and committed everything about each student to memory—name, hometown, birthday. It sounds odd, I know, but I've always had this ability to remember things. They call it a photographic memory, but that's not how it works, at least not with me. I don't take a mental photograph of what I see exactly. When I read something, it just flows inside me and stays there, whether I want it to or not. Listen to me, I am blathering on. That happens sometimes when I meet people for the first time. I get flustered and don't know when to shut up."

"Really, it's all right. You're fine," May says reassuringly. "Let's put you to the test then, Nellie Danaher. You clearly know my name. What else?"

As Nellie laughs, her nose wrinkles and her shoulders squirm like that of a young girl under the scrutiny of her first suitor.

"Testing me, are you? You don't believe me. I am bluffing, huh? Well, my powers are not just cerebral, May King. I am also schooled in the mystical arts. I wasn't completely forthcoming, you see."

Nellie takes May's hand from the dark wood of the Victrola vault without asking and turns it upward. With firm pressure, she splays the palm open using her surprisingly strong thumbs.

"I forgot to mention that I come from a long line of palm readers. One of my many, many talents."

May is momentarily paralyzed by the attractive girl's forwardness.

"You are too stiff, relax your hand, silly, or this won't work."

May's laughs nervously as the girl continues to rub her thumbs along the length of her palm and fingers.

"Now, I want you to look into my eyes and I will see not only into your past but I shall glimpse into your future as well."

Nellie's exuberant grin disappears and she stares intently into May's eyes and then glances down at the opened hand. The ethereal sound of orchestral strings fills the ballroom.

"Your name is May King, but we have already established that. You are from Richmond, Virginia, correct?" Nellie posits with a slight, tempered inflection, as she looks up again at May.

"Yes. That's right."

"Hmm. Two out of two. Let's try something more challenging," her emerald eyes dipping downward again. "You were born on...oh, this is interesting...the year is 1903, the month is July, and the day...the day is not the 4th but the...3rd. Am I correct?"

"Yes, that's remarkable."

"And you are a Kappa girl as well. Yes?"

"Yes, nicely done."

May tries to withdraw her hand but Nellie's grip is unyielding. She feels the girl's soft, slender fingers tighten and the pressure against the back of her hand grows, opening up her palm even further.

"Wait. That's the easy part. I promised a look into what the future has in store for Miss May King."

Nellie examines closely the contours of May's palm and then traces the tip of her finger along the delicate lines creasing her flesh.

"A decidedly optimistic life awaits you. Marriage to a dashing man, tall, but not too tall, sophisticated, and wealthy. You will settle in a large house, perhaps a mansion, overlooking a busy street. As for children? Yes, I foresee many, four perhaps five. Healthy and whip-smart."

She lifts the finger and places it on a prominent line bisecting May's palm and runs it lightly along its length until an involuntary shiver ripples up the girl's arm.

"You will live until you are gray-haired and hunch-backed and shuffle about with a cane, long enough to see your grandchildren and their children. But, wait—"

"What is it?"

"Hmmm. This part is a bit muddled."

Nellie leans closer until May feels the girl's warm breath pass over her open palm.

"I see a break, faint and almost imperceptible, but definitely a break. I see a trauma of sorts early in the journey ahead of you. Something will interrupt the fortune that I have predicted. Sooner than later. A crisis or loss. Perhaps an injury to body or to heart. Whatever it is, a person or an event will influence your destiny and add uncertainty to what I see."

Nellie slowly closes May's fingers into a fist, drawing the curtain down on the window into the future.

"Ta-da!" she smiles impishly at the end of her parlor game. "What do you think? Do I have talent?"

May tries to compose herself, her face suddenly hot and unsure what to say, as other girls begin to gather around the phonograph.

"I will reserve judgment until I learn more. Were your mystical powers successful on the other girls?"

"I can't say. You're the first one."

The others circling around the phonograph jostle the two about as they search for what record to play next.

"Too crowded. I'll look for you later and maybe we can dance. Nice to meet you, May King," Nellie says over the din before retreating into the surge of bodies moving along the ambulatory.

May watches her distinctive chartreuse dress weaving through the flow of girls, entranced by the chance encounter. With May's view partially obscured by the stream of passing students, Nellie stops on the far side of the room and stands before a statue of a young girl atop a pedestal, bare-chested, holding a cistern on her shoulder with one arm and gingerly grasping a cup in the other. The carved figure wears a thin, translucent skirt rippling along her waist and legs as if molded by a forceful wind. Hebe, goddess of youth, daughter of Zeus and Hera, cupbearer to the immortals. The freshman, aware that May is following her progress, holds her spot alongside the graceful carving, then turns and disappears behind the procession of young women circulating about the dance floor.

From the top floor of the ballroom the sound of the phonograph is eerie and distant, layered against a background of multitudinous conversations occasionally punctuated by a boisterous laugh or sharp exclamation. Leah has never before entered the realm of the Sweets, a moniker given to the girls occupying the ballroom suites by those students who do not. The nickname carries with it a negative connotation. Many of the girls at National Park Seminary, while themselves products of a privileged upbringing, view the over-sized rooms with their separate parlors as dens of exclusivity and snobbery set off from the shared experience of campus life. The contempt felt within the student body as a whole toward the twelve Sweets is pervasive and commonly known, even by the faculty and administration, to the point of it becoming an unwritten article in the student canon of conduct, regardless of the demeanor and character of those occupying the segregated rooms. Rather than lament the assigned stigma, the Sweets heartily embrace it, using the label freely and affectionately with one another. They relish the notion that they unofficially comprise the most exclusive of all sorority clubs on campus, a badge of distinction envied by those secretly hiding their own jealousy.

As Leah follows Mattie and Julia along the hallway to Bettina Braddock's suite, she is taken aback to see Dean Dawson and Miss Price with two unfamiliar men, one older, the other in his twenties, both dressed in dark suits, directly across the open ballroom, leaning on a balcony railing. The dean is gesturing about, talking to the older man as he animatedly points out different aspects of the building's interior design. The regent is paying scant attention to the headmaster's tour. Rather, she engages the younger of the two strangers in a separate discussion.

As her group approaches the balcony, Leah subtly steps behind her escorts so as to conceal herself. Mindful of Josephine's threatening words in her room about going to see Miss Price, Leah does not want to be noticed by the senior counselor and risk the conversation that might ensue. She watches Dean Dawson point up at the niches in the brick wall above, and the plaster busts that ring the upper reaches of the ballroom, as she passes.

160 ANDY JOHNSON

"George Washington. Christopher Columbus. Julius Caesar. Aristotle. Socrates...no, no, my apologies, Socrates and then Aristotle. And, let's see, my eyes aren't what they used to be. Plato, I believe. And then...Miss Price, do you recall the other one across the way?"

Leah does not linger to hear Miss Price's answer, thankful for the timely distraction.

The girls arrive at the door with the oval gold plate engraved Nine above the knocker. An elderly colored woman, with thick-lensed glasses framing a drawn, heavily-wrinkled face, answers the door in a black dress, starched white apron, and servant cap, and Leah catches her first glimpse of the sprawling apartments she had heard so much about. The layout is spacious, more than double the size of the rooms in Senior House. The interior is filled with polished silver and gold fixtures and plush modern furniture that make the hotel hand-me-downs and antique furnishings at the other dormitories look dated and shabby by comparison.

Mattie walks over to the plush couch where the host sits dangling a cigarette holder in the middle of a group of girls and bends over and kisses her on the cheek. Leah waits with Julia by the entranceway and admires the ornate, carved mirror glass bordered with gold leaf and the shimmering black lacquer writing desk against the near wall, trying to take in each extravagant detail of the room. Two other girls from the chorus sit by an upright piano listening to another of the Sweets play a movement from a Liszt concerto from memory. At a table across the room, a group plays cards while dining on small plates of hors d'oeuvres and fingering long stem crystal. Some of the girls in the suite take notice of their arrival while most continue what they are doing uninterrupted.

Bettina uncoils from the sofa and makes her way over to greet Leah. Despite three years on the chorus and numerous classes together, their relationship never progressed much beyond the occasional pleasantry or greeting. Leah considers her a competent but unspectacular alto, possessing a reputation outside the practice hall and classroom of a girl who is not to be crossed. Her family wealth comes from Northwest timber and because of the travel distance back home she typically spends her summers on Long Island Sound with relatives and decamps to the Willard Hotel in the city for winter break. According to a rumor from a reliable source in the Seminary intelligentsia, she is soon to be engaged to the son of the French ambassador and will leave school before her senior year ends for a life on the continent. The fiery-haired girl with pale skin sizes up Leah as she skirts across the floor, a pendulous tip of ash hanging miraculously from her cigarette as she approaches.

"Here is our heroine!" she proclaims to the room. "Where in the world did you find such audacity this afternoon? I hope you won't take this the wrong way, but of all the girls in chorus, you would be the last I would expect to tell off ol' Frau Kaspar. Please come in girl, and tells us *all* about it."

Leah hears the door shut behind her as she is guided by Bettina into the heart of the gathering.

"I like to have a small soiree on Wednesday nights and I thought tonight would be an ideal opportunity for you to get to know some of the girls from the third floor a little better."

Outside the door, Dean Dawson ushers Mr. Stratton along the hallway to the elevator that will lead them to the first floor and a survey of the art studios off the ballroom. They are closely followed by Mr. Carter and Miss Price.

The financial titan had placed a call to Dean Dawson late in the afternoon asking permission that he and Mr. Carter be allowed to tour the school as it had been a while since his last visit and his familiarity with the buildings is not what is once was. The dean, rejecting the notion that the prospective purchaser of National Park and his assistant would be left on their own accord to wander around the campus unaccompanied, sent notice to his wife that he would not be home for dinner, and quickly set up an impromptu walking inspection of the Odeon theater, Recitation Hall, the chapel and finally Vincent Hall and the ballroom.

The dean overlooked Mrs. Martin and directed the senior regent to join him so she could outline the scholastic vision of the curriculum and address any questions about residential life of students. The prefect's attitude has become increasingly temperamental, he thought, too unpredictable, and at times her opinions have been outright caustic. Moreover, based on what the headmaster observed at the morning meeting, the businessman seemed at ease and conversational around the youthful regent. The stakes are too high to risk the prospective sale over academic protocol, Dean Dawson concluded after Mr. Stratton's call.

"You seem to have a spirited group of girls to oversee, Miss Price," Mr. Carter observes, continuing his steady stream of comments and questions since they paired off at the Odeon when the dean pulled the wealthy New Yorker into a more confidential exchange of thoughts. For more than an hour, the two trailed behind their respective employers, largely ignored and left to their own devices to keep entertained as one edifice after another was explored.

"Almost ninety in the senior class. Nearly three hundred in the school all together. We assess each girl's needs and then tailor her course work to meet those needs. We teach each student to be confident but respectful. We believe building strength of character to not only face adversity but overcome it is the key to success, Mr. Carter."

"Most certainly—the sort of progressive ethos we need for a modern world. I wonder though, do you find your students willingly accept these tenets of self-sufficiency? I mean, it is not exactly second nature for girls of this class to fend for themselves."

"It's our mission to locate, unlock and cultivate potential in all of students, regardless of the circumstances of their upbringing before coming here."

The dean halts once again to give Mr. Stratton a commanding view of the crowded dance floor below, sidling up next to his guest's shoulder so as to be heard above the din.

The regent watches as Mr. Carter pulls his cigarette case out his jacket pocket.

"The students are forbidden to smoke, and we discourage it among others in their presence, particularly when inside."

"Oh, of course. I apologize," he says with a look of embarrassment, fumbling to put away the silver case.

Miss Price smiles at his clumsiness.

"Any other rules you've broken since you arrived, I should know about?" she jokes.

Mr. Carter smiles and glances over at his employer, who, he can tell from his rigid expression, is losing patience with the dean's long-winded tutorial.

"I'll never confess."

The two lean over the balcony railing and look down at the impeccably dressed students gliding across the lustrous floorboards in harmonized motion.

"It excites me to think about what awaits them when they leave here. Each girl is encouraged to be an agent of change. Each is taught she has a responsibility to shape the world around her. You are looking at the vanguard of their generation, Mr. Carter."

Mr. Carter watches the elegant dancers move along the ballroom floor and is privately shamed by a more base admiration than that espoused by his escort. Like a school of fish before the ravenous fisherman, they are too plentiful for him to target his attention on just one.

"You make it sound as if you are working in a laboratory, Miss Price, and your charges are the experiment, test subjects to be conditioned and ultimately released into the wild. Of course, I don't mean that literally."

"A provocative analogy, but one that couldn't be farther from the truth. Individuality is what we seek to instill in each girl, not conformity."

"But surely you are aware of the school's—how should I put it—less official reputation?"

"And what would that be?"

"The spouse trap," he deadpans.

"Oh, yes, that I have heard, and other not so complementary characterizations as well."

"Does it bother you, you know, the suggestion that this is all for show, that your efforts, boiled down to their most basic element, to the simplest of forms—what we call on Wall Street, the bottom line—is all about marriage, about young women ensnaring a husband, and in the process, advancing themselves through more traditional means?"

"I wholly reject the slanderous notion, Mr. Carter," she says adamantly, the raw tone of resentment punctuating her words. "It boils down our work here to a most prejudiced conclusion, that all the female sex desires in life is a mate that will provide for her and protect her. But don't rely on my words. Accompany me to the Mr. Shelby's office tomorrow morning. He is the Resident Secretary of the Alumnae Association, and he can dispel that canard with ample proof of what our graduates have accomplished outside these walls.

"National Park Seminary has produced many women who are leaders in their vocational field. Now that the Nineteenth Amendment is finally in hand, and the suffrage battle has been won, the mission of an institution like ours to produce strong and disciplined minds is even more relevant than ever,

I would argue. Whether our girls marry or not upon leaving here is irrelevant to the work that we do and the results we achieve. We tell our students that the life ahead of them is an unpainted canvas and that they must be the ones to pick up the brush and decide how it shall look."

His provocative question has stripped off the regent's mask of placidity, and she stands before him infused with emotion, red-faced and energized, her eyes wide and defiant. He returns her challenging stare unblinkingly.

So, after an hour of dancing around it, we are finally here.

He is the first to break the stand-off with a disarming smile.

"I wholeheartedly agree, as does, more importantly, Mr. Stratton. If he didn't, he would never have made this trip. I did not intend to poke a hornet's nest, but I do enjoy seeing that you are passionate about your calling, Miss Price. I have no doubt that the girls under your tutelage benefit greatly from the fervor you bring to the classroom. They are lucky to have you as their teacher."

She returns the smile and contemplates the sincerity of his soothing apology.

"Fear not, Mr. Carter, the hornets have retreated back to their nest."

"Can I ask a favor of you, however? The day has been long and I am dead on my feet, and when I feel this way I have a tendency to speak my mind. So, I would greatly appreciate it if you would dispense with calling me Mr. Carter. Every time I hear it I expect my father will pop out from behind a plant or a couch. Truth be told, I detest formalities. So, if it wouldn't result in you being fired or something else grave, would you call me Charles when we are out of earshot of you know who?" he asks with a nod and arching eyebrows toward the two men standing before them, both lost in an earnest discussion of mortgage liability.

The drop in pretense pleases the young regent. She is attracted to the man's blunt demeanor and willingness to speak his mind.

"That would be fine. I find it cumbersome at times as well. But only on the condition of reciprocity—no more Miss Price. Until such time you enroll in one of my literature classes, you will call me Katharine. Deal?"

"Deal," he answers, and they seal their compact with a quick hand-shake. The shaking motion of their arms pulls Miss Price slightly off balance while they walk and for two steps they lean tantalizingly against each other before finding their balance and restoring the space between them.

INCIDENT AT FOREST GLEN 165

At the elevator, the group halts and Mr. Stratton turns to his assistant.

"We should head back to the hotel now. There are a few business matters we still need to go over before tomorrow. I am afraid we will have to see the art studios another time, Porter. I have a number of appointments in the morning and I think it best if we curtail our visit. I will need to rise early and I never sleep all that well when I travel away from home."

"Of course, Douglas. We can finish the rest of the tour at your convenience."

"And thank you, Miss Price, for keeping young Mr. Carter occupied tonight. I trust he was well-mannered throughout your time together. He can be socially awkward at times, a little rough around the edges, if you know what I mean. Oh for goodness sake boy, why are you blushing? And stop slouching, will you. Like others of your generation, your posture is atrocious."

"We had a lovely time, Mr. Stratton," Miss Price replies warmly to the man's jibe. "Your colleague was a most entertaining escort for the evening."

"He's my *assistant*, not my colleague," a slight grin belying his gruff retort. "Perhaps then I can impose on you further, Porter? I do not require the services of my *assistant* tomorrow while I am in Washington. Would it be too much to ask if you he tagged along on the morning trip you mentioned earlier?"

"Our annual Christmas visit to Walter Reed Army Hospital," Dean Dawson answers enthusiastically. "An excellent suggestion. Mr. Carter can witness firsthand the fine philanthropic work our girls do in the community. Coincidentally, Miss Price and the other class regents will be chaperoning a group of girls representing each of the school's sororities."

"Is that so?" Mr. Stratton asks pretending to be surprised, as he buttons his overcoat and glances at the floor indicator about the elevator doors. "Are you sure he won't be a hindrance, Miss Price?"

"Not at all, Mr. Stratton," Miss Price assures him with a playful smile. "We can use his strength to carry the gifts the girls have wrapped for the convalescing soldiers. You have my word; we will make use of him."

Mr. Carter, more than slightly annoyed over how he is being excluded from the conversation, startles as he suddenly realizes he has left his hat back on the table by the balcony. Not wanting to hold up the group, he tells them to go ahead when the elevator arrives and that he will take the stairs by the balcony overhang and meet them at the front lobby entrance.

Retracing his steps briskly along the red runner he finds the forgotten hat where he left it just as a lone student turns the corner and nearly collides with him. Out of reflex, he raises his hands in front of his body and dodges to the right, nearly toppling the table in order to avoid colliding with the fast-moving girl. She does not stop or even hesitate, but turns her head to watch the stumbling man as she passes.

"Nice suit. It looks delicious on you," she purrs, her stride long and languid.

Before he can reply, she turns back around and continues down the empty corridor, confident she is being watched. Mr. Carter fumbles with his hat as she reaches one of the suites and enters without knocking, the trail of her chartreuse dress skimming along the paneled wall and then slipping past the corner just as the door closes behind her.

"If the old man saw me blushing now, he'd have a field day," he mutters.

He looks up and sees his employer, Dean Dawson, and Miss Price enter the arriving elevator across the atrium. But he waits, content for a few moments to regain his composure and observe the activity below him.

The dance floor is more crowded than before as the assembled girls move across the floor in rhythm with the musical cadence. The spectacle from above is captivating. A hundred or more young women, hands clasped, arm in arm, dressed in the finest frocks and adorned with glittering jewels. And not a single man in sight. Mr. Stratton is right: this place is a gold mine.

Just as he is about to push away from the balcony railing and head for the stairs, he notices two girls through the frame of the suspended ornamental wheel, positioned near the edge of the dance floor, moving slower than the rest. They are caught up in an animated conversation of some sort and paying scant attention to their steps. Half-heartedly they move along, drifting in the wake of the central current of dancers. For a few seconds his sight of them is obstructed by the decorative candelabrum. When they reemerge, the face of the shorter of the two girls comes into full view. He is instantly smitten by her radiant features and studies her intensely from afar. Her golden hair, curled and pulled back away from her face, bounces against her shoulder as she tosses her head to one side. The delicate line of her jaw and porcelain skin stand out against the embroidered collar of her black dress. A strong nose leads to curved lips, plush and pink and slightly parted to offer a glimpse of white.

A familiar pain twists inside his chest as he tracks her through the crush of bodies. He desperately wishes he were down there on the floor, at this very moment, in place of her partner, listening to her voice and feeling the touch of her slender wrist and gloved hand on his shoulder. He imagines the sweetness of her perfume and scintillating sound of her dress rustling as he places his arm against her back. Brilliant cerulean eyes look up at her partner, expressive and inviting, and pull the clandestine watcher in further still. He feels as if he is observing from a distance a flawless work of beauty, a living embodiment of a master artist's work, an exquisite composition of femininity meant to effortlessly capture the hearts of men. A modern Helen of Troy.

He does not dare look away or leave his place at the balcony railing and risk losing her in the crowd. Hopelessly, helplessly, shamelessly, he follows the girl's every movement and every inflection, and drinks in every small physical detail of her being until he is intoxicated with her presence and incapable of breaking the spell he is under.

Was Mr. Carter able at that moment to turn away, or simply shift his narrowed line of sight a few degrees to the right, he would have noticed his agitated employer, standing next to Dean Dawson and the fawning regent in front of the elevator, excitedly waving his arm trying to gain his aide's attention so he can leave.

Less noticeable in the frenetic ballroom scene is the solitary figure standing on the lip of the dance floor also looking upon Mr. Carter's object of desire, the short, portly girl with the pinched brow and sour scowl who has given up searching for the dance partner she arrived with, and who is now content to train her raging anger elsewhere.

She watches and learns. She translates the movements of their lips. She gathers information that confirms her conspiratorial thoughts. She watches and plots. She is contemptuous of their callous indifference and their manipulative ways. She scorns their narcissistic behavior. She watches and waits. She watches and waits for their fall.

Chapter 6
Guardians at the Gate

It is pitifully true that the average girl graduates from school and enters life with no means of self-support—possessing neither the potential power gained by rigorous application, nor its substitute, specialized knowledge of some one subject. How parents dare to take the risks for her, in this day of fortunes unmade overnight, is a marvel. The girl of eighteen or nineteen is expected to have completed her general education, to have perfected her accomplishments, to be ready for life. The boy of eighteen is just entering college, barely beginning his preparation for life. Is it fair? If parents wish to keep their daughters from the class of helpless inefficients, they must prolong their school-life. They must make for their daughters the choice between the dissipations of social life and preparation for serious life, through the acquisition of some practical training which will be a safeguard long after the shielding hand of the parent is helpless to defend.

In the nadir of night, a black locomotive hurtles through the lifeless gloom and shatters the ghostly stillness of the abandoned land. Unfettered by cars and its head lamp doused, the muscular engine races past one empty station after another unrestrained by signal or brake. Steel wheels vibrate and strain and vaporize the frost accumulated along the silvery rails stretching toward an unattainable horizon. Through a narrow slash carved into walls of jagged, weeping rock the iron beast rockets along. Its stovepipe cold and cabin vacant, the speeding train rushes past fields of gray homes and skeleton forests on its journey to Forest Glen.

The guttural rumble of its arrival awakens Mr. Stratton in his suite at Glen Manor. He dons slippers at his bedside and shuffles across the floor rug in the darkness. Pulling the window drape aside, he sees the haunting, shadowy form in the distance, motionless and silent.

The station building closed for the evening long ago and a lone pole light illuminates a nearby portion of the platform. A woman steps into this pale yellow cone and then stops. She is wearing a heavy cloak and a fur-brimmed hat and expectantly searches the pervasive emptiness that surrounds her. The awakened man rubs his eyes and directs his gaze back on the solitary figure. He struggles in the fog of his sudden rousting to understand why a train would be arriving at such a late hour, a train bearing a single passenger nonetheless.

The woman places a suitcase on the ground and burrows her hands into a muff along her waist. As she moves about the platform to warm herself, she slips in and out of the blackness of the night intermittently, emerging and then receding repeatedly. Each time the mysterious passenger reenters the light, Mr. Stratton catches a fleeting glimpse of a different aspect of her countenance. The motion quickens with unnatural rapidity until her face blinks and jumps through the beam and offers the mesmerized man one fractional clue of her identity after another with zoetropic effect. Faster the progression of partial images continues until all motion ceases and the mosaic pieces of the disorienting ocular phenomenon gradually combine into a unified composite, a singular image of a face that grips his throat and wrenches out every particle of air.

Can this possibly be real? Is this the end of my torment? Is this my salvation?

Mr. Stratton releases the window curtain and frantically pushes through the lightless room in search of the door. He must go to her. He must reach her before she leaves. Nothing else matters at this moment. Nothing else ever mattered as much in his sixty-three years of life. In the disorienting emptiness he slams against the bed frame and then reaches the wall and blindly runs his hands along its length feeling for the door or the light switch to free him from his unbearable confinement. In his frantic fumbling about, his arm swings against the table lamp and in a heartbeat an explosion of glass and porcelain on the floor shatters the silence. Precious time passes excruciatingly as he feels about the room looking for a way out. In a burst of desperation he lunges for the soft outline of the window and rips the curtains and rod from the wall letting in enough diffuse light to reveal the exit along the far wall. Just as he turns to leave, his panic spikes—the platform is empty. She is gone.

The frenzied man struggles momentarily with the balky door knob and finally reaches the hallway. As he emerges into the night, he instantly feels the bracing cold penetrate his night clothes and tighten his muscles. He runs wildly toward the distant pole light hoping to find her and feels the stabbing pain of the chilled air in his lungs grow more acute with each stride. The sound of his steps on the soft gravel of the rail bed breaks the silence as he rushes toward the wooden platform. He looks about but spots no trace of the nocturnal traveler. The foot bridge across the glen is empty, the silhouetted school on the hilltop exanimate and foreboding.

The bones in his shoulders and along his upper back subtly shift and then pop as he feels a supernatural force pull him in the direction of the ominous form. He takes half-steps in the still night toward the locomotive and can discern no detail in its exterior, no break or bend in its smooth, sleek contours. There is no patchwork of iron and bolts and rivets and rods. It is cast in one large piece of metal and bears no imperfection. He approaches apprehensively, fingers extended at arms length, reaching out to touch the spectral machine. Inching closer to the obsidian surface of the monolithic shape, he feels the tips of his fingers tingle and instinctively pulls away.

In the faint starlight he sees the parallel rails stretching out in front of the locomotive. Something, faint and distant, moves in the gray emptiness. There, oblivious to his presence, the woman is walking down the tracks.

"Stop! Wait! Wait!" he calls out as he runs after her.

But she does not stop or wait, nor does she heed his call, her feet striking the timber rail ties as a small bag swings at her side and keeps cadence with the sway of her hips. Into the lonely night she walks, the outline of her coat and hat and bag growing fainter with each step under a canopy of stars. He follows as he must.

"Please, turn around. Come back," he implores as he runs after the phantom traveler.

Exhaustion sets in and his legs grow weary, but he pushes on through the building wave of nausea, hoping that she will hear his voice and turn around. Staggering and out of breath, he falters and his knees and palms smash against the bed of jagged stones anchoring the creosote covered ties sending a shock of excruciating pain throughout his body. The desperate man tries to shake off the burning agony and looks up just as the receding figure is absorbed in the enveloping night, leaving only the sound of her footsteps, which wane and then die.

"Don't leave," he cries out, his plea swallowed by the void.

When repeated, his words waver, bled of urgency, and reverberate about him with a reedy, mocking tone.

A searing beam of light from the station suddenly appears and cuts through the heavy winter air, brightening the rail bed. The distraught man's prone body casts a distorted, elongated shadow along the empty track ahead. The cold steel trembles with a low-throttled hum and he can feel the ground come alive beneath him.

He is too late. The moment is slipping away. She is gone. Again.

The tormented dreamer jerks upright and violently kicks away the bed sheet twisted about his legs. For a fraction of a second, he can still feel the rough bed of stones under his bleeding palms and knees. And then nothing. The last traces of the nightmare, so vivid and so traumatizing, evaporate, leaving behind only a residue of perspiration along his neck and chest.

He leans over and buries his head in his hands. The morning sun pours through a slight part in the curtains and he can feel it warm the moisture ringing his collar. Once composed and grounded in the disappointed reality of his surroundings, he fumbles for his glasses on the night stand and then picks up a brown pharmacy bottle. A quick shake confirms its few remnants. Not today, he decides, and places the bottle back on the table between the framed picture of his wife and the diminutive box he brought with him to Forest Glen.

Mr. Carter waits on the steps outside Vincent Hall and draws deeply from his third cigarette in a desperate attempt to fend off the frigid morning air. He is not alone, flanked on both sides by twin copper gryphons resting atop granite pedestals, their wings unfurled and beaks turned upward.

He is purposely early and has stationed himself at the front entrance so as to not to be left behind by the others traveling to the army hospital. Inside, a small group of students congregate in the main parlor, lounging on Victorian furniture left over from the building's bygone hotel era. The solitary man spies through a nearby window a huddle of girls positioned around the pulsating fireplace.

As he waits outside, the resentment he feels over being sloughed off by his employer the night before hardens like the ice on the porch stairs. He finds

Mr. Stratton's mercurial behavior often eccentric and difficult to accept. But he has never been excluded from the arrangements of a business deal before as he has with the offer to purchase the National Park Seminary. He worries that something unknown to him has severed the bond of trust between the two of them. Why else would he lock me out, he frets, as he positions himself in a band of sunlight creeping along the veranda for warmth?

A girl wrapped tightly in wool and fur ascends the stone steps and rushes past him to join the others inside. Soon, the stream of arrivals is steady and Mr. Carter is called upon to repeatedly grin and offer pleasantries, eventually manning the entrance with the aplomb of a Park Avenue doorman. At the end of the parade of chilled students, he is met by Miss Price's bemused expression, her cheeks flush and her eyes sparkling in the unfiltered light of the new day.

"This just won't do, Charles. You are our guest. Come inside immediately and stop coddling the girls. Have you been waiting long? You have, I can tell by looking at your lips and complexion. You are positively blue."

"Good morning, Katharine. I didn't want to create a row by roaming the building unescorted."

"Don't be ridiculous. You are the one who might be in peril," she chides him good-naturedly. "Some of the girls are at the station already with the gifts. Come in and let me introduce you to the students and other chaperones."

Making sure that no one is looking, Mr. Carter takes the cigarette hidden in his cupped hand and rubs it against the back of the nearby copper chimera, flicks it behind the row of shrubbery lining the foundation, and follows the cheerful teacher into the welcomed warmth of the parlor.

The hallways inside Senior House grow crowded as students shuttle to and from the bathrooms and prepare for morning classes. Uniforms are donned and room doors are opened allowing residents to mingle about before heading off to the dining room. Margaret waits inside her room for the others to leave so she can enjoy more privacy to prepare for class. More than the typical morning malaise affects her. She awoke feeling lethargic and sore all over. Her body is warm to the touch and a dull ache throbs along her forehead. A bilious feeling rises and falls inside her stomach making breakfast out of the question. The mere thought of food brings a sour taste to her mouth. Still dressed in her night gown, she sits before the table mirror and studies the puffiness above her cheeks and the thin red capillaries in the corners of the eyes, and then thrusts out her tongue for inspection. An unexpected memory, buried deeply in her psyche, emerges and brings about a bittersweet smile. In the reflected image she makes out the contours of a smaller, rounded face, that of a precocious girl with thin lips and a banner of freckles draped across a button nose. Untamed curls pulled behind slightly protruding ears. It is the face of a headstrong, temperamental girl in the midst of adolescence and ignorant of the complexities of life awaiting her.

She remembers with a flash of passing embarrassment how she used to stare into her mother's oval pearl-lined hand mirror pretending to be a doctor diagnosing a patient of a multitude of imagined ailments and exotic tropical diseases. Both doctor and patient. Twin roles spliced together in the same image, separated by the length of the young girl's willowy arm.

Is it really possible that she played the game alone until time lost meaning? The sensation of her right arm growing weak and unsteady holding the ornate mirror punctuates the recollection.

Margaret's eyes soften and her reflection recedes and she is drawn back to a cherished time of innocence and simplicity, when she roamed the floors of her family's Fall River mansion with inexhaustible delight.

Among her earliest memories is that of waking in the morning and sneaking into her brother's nursery for a glimpse of Frank the Great, the sudden household presence that both she and her mother claimed to be their baby. There she would find her mother rocking in a high-backed chair with Frank wrapped tightly in a blanket and nestled in her arms. She was smitten by her mother's graceful beauty and nurturing ways and the idea that she would have to wait many lifetimes to be like her was unbearable and too much for young Margaret to accept.

"Why must I wait?" she would demand in the dark of her bedroom, her face buried in a twisted pillow. "Why must I wait? It's not fair."

As much as Margaret worshiped her mother, her fascination with motherhood weakened predictably as she grew older. In its place, she became enamored with her physician father and the practice he operated out of the family residence. She idolized the profession of doctor, and the heroic remedies her father was able to prescribe to cure the sick, and dreamed of one day following in his large footsteps.

"Keep out of father's way, Margaret," was her mother's familiar refrain, spoken repeatedly from the day's first appointment to when the gas lamp at the end of the front walk was lit.

She remembers the worn doctor's bag made of black leather with the handle broken at one end. How she came to possess it is a mystery. Had her father given the old bag to her or had she found it among the musty collection of old clothes and oddities stored in the attic? Over time, it came to hold an impressive collection of purloined medical supplies—long yellow tubes, bandage rolls, empty apothecary bottles, even a rubber reflex hammer. Retrieving it from underneath her bed, she would rush down the stairs in the morning, look through the sheer foyer valances, and wait anxiously for the first patient to arrive.

Much to the amusement of many who frequented the general practice of H. Everett Cleary, Margaret would faithfully and with the utmost seriousness play the role of doctor's assistant. She would follow her father about the house swinging the shabby bag and listen intently when her father greeted his patients. She positioned an end table from the family parlor outside the door to the examination room and fashioned an auxiliary clinic replete with medical books borrowed from the study and a green bound ledger showing in meticulous hand the name of each patient, the date they were seen, the clinical diagnosis of illness (based on Margaret's visual assessment of symptoms as a patient was brought in), the charge for treatment, and, in the far-right column, the annotation of "paid" or "collect."

Any annoyance her father felt at being shadowed by his young doctor in training was, for the most part, kept in check, and on more than one occasion during hosted dinners at their home she basked in the glow of his proud expression as she recounted for the assembled guests her knowledge of tongue-twisting medical terms and professed her passion for the power of healing the ill and mending the wounded.

She still cherishes one particular Easter Sunday dinner, when she was seven, standing next to her father at the doorway holding his hand, bidding farewell to their visitors, and how a well-dressed man with a ruddy complexion and bristly moustache bent down and took her face gently in his rough hands and gleefully proclaimed her destiny.

"There is no holding this one back, Everett. She will be the heir to the family practice. Mark my words. She will be the first woman doctor in Fall River."

She recalls how the man's words drilled into her and filled her body with a heavy fortifying weight. She lay awake that night long ago, staring at the ceiling of her room and fanaticizing about the prophesized day, of the good life, just a dream away.

Her devotion to her father's vocation grew more intense from that time forward, and when the family dog would no longer cooperate as a patient, Margaret set her sights on young Frank as a more than satisfactory substitute, which soon prompted stern warnings from her usually implacable and even-tempered mother. When, on a particularly uncomfortable summer afternoon, Margaret was caught pushing her brother in a carriage out the front door to, as she would later explain to her horrified father, treat his asthma by the river, a tipping point had been reached that required stern action.

In the hard wooden chair across from her father she sat, crying and pleading, tears dripping onto the front of her dress, begging him, over and over, until in a spiraling fit of hysteria she could barely breathe. She refused to leave when ordered. She would not let her feet touch the floor until he saw the unfairness, the cruelty of his misguided order, even if it meant she would expire on the very spot.

"Please, father, please," she sobbed repeatedly, his stern, unyielding expression barely visible through the blurry cascade of tears.

"Please, father, please."

Why did he not understand? How could he be so cruel?

"I promise I will leave Frank alone. Why won't you believe me?"

But he refused to yield and waited her out until exhaustion quieted his red-faced girl and she sat staring down at the laces of her shoes dangling before her, occasionally sniffling and wiping the residue of her pain from her eyes.

After a prolonged standoff, the grating sound of her father's chair pushing back away from the desk jolted her out of her melancholy stupor. He took his suit coat off the nearby rack and leaned back against the front of the desk, looking down upon his inconsolable daughter.

"Margaret, before long you will be old enough to understand. Childish games are just that, games. It is time you move on, to something else. There is no place in the world for what you want to be."

He closed the door as he left, leaving Margaret alone and devastated.

INCIDENT AT FOREST GLEN   *177*

Her mother carried her to bed sometime that night and placed her unchanged under the sheets, and when she awoke, the worn black physician's bag was gone. The end table was put back in its proper place. And the green ledger, filled with page upon page of precise records, disappeared, never to be found.

This distant, painful chapter of Margaret's youth would periodically surface in the years to come. In time, the hurt dissipated and she came to view the episode as little more than a juvenile fixation best forgotten. But as much as she wished to relegate her dream of being a doctor to a dusty bin of innocuous remembrances, she couldn't. Simple things would trigger the buried resentment at unpredictable times, such as when reading a passage of her biology text or visiting the school infirmary. Then came the rambling letter last spring from her brother in which he mused about his direction in life and how father was encouraging him to consider the medical profession. Margaret fumed when she read those words, eventually tossing the offending sheets of stationary into the fire. Of course, Frank was too young to remember and couldn't possibly understand how devastating the revelation might be to her, but her father's duplicity gnawed away at her for days until she was nearly frantic with rage.

That very weekend, after the Seminary's annual maypole celebration on the lawn of Edgewood, the dean's residence on the western lip of the campus, a large contingent of boys from Georgetown Preparatory School arrived for a chaperoned dinner dance at Forest Glen. Tables were brought into the ballroom and hosts and guests were randomly assigned in alternating seating to facilitate social interaction.

Margaret sat next to a stunningly handsome boy that bore a remarkable resemblance to a young Douglas Fairbanks. Throughout the evening, his attention toward her grew as he shunned the girl next to him as well as the group conversation around the table. They danced and flirted throughout the evening and the physical space between them narrowed as they drew closer around a shared feeling of attraction. The random coupling looked increasingly promising until, during the service of dessert, the topic of discussion turned, as it always did, to what lie ahead after graduation. As he held forth on his future plans, Margaret listened intently, her seductive brown eyes locked onto the boy's square jaw, devouring every word coming from his smooth, curved lips. Or so the misguided visitor thought at the time.

Enthralled she was, but for a different reason. Listening to his plans, she wondered how often he had spoken them to other girls in the same confident way, and how they most assuredly were captivated to hear that the young man, in addition to being strikingly handsome and wickedly humorous, was on a trajectory of profitability and nobility, as a medical student and then a doctor. But she listened with rapt attention just like the others before her had. And she carefully scrutinized his words and, without showing any outward sign, silently corrected his clumsy pronunciations and mocked his shallow understanding of medical terms she had mastered on her own a decade before. When the boy eventually finished his discourse with a smirk of self-satisfaction, Margaret could no longer contain herself and overcome by the ludicrous, maddening irony of the moment let out a delirious burst of laughter that stunned both of them. It was all she could do to not yield to the desire to take the dessert fork in front of her and use it to point out, for the boy's edification, the names of bones in the human body, beginning with those inside her fingers tightly twisting the napkin on her lap.

Embarrassed and overcome with emotion, Margaret abruptly excused herself from the table and made a quick exit from the ballroom, not stopping until she rushed past a ring of girls congregating outside the hall and into the cool air of the night. Once clear of the others, she began to sob uncontrollably, amid a flurry of newly hatched mayflies hovering above the lawn. She did not return to the ballroom, and to those at the table who witnessed the blatant rudeness toward the likeable young man it only confirmed Margaret's reputation among her fellow Seminary students as being a cruel, heartless and manipulative girl.

In the luminous oval mirror frame, the soft lines of the lost girl's face fade away. The melancholy remembrance gives way to the reality of her own worsening physical condition.

Margaret crawls into bed and curls the down feather pillow beneath her aching neck. This is what I get, she grouses, for riding around in the cold and damp.

She sinks into the warm caress of her sheets and as she drifts off to sleep the image of the boathouse lingers on the edge of her consciousness. The crude, dilapidated building is anchored by thick, gripping vine stalks, and an aura of death surrounds it.

Is she walking toward it, or is it coming to her?

The hunched form of a man emerges from inside the black portal looking down at his feet, his skin is bloodless and pale, his clothes ripped and soiled. With each step he draws closer, dragging something cumbersome along the ground at his side. Just as his menacing features come into focus, fatigue prevails and extinguishes the flickering light, and Margaret descends to a deep impenetrable plateau where the memories that haunt her cannot reach.

The electric trolley carrying the group to Walter Reed leaves the terminus station at the post office road on the feeder line heading toward Woodside and the transfer point to the main track at Georgia Avenue. A middle interior aisle bisects ten rows of forward-facing wooden benches capable of being unlocked and pushed to the opposite direction, if desired, for the return journey. Every seat is claimed by chaperones and students representing each of the campus sororities. In the front row, seated behind the conductor, Mr. Carter sits shoulder to shoulder with Miss Price, extremely distracted. He nods and occasionally concurs as the talkative teacher points out sights and markers along the way, trying not to give any indication of his divided attention. As he maintains this façade of engagement, he recreates in his mind the surprising development minutes earlier at the station before the group boarded for the trip to the hospital, trying to savor the still-fresh moment before its vividness slips away.

He recounts leaving Vincent Hall with the group and walking briskly across the foot bridge. The wind was biting and made conversation along the way impracticable. As they hurried into the sheltering, wood-shingled Baltimore & Ohio station, he had to wrestle the door close in order to keep the swirling gust at bay. On the far bench, a smaller group of students were waiting with the assembled gift bags.

Was she the second or third girl Miss Price introduced? It happened so fast. How exactly did she look at him for those brief few seconds, when he gently took her hand into his when they met? She smiled slightly, he remembers. Yes, she smiled. And the words? Think, what were the words? Their order. Exactly.

Miss Price continues to speak loudly to be heard above the streetcar noise making it difficult for him to reconstruct the scene and its details in his mind. The introduction at the station was much calmer, almost serene. Mr.

Carter turns to the window, pretending to look at the passing scenery, and closes his eyes momentarily trying to visualize the moment—the moment his wish from the night before, while standing on the balcony overlooking the ballroom floor, was miraculously granted.

"And this is Miss Josephine Barnes, one of our senior girls representing Theta clubhouse. Josephine, this is Mr. Charles Carter, our guest for the day from New York City."

"Welcome, Mr. Carter. It is a pleasure to meet you."

Simple and direct. Polite yet warm.

When he helped load the gift bags onto the trolley, he lost her in the commotion inside the car until Miss Price motioned for him to join her in the front and he turned and saw her sitting against the window in the row directly behind them. Her eyebrows arched and again she smiled, this time in pretend surprise, a private communication between the two of them.

Josephine Barnes. His school boy obsession had a name. Josephine Barnes.

The streetcar shakes stiffly on a patch of uneven track cutting through the early morning chill and he strains to discern her voice in the noise of multiple conversations behind him. Thick gray clouds start to fill the sky and the wind whistles in the small gaps between the trolley's windows and roof as the car dips under a soot-stained railroad overpass and slowly climbs on its journey toward the District line.

Miss Price leans over in order to speak privately.

"If Mr. Stratton's offer is accepted, Charles, I want to make myself available to him and to you as someone you can consult with—confidentially, of course—on any administrative or staff matter related to the school. I understand there has been a commitment made to the dean to maintain current operations, but there may come a point in time when there is a need to evaluate whether the Seminary is truly realizing its potential and, if not, what changes should be made to correct its deficiencies. I want you to know that I can provide valuable insights in this regard."

"You surprise me, Katharine," he says peering discretely over his shoulder.

"If there are to be changes, I can help. There is no reason to feel *surprised.*"

"Should there be? Should there be changes?"

"In my professional opinion, yes," her last word, trailing off in a whisper.

"Interesting. You seem have given this question some thought."

"I am saying this now, not knowing if another or better opportunity will present itself for us to speak alone. But I can, if you wish."

The flustered guest gulps and considers how to respond.

"Is that what you desire?" the words nearly burn his tongue, "To meet alone?"

The streetcar bucks and rattles and two girls in the back row let out an involuntary squeal. He feels the warmth of Miss Price's hip casually slide up against his as she leans closer.

"I can be of service to you and Mr. Stratton in making our school into a world class institution. The Seminary staff, as currently comprised, cannot achieve that goal. Some changes, limited and specific, need to be made. I say this as an objective observer working here for the past couple of years."

"Changes among the staff?"

"Yes."

"I see," he responds with a nod of acknowledgement.

The conductor calls out that they will be arriving at the transfer junction soon and the girls began to rustle about and button their coats.

"Perhaps we can talk some more on the ride back to the school, Katharine. But can you to clarify something you said just now, in the beginning? You mentioned a commitment made to Dean Dawson. What were you referring to?"

"He has told me and some of the others in the know about the offer that he will continue to lead the school and control day-to-day operations if the deal is consummated."

"Of course," Mr. Carter mumbles unconvincingly as Miss Price stands and turns to face the back rows.

"All right, girls, our station is coming up. We should be at Walter Reed shortly," she announces.

When the conductor suddenly applies the brake, the trolley lurches forward and the regent's gloved hand comes to rest lightly on Mr. Carter's shoulder for balance, an innocent act that Josephine seated inches away cannot avoid noticing.

182 ANDY JOHNSON

Dingy and tattered decorations hang from the papered walls inside the entrance to Walter Reed General Hospital. Stern-faced doctors and beleaguered nurses move about, carrying on muted conversations, their footsteps echoing in the foyer. As the girls and their chaperones, gift bags in tow, are led down a dimly lit hallway by the hospital staff, an overpowering, inescapable, antiseptic stench greets them and numbs their nostrils and brings about light-headedness in some of the girls not accustom to the smell.

Over the three years since Armistice Day, the number of patients at Walter Reed has steadily dwindled as the maimed and the shell-shocked, the amputees and the blinded, the wounded remnants of the American Expeditionary Force vanguard were treated, rehabilitated, and eventually discharged to hometowns that no longer held victory parades and to families that struggled to recognize the person they once knew in the body and mind returned to them. Many of those remaining at the hospital are long-term patients requiring constant care and who will likely never leave the main hospital and the narrow wards that encircle it. Among these are the truly forsaken, men so grievously injured they hover precariously above their own mortality in a partial state of existence, some incapable of again feeling the touch or recognizing the voice of a loved one.

As the somber contingent pass a treatment room, a low, sonorous moan comes from behind a shielding white partition. Down the hallway, a man lets out a piercing shriek and then falls silent. Mr. Carter lags at the back of the group, growing more anxious as they pass one room after another of segregated patients. He peers into an open door and glimpses a man lying motionless on a bed staring up at the ceiling, brown leather restraints pulled tightly across his chest and legs. His glassy eyes are hooded and vacant.

At the end of the corridor, they reach an expansive ward filled with rows of beds evenly spaced on a bare tiled floor. The drafty hall is spartan and colorless. Drab curtains hang from the windows and bare walls, painted a muted ivory, surround the men in a sedate, dulling emptiness. The chaperones split the girls into smaller groups and they quietly approach each row of beds. Some of men rise up when the girls arrive. Other, more ambulatory patients sit in chairs or steady themselves on wooden crutches and wait their turn. Many are either asleep or unable to do more than turn their heads to check out the cause of the sudden disturbance in the ward.

Working in pairs, the girls go to each bed in turn, wishing the wounded soldiers a merry Christmas and offering comforting thoughts. Some ask the men their names and where they are from and then move on, while others linger at the bedside and engage in more personal exchanges. A single wrapped gift adorned with a fresh sprig of holly is handed to each man or, if necessary, placed on the bed sheets to be opened later.

Mr. Carter paces up and down the long aisles marveling at the tenderness of the girls in ministering to the horribly damaged men. Despite the chilliness of the building, he is uncomfortably warm and beads of sweat form along his brow and above his lip as he moves around the ward. Many of the faces are those of men his age and bear the scars of battle that he so deliberately avoided. He feels self-conscious as he walks about. The simple act of his legs stepping across the linoleum, effortlessly and painlessly, summons a wave of almost unbearable shame. He looks down on one bed and sees the cleaved torso of a heavily bandaged man, his ribs and hip along one side obliterated. Flustered and unnerved, he slips his hands in his pockets and walks on, trying to avoid looking at the desecrated flesh as he moves through the gauntlet of the tormented souls.

The reluctant participant knew the trip to the hospital would be difficult when he was volunteered by his boss the night before. But he had no choice. And he decided he would play only a supporting role in the whole affair and stay off to the side. He prepared himself for uncomfortable moments, and he knew some of what he saw might be hard to take. But this is different. This is more than he bargained for. This is his living nightmare.

He feels their accusatory eyes all around him, their silent stares judging him as he passes. One man struggles up on elbows and tries to speak to the wandering stranger but he does not respond, paralyzed by his growing panic. When he reaches the end of the row, he looks about for a door or hallway to escape the ward, but there is none. He's trapped and realizes he will need to double back the same direction he came in order to leave.

"Henry," a strong voice calls out behind him.

Mr. Carter turns to see a man in a wheelchair, pushed by a hospital corpsman, coming toward him.

"Henry. It's you."

The war wound is visible along his crown, bordered by irregularly shaped patches of closely cropped hair. The man blossoms with delight as he is pushed nearer. His intense eyes burn with anticipation.

"Henry Babcock. It is you," he marvels. "How in hell did you find me? The last time I saw you, you were covered in mud and looking scared like you were going to soil your pants. I can't believe it is you, after all these years."

Mr. Carter, taken aback, glances at the corpsman for help, but the man's attention is focused on the young women in blue uniforms who have infiltrated the ward.

"Henry, what did you bring me? Did you bring me something good? You still owe me, you know. You owe me from what I lent you back at Belleau Wood. What do you have for your friend? God, it's good to see you."

The man reaches back and taps the arm of the orderly who pushes the chair closer. He gives Mr. Carter the once-over.

"You look good," he says with a begrudging tone. "A lot better than me," he says, gingerly running his fingers across the purple ridge along his scalp. "There are a couple of others from the 23rd Infantry around this place. They come and go. Even saw that bastard Lieutenant Shipley come through here once. Can you believe it? The son of a bitch made it through too."

"I'm sorry," the bewildered visitor stammers. "You have me confused with someone else. I am not the person you think I am."

The wounded veteran stares back with a perplexed look. His eyes squint and then he shakes his head violently to one side.

"You always were the wise guy of the group. I remember..." he says with a knowing look, shaking his finger at Mr. Carter. "We've spilled blood together, Henry," his voice now agitated. "We've been to hell and back together. To hell and back. So don't play your games. It's been too long. Too long."

"Look, I am not your friend Henry. I didn't mean to upset you. I am sorry. Perhaps I bear some resemblance to him."

"Then who are you?!" the man demands.

The orderly places a hand on the patient's shoulder to calm him, but makes no attempt to resolve the confusion.

"Tell me who you are! What business do you have here pretending to be Henry Babcock!!?"

"My name is Charles Carter. I am here with the others from the National Park Seminary."

"There was a gunnery sergeant in our unit named Carter. Is that you?"

"No. I apologize for the confusion. I should be leaving.

"Then who are you? How do I know you? I know everyone here."

The man lifts his head back toward the orderly.

"Is this Henry Babcock or not? Can't anyone give me a straight answer?"

"Maybe we will see him later, sir," the distracted man politely dismisses the question.

"I am truly sorry, but I must go now."

"Wait," the soldier protests, leaning forward and grabbing Mr. Carter's wrist with surprising strength. "What did you bring me?"

"Relax, sir. Let him go. Now!" the corpsman commands as he pulls the wheelchair backwards in an attempt to break the hold.

Too stunned to react, Mr. Carter is immobilized by the man's fierce grip. He feels the soldier's fingers tighten and pull at the fabric of his suit coat, as the corpsman struggles with the handles of the chair. In the tussle, the businessman is yanked forward and loses his balance, and just before he topples over, the confused veteran releases his hold and turns his attention away from his stunned captive.

A soft voice, filled with cheer, brings the scuffle to an abrupt end.

"We have plenty of gifts to go around. But this one here is especially for you."

Off to the side, positioned behind Mr. Carter, Josephine stands clutching a package to her stomach, smiling down at the agitated man. A second, much taller student that Mr. Carter met at the train station is standing next to her.

"I wrapped it myself. And I think it would be perfect for you."

Josephine brushes past Mr. Carter and kneels down so that she is at eye-level with the pacified patient.

"My name is Josephine and this is Jennie. We are students from a school not far from here. Has anyone told you why we are here?"

The man shakes his head and straightens up in the wheelchair.

"We have come to show our thanks to heroes like you, brave men who fought in the war. That is you, right?"

The man nods, captivated by the young women.

"But let me make sure that I have the right package and that there hasn't been a switch."

Josephine lifts the tag tied to the ribbon and turns it over. Her eyes narrow and she frowns with concern.

186 ANDY JOHNSON

"Hmmm. I may have made a mistake," she says, pensively studying the brown slip. "Are you Sergeant Major Jonathan Miller?"

"Yes, yes. I am Sergeant Major Miller," he answers excitedly, "That's my name."

"Hmmm. Good. Perhaps there is no mistake after all. But the gift is a special one, so I need to be sure. The name Miller is rather common, after all."

Josephine's blue eyes dance playfully back to the tag and then to the eager face seated before her.

"A question or two will resolve it, I think. Is your hometown in Vermont?"

"Yes, yes, Traylor's Bridge. In Vermont."

"And what is the one thing you liked to do as a young man in Traylor's Bridge, more than anything else? What was the one thing that brought you the greatest happiness?"

The soldier searches his memory as Mr. Carter, the corpsman, and Jennie look on. As he moves about his seat, his emaciated, lifeless legs shift from one side of the chair to the other.

"Skate," he blurts out with satisfaction, "I skated on the canals and the lakes. I skated wherever and whenever I could."

"And why did skating make you happy, Sergeant Major?"

"I was fast. Faster than anyone else in the town. And when I went fast, it was like I was shot out of a cannon, whizzing along like a hawk running down a mouse in the field."

"Wasn't it cold skating so fast in the winter in Vermont?"

"My face would turn blue and my cheeks would freeze and my eyes would water, but I wouldn't stop. I'd skate for hours until nightfall. And then after dinner, my friends and I would build fires on the banks of the lake and we would skate some more under the stars until our legs ached and our lungs burned."

The fond recollection causes the soldier to drift away in thought. Josephine rubs her hand along his arm to bring him back.

"And it was on such a winter's night, wasn't it, that something very special happened. Do you remember that too?"

He pauses and then nods. Looking down, he wipes his hand across his eyes and draws a deep breath.

"You don't expect me to talk about it with all these strangers about, do you?" he protests in a wavering voice.

Josephine smiles and places the gift on his lap.

"Merry Christmas, Mr. Jonathan Miller of Traylor's Bridge, Vermont."

Overcome by emotion, he pulls away the paper wrap and inside the box finds a pair of winter gloves and a knitted scarf.

"I thought you could wear them on your next trip outside. Perhaps you wore similar ones on those days at the lake."

"Yes. Thank you," he mumbles, his head still tilted downward, ashamed of his weeping.

Josephine rises and rejoins Jennie and together they walk back to the unfinished row of patients they had left in order to calm the commotion.

Mr. Carter, thoroughly beguiled by the girl's deft intervention, watches the corpsman slowly push the subdued soldier along the ward, mystified by what he has just witnessed. Following the momentary lapse, he follows, hoping to catch up with his savior before she reaches the next patient. One of the school chaperones, matronly and severe in her demeanor, intercepts Mr. Carter and halts his pursuit.

"I saw how that man accosted you. I saw it all from over there. Are you all right?"

"Of course. It's nothing really."

"He practically attacked you. I've never seen that happen before, and I've visited here plenty of times."

"He was confused, that's all."

Mr. Carter smoothes his suit jacket and tries to politely extract himself away from the woman.

"Oh dear boy," she exclaims with maternal instinct, "your hand—it's bleeding."

He turns his hand around and sees that the tussle with the man in the wheelchair has left a shallow scrape mark near his wrist, so superficial he hadn't felt it in the aftermath. The chaperone springs to action and pulls a handkerchief from her purse and places it on the wound with the gentleness usually reserved for treating a little boy's scraped knee.

"Oh, yes, this will help. Why don't you press this against your hand and I will go and get one of the nurses."

"Really, there's no need."

188 ANDY JOHNSON

Embarrassed by the chaperone's fawning attention, Mr. Carter dabs the wound repeatedly and shows the woman the faint pink stain.

"See, it's stopped. Let's not alarm folks unnecessarily."

"No bother, we are in a hospital after all."

"Please, I prefer that you not create a fuss."

But it's too late. Miss Price walks over to investigate what is going on and after being given a blow-by-blow account of the assault by the chaperone she protectively leads Mr. Carter around the ward, using the opportunity to comment on the other charitable work carried out by the girls throughout the year. They are soon joined by another chaperone and a hospital doctor who provides a narrative of the patients' conditions as they move about overseeing the students distributing their gifts.

The presence of the students has brought the sedate ward to life. Supine bodies stir. The sound of laughter warms the cavernous room. For a brief interlude, the grim monotony of daily life among the patients is broken by the appearance of fresh faces and an air of the unexpected. The girls from the Seminary go from bed to bed heralding an end to their solitude of existence, living embodiments of those now lost to them.

He feels the weight of the girl seated at the end of his bed.

He breathes in the lingering scent of exotic perfume left on the pillow.

He feels her comforting touch across the card table.

He drinks in the sweet voice and tender words.

He devours the stories of life beyond the walls, and thrills at news about his hometown.

He is spellbound by the curves of youth, the affirming allure of unmarred flesh and the female form.

He smiles uncontrollably when she laughs.

He drapes a blanket over his wound and nervously runs his fingers through his matted hair as she draws nearer.

He watches when she leaves, and wonders how long will it be before another like her comes again.

Some tell the girls. Some think it to themselves. Others still can only passively look at the stranger next to them and struggle to understand by what magical force ghosts of their past have been summoned. They are sisters. They are friends. They are wives. They are lovers. And then they are gone, leaving a gift and the bittersweet taste of remembrance behind.

INCIDENT AT FOREST GLEN *189*

Mr. Carter notices Josephine's partner standing next to two other girls at the front of the ward holding a bag laden with the remaining gifts. She is clearly distressed and one of the girls has her arm around Jennie's waist and is resting her head on her shoulder for comfort. Josephine is nowhere to be seen. He excuses himself from the group and walks toward the cluster of students before Miss Price can speak up. Slowing as he approaches, he looks at the patient stations to the left and right pretending not to be aware of the three girls as he passes by.

"I couldn't do it. I simply couldn't. I'm embarrassed to admit it, but I was repulsed," he hears Jennie whisper, shaking her head.

"There, there. I can be difficult. Everyone feels it. I remember my first trip..."

Just ahead, he sees the reason for young Jennie's distress.

In a forgotten corner of the ward, separated from the neatly aligned rows of patient beds, a triangle partition made of white cotton cloth and metal rods hangs over a bed masking a still head. He can see the outline of a slight, incomplete, grievously wounded man under the tightly fitted sheet. An elaborate network of thin tubes runs along the side of the bed carrying fluids to and from the motionless patient. In a chair next to a table lamp, Josephine sits, as if posing for a painting, neither speaking nor moving, her body bathed in a golden light. Her hand rests on the bed sheet, her fingers intertwined with the man's curled and scarlet appendages.

Mr. Carter pauses at a distance and thinks twice about encroaching on the moment. Josephine, unaware that she is being watched, looks down on the man's shielded face and tenderly cradles the severely burned flesh in silence. Her demeanor is calm as she reflects on the painful existence imprisoning the sedated soldier. She closes her eyes and shuts out the sounds of conversations reverberating about the cavernous ward. Her heartbeat slows. Her breathing becomes measured and she presses slightly on the badly mangled hand.

Smooth fingers run along scarred skin, carefully probing the patchwork of purple and brown and red for the tell-tale sign of life. There, behind the thick, coarse surface of dead flesh, she finds it—a pulse, faint and distant. She breathes out and focuses on the sensation at her finger tips, slowing her breathing even further. She feels the man's pulse grow stronger, like that of a trapped miner rhythmically signaling his existence beneath an impenetrable sarcophagus of dirt and stone. In the blackness of her mind's eye, she connects with the forsaken soldier. She draws a deep breath and quietly exhales. Her heartbeat grows even more deliberate while his quickens. Her thumb rubs along the man's emaciated wrist. Back and forth. Summoning him. Waking him to her touch. The gap closes as the seconds pass, one racing to catch up with the other, until their pulses synchronize for a few beats.

I have found you.

Here is the true man. Here is the real person behind the surgical veil.

Do you remember me? Do you remember the feel of my touch?

Perhaps it's been too long.

A minute passes as the two communicate in their private sanctuary. And then the soldier's pulse begins to weaken until it returns to the sluggish rhythm of before. The silent connection between them drifts off into a narcotic cloud of nothingness.

Josephine recites the Lord's Prayer and then carefully slips her fingers from the maimed soldier's hand.

The sounds of the others in the ward around her grow louder and she slowly opens her eyes to find the solitary man from New York standing before.

While others might have reacted to his stare by turning away, that is not Josephine's nature. She meets his look unflinchingly. He is the one who eventually breaks away, embarrassed by his intrusion on the intimate exchange.

As she slowly walks over to rejoin Jennie and the others, Mr. Carter turns back around and hesitantly approaches her, conflicted as to the wisdom of what he is about to do, unsure about what to say.

When his courage falters and he is about to walk away a second time, it is the self-assured student who throws him a line.

"Is this your first time in a military hospital?"

He nods, as she walks over to where he stands.

"It was hard for me to handle the first time too."

"You could have fooled me. You are so natural around the patients."

"That's kind of you to say."

The somber reflection Josephine felt leaving the bed begins to melt away.

"Miss Barnes. May I speak with you for a moment? Charles Carter. We met earlier at the station."

"Of course, I remember. Miss Price's gentleman friend."

"I wanted to tell you that I am grateful for the way you extracted me out of the situation a few minutes ago, you know, with the man in the wheelchair. I have to admit that I was at a loss as to what to do."

"You would have thought of something, I'm sure. But, you are welcome, Mr. Carter."

"But how? How did you know so much about him? I was absolutely captivated by how disarming you were. One moment he was accosting me and the next he was practically eating out of a stranger's hand."

"It was nothing really."

"You're being modest. You must tell me how you did it, and if you don't, I will hound you until you confess your secret."

The heartfelt entreaty produces an appreciative smile and she glances over to see Jennie occupied with the others.

"There is no secret. And Sergeant Major Miller is no stranger. I met him my first year at the Seminary with my mentor from Theta. The experience was overwhelming to say the least. He scared me at first and he went on about how he reminded me of his cousin and spoke about other people I didn't know, just as he did with you. And when we left to go back to the school that day I kept wondering about his lucidity and how awful it must be for him here, to be ignored because of his madness. The next year, I begged one of the club sisters to take her place because I wanted to see if he was still here. I hoped he wasn't, you understand, but if he was, I had this plan to learn more about him, even if it meant playing along and pretending to be his cousin."

"And did you?"

"No. When he saw me the next year, I was a different person all together to him. But I persevered. I became whomever he wanted to be in order to gain his confidence. I learned much about him and then the next Christmas visit I learned even more. He trusted me enough to tell me where he grew up, about his childhood, his memories—"

"The war?"

Josephine shakes her head.

"I learned to steer away from the war and how he came to be here. He would grow belligerent and harder to reach when he talked about the fighting. But mostly, I wanted him to think of earlier days, more innocent times, when he was carefree and happy."

"Like the skating."

"He has enough time to wrestle with the demons of the war. For one day out of three-hundred and sixty-five I want him to believe that it never happened."

"Of course. Of course. You are impressively perceptive. It seems ingrained in your nature. I suspect you've done more good with the man in your short time here than all the doctors and corpsmen running about the place."

She blushes and deflects the compliment with a remark about the other girls in the visiting party. An awkward moment of silence comes between them. He knows their time together alone is running out.

"At the risk of crossing the line of patient confidentiality, as it were, what were you asking him to recall that moved him so at the end—something about a special happening on a winter's night?"

Josephine looks away at the wheelchair rolling down the far row of convalescing men.

"That our little secret," she teasingly shuts the door. "I know if I can get him to recall it, he is back and living in a moment that has meaning to him."

"You are not only perceptive, Miss Barnes, but mysterious too."

"Mysterious? I am not the one who suddenly shows up and joins our little trip, Mr. Carter," Josephine fires back cheekily, her blue eyes tugging playfully at his heart. "You should know there is a lot of talk among the girls as to why you are here. You've already told me the care of the sick is not your business."

"Truthfully, I find it extremely difficult being here. It reminds me as well of something I thought I had left in my past."

"And what would that be, Mr. Carter?"

"It too is best left a mystery for now. Let's just say that I am at Forest Glen with my employer on business. We are staying at Glen Manor through the end of the week."

"I see."

"And what is this gossip among your fellow students?" he asks in a conspiratorial whisper. "What am I being accused of exactly? You can tell me before they come over."

"Isn't it obvious? What else would school girls talk about when their unmarried teacher shows up with an unfamiliar man by her side?"

Josephine's verbal dart pops his balloon of composure and he is suddenly at a loss for words.

"On cue, here comes Miss Price now. I should join the others and hand out the rest of the presents. Thank you, Mr. Carter, for your kind remarks. Perhaps I should consider becoming a nurse after graduation. It may be the calling I am searching for."

Had time allowed and Josephine not excused herself so abruptly, Mr. Carter would have pulled himself together and been tempted to tell the captivating girl the story of another student of similar circumstances who followed such a path. He had never met her but as he watches Josephine walk away he cannot help but wonder if Elizabeth Stratton moved among her peers with such a becoming presence, also struggling to find her proper place in an increasingly chaotic world.

As the alluring young woman rejoins her partner and they head off to greet the anxiously waiting patients, the hook that pierced Mr. Carter's skin only the night before works its way deeper into his flesh.

"There you are," the regent calls out to him. "What's troubling you? You look as if you saw a ghost."

By the time the group finishes and emerges from Walter Reed Hospital, the sky is steely gray with billowy clouds and a punishing wind is blowing from the north. The girls huddle together in a tight circle at the trolley stop and struggle to hold onto their hats and push down the hem of their coats as the swirling gusts buffet them. Once on board the streetcar, they laugh in amusement at their ordeal and bring order to disheveled locks.

Mr. Carter joins Miss Price and the other school chaperones in the back rows of the car this time, away from the frivolity and animated conversations of the students. The worsening weather rocks the trolley and slows its progress along the gradual climb back out of the city and soon the row houses and storefronts bordering the tracks give way to thickets of small trees and untamed brush and acres of vacant land scored by rutted dirt roads.

Stray ice pellets strike the windshield as the car crests a hill and grow in intensity as they move northward. A violent downward push of air brings a thick wave of fat flakes that envelope the trolley and within minutes the surrounding fields are frosted white. Exclamations of delight at the dramatic turn in the weather and the season's first snowfall fill the car. The sky turns black as the squall continues to gain strength and obscures the view out of the side windows.

From her seat near the front Josephine rests her temple against the cold glass, alone with her thoughts, and wipes away the condensation with increasing circles of her gloved hand. Jennie, seated next to her, leans across the aisle and describes in meticulous detail the dress she bought recently from Woodward & Lothrop's to the girls from Delta house. A black wrought iron fence, barely visible through the snow, rushes past the window, parallel to the tracks, soon followed by an imposing gate topped with a gold painted crest. Beyond the barrier, headstones and statues and mausoleums dot the white-washed hillside.

As the pale, colorless landscape passes, Josephine reflects on Leah's eroding emotional state and how it has disrupted the normally harmonious and enjoyable end to the semester. Weighing more heavily still is Margaret's confession about the trauma she endured at the boathouse and on the frightful ride through the woods. Her friend is not prone to such abstract feelings and when she told Josephine of the nightmarish fear she felt on the morning ride it was genuine and deeply troubling. But is she right, Josephine wonders, staring past the fogged glass? Is it explained away so simply, that Leah is the problem? A girl in the free-fall of mental distress. On the verge of an emotional breakdown. How could it happen so suddenly, without any outward signs of warning?

Leah outside the Spanish Mission, alone in the night, spying on them from behind Peeping Tom. Leah running off at the boathouse. Leah stepping out from behind the shed, dazed and expressionless.

The trolley pushes on, past the field thick with concrete stones and marble monuments. The snowfall is heavier now and begins to blanket the streets and trees and stick to the sides of the telephone poles.

Josephine remembers with an involuntary tremor Leah's blank expression the previous evening in her room when she lifted her hair and revealed the mark of a savage blow along her forehead. At that moment, the girl didn't act peculiar or addled. To the contrary, her words were sharp and spoken pointedly, with an almost hostile and cutting frankness. This is the way she had been outside the clubhouse, so whatever happened to her while she was separated from her and Margaret on the ride had not changed her already curious temperament.

Josephine again rubs away a small opening in the creeping condensation and marvels at how quickly the landscape has been coated with a layer of winter white. Through the scratched out portal to the outside world, she makes out the blurred outline of figure in the cemetery, lying on a granite pedestal, just past the fence line. For a fleeting moment, her mind fools her into thinking the lifelike sculpture, with its finely carved facial lines and sinewy features, is animate. The memorial is that of a woman in repose, her face twisted into unmistakable melancholy under a rippling shroud, her hand, palm straight and opened, raised high above her head. The enigmatic gesture puzzles her. A hand beckoning back a loved one from the grave? Perhaps a protest against the approach of death? Or is the outstretched arm a warning to those who view it?

The trolley abruptly veers to the left and follows a westward spur away from the receding monument. Josephine turns and watches as the solitary figure, green from oxidation, slowly disappears behind a window streaked with melted snowflakes. Facing toward the rear of the car, she catches a glance of Miss Price seated next to the visitor from New York City, the man who she twice crossed paths with at the hospital. The encounters were anything but perfunctory, however. She could tell by the way he looked at her in the station and then at the patient ward that his interest in her was more than passing. She can't deny to herself that she not only appreciated the attention but sought it. Their exchanges, though brief, secretly thrilled her and that fact is as undeniable as it is troubling. If a complete stranger could so easily elicit such an emotional reaction, what did it say about her relationship with Robert?

Watching the teacher speak to him with that earnest expression of hers makes Josephine recall the lecture she received in her office earlier in the week. The sting of the rebuke remains. As much as she accepts her own shortcomings in what took place at the glen, she feels the regent rushed to make her the scapegoat just to placate May King's emotional protest. She watches as Miss Price continues with her one-sided conversation in the rear of the car. The unpleasant memory of their office confrontation is quickly chased away as Mr. Carter's indifferent expression and wandering eyes brings a smile to her face.

Jennie leans over and catches Josephine looking toward the back row.

"He's handsome, don't you think?" she says privately. "I think our fair teacher is quite taken with our surprising guest."

"Perhaps."

"Most definitely, I say. So I've heard from the others. What do you say?"

"About the two of them?"

"No. About my dress for Saturday's dance. Where have you been? Do you think I was right to buy the one I did or should I have gone with something white, more traditional? The others think it is too dramatic or some such nonsense. I just think a white dress is too plain for the occasion."

You remember, the white dress.

The white dress. Miss Price asked about it in her office.

You remember, the white dress.

She recalls Margaret's words from their talk in Leah's room. Leah hadn't been the same since, she said.

The dress you pulled from the creek. What became of it?

Left behind at the glen, it had disappeared, the regent told her.

Josephine offers up a supportive yet vague opinion to the exuberant girl, and then turns back to the cool relief of the window, only to find that opaque film of moisture has returned and reclaimed the opening.

The streetcar's mid-day arrival at Forest Glen is monitored closely from the window of a musty office in Miller Library. Surrounded on all sides by uniform shelves filled with rarely disturbed books, Mrs. Martin stands sipping tea and watching the brown paneled car through the thick snow as it slows to the station and unloads. Outside the prefect's office, a handful of students lounge in leather upholstered chairs reading as others meander along the mezzanine level perusing the first editions and delicately bound antiquities bequeathed to the school at the turn of the century by a prominent university professor and frequent instructor at National Park Seminary.

Mrs. Martin scans the group at the distant station with the sharp, discerning eye and meticulously identifies each of the heavily cloaked travelers. She is intrigued as Miss Price lingers on the platform with Mr. Carter while the other chaperones lead the students across the footbridge traversing the glen. The two talk for a minute or so and then part ways. Not a casual farewell, she surmises, as she follows Miss Price hurrying along to catch up with the rest of the group. She seethes at the idea that this young interloper, little more than two years at the school, has insinuated herself into a place of favor with Dean Dawson, and, in the process, leapfrogged the prefect as his senior advisor on important scholastic matters. For the dean to turn to Miss Price to hold the hand of the New Yorkers during their stay is a personal affront to her and sows more seeds of doubt about the changes afoot.

From her protected vantage point, she watches Mr. Stratton's assistant lower his head and push through the swirling snow toward Glen Manor and speculates about the role the young man will play in the operation of the school if the sale is finalized. As he reaches the hotel entrance, he is greeted by a man departing the building. They shake hands under the porch awning and Mrs. Martin instantly recognizes the wide-brimmed gray hat of the second man.

"Well, well," she says to herself, "this has just become a lot more interesting."

Placing the tea cup on her desk, she grabs her coat and hat from the hall closet and marches through the library's main reading room without saying a word and then leaves through the curved stone entryway.

Members of the hospital delegation return to Vincent Hall and shake the snow from their shoulders on the veranda and then head off to warm themselves around the fireplace in the Empire parlor before lunch is served. Special delivery letters from the morning post are arrayed along the counter top of the reception desk and Josephine finds a light brown envelope addressed to her in a familiar hand. She finds a seat in the parlor away from the others before opening it.

My dearest Jo,

I write these words a prisoner of an unfeeling and ruthless jailer. Day after day of rain has turned the Academy into a quagmire and forced us to sandbag along the river. All sailing has been canceled for over a week. The abysmal weather has done nothing to extinguish my enthusiasm about this Saturday however. I will arrive in Washington mid-afternoon, collect Caleb, and head to your school. I can only hope the depressing conditions have not set off our mutual friend. Caleb is a somewhat reluctant participant in the arrangement, so any assistance you can provide in keeping her disposition cheerful and her tongue in check would be helpful. Enough of such trifling worries. I am counting the hours down to when we meet again and when I have you all to myself, if only for one evening. I miss you dearly and think constantly about the time I will again hold you in my arms. We have much to talk about, so consider your dance card filled!

With enduring love, Robert

198 Andy Johnson

Josephine slips the note into her uniform pocket and sidles up to the others next to the fireplace. Surprisingly, the letter from Annapolis and Robert's affectionate expressions do not move her as she expects. Perhaps it is fatigue from the trip or preoccupation with Leah's worsening condition. Regardless, she leans in closer toward the fire and thinks warmly of how nice it will be when he arrives and she can jettison all else that encumbers her thoughts and suppresses her passion.

A servant enters the parlor carrying cups of heated cider on a silver tray and the chilled girls sip the cinnamon and spice ambrosia and gaze at the burning logs as they pop and sizzle.

Mr. Geary briskly walks into his office, opens his desk drawer, slips a sheet of paper inside a folder, and closes it. He takes a ledger off the desktop and within seconds loses himself in the columns of numbers and accounting annotations before him, mindlessly tapping the end of a letter opener against the desktop. He pauses and glances up at the glass paper weight in front him, just as a contorted image slides from one side of the half-globe to the other. With a suppressed gasp, he flinches backward in his chair as a hidden presence suddenly emerges from the shadowy corner of the room.

"What in God's name—Charlotte, why are you skulking about my office?! You scared me half to death."

A self-satisfied smirk appears on the prefect's face as she approaches the desk.

"You need to get your nose out those books and pay attention to what's happening around you, George. I'm sorry for giving you a start though. I came looking for you and thought maybe you were off to lunch, so I thought I would wait for a few minutes. If you don't mind a few words of unsolicited advice, that secretary of yours is worthless. She didn't know where you were or when you would be back."

"Lower you voice," he says, rushing to close the door and contain the spread of her uncharitable assessment to the outer office.

"Always worried about causing waves, aren't you?"

"I find it a more present challenge *containing* waves rather than *causing* them," he retorts, returning to his desk. "What could possibly be so urgent to get you to leave your fortress of folios and dusty reference books, especially on a morning like this? Come on, what is it? I have work to do. I don't have much time to spare. What have you come to discuss?"

"Your job," she says flatly, running her finger along the sharp edge of his walnut desk.

"My job?"

The bursar places the letter opener on the blotter and closes the ledger book.

"What's this about, Charlotte?"

"Good. I have your attention now," she continues, pacing back and forth in front of the desk. "Information has come to my attention that leads me to believe that Douglas Stratton's purchase of the school is not as it is being portrayed to us. I suspect that we aren't being told the full story of what will happen once the sale goes through. I don't believe for a moment that Dean Dawson is being straight with us. He is sugarcoating the deal."

"Wait, wait. Slow down. What makes you say this? What is this information you talk about?"

"No, please don't sit there, George, and tell me you swallowed that claptrap the dean was offering up last night."

"Yes, I believe him, and why shouldn't I? This school has been bought and sold twice before. And yet you see some sinister motive in Stratton's decision to purchase it now. I cannot think of anything more expected or in the ordinary. It is the natural course of business. Something you seem to struggle to understand. National Park Seminary is a profitable enterprise. Our financial portfolio and our capital to debt ratio are sound. Enrollment is up and demand is increasing."

As the bursar continues, Mrs. Martin rudely turns away and walks around the office and looks over the multitude of certificates and photographs hanging on the walls.

"Therefore, it is not surprising Douglas Stratton would look upon the school as a sound investment. Look Charlotte, these matters don't involve us—you said so yourself the other day. We would be best served keeping to our own lanes."

"Let's go talk to him. You and me."

"What! Talk to Douglas Stratton?"

"Yes. That is why I came here to see you. I think we should meet with him while he is at Forest Glen and hear from him directly that the jobs of the school staff will not change with ownership."

"Highly improper. Highly improper, Charlotte."

"Hear me out, George. Our approach would be much more subtle, of course, something along the lines of an expression of enthusiasm on our part and a solicitation of his expectations of what the coming months will hold."

"The bursar and the prefect of studies just showing up at Douglas Stratton's door, circumventing the dean. Highly improper."

"Mark my words, George, we are being outmaneuvered and unless we act now, we will be on the outside looking in when all is said and done. What is the harm in finding out if our jobs are secure?"

She lingers over a photograph showing the construction of the ballroom annex to Vincent Hall, traces her finger along the top of the frame, and then blows the accumulated particles of gray dust into the air.

"Again with this suspicion. What so-called *information* is feeding this paranoia of yours? Answer me that."

"I am not at liberty to say."

"If you feel so strongly, you should speak with the dean then. He is the person who can allay your concerns."

Mrs. Martin shrugs dismissively at the suggestion and completing her tour about the office stands before the bursar's desk again, looking down upon him.

"I have serious doubts that Dean Dawson would be willing to reveal to me his own part in this affair."

"Then I can't help you, Charlotte. I am not going to approach Douglas Stratton as you suggest. There, you have your answer. Even in the slim chance your suspicions are right, what could be done at this point? The Board of Trustees meets tomorrow morning. At that time, the fate of the sale will be decided and the issue will be moot."

"Conditions could be placed on the sale by the board. There must be someway to ensure that the staff is held harmless."

"No purchaser would agree to have his hands tied in that way. Let it go, Charlotte. The dean told us there would be no changes in operations. I believe him, and so should you."

"I see."

INCIDENT AT FOREST GLEN *201*

"And when the spring semester comes and you are squirreled away in that cramped hovel you call a library working away on your curriculum plans, I will resist the temptation to remind you of this day and how you spun such strange tales of intrigue and duplicity."

"I hope you are right, George. For your sake, and mine, I hope you are right."

Leah reaches out, grips the horizontal support bar, and gently lowers her body into the shallow end of the gymnasium pool. The tepid water envelopes her and chases away the goose bumps that formed on her arms and legs on the walk from the changing room. She pulls the cap firmly down on her head and turns her back and floats away from the side of the pool. Above her, on the other side of the white stucco ceiling, girls run about a track on the upper floor, their muffled footsteps marring the tranquility of the calming water. A few swimmers paddle about Leah's drifting body, while others at the deep end hold onto the sides of the rectangular pool talking, their white caps bobbing in front of ceramic tiles painted with brightly colored flower blooms.

A rumbling sound runs along the length of the ceiling followed by a sharp crash, a sound that will be repeated throughout the hour as the students take to the bowling lanes adjacent to the track.

But Leah floats on, undistracted by the disturbances, listening to the low lullaby of the heating pipes humming in the water below her. The soothing sensation against her skin is rapturous and she exists in perfect harmony with her surroundings, detached from the world she knew seconds before, floating in a liquid embrace that lightens the pull on her muscles and melts away the tension in her joints. She pulls her chin slightly up toward the drifting ceiling and feels the relaxing warmth spread along her protected scalp and brush against the tender patch of skin at her temple. She draws a deep breath and holds it, causing her clavicle to spread and her chest to lift out of the water. Her arms extend out from her side and she relaxes her fingers and they float limply just beneath the surface of the shimmering blue pool.

Still and suspended, exerting no effort, employing no muscle to guide her direction or maintain her position, she drifts lifelessly, staring at the rough interior surface overhanging her body. Nothing permeates the embryonic bubble surrounding her. Not Madame Kaspar's shrill, incessant commands. Not Josephine's domineering ways and threats. Not May's weak and whimpering insecurity. Only the distant mechanical drone of the water pumps soothing her mind.

For the first time in days, Leah feels at peace, no longer plagued by the disturbing specters persistently probing her thoughts and tormenting her sleep. The tips of her fingers go numb and then she loses the feeling in her toes as she succumbs to the calming power of the pool. A dulling sensation runs up her arms and her legs and encircles and anesthetizes the submerged portions of her body. Her torso tingles and feels detached from her heavy limbs. And on she floats, wallowing in her asylum, the minute ripples in the water lapping against her cheeks and along her neck.

She exhales the captured breath and feels a gentle pull along her abdomen that opens up her diaphragm. Her back arches as the downward pressure against her hips grows. The ceiling begins to move gradually before her eyes and her shoulders roll forward ever so slightly. She relents without protest, giving over her body to the opiate feel along her skin. Water breaches her parted lips and a bitter, chemical taste rolls over her tongue.

So this is how it feels.

No panic.

Just acceptance.

And welcome relief.

Sinking slowly, she does not draw another breath, satisfied to let the languid water enter her. She does not struggle as the warm liquid fills her mouth and nostrils and ears and coats her unblinking eyes. Waves of light dance in a sea of endless pale blue and then dissipate. She is no longer able to command her body and waits for the comforting blackness to arrive.

Is this how she felt?

The weight grows along the length of her thighs to her deadened feet. Her arms rise above her head as her upper body slowly drifts to vertical. The pull of the water intensifies and her descent quickens. She calmly watches the shimmering surface of the pool overhead recede. Her mind is clear. A large bubble of air erupts from her mouth. And then another. A dull ache grips her chest. Darkness encroaches around her and she closes her eyes in a final act of submission.

Please God. Teach me how to die.

A powerful force wraps around her chest and squeezes tightly until the remaining air is pushed out of Leah's lungs and bubbles stream over his face. The sinister grip, the malevolent sensation of a cold body against hers is familiar—the avenging angel of her dream! On the edge of consciousness, she struggles to suppress the instinctual urge of survival, and gives herself willingly to her insatiable captor.

Don't fight. Don't fight. You must not fight.

And she doesn't.

May, still dressed in her school uniform, walks about the gymnasium clutching a book of poetry and casually observing the girls in her class. She is usually partial to bowling during indoor activities followed by fifteen minutes in the solarium, but not today. She is in no mood to participate given her foul disposition and elects to spend the period walking about the spacious complex, inconspicuous and alone with her book and her brooding thoughts.

As she does, she makes notes of which girls are together in groups and which are being friendly and which are withdrawn. She keeps a tally of the social alliances at the school and takes notice when fissures begin to appear or when disagreements or jealousies sever the bonds of sisterhood. This role of discreet observer is almost second nature for May—a compulsive hobby of sorts—and she keeps a mental scorecard, meticulous and nuanced, of who spends time with whom outside of the classroom, the overtures and the slights, who is accepted into which circles and who is turned away. She has never confided to anyone the extent of her work mapping out the elaborate web of friendships at the Seminary. To do so would diminish the sense of empowerment she derives from her clandestine eavesdropping and the satisfaction that comes from privately judging those around her for their myriad faults—the insincerity and the insecurity, the manipulation and the gullibility, the followers of fashion and the slaves to the society page, and, of great anthropologic fascination to May, the queens and the drones that labor to please them.

May sidles up to the railing overlooking the side of the pool to see who is swimming on such a wintry day and spots Leah in the water surrounded by three girls laughing and splashing about her. She immediately identifies the broad shoulders and athletic build of Mattie, one of the girls from chorus who interrupted them at dinner the night before. She and the other two paddle in a circle around Leah like playful sirens taunting her with their words and probing touches. Leah smiles at her tormenters and tries to swim away but they pursue her with effortless strokes hidden beneath the water's surface.

As they draw nearer to the side of the pool, May recognizes Bettina Braddock's fair coloring and pronounced aquiline nose. She swims about, laughing and darting her pinching fingers at Leah's exposed ribs as she tries to escape her relentless pursuers. Exhausted and pleading for surrender from the pack, Leah glances up and catches sight of May at the railing.

"May. You must come in. The water is absolutely wonderful. The temperature is perfect," she calls out, her cheeks flush and her chest rising spasmodically from exertion. "Come in, will you? Go change out of that drab uniform and join us."

"I don't think so, Leah," she replies, reticent to speak in front of the others.

"I think it would do you some good. I do. I really do," Leah begs. "You must trust me. When you feel the warm water on your arms and legs, you will thank me. Come in. Please, May. Come and join us."

"I thought you were resting your voice."

"I am. The steam is good for my throat. Now get out of that dress and come in."

Before she thinks twice, the words erupt from May's lips, blunt and unabashed. She doesn't care any longer. She doesn't care even if the others overhear her.

"Leah, what happened to you last night? We went to the ballroom after dinner. And...and then you just...just disappeared. You went off without a word and left me standing there. I waited—"

Leah's encouraging smile melts away as she recognizes the hurt in May's eyes.

Not again. Not again, May. Not the pity play.

"I waited for you. And you never came back."

"May, you shouldn't—you don't understand."

"After what I told you, I thought—"

Bettina, eyes wide, her lips pulled back revealing oversized teeth, drifts up from behind and slips her arm around Leah's waist and rests her chin against her bare shoulder, looking up at May leaning on the railing.

"After what I told you, well you have *my* interest."

INCIDENT AT FOREST GLEN   *205*

"I am sorry," Leah says half-heartedly as May looks away from Bettina's brazen stare.

Mattie and the other swimmer close in on Leah, as if to support her in the water and look upon the insecure girl. A few minutes before May's arrival, it was the muscular swimmer who spotted Leah drifting in the deep end and dove into the water to pull her to the surface.

"Never mind," May says defiantly.

"You are May, aren't you," Mattie asks, "the girl with Leah at dinner last night?"

Bettina, not waiting for a reply, zeroes in and says into Leah's ear cruelly, "Do I know this girl? For the life of me, I don't recognize her. Is she new to the school?"

The others laugh on cue at the cutting remark and May pushes away from the railing and leaves hurriedly. Leah separates herself from the clutch of arms, swims to the pool's edge, and hoists her knees up onto the concrete lip.

May rushes past some girls headed for the changing room and pauses in the empty solarium. Beyond the double glass windows, a shower of heavy flakes floats down from a flint gray sky. The room has been robbed of its usual infusion of warmth by the clouds and a cool dampness hangs in the air. The incensed girl throws herself down on a wicker chaise lounge, opens the book, and stares at the fine print trembling before her.

The door opens behind her and for a few seconds the silence is broken by the revelry of swimmers before it shuts again.

Leah leans back against the wall, wrapped in a robe with a towel around her shoulders, looking at the girl pretending to ignore her presence.

"Is that all it takes to send you running? Are you that easily pushed around?"

The accusatory words enrage May further, but she bites her tongue as Leah walks along the beveled glass walls, leaving faint foot prints of moisture on the tile floor as she goes.

"They treat you like sport. You're like a quail cowering in the brush waiting for the hunter to flush you out. And off you fly, so predictably, an easy shot."

"You are no position to speak to me in such a way!" May fires back, slamming the book down on the lounge cushion. "The opinions of those wasps are beneath me. What they think and what they say means nothing to me."

"But of course it does," Leah responds coldly. "Everyone, including me, can see it."

"And what about you? Do you deny that you crave their attention? Now that the Sweets are enamored with you and your newly discovered rebellious ways, I suppose this changes a lot for you."

Leah stares out the window, lulled by the thick curtain of precipitation, and considers the verbal challenge. The road running past sorority row is blanketed in a softening white and the limbs of the evergreen trees in the grove beyond the Chiopi Pagoda have begun to sag under the weight of the accumulating snow. Outside Beta house, a group of girls run and slide on the slick ground beyond the drawbridge while others at the castle ramparts hurl snowballs down upon them. Further on toward the glen, in front of the Villa, barely discernable through the snowfall, a student chases another around the gargantuan concrete statue of an Athenian woman draped in a tunic and seated on a throne, her eyes covered, a downward sword in one hand and the scales of Justice held aloft by the other. Dodging from side to side, the pursued girl shields herself from her attacker until they both run away and continue their game of tag in the labyrinthine paths of the washed out gardens.

"Change? Yes. Much has changed."

"It suits you, Leah. You seem to enjoy toying with the emotions of others. You will fit in well with those girls."

"You may not believe me, May, but we do share something in common. Contrary to appearances and your oh-so predictable, thin-skinned protests, we are both misfits in our own way."

"Why don't you just leave now?"

"Loners. That's what we are," Leah calls out as she steps closer to where May sits.

"I said, leave me!" she yells back.

Leah raises her arm and points to May as she approaches.

"Oddities."

The besieged girl takes up her book and opens it again.

"Defective."

With alarming swiftness she grabs May violently at the base of the neck and jerks her forward until their faces almost touch.

"Defective!"

May turns away but cannot break the sure grip. The wet towel slides off Leah's shoulders into the girl's lap.

"What are you doing?! You are mad! Let me go!"

"Wake up, my little quail, for the hunter is afoot."

"Leah, let me go this instance!"

"Wake up," she repeats, inches from May's straining face. "Wake up, before it is too late."

Leah releases her hold and May, still resisting, falls back in the lounge sending the tome onto the floor.

"What in the world has come over you?!" May exclaims, stunned by what just transpired.

The solarium door opens just as Leah is backing away from the wicker davenport.

"There you are, my dear. We weren't sure where you went to," Bettina says, amused by the scene of the two flustered girls in the solarium. "We are going to change now. Are you coming?"

By the time May retrieves her book off the floor, she is once again alone. The physical confrontation with Leah leaves her shaken and she can feel her heart pounding. She smoothes out the folds in her uniform and composes herself before leaving the solarium. Running her fingers back through her hair she feels a surprising sting on her neck and rubs it lightly. She touches something moist and warm and when she looks down at her hand she is shocked to see a smear of crimson along her finger tips.

Chapter 7
Warrior, Resolute

It is of the utmost importance in the accomplishment of a woman's work in life that her physical condition should be perfect. Neglect in this respect is criminal. She who, by neglect, renders herself incapable of performing the duties which are coming to her in later life, is responsible for all the miseries which she thus inflicts upon herself and others. We wish to inculcate reverence for the body and the duties it is intended to perform. A distinctly womanly future is pre-supposed and plainly discussed, and is made the incentive of a delicate and reverential regard for the high destiny of woman and of adequate preparation of it.

By mid-afternoon, the snow stops and Mr. Stratton, feeling his attentiveness beginning to flag, orders coffee service brought up to his suite at Glen Manor. A set of legal papers are arrayed on the table before him, next to a tray filled with cigar ends and ash. Mr. Carter sits nearby making notes in a small notebook bound in moleskin as his employer paces about dictating his directives.

"Arrange for a courier to be here in an hour to pick up the contract and deliver it to the lawyers so that my changes can be made without delay. I want the revised document in the hands of the board first thing tomorrow morning. They will need time to review the alterations before the meeting, minor though they may be. I want it spelled out to everyone that clerical delay is not acceptable, under any circumstances. Also, confirm my train reservations for tomorrow morning. This weather is making me antsy. Do you know if they are getting the same weather in New York?"

"No, sir, I don't. But I will check on that too."

"You are to communicate with me immediately once the Board of Trustees reaches a decision. You can wire me in Philadelphia and have it delivered to my cabin during the stop there. If I don't confirm receipt, then send it to Grand Central as well. Then I will see you Monday morning at the office."

"Any other preparations before the board meeting you need me to handle?"

"No, the groundwork has been laid."

"Because, I am more the willing—"

"Not necessary, Charles. My agent has been working on the inside and assures me that everything has been taken care of. Look, I know it is killing you, not being brought in on some of the details, but that's how I want to run this one. Where is that damn coffee?"

"Do you want me to check on it?"

The agitated tycoon shakes his head and points to the chair for his assistant to sit.

"Where was I? Oh yes, tonight. Dean Dawson has invited me to dinner at his residence. Just the two of us and Mrs. Dawson. He lives just off campus and a car will be picking me up at six. So, you are on your own again for the evening. You are free to head into the District or do whatever you please."

Mr. Stratton lets out a prolonged yawn and then shakes his head before dropping down into a chair.

"So, how did it go this morning, you know, your trip?"

Mr. Carter shrugs off the probing question and pages through his notebook.

"My two sons have started their own lives and I don't have the chance to see them very often, Charles," he says with a wistful expression. "So indulge me the role of the prying father figure. It is perfectly acceptable for you to open up to me. I may judge you harshly, but it will always be in private."

"You do instill openness, Mr. Stratton," he says with more than a hint of sarcasm.

"Loosen up, boy. We are about to complete a sizeable investment with an appreciable upside. You should be happy and relaxed, enjoying the moment. But, instead you are acting like an over-wound watch. Come on, tell me about your morning in the company of Miss Price. I may have forty years on you, but we are both men. And the laws of attraction are universal and immutable. She's quite attractive, is she not?"

"Yes, she is an attractive woman."

"An attractive woman who is attracted to you based on what I have observed. My eyes have weakened with age but it's as obvious as the nose on your face, son. Surely you have picked up on the signs. Hell, I could see it right off the bat last night. I told you your odds were about to improve. Don't clam up, son. Give me the story."

Pressed for details, the young man is torn over what to say. True, he is aware of Miss Price's interest in him. The easy familiarity between them and the intimate conversations over the past day are clear signals that their rapport is more than cordial. But are these personal expressions or the designs of a woman seeking something different all together, something more aggrandizing? Mr. Carter considers the import of her offer to him on the trolley, the overture to work with him and his employer behind the scenes to refashion the school's operations, and wonders whether he should share it with his boss. He looks up to see a quizzical look on the man's face, his shoulders shrugged and hands upturned, waiting for an answer.

"Well?"

"I think Miss Katharine Price is more devoted to the affairs of the school at this point in her life, understandably so."

"Katharine. Nice name. Always liked it. Are you sure you're not being thick-headed and overlooking her interest? A woman isn't simply going to fly her heart up a flag pole for all the world to see. Subtlety. That's the ticket."

"All she wanted to talk about on the streetcar ride to the hospital was the sale of the school."

"What did you tell her?"

"Nothing. I mostly listened. But she is angling for something more after the deal is completed."

"Really. This is fascinating. You have now piqued my interest. What exactly is she *angling* for?"

"I am not sure," he lies.

"Hmmm."

The wealthy industrialist leans forward and spins a Wonderlite on the coffee table.

"Surely you have considered the other rationale for her interest?"

"I think she is curious and just a bit scared about what changes the sale may bring about. She strikes me as an ambitious woman."

"An ambitious woman presented with access to a man who himself is close to the very power that can make or break future prospects. A bit of palace intrigue. I have not given Miss Price suitable credit. There is more to this woman than a sharp mind and fetching appearance. This too is a lesson worth imparting, Charles. The opposite sex can be as calculating in matters of business as men. Their minds are just as capable at recognizing the bottom line and employing the means necessary to get what they want. In fact, some women have an advantage we don't enjoy. You need to be mindful of one thing above all in your dealings with people, whether in business or your personal life?"

"What would that be?"

"Motive."

"And Katharine Price's motive is to promote her own standing through me?"

"I'm in no position to judge. What does your head, not your heart, tell you? Is she interested in Charles Carter, the man, or Charles Carter, the businessman?"

He mulls over the choice until a knock at the door interrupts them. He stands and moves to answer it wearing a look of mild bewilderment, and then hesitates momentarily next to his employer's chair.

"I think it is both, Mr. Stratton. I think her attention toward me is part emotional and part calculated. I just haven't figured out if they are inseparable."

A derisive bellow of delight bursts from the tickled tycoon, as he squirms about in his chair, rolling in the absurdity of his young charge's answer.

"Fetch the coffee before it gets any colder. You are a font of amusement for me, you know that, Charles. A font of amusement."

Once the tray is retrieved and the coffee poured, Mr. Carter slinks back to his chair, cowed and confused.

"Don't go off and sulk now, boy. It's admirable to believe that the two worlds can coexist, though a bit naïve for someone your age. I don't want to send you into an emotional tale-spin, but from what you have relayed, Miss Price has given you a peek at her cards and it seems she is looking to use you to further her own cause. Don't give her another thought. Speaking of cards, I will need my best poker face for tonight's dinner with the dean. He will be pumping me for information, I suspect. Who knows, maybe Porter is behind young Miss Price approaching you like she did."

"If you permit me to say, sir, that's a cynical take, don't you think? I've been very impressed by what I've witnessed at the school since we arrived. Your familiarity with the school and its accomplishments are long-standing, what with your three daughters being schooled here. But for me, it is a revelation. In a short period of time, I have come to appreciate the merit of the Seminary's educational course and the value it is providing in energizing the minds of these young women. I was skeptical when I arrived, but after yesterday and the trip to the hospital this morning, watching the students outside the classroom, I now better understand the allure of this peculiar place."

"So what exactly are you saying, Charles?"

"I think Dean Dawson and his staff, including Miss Price, are truly vested in the future of the National Park Seminary. Their concern over what the purchase offer portends is understandable, if not laudable. You of all people know its worth. Like an apartment building or a paper factory, the school is an investment for you. It is business. I understand that. But its return is not simply financial.

"I witnessed it at the hospital this morning. It is hard for me to describe. Mr. Stratton, I saw the living embodiment of your words to Dean Dawson the other day while I was watching the girls visiting the wounded soldiers. One of the students, in particular, was so confident and disarming around the patients, it was remarkable to behold. You told him that the purchase was in the name of your daughters. Their legacy is not in the past. It is here. It is happening now. I witnessed it myself. Forgive me, sir, if my words are impertinent, but to see this capable young woman moving about the hospital ward going from one patient to the next, tenderly comforting each one, it was if I was watching Elizabeth herself."

Mr. Stratton stares implacably at his enthusiastic, wide-eyed assistant and in the prolonged silence his eyes slowly moisten. The light-heartedness, so evident seconds before, is gone, bled away from his sallow cheeks.

"Interesting, Charles. Very interesting."

He retrieves a cigar from a leather pouch and searches his vest pocket and finally produces a silver cutter.

"I remember reading a story as a child, some ancient fable about a sultan or emperor. When he assumes the throne of power, he orders that a giant rock be wrought out of the quarry and hung above the bed of state of the previous emperor. Through great toil and labor, the heavy slab was carved out, tied with thick rope, and hoisted onto the roof overtop the magnificent and ornate bed. The rope was then painstakingly carried through a long tunnel hollowed out of the quarry stone and anchored to an iron ring."

The reflective businessman stops and wets the end of the cigar with his lips and retrieves a tiny particle of tobacco from his tongue.

"Once this task of prodigious engineering was completed and final preparations were made, the emperor was woken in the middle of the night and a sharpened axe was placed into his hands. The ruler raised the axe high and with a single, mighty blow, severed the rope, watched it rush away, and the slab of stone fell."

Mr. Stratton slips the cigar into the cutter hole, snaps the blade down with his thumb, and snips away the end, which he then brushes off his pants leg to the floor.

"Imagine all the work. And for what? As I child, I was struck by the imagery of the tale, but I didn't have a clue what it meant. And I haven't figured it out in all the years since. But for some peculiar reason, it comes to mind now."

He uses the Wonderlite to start the tightly-rolled tobacco. Mr. Carter sips his coffee and watches the old man turn the cigar in his mouth and send a pungent cloud of gray smoke up to the ceiling.

"You have a chance to build something great here, Mr. Stratton. National Park Seminary will be a prized jewel in the holdings of Stratton Enterprises. I understand that now in a way that I didn't before. There will be naysayers who question the wisdom of buying this school, but they will be proven wrong. I am confident in time you will be celebrated as an educational reformer and visionary in the promotion of women in society. I have seen the results firsthand. Under your auspices, with your money, this school will grow and prosper, as will your standing as a public figure."

"Charles, Charles, slow down. You are getting carried away."

Mr. Stratton looks at the excited man and contemplates his mistake.

"This can't go on. I kept you and the others in New York at a distance about the deal for a reason—"

"But you were wise to do so, Mr. Stratton. The circumstances justified a certain amount of compartmentalizing, as it were. I am only embarrassed at my initial misgivings. I should never have allowed doubt and suspicion to creep in to my thinking. You spoke of lessons learned earlier. Well, you have taught me a valuable lesson on this trip. I want you to know that."

"You are not making this easy, son."

Mr. Stratton shakes his head and places the cigar in the ashtray.

"I wasn't going to say anything until after tomorrow's board meeting and the execution of the contract and title transfer. But hell, the way you are going on..."

"What? What is it, sir?"

The aging lion of industry realizes he can no longer continue the charade.

"I am not buying the school, Charles. I am buying the land," he says matter-of-factly, and pauses to gauge his young assistant's reaction.

"I am confused. The contract of sale says that you are—"

"Yes, yes, I know what the damn contract says. It's the land I am interested in, not the school. I am buying a ninety acre parcel to subdivide it and build upscale homes for the wave of buyers from the city that's already on its way. That's where the money is. With both the railroad and trolley running to Forest Glen and a new road being built every other week by the county, this area is about to explode and the National Park Seminary sits here prime for the picking."

"And the school?" Mr. Carter weakly asks, blindsided by his employer's mendacity.

Having prematurely revealed his secret, Mr. Stratton feels he can no longer hold back or shade the truth and levels with him.

"The school will close and in time the buildings will be demolished."

Stunned by the revelation, Mr. Carter walks to the window and looks out over the glen at the sprawling village carved out of the woods. The passing storm has blanketed the grounds completely and coated the rooftops and eaves and balconies in a soft white giving the campus a fairy tale-like patina. Through the distortion of the streaked window, the school appears as a miniature world inside a glass globe, fragile yet protected.

"I didn't mean this to be such a shock, Charles. But the way you were going on about the Seminary and your girl at the hospital, I felt the time had come for me to be straight with you."

"And none of them know anything about your plans?"

"The dean and the rest, you mean? Of course not. And that is the way it will stay until after the purchase is final and we and the building developer announce the construction plans at a time and place of our choosing."

"And the students?"

"Important details, yes, to be sure. But these will all be worked out at a later date, Charles. Our focus now is on the next twenty-four hours. Understand?"

Mr. Carter feels the sage investor's hand land on his shoulder and the aroma of smoldering tobacco permeates the air around him.

"I almost told you yesterday when I was putting my boot to your pants about all of the desirable and eligible girls across that bridge. I told you National Park Seminary was a gold mine. And that time was short. Do you remember? If my hunch is right, this project will make us a lot of money," he says with a reassuring shake.

"I have no doubt it will be extremely profitable," Mr. Carter replies flatly, remaining turned toward the window, pondering how his boss' unexpected admission has now transformed him into an accessory in the school's premature and swift demise.

In the eyes of Katharine Price he will be nothing more than a duplicitous scoundrel, an unconscionable mercenary whose sole purpose is to ready the execution. And what will be said among the students when the sentence is announced and their fate revealed on that not so distant date after his return to New York City? What curse of infamy will be assigned to him, the enigmatic visitor who arrived days before Christmas break, the stranger whose sweet words of praise masked the perfidy of his heart? Certainly *she* will look back on their brief interlude at the hospital and realize it was him and, upon doing so, who would blame her for heaping scorn on his name, the wolfish man who infiltrated his way into her confidence bearing secret malice?

Mr. Stratton steps forward, unties a golden tasseled rope, and the curtain falls across the window.

"Let's get back to work, son" he commands, walking back to the table covered with legal documents. "You need to get busy and arrange for the courier. And I am going to take a long bath before my dinner at Edgewood."

And in that instant, the blow is struck, and the roof of Charles Carter's stronghold drops upon him.

As word of Leah's defanging of Madame Kaspar spreads, speculation runs rampant about the incident's ramifications. The prevailing opinion among the students is that Leah will be suspended from the chorus and prevented from singing at the winter concert as punishment for her impudence. After all, such a sanction has been levied against others girls guilty of similar insurrections in the past. Some of the chorus members surmise that suspension is not only too severe but that their instructor, fanatic as she is about the sanctity of the performance, will hesitate to remove her best pupil on the eve of the concert. Taking away Leah's solo will be the compromise, they insist. Still others, such as Bettina Braddock and her faithful minions, Julia and Mattie, hope against any punishment at all, not out of any strong defense of Leah's actions or overriding concern for her welfare, but because they eagerly anticipate a reprise. The clash has left them craving more. Only a continuation and escalation of the high drama will do.

The air of anticipation grows as Leah enters the Odeon alone and walks to the stage to join the others who are early for the final practice. Madame Kaspar has yet to arrive and the sound of whispering circulates around Leah as she ascends the short flight of steps.

Has she come to challenge her suspension? Has she been given preferential treatment and allowed to sing? Has Madame Kaspar been overruled by the dean? Or is she the one who has been removed over the brush-up by an administration tired of chronic complaints about her demanding teaching style?

Bettina stands up from a circle of girls seated at the edge of the stage and looks around the auditorium and seeing no sign of their instructor claps her hands just loudly enough to be heard by Leah and a few others. Another student follows her lead and eventually all the rest join in the acclamation. Bettina wraps her arm around Leah's shoulder and squeezes her firmly, but the reluctant hero looks away, uncomfortable with being singled out on stage by the applause and all that it implies. She harbors no animosity toward Madame Kaspar and shrinks from the attention her outburst is garnering.

"This is how revolutions start, you little Bolshevik!" Bettina whispers into her ear.

"Enough" she protests, sliding out from underneath Bettina's hold.

"Well, you are a fickle one. Still no word from Kaspar? I bet she is just waiting for you to slip up or commit some imagined transgression and then she will tear into you. She rules the stage with an iron fist and I expect she will come back prepared to show us all that her grip is as strong as ever."

"Enough already, Bettina. I only want this to be over with. The concert. The semester. Everything. I want all of it to simply go away."

"I thought the swim would have relaxed you. But you are as contrary as before. You also don't look very well, my dear. Your face is—"

"I'm fine."

Other members of the chorus begin to circle around the two girls interested in learning more about the rumored suspension, careful not to insert themselves between Bettina and Leah, a gesture that the would be viewed by the red-haired leader as a challenge to her defacto rule over the group. Words of encouragement and support are offered in rapid succession as the cordon of singers closes in around Leah.

"Don't back down, Leah. It's time someone stood up against her."

"If I were you, the next time she points the stick in your face, grab it out of her bony fingers and break it over your knee."

"She won't drop you from chorus. She needs you too much."

"If she does, don't leave. Just stay here and wait her out. She is all bluster."

The overhead lights of the auditorium come to life with the loud snap of the electrical switch backstage and illuminate the congregation of singers on the stage. The conspiratorial circle, tightly drawn and feverish, begins to dissolve away under sudden brightness, and the girls move lethargically toward the risers to take their assigned places.

Leah watches as Bettina and the others walk away, but she holds her spot.

Madame Kaspar appears from behind the curtain and walks briskly toward center stage, followed by a student pianist carrying a folder of sheet music. Seeing the teacher for the first time since their confrontation produces neither loathing nor trepidation in Leah. Her heart is calm and her expression placid as the teacher herds the girls to the risers with the silent efficiency of a border collie corralling a flock of sheep. Once the chorus members find their proper places, the commotion quiets and Madame turns her attention to the assembled rows. She immediately notices the gap in the center of the first row and turns around and sees that Leah remains rooted to the wooden floor, stationary and isolated.

Madame Kaspar's soulless eyes narrow behind her black rimmed glasses and her mouth puckers, producing deep, furrowed creases along her concave cheeks and severe lines around her dry, pale lips.

"Are you joining the group today, Miss Hathaway?" she spits venomously.

Leah can see Bettina and a few of the others standing behind Madame Kaspar struggle to suppress the anxious laughter brimming up inside them. One of the girls holds her hand against her mouth and stares wide-eyed at the rebellious girl in anticipation of what will come next.

Leah walks in a direct line toward the scowling, unblinking teacher, as if reeled in by an invisible fishing line. In Madame Kaspar's hand she sees the offending rod, clutched tightly, pointed at the floor. She senses the collective wishes of the chorus filling the space between her and the teacher.

Bettina leans over and whispers giddily to Mattie in the middle row.

"She is going to do it. I can't believe she is really going to do it. The girl is suicidal."

As Leah steps before Madame Kaspar, everyone on the risers, as well as the student positioned at the piano, hold their collective breath. Some girls anxiously hold hands as the moment of battle arrives.

"No," Leah says firmly.

Madame Kaspar's blistering gaze intensifies and her gnarled hands, claw-like and marred with raised purple veins and brown liver spots, squeeze tighter still.

"Not until I apologize to you, Madame, in front of the entire chorus. My words yesterday were rash. My behavior was unacceptable. I was feeling sick and ill-tempered. I tell you this not as an excuse for my actions but so that you know that it is not my true nature to speak rudely to my teachers. I ask your forgiveness."

Madame Kaspar does not immediately react to the surprising offer of contrition, and remains in her frozen, slightly crouched pose, as if prepared to fend off the attack of a mad dog. She searches the girl's expression for indications of insincerity. Leah looks downward signaling to the glowering teacher both regret and submissiveness.

"Take your place, Miss Hathaway, and delay us no more."

Under the proscenium arch, the chorus is put through their paces in the final rehearsal. Their blended voices fill the Odeon's grand interior with lyrical beauty that pleases even Madame Kaspar. Mid-way through the practice, Dean Dawson unexpectedly arrives and listens to the choral group from one of the luxurious side boxes decorated with overhanging balloon valances. Behind him, standing against the door unnoticed, Miss Price waits for a break in the rehearsal to speak with the dean, fingering impatiently a folded sheet of paper held against her body.

Rapturous notes rise and fall in a vocal tapestry of sublime purity. The exalted chorus breathes life into the empty hall. The glorious sound takes wing, swells over the ornately decorated façade hanging above Madame's diminutive figure, and reverberates against the back wall of the balcony. Here, at this elevated tier of seats, the enormous face of a Greek goddess hangs above scenes of pastoral beauty painted on plaster, centered perfectly with alignment of the stage, looking down on the singers. Cast against a clamshell-shaped corona, the head of shiny alabaster looms high above the stage, peering over the audience seating with narrow slits for eyes and full lips rendered in a contented smile. When the concert hall lights are doused and the curtain is pulled back, the proscenium goddess emanates an eerie, silvery lunar glow that can be seen from any seat inside the Odeon.

Impressed by the performance, Dean Dawson remains longer than he originally planned. As the beginning notes of Silent Night are sung, he is spellbound. The immaculate, seemingly effortless sound makes his spirit bloom as he drifts back to the Christmas services of his youth. He grins widely as he listens to the angelic chorus. He is slightly embarrassed by the rush of emotion that comes over him. But rather than denying it, he embraces the tinge of melancholy that nips at his heart as the powerful notes recall the simpler time of boyhood, when the acute anticipation of Christmas morning was unbearable and stung more harshly than the prairie winds of winter.

Leah, her voice strong and feeling no ill-effects from the cold during the rehearsal, steps forward from the group, finds her mark, and waits for her moment, along with the other two soloists, her chin raised slightly, her gaze trained on the mezzanine, as Madame Kaspar has instructed them to do, to help project her voice.

Despite her effort to remain focused, the memory of the nightmarish images conjured up the last time she stood on this spot slowly take over her thoughts. Standing apart on the cold stage, she can almost feel the icy hand around her waist and the unyielding hold placed on her as she was borne away

INCIDENT AT FOREST GLEN   *221*

from the dark and cruel waters. Leah instinctively rubs her hand across stomach as if to check that the haunting sensation is indeed imaginary, before moving it quickly back to her side in the hope Madame Kaspar did not notice the break in form. The fleeting touch across her mid-section reminds Leah of Mattie Bishop's powerful grip earlier in the pool. If she hadn't been there, if she hadn't dove under the water, what would have happened, Leah wonders? Would I have allowed it to happen?

She pictures their faces—Bettina, Mattie, Julia, and the all the rest—looking at her, knowing that she is now different in their eyes, after what just happened—or to be more precise, didn't happen—between her and Madame at the beginning of practice. She imagines how they study her, dissect her, examine her, their interest driven by the need to judge and to mock and to render inferior. How she loathes their ways and their pathetic realm of existence.

While holding her position, Leah sees something move in the upper level of the hall, a small disturbance in front of the mural of verdant fields, its form concealed in a thin shadowy band running the length of the back wall. Why would someone be walking there now?

She focuses her attention back on the progression of the music, but her eyes remain fixed on the loft. She detects no more movement in the dimly lit recesses of the balcony. An illusion perhaps. As she stares off in the distance, she relaxes her eyes and waits, hoping to catch another glimpse of whoever might be watching from above. But the phantom does not reappear. The cramped rows are empty seats are still. She does not dare turn around from her front position to see if others in the chorus saw it too. Instead, she holds fast, her body rigid, and waits.

When her solo arrives, Leah sings effortlessly, her annunciation crisp and her voice rich and full. As she continues through Silent Night, she feels the creeping malaise lifting. A pleasant lightness, like that which she experienced in the gymnasium pool, comes over her as she sings, and for the time being the malignant thoughts that poison her waking moments and deprive her of sleep at night are held at bay. She gives herself over to the music and lets it inhabit her being, and when the final notes are sung and slip away into the lofty space above the Odeon stage, the sound of spirited clapping erupts from the side box.

"Excellent. Truly magnificent," the dean exults cheerfully. "Madame Kaspar, you and your assistants have prepared a program of unparalleled excellence. Excellent. Girls, everyone has worked hard to get to this point, I know. But the end result is truly inspirational. Our guests are in for quite a treat tomorrow night. And I have a bit of good news to pass along. I am assured that a representative from the newspaper's music review will be in attendance, and I can only imagine the review he will write after hearing such a moving performance. Thank you girls for affording me the privilege of previewing the concert. Thank you again."

As the dean departs, the chorus buzzes with giddy chatter over the revelation that the concert will be reviewed. Madame Kaspar nods to the box, glowing with satisfaction over the headmaster's praise, and calls a ten minute break in the rehearsal.

Leah remains separate from the rest of the chorus in her solo position as the girls noisily step down from the risers, some heading to the powder room, others socializing in impromptu groups around the stage. She watches as Madame Kaspar strolls over to the pianist and begins critiquing the accompaniment, pointing a knotted, slightly bent finger emphatically at a sheet of music. None of the girls who circled around Leah before practice approach her now. To the contrary, they move about her as if she does not exist, a pariah in their midst. Even Bettina and the other Sweets, the ones who were so anxious to claim her and bestow their favor upon her after the row with Madame Kaspar, walk past without speaking a word or acknowledging her. She watches perplexed as Bettina leads them down the stage stairs and up the center aisle to the entrance doors in the back of the hall, like a mother duck leading her young, to report the latest on the passing storm.

As the group disperses, a sharp, high-pitched squeal of metal striking metal comes from the balcony and startles Leah. She looks up quickly and struggles momentarily to adjust to the change in lighting. She catches a fleeting glimpse of someone disappearing through the doorway leading to the upper rows. She looks about her to see if any of the others heard the disruption or spotted the person in the back of the auditorium more clearly, but the rest of the girls have either left the stage or are busied in conversation. She hesitates, unsure if she should say something or call attention to the balcony, now empty and quiet.

Looking back, she notices something else in the theater overhang, a small, out-of-place object that escaped her notice earlier, a vision that makes her gasp and stiffens her joints. Leah's eyes widen and strain to capture all the light possible to bring the slender effigy resting against the far balcony wall into focus.

The heavy wooden doors in the back of the hall are cracked and a biting wind, bearing confetti of blown snow and stray leaves, rushes into the Odeon before they are secured again.

Leah hugs herself to suppress an involuntary shudder and feels the gallop of her racing heart against her rib cage.

Why won't you leave me alone?!

As Dean Dawson prepares to leave the Odeon and return to his office he is waylaid by Miss Price. Outside the viewing box, in a private corridor out of sight and ear-shot of Madame Kaspar and the members of the chorus, she asks for a moment of his time as he buttons his coat in preparation of the short walk back. She waits patiently for him to finish as he gushes on about the rehearsal.

"Listening to the girls sing was inspiring, Miss Price. It put me deep into the spirit of the Christmas season. The chorus is extraordinary this year, many of the star singers are from your class, yes? With everything going on now, with all the craziness of Douglas Stratton's visit and his proposal for you know what, and then the board meeting tomorrow, well, it was the perfect tonic for me I suppose. You know, I am most contented when I am among the girls, in the classroom, in the recital hall, during assemblies, watching how they apply themselves and seeing how much they have progressed. The love of teaching has never left me. I miss it. I envy you and the other instructors. Seeing the affirmation of your labors. I know it is quite rewarding."

"But we are surrounded by the affirmation of your labors, Dean. We are constantly reminded of your work in these magnificent buildings and at the students who leave us upon graduation as capable young women. They are as much products of your work as they are ours."

"Thank you, Miss Price. Trust me when I say that I was speaking from the heart and not fishing for compliments. But it means a great deal to me that you understand the worth of what we are doing here. I personally value your insights and your counsel. I have from the beginning of your time at the school. Now we must make sure that nothing deters us in our mission. I will be insisting at tomorrow's meeting of the Board of Trustees that any sale be contingent upon their being a free rein in continuing the work that is underway. There shall be no bit placed in our mouths, so to speak, right Miss Price?"

The headmaster chortles at his coarse metaphor and playfully shakes the regent's upper arm.

"You have put your finger on why I have sought you out."

"Really," he says in a surprised tone, fumbling with the button of his overcoat. "You have something to give me, Miss Price," glancing down at the paper she has brought with her.

"Yes. But I think it would be more helpful if I show you something first on the walk back to Vincent Hall."

The dean arches his eyebrows and smirks.

"Given your mysterious way in getting to the point you would be a perfect fit working for Douglas Stratton."

Miss Price flashes a polite smile and the two walk out a side entrance to the Odeon and past a long row of towering Ionic columns running the length of the imposing three-story structure. Atop the roof, aligned with each column, Grecian statues keep silent watch over the campus from above.

The walkway in front of the Odeon branches off, cuts through twin topiary hedges, beaten down and limp, and continues on toward Senior House and then Vincent Hall. They are alone on the path, as classes are in session and not scheduled to end for another twenty minutes.

"You realize I am suppressing the urge to ask what this is about," Dean Dawson yells into a brisk headwind. "I have a lot on my plate and I am hosting Stratton at Edgewood for dinner this evening."

"Yes, I know. I ask your indulgence for only a moment, sir. It will be worth your while. Trust me."

"What, we are going inside the senior dormitory? If we are to meet with one of your students, Miss Price, propriety would dictate a meeting in my office or yours."

Miss Price stops at the red sandstone column at the base of the entrance steps.

"No, sir. What I want to show you is here. It concerns Mr. Stratton, actually."

"Nothing I haven't seen many times before. I am perplexed by your circumlocution."

She can see in his face, bundled tightly against the buffeting wind, the impatience he feels turning to anger.

"My apologies, Dean. Allow me to explain. Yesterday morning, at your direction, I spoke with Lucille Wilhoit, one of our seniors, about her chance meeting with Douglas Stratton when he arrived at National Park. You may recall, he walked across the foot bridge—"

"Of course, I remember. I watched him myself. You told us about it."

"There were a few details omitted from my recounting to the group, some known at the time, one fact unknown to me until this morning."

"Really?"

"He spoke to Lucille and a couple of other girls about that statue over there," Miss Price gestures to the right of the building while maintaining eye contact with the dean. "It's a replica of Joan of Arc at Domremy."

"And?"

"Mr. Stratton was taken by the statue, according to the girls, though it is an ordinary and somewhat pedestrian copy. He later told Lucille in their short walk to Vincent Hall that he had seen the original in Paris at the Louvre and how passionate he was of the great works of art there."

"Miss Price, I ask for clarity and a linear explanation and you respond by careening off in the opposite direction with disjointed fragments of a past conversation that has no meaning to me. Is it your design to have me catch a cold standing outside here just days before Christmas?"

Miss Price steps closer, reaches into her coat pocket and produces the lapel pin in her palm.

"It's a Red Cross pin. Mr. Stratton gave it to Lucille Wilhoit. When she told me, I didn't understand what reason he would have to give it her. So, I made some phone calls and asked a few questions about the Strattons."

The headmaster takes the red and white pin in hand and scrutinizes it closely for some hidden meaning.

"That's most irregular, Miss Price. It is not our position to snoop around in the personal affairs of a man of Douglas Stratton's stature."

"Not Douglas Stratton—his daughters who went to school here. What I found I thought you should know, if only so that you may act accordingly, provided it is not too late."

Miss Price opens the sheet of paper in her hand and struggles to hold down the flapping edges in the wind as she reads.

On June 4, 1918, the troop transport ship USS Piscataway departed New York harbor for France. Three days later, while in transit in the Atlantic, the converted, iron-clad ship was torpedoed by a German U-boat. The USS Piscataway began taking on water and the passengers aboard were ordered to abandon ship. Though a larger loss of life was avoided due to efficient and heroic actions of those who remained onboard to save the ship, seventy-six deaths were reported in the attack, including those of nine volunteer US Army nurses.

"Douglas Stratton's oldest daughter, Elizabeth, was on that ship. She was one of the nine nurses who drowned in the attack at sea three years ago. Her body was taken to France where she was buried. This tragic event occurred only weeks after Douglas Stratton was here for the graduation of his youngest daughter Claudia. He never returned to Forest Glen. Until now."

"Oh my God, this cannot be so. I cannot believe it. I remember the girl. Elizabeth. She was nothing short of remarkable. How is this possible? How were we not informed of this tragedy before now?"

"Evidently, the Strattons, grief-stricken, kept their loss as private as possible and restricted discussion of the tragedy to a close group of family friends. Her death was reported by the newspapers at the time of course, but from what I have been able to uncover there was no broad dissemination of an obituary noting she was the daughter of prominence. The family waited until after the Armistice to travel to France for a funeral service. I spoke to the president of the school alumnae chapter in New York yesterday and she was shocked to hear about it. She could not recall any mention of Elizabeth's death within their circle at the time. The Stratton girls were never members of the alumnae group, but she was thoroughly embarrassed that news of the woman's death would have escaped the attention of the chapter membership."

"How sad for such a fine woman to be cut down in the early bloom of life. It must have been a devastating blow to Douglas. I can't comprehend it myself. To lose his first born so suddenly..." Dean Dawson trails off, overcome by emotion, and then turns to look at the stone girl seated upon the pedestal.

"As disturbing as the news may be, I thought it best that you know. To my mind, it brings clarity to the question of why he is seeking to purchase the school. He spoke of doing this in the name of his daughters. I have no doubt that it is the memory of Elizabeth Stratton he seeks to venerate."

"Yes, of course," the dean weakly acknowledges, still stunned by the news.

"I propose that I hold on to the pin and that this unfortunate information about Elizabeth Stratton not be circulated among the staff for the time being until events play themselves out."

"But what do I say, how do I act around him now that I know about his daughter? I cannot possible feign ignorance around him. This puts me in a difficult situation, Miss Price. I said nothing, I made no offer of condolence, when he arrived. If I acknowledge his loss now it will come across as being an afterthought. I will seem callous and insincere. But pretending not to know is out of the question too. The truth is no better, how the senior regent has been digging around in his past—"

He cuts himself off, recognizing the unfortunate characterization of his words.

While looking upon the statue of the martyr, the dean's eyes well-up and he turns to shield his face from the biting wind.

"My God," he mutters. "I have completely misjudged the man."

"I have an idea or two how the information can be used to your advantage.

"What are you talking about? How is that possible?"

"A gesture can be made that will ingratiate yourself to Douglas Stratton and at the same time lock in place an advantage in your negotiations."

The headmaster is taken aback by the regent's calculating remark, surprised that the woman is not similarly affected by the shocking revelation.

"This is no time for a ruse. Not now, not after such horrible news."

"We have no choice. Here me out, Dean."

"All right. Tell me what to do?"

From the recesses of the glen, the black bird gives out a solitary lament and launches from the cracked branch of a river birch and rises from the ravine, passing over the skeletal trusses of the Honeysuckle Bridge as it flies over the creek searching for a meal left along the banks by the receding waters. Nothing entices its senses and it circles over the landscaped grounds of the Villa before landing on the field adjacent to the lake, where it marches across the dormant lawn looking for dried beetles and hardened worms beneath the concealing blanket of snow. Its shiny beak searches the ground repeatedly but the crow grows impatient and again takes flight, beating its wings frantically against a stiff gust blowing from the north. Above the rooftops, the invisible tide grows in intensity and the bird is suspended in the air, flapping harder, unable to progress against the relentless force. The struggle tires the crow and it peels away, pushed along a stream that takes it effortless along the length of the colonnade connecting the gymnasium to Recitation Hall and past the chapel steeple where it catches an updraft and catapults skyward, toward quilted clouds with pendulous, ink-black bellies.

A faint trace of decay tickles its beak and the hungry creature turns and glides to the cupola atop Vincent Hall. Grasping the lip of the rain gutter, the crow side-steps hesitantly along the curved drain, its feet scraping against the mottled tin as it tries to maintain its hold. Once it reaches the end the gutter, it contorts its head sideways and drives its beak into the eaves repeatedly until it feels the compacted mud of an abandoned swallow nest. With the fearlessness and dexterity of a circus high-wire performer, the acrobatic bird lifts one leg off the curved surface, flaps its right wing, and twists its neck even more, until its beak is positioned to strike more cleanly. Over and over, the crow jabs blindly into the dark, hidden recess until the wall of the nest, dried and weakened over the months since it was built, begins to crumble and light brown remnants fall away and litter the walkway below. A sliver of broken egg shell is pulled out from a bed of stray feathers and chalky guano. The persistent scavenger senses it is close to his uncovered treasure and pushes its head further into the underside of the roof. A second egg, tiny, blue and intact, its embryo spoiled and hardened, is retrieved through a narrow opening created by the stabbing blows and carefully held in parted beak as the crow walks back along the edge. The triumphant bird, its prize secured, hops along the shingles until it reaches the protection of the cupola just as the tolling of the chapel bell calls students to vespers.

Before dismissing the chorus at the end of practice, Madame Kaspar reminds the girls of the importance of getting plenty of rest, which foods and drinks to avoid, and the necessity of protecting their throats against the inhospitable elements outside. As she is about to release them, she taps her rod against the stage floor boards, pauses for effect, and looks over the singers, a slight smile, barely perceptible, cracking her stoic countenance.

"You impressed our guest today. It shows the heights you are capable of achieving through dedication and discipline. Be here an hour before the concert. No exceptions. No excuses. You can go now."

The spare praise buoys the girls as they disperse, tired after two hours of rehearsal. A collective relief comes over the group as their sequestered time with Madame Kaspar over the past three weeks ends and the culmination of their work is nearly at hand.

As the other girls slowly collect their belongings and walk along the aisles toward the front entrance, Leah gathers her coat and hat and slips out behind the stage curtain, taking a quick glance to be sure she is not seen by the others before disappearing backstage. She walks past dusty boxes and a gauntlet of scenery boards from forgotten drama productions, navigates the stacked chairs in front of a makeup table and mirror, and then takes the door to the instructional wing of the Odeon. Her gait quickens and she starts to run down the long, dim corridor, past empty music rooms and dance studios.

Leah reaches the carpeted stairs and takes them two at a time, grabbing the interior banister to slingshot her body around and maintain momentum as she ascends the next flight. At the balcony level, she stops and looks around the florid anteroom, her ears filled with the sound of her labored breathing. Slowly she walks on, past grim-faced portraiture hanging from the walls, past oriental vases and upholstered sitting chairs, past marble tables and the chrysalis lamps, until she arrives at her destination.

Leah stands before the red door and starts to lose her nerve. Doubt seeps into her mind about what she saw from the stage during rehearsal. Alone on the upper floor, she feels suddenly vulnerable and afraid. Afraid of what is beyond the door. Afraid that she might find something. Afraid that she might find nothing.

She places her hand on the brass knob and closes her eyes trying to quell the growing timidity that threatens to consume her resolve. Only a short time before, standing on the stage, she had shed the dark thoughts and pangs of nervousness that infected her emotions and feasted on her sanity. She felt free on the stage. The malignancy that had so swiftly driven her to despair was gone, relinquishing its insidious hold on her. She savors how good it felt then to be...normal again. And now this.

Think Leah. Think before you act.

Turn around and walk away.

Don't open the door. Don't allow it back in.

You can decide.

You must decide.

She removes her hand and cautiously backs away from the doorway.

Turning around resolutely, she sees her hat at the tops of the stairs, dropped in her rush up to the balcony. She bends to pick it up as she leaves, and in that momentary pause, in those few seconds of delay, while she is crouched down, a bubble of self-doubt squeezes through a slender fissure in her willpower and paralyzes her from going further.

She falls backward clumsily, collapses on the step, and buries her head in her hands. Rocking back and forth in a curled position, knees to her chest, she emits a low groan from her covered mouth, like that of a wild beast snared in a hunter's trap. Her cheeks burn as the muscles along her neck strain violently. The plaintive moan erupts into a spiked high-pitch shriek and Leah pulls her hands away from her face and pounds them, clenched tight into fists, against the step again and again, without regard for injury, until her blind rage gives way to the throbbing pain of her swollen purplish palms. A strand of hair, fine and damp with perspiration, hangs over her flush forehead.

The door opens to silence. The delightful notes that filled the hall minutes earlier are gone and a solemn eeriness inhabits the vast interior. Leah sees no sign of Madame Kaspar or any of girls on the stage or in the audience seating below. She quietly walks down an empty row of seats on her toes until she reaches the center aisle of the balcony.

The uncertainty she felt before entering is wiped away in an instant. The object, small and imprecise when viewed from the lit stage, is unmistakable up-close. Leah summons the courage and slowly ascends the rows into the dim recesses of the balcony.

Under the fixed, approving stare of the proscenium goddess's gargantuan face, she bends down and picks up the offering left leaning against the wall. The cloth doll is crudely stitched and roughly rendered, and its arms and legs go limp as Leah lifts it off the floor. The misshapen body is made out of white cotton bearing brown water stains and stuffed unevenly with down feathers that pierce the fabric here and there. Its head and limbs are fashioned from faded black cloth, more coarse than that used for the body. On its face, a primitive set of eyes, nose and mouth are embroidered with soiled white thread by an unskilled hand.

A door slams close in the distance and she hears the hollow sound of heels striking against wood.

"Miss Hathaway, are you still here?" the voice intones below, the accent unmistakable.

Leah does not answer or look back, but instead quickly presses her body against the wall and freezes to avoid being seen from the stage. Cheek flush against the painted mural, eyes shut, she follows the sound of Madame Kaspar's footsteps across the stage.

"Leah, have you left?"

Her steps, severe and louder, ring out and then cease. She is at the edge of stage, Leah imagines, looking around, searching the empty concert hall. She visualizes the teacher looking left and looking right. Then looking up.

"Leah," Madame Kaspar calls out and waits for a response.

Convinced that she is about to be spotted, Leah presses closer still against the wall as if she wants to enter the two-dimensional scene of an Italian village and walk unnoticed among its cheerful, miniature residents. It's too late to turn around and answer now, and she holds her breath, pinning the pliable form of the doll against the cool surface with her chest.

The unnerving silence ends as the teacher resumes her walk across the stage, mumbling in her native tongue as she goes.

Another door opens and closes. Then silence.

Leah waits for Madame Kaspar's return, and then waits some more just to be sure. Once convinced that she is alone, Leah stuffs the simple cloth figure inside her coat and hurries from the upper balcony, fighting the urge to look back and see if the narrow eyes of the alabaster goddess follow her retreat.

Heading westbound along the county road bordering the National Park Seminary campus, travelers are likely to overlook a small opening in the scrub brush just beyond the Spanish Mission as they bear right and anticipate the visually stupefying Japanese Pagoda and Swiss Chalet clubhouses around the corner. These incongruous architectural wonders, like their sister sororities situated along the drive bridge, create a mystique of exoticism that belies the otherwise ordinary brick and stucco buildings hidden behind false facades and elaborate exterior decoration. Not only do these curious and extravagant edifices give the school the elite cache to the outside world its owners meticulously cultivate, they also serve to obscure the land's authentic and, from the administration's perspective, somewhat problematic history.

While the campus buildings and infrastructure contain reminders of its colorful, albeit brief, past as a struggling hotel and casino, no vestige exists of the property's original use, of the time when the sweat of labor, both human and animal, plowed deep furrows in the ground and tobacco leaves, broad, green and profitable, sprouted abundantly from the soil. The ignorance of parents and students to Forest Glen's complete past is excusable, for there is no painting or photograph, no engraving or monument, no rendering or written depiction inside the school recounting it. Visitors are left to assume that the National Park Seminary rose from virgin land divinely reserved for the construction of a modern educational Xanadu. So it is unofficially.

If one was disposed to inquire further, a search of the county land records will be of limited insight, offering only factual information such as boundary coordinates, ownership, and parcel size. The past lives, however, in the memory and in the blood of those residing beyond the gates of the exclusive institution.

Ask a local resident at the country store just north of the school or at the nearby roadhouse produce market, and they are likely to point you to the unmarked driveway carved out of the brambles and wild roses for proof that for more than a half-century the land was a highly productive plantation where slaves cultivated and dried tobacco to be placed in hogsheads rolled along the old corduroy road and floated down Rock Creek to be sold at the Port of Georgetown. All that's left of this forgotten era is Edgewood, the old plantation house down the road. It's owned by the school now, and it's seen better days, they might opine.

At the turnoff, a rutted dirt drive leads to the ancient manse, sheltered by a magnificent spread of trees that took root before European explorers left their mark on the land. On the approach, Edgewood, with its six towering columns and sloped, overhanging roof, is an out-of-place vision of antebellum architecture, the type of grand structure more likely found in cotton planta-tions in the deep South than in the border state of Maryland.

Built in 1790 by a descendent of Lord Baltimore on a generous swath of land that stretched over the creek and well beyond what would become the railroad right-of-way on the other side of the glen, Edgewood was the most prominent residence in the county when completed, though neither extrava-gantly spacious nor opulently decorated. Situated at the crossroads of agrarian commerce, the estate was a distinctive island rising up out a sea of bountiful crops and could be seen for miles in all directions by farmers transiting crops and livestock to the newly-established capital city.

The mansion now overlooks an expansive front lawn where cows once grazed after decades of growing tobacco robbed the soil of nutrients and the plantation took to dairy farming. Widely spaced elms dot the erstwhile pasture and the exterior of the once-pristine building, painted a brilliant white with black shudders and trim in its heyday, is a dingy gray, its sloping roof pocked and stained by the pollen and leaves and decay that has fallen upon it over a generation of neglect.

As the headmaster leads Mr. Stratton to the first floor parlor, a colored woman dressed in a starched indigo dress and apron and wearing a ruffled cap files into the vacated dining room and begins removing the service and unfinished trays of beef and quail under the watchful supervision of Mrs. Dawson. The two men, close in age, one a disciple in the millennium-old pursuit of knowledge, the other a captain of industry, settle into their respective chairs and consider the other, alone together for the first time since the tycoon's arrival the morning before. A fierce blaze casts a yellow glow against walls neatly lined with leather bound books while outside the parlor windows tree limbs sway languidly against a violet sky. In the far corner of the room, sandwiched between a neglected piano and a chestnut writing desk, a cloth-covered object sits on a pedestal unnoticed by the satiated guest.

"A sumptuous meal, Porter. Your wife is a delightful conversationalist. Most enjoyable. You must let me reciprocate soon. Do you and Mildred ever have reason to travel to New York?"

"On rare occasion. Let me see, it's been nearly four years since we were there last."

"The next time, you are my guests. My offer is an open one. Any time of year. The clubs in Manhattan are practically culinary orgies. You would be astounded by the size of the cuts of meat they serve and how tender they are. Shockingly good. I ate a steak at one club last month that I swear was more meat than I had in an entire year growing up as a young boy.

"Everything these days is bigger. Bigger. More plentiful. Faster. Before long, planes will be taking us where we want to go in hours, not in days. The world is opening up to us, Porter. Just as we are getting too old to enjoy it, wouldn't you know it? I get shivers thinking what it will all lead to. But I know this much: there will be opportunities that you and I and those of our generation never had. Opportunities that will make men with the vision to see beyond the horizon and have the courage to follow it extremely wealthy."

"Is the National Park Seminary such an opportunity?"

"Yes, I believe so. I've been outspoken about what you have accomplished here."

"But may I press the point a bit further, Douglas?"

"Of course. We must speak freely with one another. I want it no other way. Let's not stand on pretense or guard our words on the eve of our partnership being consummated."

The dean leans forward and addresses the grinning businessman in a deliberate yet emphatic tone.

"The Board of Trustees wants to know what a prospective sale will mean to the direction of the school. They will turn to me to report tomorrow on what changes are anticipated in the running of the school. As you know, we have embarked on an ambitious capital plan of expansion and the staffing rolls are likewise being increased to accommodate the growing enrollment. Our investment strategy has been aggressive and, if I may say so, wildly successfully. The outstanding debt, though considerable, will be retired on schedule if not early as National Park takes steps to bolster enrollment even more through improved marketing and primary school recruitment around the country. All this is underway while we are mindful of the need to maintain our reputation of exclusivity."

"Yes, National Park Seminary is indeed a successful venture, one I have enthusiastically supported through a not insignificant contribution of my own over the years."

The host bows his head in appreciation.

"And the future profitability of our venture is contingent upon these elements of success being in place and working in the future as they have done so well in the past. You would surely agree, Douglas. To disrupt or remove the efforts now underway would not only undercut our success as an educational institution, it would be injurious to keeping the business side of our house on the straight."

"Certainly."

The dean waits uncomfortably for an elaboration that does not come. He hears a commotion in the adjacent dining room that hints that their private exchange may soon come to an end. Frustrated that he cannot bring himself to be more direct in explaining his request, he stares down at his hands as the businessman looks on expectantly.

"What is it Porter? What are you seeking?" Mr. Stratton asks, knowing full-well the bush the dean is beating about.

"Very well. Will you accept, as a condition of sale, clear language that vests all matters of school operation and administration in the headmaster?"

"So that we are clear, that would be you?"

"The board will expect such an assurance."

"Are you are speaking on behalf of the Board of Trustees in this matter specifically or in all matters related to their consideration of my purchase offer?"

"I am not only the school's dean. My name is on the property title. I am a trustee as well."

"And, as such, you, more than the rest, will profit handsomely once our deal is concluded."

"That is secondary. I am not one to cash in, sir! I speak to you as the head of this school. I am not an idle participant in this affair. I must have your word that our work here will be done. This is not an inconsequential point. I know the board will want certain assurances spelled out before endorsing an agreement."

"And, if I understood you, they will be asking you tomorrow to report on whether these assurances have been mutually agreed to in principle? You have been authorized to negotiate the particulars? That is what we are discussing now?"

"Why such skepticism?" Dean Dawson defiantly blurts out. "I have led this school for nearly the past ten years and built it into the elite institution it is today. The board is well aware how essential my hand at the wheel has been in charting a course of profitability and excellence. They would no more want to lose my expertise as a surgeon would expect his patient to live without a heart. Outlining such parameters should not even be topic of discussion. Even the most uninformed purchaser of National Park Seminary would recognize how critical my continued leadership is to his investment. He would realize that the smart money would be to lock up the continued services of everyone in the administration or otherwise risk watching the bottom fall out.

"I have seen it at other schools, in other places. I have watched established schools, venerated institutions, held in high regard and in higher demand, wither away from poor, unconscionable stewardship. Schools with unshakeable reputations built over decades shuttered and bankrupt after only a few years of mismanagement. From my where I sit, it behooves the buyer more than the seller to seek an arrangement that protects his investment after the ink is dry."

"So you are now representing *my* interests in this affair as well?" the sage businessman tartly retorts, which only worsens the host's exasperation.

"This is not how I planned our discussion. We are not adversaries across a negotiating table. I speak of shared interests, Douglas. We have known each other for many years. You can trust my professional judgment on the topic of how to run a profitable establishment of higher learning. Look about us."

His guest leans forward, his tone stern.

"In truth, we do not know each other, Porter. Many years ago, my daughters attended your school for their education. We were acquaintances at that time. Our meetings were few and our dealings then were superficial. We shouldn't misconstrue the past into something it isn't. It is a common mistake—one I myself have made. I will consider your request. You should know that I have given it considerable thought already. But I make no commitment here tonight."

Stung by the Mr. Stratton's cold rebuke, the dean backs down, seeing that the door is closed to any further discussion of the matter.

Mrs. Dawson pokes her head in the parlor.

"Porter, we should be ready in two minutes," she says with an oddly mischievous look that escapes the attention of the distracted men.

The dean sighs audibly and labors to shake off the harsh exchange.

"Before we go in for dessert, I have something to present to you, Douglas."

"You have been too generous as it is, Porter, with the hotel room and now tonight's dinner."

Dean Dawson walks solemnly across the room and retrieves the wheeled cart holding the hidden object and slowly rolls it to where his guest is seated.

"I wanted to wait for the proper time to present this to you. With everything happening since you arrived, the time hasn't been right for me to express to you, in private, the appropriate sentiment. I wish, in retrospect, that our pointed words about the school's sale had not preceded what I am about to say."

Mr. Stratton looks curiously at the asymmetrical shape of the cloaked item.

"At the beginning of the spring semester, I am renaming Senior House after your daughter. It will be known as Elizabeth Stratton House as a lasting memorial to the tragic sacrifice she made in service to America. The news of her death left everyone stunned. Even now, I cannot accept it. Her brief life must serve as a reminder to all the girls who attend National Park of the virtues of womanhood and the heroic deeds they are capable of achieving."

"Really, Porter, that is not necessary—"

Dean Dawson raises his hand in silent protest and then lifts the sheet.

"This bronze statue will be placed prominently in the dormitory's reception parlor and will bear a plaque describing Elizabeth as an eternal daughter of the National Park Seminary and martyr to our Nation."

The miniaturized cast of an Amazon warrior riding atop a stallion, under attack by a panther, shines lustrously in the fire light. Caught in a moment of perilous violence, the unsheathed warrior, her skin taut and glistening, rears back with her spear and prepares to strike at the ferocious cat that has set upon the neck of her wounded mount with tooth and claw. The German chancellor presented the replica to John Vincent, Dean Dawson's predecessor, following his visit to Berlin in the summer of 1909. The provocative piece, delivered with fanfare by officials of the German embassy, was deemed by the dean to be too explicit for public display and was kept in his office until the war on the continent five years later made its presence there unpalatable. It was quietly removed, wrapped and placed in the storage house next to the servant's quarters. The irony—if not questionable taste—of presenting a replica of a work on display on the steps of the National Museum in Berlin, as a commemorative to Elizabeth Stratton is lost on Dean Dawson, who waits breathlessly for some reaction from the man seated quietly before him.

Mr. Stratton rises and looks over the dynamic work of art, contemplating the unexpected gesture, for the moment unwilling to make eye contact with the host.

"I can only imagine how painful Elizabeth's loss must be still. There are certain burdens that cannot be lightened with the passage of time. Let us keep her name on the lips and in the hearts of all of the girls who come here so they shall never forget her selfless deeds. This is my gift to you and Mrs. Stratton and your entire family."

"Your gesture is deeply moving, Porter," he says, pausing as he runs his fingers over the warrior's poised weapon. "I was at my home on the day we received the telegram about the attack on Elizabeth's transport ship. I remember that day so vividly, though I would erase it from my memory if I could. The sun was bright and there was not a cloud in the sky. The flower beds were lush and in full bloom. The windows were thrown open and a cool, dry breeze circulated throughout the house. It was one of those impossibly beautiful days that make you wonder if this is what heaven looks and feels like.

"When the door bell rang and the envelope was delivered, I was sure—absolutely positive—it was a mistake or perhaps even a dream. I kept telling myself over and over that it was not possible, not on a day so beautiful. I would not believe it. I simply could not accept that my dear Elizabeth was gone, not on a day like this.

"And then I heard Norma wail and the sound of her grief sliced through my heart like a knife. I knew then that it was not an imagined nightmare or an unfortunate clerical error. The panicked calls from my other daughters rushing down the stairs to their mother followed and I ran out of the house, out of my mind with madness, everything under the brilliant sun went dark and I paced back and forth in front of the house in a blind rage ripping out every single flower and plant until the yard was covered with broken stems and mangled blossoms. That was over three years ago and the memory of that day feels as new and as raw as if it just happened."

A melancholy smile comes over the businessman's face.

"I can remember sitting on the ground, stunned and barely able to marshal the will to breath, looking at the dirt and cuts on my hands from my frenzy when the voice of a boy beyond the fence called to me offering his services to dig up the rest for a nickel a plant."

For the second time, Mrs. Dawson enters the room and interrupts, her voice now forceful and urgent.

"Porter, it is time."

The dean shoots her a perturbed look that chases her back to the hallway and then he glances out the window. Placing his hand on Mr. Stratton's shoulder, he guides him from the room in silence and before they reach the dining room he stops and gestures toward the door, where Mrs. Dawson stands, fidgeting nervously, her eyes moist with tears.

"On this, your last evening at Forest Glen, we...we...we wanted..." her voice quivers and fails as emotion overcomes her.

Drawing a handkerchief to her mouth and nose, she does not try to regain her composure and instead pulls open the front door ushering the cold air into the foyer. Past the carpeted entryway and framed by the porch columns, a multitude of flickering kerosene lamps are positioned uniformly on the lawn in a rectangle. Inside this outline of white lights, lamps with red-stained chimneys are shaped in the form of a cross.

"The handiwork of some of our girls over at Zeta sorority."

The businessman looks out at the symbol shimmering under the night sky and then gives Mrs. Dawson, who struggles to suppress her sobbing, a reassuring look.

"Tell the girls their tribute is a moving one, and one I will never forget for as along as I live."

The words are enough to crumble the levee holding back the torrent of emotion inside the dean's wife causing her to flee to the refuge of the upstairs bedroom.

By tradition, the last—and best attended—tree trimming party held during the Christmas season is hosted by Chiopi sorority. An open invitation is extended to all of the Seminary girls and admission requires only that attendees dress as geishas or other outfits befitting of the Japanese Pagoda and its oriental motif. The costume lockers and makeup stashes of the drama department are raided and girls scour their closets for odds and ends to adorn satin robes and old bed sheets hastily tailored into suitable period dress.

Over the years, the costumes have grown more elaborate and carefully crafted as girls attempt to out-do one another. Outlandish masks of thickly-applied white powder and face paint are worn by many to conceal their identity and trick their classmates. The school administration, while typically attentive to regulating all social activities on campus, has come to recognize the Chiopi clubhouse geisha party as a well-earned release at the end of three months of classroom work and study, and, as such, has unofficially waived the requirement that chaperones be in attendance on the condition that outside guests not be invited. Though portrayed by Dean Dawson as a magnanimous gesture of trust, the decision is commonly thought of among the girls of the sorority as a bow to the administration's stodginess and the mockery that would be invited if the regents and teachers were to don silk robes, rouge their cheeks, and pin their hair up with wooden sticks.

At precisely eight o'clock, the stone lanterns on the Pagoda steps are lit to signal that the faux temple, with its up-swept, three-tiered roof, is open to guests. Soon a steady procession of girls file out of the dormitories huddled together for warmth and protection against the relentless wind, some dragging loosely secured cloaks along the snowy ground as they make their way. Upon reaching the Pagoda, guests enter through a vaulted archway and are greeted by a host who hands each a pair of worn, cheaply manufactured open-toed slippers, purchased in bulk at a shabby Chinatown market in the city years ago, and directs them to line their shoes along the near wall.

The popularity of the geisha party has grown over time, the exotic silliness serving as a break from the solemn tradition that hangs heavily over the campus in the weeks leading up to Christmas, and the sorority is soon packed. Delicate, brightly-colored lamps made of balsa wood and rice paper hang from the ceiling and clip the heads of the taller girls as they mingle about. At a table next to the corner phonograph, a punch of steaming apple cider and citrus slices is served in cups bearing the NPS monogram alongside twin silver serving trays with plates bearing generous slices of Lord Baltimore cake baked earlier in the day by the kitchen staff. The dessert, with its light yellow layers separated by a dense filling of pecans, almonds, cherries, and macaroons, and topped with fluffy white icing, is a staple of school socials and birthday celebrations. The cake is a favorite among students, many of whom try but fail to replicate the exquisite recipe when home between semesters.

In the center of the room, under a golden lantern with red silk tassels, the clubhouse Christmas tree has been removed and a terra cotta Buddhist statue, decorated with garlands and gaudy dime store necklaces, put in its place.

Margaret, dressed in a green silk robe embroidered with a fire-spewing dragon on the back, hugs the far wall trying to avoid the crush of bodies, her legs weak and unsteady from the persistent fatigue and waves of nausea throughout the day. Exaggerated charcoal lines accentuate her almond eyes and her hair is pulled back tightly giving her face a severe, feral look. She reluctantly agreed to come after Josephine insisted that staying in her room all day was doing her no good. The crowded room is suffocating and the air humid and she contemplates escaping out to the porch so she can feel the cooling breeze against her clammy neck. The noise is unbearable and makes

Margaret's aching head throb. With each new arrival to the party, the room shrinks further and the sound of praise and laughter over the girl's ingenuity in fashioning her outfit ratchets up the din.

Josephine socializes nearby with a closely bunched group of costumed girls, nearly unrecognizable in an oversized black wig, ghostly white face and scarlet lipstick. She has cinched a pink satin pillow around her waist so that it rests against the curve of her lower back. Two girls from Beta clubhouse wearing false mustaches and bulky samurai outfits made out of opera helmets and baseball chest protectors borrowed from the gymnasium equipment locker pinball through the crowd and join the circle of conversation. The discussion grows animated and Josephine, spotting Margaret leaning against the window sill, waves her over. Josephine seizes her by the arm as she reluctantly approaches and pulls her close so she can hear.

"So Phyllis and Evaline here have offered up a challenge. A friendly wager that they can take us on in a game of bowling. Alpha house against Theta house," Josephine explains at a volume level just below yelling as the music is suddenly turned up.

She playfully pokes a finger at the chest of the makeshift warrior standing across from her.

"Now, our regally dressed samurais, having got wind of the pathetic challenge, have thrown in their lot in a valiant attempt to show that the girls of Beta can do more than flirt with passersby from the rooftop of their silly castle."

Phyllis and Evaline giggle at the characterization.

"High-handed mockery won't help you win," Marion Kittle answers behind the tilted strands of horse hair on her upper lip. "I've seen you bowl at the gymnasium, Josephine. You throw the ball like you are hurling a sack of unwanted kittens into the river."

The girls from Alpha laugh some more, thoroughly enjoying the two facing off against each other.

"Touché. But I told Marion and her swarthy looking companion, Audrey, that I remember similar talk around the courts not long ago. A blustery challenge to a match of doubles and then a quickly dispatched pasting followed. I am not sure it is worth our while. What do you think, my dear?" Josephine asks, hoping to provoke the ire of her prospective opponents.

Margaret looks at the bright, exaggerated makeup on the faces around her.

"It's hard to take any of you seriously dressed the way you are. You look like refugee clowns from the circus."

Phyllis and Evaline snicker uncontrollably, even though they too are the target of derision from the willowy, acid-tongued girl.

"But if the gauntlet is thrown down, we shall pick it up."

"Then it is set," Audrey exclaims. "Marion and I representing Beta. The giggle girls here will represent Alpha. Against the best Theta has to offer. Monday at noon. The highest combined score wins."

"Agreed," Phyllis accepts on behalf of her team.

"Fine," Josephine concurs.

"And what of the wager?" Margaret poses abruptly to the group. "I mean, if I am going to dress and drag myself to gymnasium on our day off, there should be something at stake."

"What did you have in mind?" Evaline asks.

"Something more substantial than the tepid handshake we got across the net after winning at tennis, three and one," she answers, glaring pointedly at the twin warriors.

"Well, I feel confident in our chances, Audrey. Sure, let's place a wager. It will make it more interesting. It's all for fun anyway, right?"

"Count us in too!" a voice announces over Josephine's shoulder as Bettina, dressed in a flowered white robe and wearing pale green eye shadow, shoe-horns into the circle, with Mattie in tow.

The sophomore class president has been a favorite of the carmine-haired ruler of the ballroom suites soon after her arrival at the Seminary and was convinced to not only join Bettina on the chorus in her first year but also to pledge Zeta on the assurance that the quaint Swiss chalet was "the only choice of the high society girls on campus."

Mattie's physical poise and effortless skills separate her from most of the girls at the school who, stunted by years of athletic neglect and handicapped by deficiencies in their self-confidence, struggle to paddle a canoe in a straight line, fumble about on the basketball hard court, hesitatingly bring the epee to en guard, and panic when instructed to sprint twenty yards down chalk-lined lanes against their classmates.

"Excellent!" Evaline says as Audrey hugs Bettina and then Mattie. "Two westside clubs and two eastside clubs. Four bowling lanes and four teams. We have reached full capacity!"

INCIDENT AT FOREST GLEN *243*

Bettina looks over the samurai costumes, toys with the wig made of straw jutting under Evaline's helmet, and smiles.

"You have outdone yourselves girls. By far the most original I've seen tonight. You put us to shame with your creativity. When I heard you talk about a bowling tournament, I had to stop. What fun!"

Margaret scowls at the interloper, annoyed at the way Bettina has included herself in their friendly challenge. Her scalp burns as a wave of light-headedness sweeps over her.

Having seized control of the conversation, Bettina lays out her proposal for the stakes.

"It's a bit complicated with four teams, but what if we take turns and one house sets the bet for the other. The winning team decides which of the three bets it wishes to collect."

Margaret's eyes narrow and she speaks without thinking twice.

"I think it was a lot simpler when there were three teams."

Bettina brushes off the slight and shoots a condescending grin back at Margaret, too crafty to rise to the bait.

"More the merrier, isn't that right, Lizzie?"

The name burrows deeply under Margaret's skin. Josephine places a hand on her friend's shoulder to steady her.

In the jostling around them, a girl is bumped and drops her cake. The plate shatters, sending shards of frosting-covered china across the floor.

"So, let's see," Bettina continues on. "Why don't we start with our merry swordsmen, Marion and Audrey? If we lose, what price should Zeta house pay?"

The girls confer privately, their helmets pressed together, long wooden rods bound by twine to tortoise shell comb handles, jutting out from their belts at an angle threatening to others nearby.

"If Zeta loses," Audrey offers, "you agree to hang Beta's pennant on the front of your house for a week."

"A dare. How interesting. We accept. Now it's your turn," Bettina commands, pointing at Evaline and Phyllis. "You understand how the game's played. What should Marion and Audrey put up?"

Evaline is prepared and looks at the twin warriors with a devilish grin.

"If you lose, both of you must run down to the Honeysuckle Bridge at midnight and stand next to Cleo and Leo and roar like lions—"

"Ooh, ooh," Phyllis interjects, "in your nightgowns. At midnight. In your nightgowns at midnight. Roaring like lions."

"Yes," Evaline enthusiastically endorses. "Perfect touch, my dear."

"Wait a second," Marion objects, "that's much more than what we proposed. I want to change ours."

"Too late. Do you accept?" Bettina officiates.

"We accept," Marion answers confidently. "We are not going to lose. None of you can beat us. I haven't even seen Bettina bowl before. You do know you have to wear old bowling shoes that have been worn on the feet of other girls, don't you? I think it is even odds that you balk at putting them on."

"Maybe I have my own personal pair in my room."

The idea of Bettina Braddock, socialite and heiress to the family timber fortune, owning her own two-toned bowling shoes is enough to launch Evaline and Phyllis into an uncontrolled fit of snorts and laughter.

"All right. Josephine, your choice. What do you want Evaline and Phyllis to wager," Bettina says matter-of-factly, trying her best to ignore the guffawing next to her.

"Why don't you and Mattie go first, Bettina?"

"Because I am being polite and allowing everyone to go before we do."

"Hardly," Margaret spits out. "You want to use going last to your advantage. You want to propose the final bet. And you have gamed it so that it is our bet. Your designs are transparent."

"What has gotten into you, Lizzie? You have such a suspicious mind."

Audrey looks puzzled.

"What do you keep calling Margaret *Lizzie?* It's the second time you've called her that."

"Just an inside joke between the two of us, right?" she says to Margaret with a contemptuous, leering look.

"Tell us. What's the joke?" Audrey presses.

"Margaret doesn't like it when I call her that."

"Fine, let's just finish this," Josephine interrupts impatiently. "If Alpha loses, you present Peeping Tom with an offering of tribute. Three times— once in the morning, once in the afternoon, once in the evening—you will lay a tray of treats and candy before his feet, for all of the Theta club to enjoy."

"How mundane," Margaret grouses.

"Indeed," Bettina echoes, continuing to needle the sour girl.

"I suppose we can accept that," Evaline says after receiving a nod from her partner.

"Well, what do you say, Mattie, what is a fair wager for the alley cats of Theta?"

Though intrigued by the game being played, Mattie, sensing the tension between Bettina and Margaret, thinks twice before offering a suggestion and shrugs.

"Hmmm." Bettina ponders aloud for effect. "How about if you lose, you have to skip rope out in front of Vincent Hall while you sing a school yard rhyme?"

"I've told you before to stop, Bettina," Margaret warns gravely, the severity of her tone unambiguous and menacing.

"Don't let her get to you," Josephine counsels, sensing that Margaret, already in an ill-tempered mood, is about to erupt.

"I don't understand," Audrey persists. "Is this about the name Lizzie? Is it your middle name or a family nickname?"

"Oh, you don't know, do you?" Bettina dangles before the group like an enticing morsel of meat.

Mattie feels increasingly uncomfortable with the turn in the conversation and looks to extract herself from both Bettina and the wall of bodies pushing the group closer together.

"If you insist, Audrey. Margaret is from a Massachusetts town of some notoriety. As the story goes she was teased when she was young by other children who said she had the looks and temperament of a woman who just a few years before Margaret was born walked the very same neighborhood streets in Fall River. You wouldn't know it now, but evidently Margaret had quite the temper at a young age. Strong-willed and defiant. You know how children can be so cruel when they find weakness in another.

"You see, the despicable acts of the woman to whom she was compared were the stuff of lore. The images and the acts were so gruesome that they robbed many a child of sleep. And the idea that the perpetrator of the brutality, to this day, walks freely among the residents of Fall River surely scared and fascinated Margaret's tormentors.

"The relentless teasing bothered our school mate terribly. Over and over the children would sing the playground rhyme until they chased poor

Margaret back inside her house in tears. I am told the nickname of Lizzie stuck and it follows her to this day. Do I have it more or less right, my dear?"

Margaret directs her attention to the girls crowded around the statue of Buddha pretending to ignore the Bettina's reptilian expression of delight. The air has grown thin and she feels her skin tingle as if tiny soda bubbles are popping along the length of her arms.

"Enough!" Josephine demands.

"It's all in the past, of course," Bettina offers in a softer, more conciliatory tone. "We are mature now. What harm can childhood taunts do us now, am I right?"

A host from Chiopi dressed in the garb of a Japanese princess interrupts Bettina and reminds the group to get some cake before it is gone. The samurai twins start to break away from the circle but stop when Bettina launches the coup de grace.

"Based on what Mrs. Tulkingham taught us this semester in psychology, I would think skipping rope to the rhyme might provide a therapeutic outlet for you, Margaret, a chance to chase away the demons of your past."

She pauses and then begins striking her hands together in a slow cadence.

"Tell us how it goes," she teases. "Come on. You know the words."

The sound of Bettina's clapping grows louder.

"Come on."

"Stop it now, Bettina, or we are leaving." Josephine's ultimatum is delivered in a harsh, forceful tone.

Mattie pulls at her friend's arm and whispers a private plea that the others cannot hear over the noise in the cramped room.

"You are being ridiculous, Bettina. Stop the clapping," Josephine chides the persistent interrogator. "The only person you are embarrassing is yourself."

"Really? Is that so? At least I have the decency to speak what I have to say to her face. I don't go around other people's backs and run them down with wicked rumors. That's the difference between you and me, Margaret. I look the girl in the eye when there's a problem and tell her what I think about her."

Margaret, embarrassed by Josephine's rush to her defense, stares coldly at Bettina's goading expression, as other girls near the circle, attracted by the odd, methodic clapping in the corner of the room, begin to take notice of the disturbance.

"Your desperate need for attention and acceptance is none of my concern, Bettina. For someone who constantly reminds everyone at this school of her family's fortune and society page prominence, I find it most peculiar. So go ahead and clap like a monkey on the shoulder of an organ grinder, if you want. This is a dull affair and could use some entertainment, no matter how primitive. I'll have no part of your debasement."

"No? You don't remember the words?"

"Does this mean the bowling match is not happening?" Evaline asks to no one in particular as Margaret slips past her and hurries away.

"Let me help you then," Bettina calls out, unaware that Mattie has left her side as well.

The words of the nasty little rhyme, synchronized to the beat of the sharp clapping, ring in Margaret's ears as she presses through the hot wall of silk and powder separating her from the oriental doors of the Pagoda.

Lizzie Borden took an axe
And gave her mother forty whacks.
When she saw what she had done
She gave her father forty-one.

Josephine retrieves her shoes and coat and rushes along the path leading to Senior House trying to catch up with Margaret. The night air is exhilarating after the oppressiveness of the party and she draws it in hungrily, the cleansing feel in her lungs welcome as she runs along, passing a few latecomers as she goes.

Just as she is about to head inside the dormitory, she notices a solitary figure in the gardens further on near the footbridge over the glen, partially obscured by the waist-high bank of boxwoods. Margaret, coatless and wearing only her green robe, stands next to the statue of Cyporissus with her back turned, illuminated under a pole lamp against the cold emptiness of the ravine beyond, a black abyss without form or definition, dotted only by the distant, twinkle of lights from the train station and the Glen Manor Hotel.

As she makes her way over to Margaret, Josephine notices out of the corner of her eye the pin-prick glow of red burn through the darkness. A man, the smoke of his cigarette spewing between clenched lips, steps into the light and begins to remove his overcoat. The stranger's appearance out of nowhere gives Margaret a start and she takes a step away from the advancing man. Josephine calls out to her as she hurries down the walkway. The man turns in the direction of her voice, shakes his head, and begins to laugh as Josephine draws near.

"I am speechless," he stammers at the sight of the two girls dressed inexplicably in the garish, foreign costumes. "I mean, what goes on at this school? Do you girls ever attend class or study?"

He can hardly suppress his incredulity as he drapes his coat over Margaret's shoulders. Josephine is able to tell from the man's tone and mannerisms that, dressed as she is in the dark, he does not recognize her.

"I apologize if I startled you, but imagine my surprise when I saw... when I saw...what are you dressed up to be exactly?"

"An oriental geisha," Margaret answers, throwing open the folds of his oversized coat to reveal the richly embroidered robe and still wearing the bamboo sandals, two sizes too small, given to her at the party.

"A geisha, I see. The sort of vision you expect to see when you are out for a walk in the freezing December night. You looked like you were in need of some protection."

"Quite gallant," Margaret coos, wrapping the surrendered coat around her thinly-covered, slender frame.

She looks over the confident, forward man.

"And out of the dark night a stranger appears to rescue a geisha girl in need. How fortuitous. Do you make a habit of prowling around the grounds under the cover of night?"

"Perhaps I am an art connoisseur just taking in the statues and monuments."

"Then that would certainly explain it. To see them all would take a day *and* a night. But you look like a man of more refined tastes than what National Park can offer," Margaret says flirtatiously.

"Wait a moment. You look vaguely familiar," he says with a quizzical expression, casting a more discriminating look upon Margaret.

"Not unless you had reason to travel to the Orient recently."

Josephine moves closer to the two so that the overhead light shines fully on her.

"Mr. Carter, let me introduce you to Miss Margaret Cleary, the student body's unofficial mistress of deception and intrigue."

The stunned man turns toward Josephine and does a double-take, his jaw left gaping at hearing his name spoken. He narrows his eyes and tries to recognize the person hidden behind the white theater paint and broad, upswept onyx wig. For a moment, Josephine feels strangely empowered in her disguise, drawing perverse enjoyment as Mr. Carter stammers about.

"I'm sorry, but you have me at a disadvantage. Your disguise makes it difficult…"

"Miss Barnes. Josephine Barnes. We met this morning during the visit to the hospital."

"Why, I would never have recognized you with the—" he stares at Josephine in shocked surprise circling his fingers around his face, "and with the—" and then points to his head as he looks over the wig.

"I know. It's a ritual at the Seminary. The week before Christmas break. Rather silly, isn't it?"

"The two of you know each other?!" Margaret exclaims, suddenly and unhappily cut out of the conversation.

"So it seems," Mr. Carter answers, still on his heels, glancing back at the tall, distinctive looking woman he now recognizes as Josephine's dancing partner from last night when he first saw her from the ballroom balcony. "The two of you look stunning, very exotic."

"You are kind—and a convincing liar. I feel a bit foolish. It is one thing to parade about like this among other girls also dressed this way. It an entirely different matter all together to be seen dressed up like a china doll around strangers."

"Luckily we are not strangers," he offers with a comforting smile, his words, casually spoken, grab Margaret's interest.

"We should go now."

Josephine removes the coat from Margaret's shoulders and hands it back to its owner.

"Thank you. We need to head inside."

"Of course. It's frightfully cold. You should go find a nice fire to warm yourselves. The word is that it is about to get even colder tomorrow."

Intertwining her arm in Margaret's, she leads the way back toward Senior House, saying good night over her shoulder as she leaves.

"It is a pleasure to meet you Miss Cleary," Mr. Carter calls out, the vapor of his breath rising up toward the yellow bulb buzzing overhead. "And, Miss Barnes, perhaps our paths will cross again soon."

Holding his coat over his arm, he draws the last of the cigarette and watches the two women dissolve into the night until all that is left is a faint residue of gray for him to follow. He turns and heads across the Honeysuckle Bridge to return to his room, not breaking stride as he flicks the smoldering butt of tobacco over the railing and into the hidden fast-moving waters below. The bell of an approaching streetcar rings in the distance heralding the last arrival of the evening into the station.

On the short walk to Senior House, Josephine is quiet and Margaret senses she is unwilling to discuss what just transpired. She feels the defensiveness in her friend's body language, a fortress of clenched muscles, tight like rigor mortis. As the girls ascend the stairs and hurry toward the door, Margaret, intrigued by the chance meeting by the bridge, can no longer hold her tongue.

"A pleasant man, wouldn't you say?"

Josephine shrugs unconvincingly without saying a word.

"Just as I thought. We must definitely talk. Your room or mine?"

Chapter 8
Proscenium Goddess

Not infrequently has a mother brought to us a shy, diffident, self-conscious daughter, saying in her presence: "It is useless to give my daughter lessons in music, art or elocution. She has no talent. She can take only a plain, common education." Talent is largely a matter of awakened emotion. The ability to feel must come before the ability to do. Such a daughter needs, above all, to see and feel the universe of beauty around her; to lose sight of self in contemplating the great ideals of others; while her heart should respond promptly to the story of life expressed in its finest forms. We plead for the girl who has not talent, but who needs culture. We feel that music itself is more than its performance; that the highest gains from music study are the perception of the beautiful, the cultivation of the imagination, spirituality and expression, the accurate observation of those points of touch, structure and significance which—though trifles in themselves—lead to that perfection which is no trifle.

Shadows of shadows awaken. Over the soil hardened by the killing frost they move. Across the virgin ice crystals that calm the brackish lake they sweep. Arcing over slick rooftops and around dying chimneys they soar. Shadows of shadows. Passing over a still and lifeless landscape undetected.

The chapel clock strikes ten. The lanterns in front of the Pagoda are snuffed out and the doors of the clubhouse are secured, the job of cleaning up the remnants of the evening's festivities left for the morning. The last of the Chiopi sisters hurry off to their dormitory rooms, fatigued but gossiping giddily about the best and worst of the costumes worn by their classmates.

Up the road, a hunchbacked grounds worker wearing thick wool gloves and a moth-eaten scarf leads a horse and cart down the narrow driveway to Edgewood. Many of the lanterns positioned on the plantation lawn in tribute

252 ANDY JOHNSON

to Elizabeth Stratton have run out of fuel, while the flames of others flicker under the light of a rising moon. The worker methodically retrieves the rows of lamps and places them into the flat bed, careful to not disturb those inside the quiet mansion.

Beyond the drawn curtain on the second floor, Mrs. Dawson, dressed for bed, combs her hair seated in front of the vanity mirror extremely pleased with how well the dinner for their famous guest went. With every few strokes of the tortoiseshell brush, she recounts out loud in the most favorable terms a different chapter in the evening's events, while down the hall, the dean, still dressed in his vested suit and tie, half-listens in his study. School annuals are arrayed on the desk before him and as he pages through them, looking at the sepia photographs and the names from the past, an oppressive weight of despondency settles on his heart. He lingers over one page. A collage of photographs, entitled *Domestic Science Department*. One of a sewing class. Another of students wearing aprons and lace caps positioned around a cooking class counter. The spare description beneath the picture of the school infirmary reads:

In sickness, as in health, our girls are our daughters to be cared for as our own. We also teach the care of the sick, invalid cookery, emergencies, etc.

The dean reaches down and retrieves the glass carefully positioned on the floor by his feet, concealed within the interior of the desk. He places the nearly empty crystal lightly against his lips and draws a quick sip, so as to not let the burgundy liquid rest on his lips longer than necessary, and feels the fragrant, forbidden offering from Douglas Stratton fill his mouth and slide down his throat. A warming sensation travels through his pleasantly numb body as he studies the miniature world of the first floor infirmary in Vincent Hall.

There she is, next to the grim, older faces of the nursing staff. The flawless skin, the pronounced cheek bones. Her posture erect and resolute. The fiber of youth exuded in her presence. The world, new and green, in her eyes.

"I've hung your suit and shirt on your valet for tomorrow, Porter," his wife calls out. "Don't stay up too late. Good night, dear."

The room down the hall goes dark and his reply is weak and slightly slurred.

Miss Price climbs the stairs to the third floor of Senior House on her rounds to ensure that all students are accounted for after the party. Some girls have gone to bed already, while others labor in the hallway bathroom removing layers of greasepaint and makeup. As she walks down the corridor, she stops at Josephine's room, the door slightly ajar, and listens to the animated voice of Margaret inside. She hears passing mention of a man in the flood of words. Leaning closer, she hesitates in pushing the door open, satisfied for the moment to keep her presence hidden.

"Don't be dense. I could see immediately in his reaction that he is smitten with you. If you took off your puritanical blinders and you would see it too."

"How can you be so sure after a grand total of sixty seconds?"

"Because he treated me like a smelly two-day old fish when you showed up?"

"Ha! I knew you would figure a way to bring it back to you."

"What! It's true."

"Of course, what possible reason could there be for a man not making a run at Margaret Cleary's affections other than he is madly in love with someone else?"

"I said nothing of love. This is an opening gambit on his part. More likely a question of lust really."

The regent can't help but smile and decides to linger after she sees that no one is around to witness her eavesdropping.

"And let's say this isn't another instance of your pathological preoccupation with the desires of men. What exactly would you have me do?"

"Start by not being so dismissive of his advance. This is how men go about pursuing a woman. Most of them have barely evolved beyond the stage of presenting women with a leaf filled with roots and berries as a sign of their interest. When he makes the first move, you have to give him a reason to believe he is not out of line. It's a miracle you didn't chase off Robert behaving like that."

"Speaking of Robert."

"What's the harm with a little flirting now and again? You are not engaged. You are almost nineteen. What is the point of tying yourself down?"

"And encourage the affections of a man I only just met?"

"See where it takes you. You may be surprised by what you find."

"I barely know anything about him. We talked in a ward filled with hospital patients for no more than a few minutes. Hardly the type of first impression that is likely to produce the passionate interest you claim."

Miss Price rears back at Josephine's mention of the trip to Walter Reed that morning.

Had she misunderstand what was said behind the partially closed door? She searches her memory and the disparate clues begin to pull together into one devastating conclusion. Now it makes sense, she realizes. She remembers losing track of Mr. Carter's whereabouts in the patient ward and then coming upon him talking alone with Josephine at the back of the room. She thought nothing of it at the time. The revelation that the girls' bedside chat is about the visitor from New York catches her off-guard. As she pulls back from the door, she is wounded by the surprising sting of jealousy.

As Miss Price continues along the hallway, stunned by what she has inadvertently discovered, Margaret's lugubrious words follow her, tormenting her ears.

"Seeing you as a Japanese tart dressed in satin and ribbons certainly grabbed his attention."

Further down the corridor, May lies quietly in bed reading her book of poetry by lamp light, oblivious to the sound of the girls outside readying themselves for bedtime. The book, her constant companion throughout the day, has a profound hold on her. She read it walking between classes and even spent lunchtime holed up in the Empire parlor reading to escape the distraction of the dining room. She returned to her room after dinner anxious to finish the leather bound volume, plucked from the shelves of Miller library the day before out of boredom. As daytime gave way to night, she immersed herself in the mesmerizing tales, stopping only occasionally to count the number of pages remaining.

The sound of knocking nearby breaks the spell and she looks up from the enchanting verses to see that the hour is late. She hears Miss Price's distinctive voice across the hallway calling through the door to Leah's room and listens carefully. But there is no answer.

Miss Price looks down between the door and the floor and sees that the quiet room is dark.

"It's been a long night girls. Lights off," the regent announces down the hallway, followed by a softer, more personal entreaty just outside her door. "Lights out, May."

She does not respond to the disembodied voice and waits for Miss Price to walk on before returning to her reading. As she dives back into the open pages, tantalizingly close to finishing the thin volume, she unconsciously picks at the ends of the bandage taped to the back of her neck. The narrow strip of gauze and cotton is caked with a dollop of dried blood where Leah scratched away the skin during their confrontation at the solarium.

Across the glen, Mr. Stratton finishes packing for his early morning train back to New York City. A stack of telegrams litter the writing desk in his room, retrieved by his faithful assistant from the post office next to the train station while he was dining with the Dawsons, clipped communications from his headquarters office and associates of the legal firm representing him tomorrow before the school's Board of Trustees.

He takes the framed picture of his wife from the bed stand and slips it securely between layers of clothes in his luggage bag before closing it. Feeling his energy beginning to wane, he draws a blank sheet of stationary from the desk drawer and writes a last minute note to Mr. Carter. Once completed, he reads the instructions over twice and satisfied with his decision slips the paper into an envelope and places it on top of the slender box next to the ashtray. He turns off the lights, slowly reclines onto the uneven mattress, and pulls the sheet and blanket close to his chin.

Bare tree limbs outside his window, back-lit by a gas lamp in front of the hotel, cast exaggerated shadows across the ceiling and he watches the thin, crooked branches sway silently above him until his eyelids grow heavy and a peaceful sleep sweeps over him.

Beyond the rail bed, deep in the wooded recesses of Rock Creek, a restless presence moves swiftly along the old corduroy road. It travels in silence down the winding trail moving with preternatural strides and suddenly turns and heads off into the concealing heart of the still forest. Pushing through twisted towers of sharp-blade grasses, it accelerates across an open field, rushing down a snow-covered row of decapitated corn stalks. The ramshackle building appears in the distance. As it draws near, the solitary figure passes weed-infested livestock pens and discarded farming tools claimed by rust long ago. Nearby, the tortured creature rests fitfully in a shallow state of unconsciousness, tethered to a splintered railing by a short rope, the glaze of the biting frost noticeable along its dull withers and sloping backside.

The uninvited presence ascends the broken porch steps and hovers outside, watching over the man seated in the chair, his back to the window, rocking slowly before a dying fire inside a wood stove. Dingy mattresses, illuminated in the weak light, are spread across the floor, covering half of the sagging floor. Shrouded forms, concealed under layers of thin blankets and soiled clothes, lay upon them, motionless except for the slow breathing that causes their makeshift cocoons to rise and fall in halting, unsynchronized rhythms.

As the last of the embers in the stove pulsate and slowly die, the surreptitious watcher slips away and traveling along a stiff breeze melts into the nearby maze of trees. Over consecrated ground, unmarked and forgotten, the specter travels toward the glen, navigating the lightless contours of the somnolent world effortlessly until the scent of saturated soil and rotten timber presages the approaching waters.

It drops down from an outcropping of rock without hesitation and continues along the eroded edge of the black water. A thin, crystalline mist floats above the creek like a swarm of shiny gnats frozen in suspended animation by the cruel hand of winter. A silvery object glimmering in the tall grass next to the concrete ramp is retrieved and carried off into the dense brush lining the banks.

In the flurry of activity leading up to the last weekend before Christmas dismissal, the re-emergence of the mermaid fountain from the receding flood waters escapes the notice of the Seminary students and teachers alike. The harsh conditions make walking the stone path treacherous and deter students from visiting the Grotto and those crossing the glen are in too much of a hurry to escape the wintry winds sweeping along the ravine to see that the cast-iron figure has slowly risen out of tumult like a primordial fossil.

Leah stands on the creek's edge in the dead of night, peers into the abyss, and contemplates how to reach the fountain. A necklace of accumulated branches and leaves surrounds the marred statue and an uprooted tree trunk rests on top of the mid-stream island. After careful consideration, she takes an elongated step and lands on a rounded stone only a few inches above the fast-moving water. She extends her arm out in front to steady her precarious footing on the slick and narrow perch. Turning to her right, she finds the second step and without delay leaps forward, her legs spread in flight like those of a dancer, and finds the flatter, wider stone. Overconfident with success, her next step is careless and she lands on the icy surface and rolls her ankle in an explosion of excruciating pain. Struggling not to lose her balance, she bends down and grips the splattered rock but not before her wounded foot splashes into water so cold it steals her breath. She continues on in a frantic rush, adrenaline driving her clumsy steps until she reaches the grouping of large rocks in the middle of the creek.

Leah limps over toward the fountain whimpering with pain, dragging her foot as if it were a ponderous anchor, looking for a suitable spot to rest. Using her hands to guide her in the darkness, she cautiously lowers herself down onto the rocky surface, panting rapidly from the shock of the slip. She rubs her hands along the length of her soaked stocking and grimaces when she reaches the tender, swelling ankle, suppressing the urge to cry out in agony.

She waits a few moments to allow the pain to subside and to calm her thoughts. The outcropping is exposed and the night air is frightfully cold. All she hears is the sound of the water surrounding her, lapping at the rocks and rushing along the length of the glen. She struggles to stand upright and hops along the loose scree of the creek bed, using the pedestal to steady herself as she passes by the diminutive storybook figure. She kneels with care next to the water's edge and slides a cloth satchel from her shoulder and rests it on a bar of sandy loom churned up by the flood. With barely enough ambient light to see the thin drawstring, Leah fumbles to untie the bag until the troublesome knot is finally solved. She reaches in and carefully draws out the deformed doll left in the theater balcony, now wearing the oversized white dress retrieved by Josephine from the flood.

The unveiled fabric glows. The figurine's stitched eyes and mouth are prominent in the darkness.

The wind along the ravine swirls and shifts as if the trees are collectively breathing and exhaling around her. The sumptuous song of the woods fills her ears with sweet, unrestrained notes. She revels in the discordant sounds, swims in the collective aura that surrounds her. It is new and invigorating to her senses—so different from the rigorously and meticulously formed melodies she has labored to produce over the years toiling inside the Odeon.

Now I see. This is my destiny.

Kneeling at the water's edge, the feel of moist rock and sand beneath her, she finally has clarity, a higher calling to quell the turmoil of the past few days.

Out of chaos, there is now purpose.

Her hands tremble as she places the limp effigy tenderly on the murky, ebony surface. The swift current spirits the offering away into the maw of the bleak night.

I have done what is asked of me.

Retracing her steps in preparation to ford the creek back to the banks of the Grotto, Leah pauses at the base of the fountain and looks up at the outline of the mermaid silhouetted against a sky robbed of its stellar brilliance. Stabbing pain rockets up her leg as the rush of blood reaches her enlarged ankle. She has never before been so close to the fountain, never touched it or closely inspected its inspirational form. The mermaid's facial features, looking at the graceful arm pointing upward, are delicate and enchanting. Even in the scant light, Leah can make out the clear line of the myth's chin and jaw, the youthful curve of her neck, the rounded protrusion of her pubescent breasts. The fixture's rapturous beauty momentarily calms Leah's frantic mind and settles her heart.

The soothing sound of the creek caresses her ears and the burning pain consuming her foot, so urgent and insatiable moments before, ceases. A gust of wind ripples along the length of her coat and lifts the hair off of the back of her neck. In the gap between her gloves and sleeves, her slender wrists, exposed to the bitter air, grow numb, engorged purple veins prominent beneath translucent skin. Leah feels the internal tempo of her body slow as the gusting vortex grips the bones of her body and pours into her chest cavity. Fine droplets of mist coat her flush cheeks, dot her eyelashes, moisten her dry lips. The sedative embrace dulls her senses. Her speeding pulse quiets.

Animate.
     Inanimate.
          Silence.
               Blackness.
                    Regeneration.
                         Animate.

The beguiling visage turns slowly toward Leah. The delicate upturned nose, the thin, finely sculpted lips, the rounded chin, cast against the blank backdrop of the heavens, gradually disappear as the linear profile transforms into an oval shape without defining features, a dread-inducing oracle of nihility gazing down upon the frightened girl.

"No, dear God, no!"

Leah panics and rushes headlong into the open water, making no attempt to find the stepping stones. The soles of her leather shoes slip and slide along the submerged rocks forcing her to slow and steady herself or risk falling into the stiff current that pushes against her legs. In seconds, she loses the feeling in her feet and toes. After a near-fall, she rights herself and pushes on through the shifting, disorienting water. Reaching the shore, she grabs onto tufts of overgrown grass jutting out from the bank and hoists herself onto land, breathless and soaked from the knees down.

Terrified and unable to climb the lengthy flight of steps back to the school, she frantically limps over to the spring niche next to the Grotto's amphitheater and crawls into the dank nook. An inescapable cold emanates from the walls of the shelter and her shoulders begin convulsing. Leah draws her knees tightly against her chest as she used to do as a young girl and looks out into the pervasive darkness, panting, trembling, and waiting.

"No, no...it can't be real! It can't be."

From inside the sheltered alcove, she can no longer see the statue. Nor is the formation of rocks visible. She closes her eyes and listens intently for some sign that her hasty escape was followed, for some indication that the statue, suddenly brought to life by Leah's presence, seeks her out.

But nothing moves in the gloom. The only sound is the deadly current.

The throbbing of her ankle is now more intense after the frantic escape and she winces as her foot scrapes along the mortar and brick.

And then she hears it.

Far in the distance, beyond the misty veil, a chilling solitary cry, high in the treetops above the water, echoes down the glen and is swallowed by the night.

Dean Dawson sits despondently on a park bench and watches the early morning traffic of automobiles, horse carts, and streetcars jockey for the position along the avenue. Beyond the hustle and bustle, the grand portico of the

White House is awash in a pink glow as the sun peeks through a narrow rip in the thick, moisture-laden clouds rolling across the horizon.

Squirrels with wire-brush tails hop around the lawn under towering oaks holding onto the last of their withered leaves, scratching and probing the hardened soil for forgotten stashes. One precocious creature among them, young and missing the tip of its tail, cautiously approaches the bench along the crushed-stone walkway hoping for a handout, only to be sent away with abrupt kick of the dejected headmaster's shoe.

Across the square, a man stands on the steps of the marble bank building and scans the park until he spots the dean's slight build hunched over on the bench. He walks toward him unsure of what to say, though he knew all along that this moment was inevitable and the unpleasant conversation he is about to have unavoidable. He approaches the bench unnoticed, ignoring a street vendor hawking cooked sausages from a steaming cart. At least the exchange will not be at the Seminary. The abandoned park is ideal just in case their meeting turns contentious.

Why wouldn't it, he asks himself? Should he rightfully expect anything other than disbelief and rage? If their positions were reversed, how would he react? Would there not be heated words? Accusations of perfidy? The grabbing of lapels? Unrestrained anger?

The anxious man feels a nervous tingle inside as he draws near, as if he is approaching the moment of his own judgment. Wiping away a dusting of snow from the wooden slats, he sits at the far end of the bench and places his leather satchel between them, a symbolic dividing line of sorts, and waits for the dean to speak or to at least acknowledge his presence. But the reflective headmaster just stares ahead at the chaos unfolding before him, satisfied to share the bench in silence.

He waits until he can no longer bear it. His conscience will not let him rest; he must face the music and hear from the one he betrayed.

"Dean Dawson, the board has appointed me to act on their behalf to handle the execution of the sale. I will work with the lawyers, of course, to prepare and file the necessary papers. But I thought you should know that the board has voted that I am to report to them directly on all matters related to purchase. They took these actions after you left. They are prepared to proceed with the sale of the National Park Seminary."

The inconsolable dean refuses to look over, maintaining his gaze toward the executive mansion.

"Do you understand that from this point forward, I am no longer to report to you in carrying out these duties?"

"George, are you aware that a graduate of our school works in the protocol office there? Mrs. Beverly Clouse. The class of 1915. Quite a remarkable woman."

"I was not aware, sir."

"She is living proof of the how we take in girls, immature and bearing the unpolished edges of youth, and make them into strong, capable women."

"Yes, sir, there are many."

"And yet, my colleagues on the Board of Trustees believe it is not prudent to allow me to continue to lead an institution that I am principally responsible for rebuilding to its current state of excellence after years of absent leadership! Are they blind to the consequences of their action?!"

"They *do* wish to see you continue as school administrator. They just were not willing to make it a condition stipulated in the sale contract. Douglas Stratton made it known to them that he would not be bound in how the school is to be run and who will run it. Forcing their hand by demanding a vote on the question was not wise. And leaving the meeting when the motion was defeated was a desperate act of hubris on your part. It was not the time to be headstrong. There is a new reality in play, Dean Dawson, and we must bend to it. In this age of industry and capital, we must adapt."

"George, if only you were behind me whispering *'all loyalty is fleeting.'* How can I continue on after such rejection by the board members? I considered each and every one of them to be wholly supportive of my tenure as administrator. There is principle at stake here. How could their loyalty be so shallow? It was all I could do not to yell out *'Et tu Brute.'* Their decision is unconscionable."

"Are you understanding me, sir? The board made a financial decision. The offer was too attractive to ignore. Once settlement is final, all decisions affecting National Park Seminary will rest with Stratton Enterprises. The board's legal powers will dissolve. It is to remain on in an advisory capacity only once the transfer is complete. The days of past have fallen victim to the modern ways of business."

The dean rubs his temples vigorously, racking his brain over the swift repudiation by those he thought of as allies.

"There is something not right here. My case fell upon deaf ears. There was no discussion, no serious discussion at least. Somehow Stratton insinuated himself into the meeting. His influence was on their lips; it swayed their consciences. I could see it on their faces. Many of them would not even look me in the eye when I spoke."

"Perhaps I can be an advocate for your interests moving forward."

The dean turns toward the bursar, tired looking, though he awoke only a few hours ago. He no longer wants to launch his arrows of exasperation and recriminations into the inhospitable morning air.

"'*An advocate*,'" he repeats softly, before slipping into reflective thought.

Mr. Geary slides closer on the bench.

"You have turned a fortuitous development inside out. Instead of recognizing the financial benefit the sale will provide to both you and the school's future, you are needlessly focusing on a narrow question that by the beginning of next semester will seem silly and inconsequential."

A loose page of newsprint floats past the two men and pirouettes before being borne away by a stiff gust up toward the gray clouds overhead.

"Are you to be my advocate, George? Are you to be my advocate with Douglas Stratton?"

"I will be, Dean. I will do whatever I can to maintain your hands on the tiller."

The stunned headmaster looks intently at his financial officer and considers the pledge.

"The first order of business, however, is for you to communicate your congratulations directly to Mr. Stratton with words sufficiently laying out how enthusiastically you look forward to working for him."

The dean thinks back to last night's dinner at Edgewood and the testy exchange between the two of them.

Mr. Geary continues on.

"I, of course, will make sure that your message is expeditiously sent to him and that he knows he can count on you four-square."

Dean Dawson's head swims with nagging questions making it difficult to reconcile the raw emotions he is experiencing. He feels a broken fingernail hook onto the wool lining of his glove, a maddening, irritating sensation that makes his teeth grind. Over and over the odious, maleficent utterances cycle through his mind, slashing at his sensibilities, altering his perception of what constitutes reality.

Act of hubris.

New reality in play.

Advocate for your interests.

He can count on you.

The persistent squirrel reappears, hops in front of the bench, and rises on its hind legs, positioned far enough away to escape the reach of the men but close enough to grab their attention. Its nose and whiskers twitch to discern if they are in possession of food. Large brown eyes look over the visitors and silently communicate the creature's desire.

"Someone is looking for a handout," Mr. Geary says, amused by the animal's begging posture.

He reaches across the bench and places his hand on Dean Dawson's shoulder.

"Come on, Porter. It's Christmas. Let us enjoy the season."

As they walk down the hardened pathway, unintentionally chasing the retreating squirrel as they go, an odd, singular thought worms its way out of the dean's wounded ego:

Since when did George Geary start calling me Porter?

A festive, light-hearted mood fills the dining room as the girls talk about the upcoming weekend's events and the winter dismissal. At a table near the crackling hearth, Josephine shares tea and rolls with Jennie and a group of underclassmen. The class work of the day is an afterthought as talk of tomorrow's formal ball fuels the spirited discussion.

Josephine listens to the girls' unbridled excitement and thinks back to when she and others in her class used to sit around the very same tables and spend countless meals endlessly talking about boys and the prospects each girl had or hoped to have.

Her current relationship with Robert has steadied those waters, as unpredictable and thrilling as they were at the time. Listening to the younger girls talk now, an unexpected twinge of sadness moves her heart. Beneath the outward appearance of approval and her engaging smile, Josephine feels the slow bleed of lost innocence as she remembers what it felt to be like them again—the pin-pricks of excitement, the palpable nervousness around boys, the drunkenness of infatuation that followed her to bed at night and was with her when she woke the next morning.

Wasn't that how she felt last night at the statue of Cyporissus? The ridiculous, chance meeting in the cold of night. She, of course, knew Margaret was right, her assessment of the man's interest dead-on. She would never admit it though, not in the way her friend wanted her to. That was one of the many differences between the two of them. Unlike Margaret, she does not possess the ability to speak freely, even in confidence, about the deepness of her affections or confess intimate secrets.

And Miss Barnes, perhaps our paths will cross again soon.

A surprising rush of adrenaline swims through her veins as she recalls his parting words. Is it the effect of flattery or something more, she wonders?

Jennie steers the conversation abruptly to Josephine, proud that her senior mentor, the most popular girl in her class, has joined them for breakfast.

"You must be thrilled to see Robert tomorrow. Has it been long since the last time the two of you spent time together?"

"Yes, I am looking forward to it. It's been many weeks."

"Girls, you would not believe how striking Josephine's midshipman is. I am not kidding. He commands the room when he enters in his dress uniform. I met him at the music recital in October. It was then that I knew that I made the right choice coming to Forest Glen!" Jennie says a bit too loud, causing Josephine's face to redden with embarrassment.

"I remember him!" one of the girls exclaims, "Oh yes, tall, dark and handsome. I *definitely* remember him."

The others around the table laugh at the girl's enthusiastic seconding.

"Well, is that how it is?" Josephine responds with a sly smile. "Perhaps I should raffle off dances with my —with Robert—if he is such a highly desirable commodity with all of you. I stand to make a tidy sum. What do you say?"

The girls call out their approval all at once as a server brings another plate of pastries to the table.

Jennie leans over to Josephine as the rest of the girls set upon the sweet confections and continue talking about the upcoming weekend.

"Is there any chance I can lure you out to California for a couple of weeks during the break? You would love it there. My parents could speak to yours and make all of the necessary arrangements. It would do you good to escape this dreary weather. Nothing but sunny days and glitzy nights in Hollywood. We can lie out on the beach in the morning and then go to the studios and meet some movie stars. Won't you please come?"

"That's an enticing offer, Jennie. And very sweet."

"You don't have any other plans, do you? At least nothing you can't break."

"I'm not sure. Give me a chance to talk with my parents. They can become over-possessive during the holidays to the point of practically suffocating me when I am home. I'd like to. I just don't know what they would say."

"I understand. Talk to them. Promise? I would love for you to come out West and meet my family and friends. I know they would absolutely adore you. I don't want to miss the chance before it becomes too late."

"'Too late? How do you mean?"

"You know, next spring you will graduate and then you will be married, unless Robert has lost his sanity in the time being. You know it's going to happen. You are a perfect match for each other."

"Really, Jennie. I think you are getting ahead of yourself."

"Deny it if you wish. All I ask is that I have you for a couple of weeks in California before then. We'd have a blast. Consider it a pre-marriage fling."

"Good morning, Miss Price," one of the girls abruptly announces, followed in turn by the rest around the table.

Josephine looks up and sees the regent standing behind one of the girls across the table, her hands resting on the shoulders of the surprised and visibly uncomfortable girl.

"Good morning girls. It is encouraging to see that you haven't let the weather dampen your spirits. Are you counting the days until you are free of this place?"

A few around the table nod while others laugh nervously, unsure as to whether or not the teacher is joking.

"Well, I will see some of you—Barbara, Jennie, Norma—in class later this morning. For the rest of you, if I don't see you again, enjoy the dance and merry Christmas to you."

A chorus of greetings answers back. Miss Price nods back politely as she makes her way around the table, stopping at Jennie's chair.

"Miss Milburn, I wanted to let you know that I was impressed with your essay on Rossetti and the Pre-Raphaelite Brotherhood. You showed genuine enthusiasm for his work. Have you given any thought to the criticism of the Modernists who find the verse of the Victorians antiquated and repressive and a tad irrelevant to twentieth century existence?"

"I am not sure, Miss Price. I suppose Romanticism has fallen out of fashion in some academic circles. But I think there must be some accounting for nature and the spiritual in art, even in today's world."

"To include mysticism? Is there value in contemplating the forces beyond the conventional and physical worlds to explain aspects of the human condition? Rossetti and others like him pushed a medieval revival that linked the sensual with the mythological. How do you view connecting the two?"

"Would you like me to amend my paper, Miss Price, to address the point?"

"No, dear! I was just curious as to your thoughts on the topic, that's all. I did not mean to catch you off guard, early in the morning at that. As I said, overall, your essay was a strong effort. Perhaps we can discuss it further after class today."

Jennie's concerned expression turns to relief.

"Miss Barnes, good morning to you as well. I am heartened to see the classes mixing. We could you more of it around here. Would you mind stopping by my office for a quick chat before first period, let's say at 8:30? I promise I will not subject you to a quiz on 19th century English poetry," she says almost as an after-thought as she turns to leave.

The regent's casual, friendly demeanor in the dining room is gone when Josephine is waved into her office by the secretary sitting out in front of the faculty offices. She drops the paper she is reading onto the desk and begins rubbing her forehead as Josephine enters, as if the trials of the new day have already overwhelmed her.

"You know, Josephine, there are a number of duties I need to be concentrating on before the semester ends. But instead I am continually distracted by complaints concerning members of the senior class."

Her voice is higher pitched than usual, the exasperation she is feeling evident in her tone.

"Sometime after I left my office yesterday, a student slipped a note under my door claiming that Leah Hathaway had physically assaulted May King in the gymnasium. This, mind you, came on the heels of a different report I received from another student this morning who said that Margaret Cleary had threatened a girl at last night's Chiopi party. What has come over you girls that is turning you into savages?!"

"I don't know anything about these reports, Miss Price."

The regent slams her palm down on the desk and shoots daggers at the girl standing before her.

"It is not lost on me, Josephine, that the three girls I am talking about are the very same three who went with you to the glen Monday morning. And as much as I am willing to accept a certain level of statistical improbability in life, the fact that the same three girls out of a school of three hundred are involved in these reports leads me to believe that you do know something about these incidents. So tell me what the hell is going on, and why, after our earlier discussion, I find it necessary to call you to my office again!"

Josephine, having never before heard the regent curse, is shocked by the unexpected volcanic outburst and responds defensively.

"I am being honest with you. You must believe me, Miss Price."

"But I don't. Sadly, I have my suspicions that you are not being straight with me and haven't for some time."

"Have you spoken to *them?*" Josephine asks pointedly, wondering why she is the one being subjected to the withering interrogation.

"You see, that is something of a problem."

Miss Price stands up and steps around from behind the desk.

"I can't find any of the three. No one has seen Leah since chorus practice yesterday afternoon. The girls at Chiopi don't remember seeing her at the party last night. And when I walked through Senior House for lights out, her room was dark. I assumed she was sleeping. This morning I sent one of the administration staff to her room and she wasn't there. Her bed was made, but she was gone. She hasn't been seen in the dining room this morning as far as I know either."

Josephine quickly scans her recollection of last night's events. Had Leah been at the geisha party? She didn't see her there, but it was so crowded and with the elaborate disguises and heavy makeup worn by many of the attendees she might have missed her.

"Now as to my ongoing project, May King, she too has vanished."

Miss Price's unguarded sarcastic characterization surprises Josephine and she now sees that the young teacher's emotional fit has jettisoned any semblance of decorum.

"Our churlish, alleged victim, the girl according to this unsigned note Leah Hathaway assaulted, is not in her dorm room either. Nor is she camped out at her usual spot for breakfast. I checked myself. What transpired between the two of them, Josephine? They live across the hall from each other and I have not heard of any friction between the two before. Were you at the gymnasium yesterday with them?"

Josephine hesitates in replying, distracted by thoughts of Margaret's yet unexplained absence and the report to the regent that her friend had threatened Bettina.

"I expect that you will be completely honest with me, Josephine. What is going on between Leah and May?"

"I don't know what happened between the two of them. They've been keeping to themselves lately," she answers, trying her best to conceal the depth of concern she has felt over Leah's increasingly disturbing behavior. "I will go and try to find them. Perhaps they left early for class or are out for a walk."

"Not so fast. There is the matter of your friend, Miss Cleary. I was approached a little while ago by a student, whose name I will not mention here, who claims that Margaret threatened another girl at the Chiopi party. Now before you claim not to know what transpired, I know for a fact that you were at the party, Josephine, and that you were there with her when the incident occurred."

"This is absurd. Margaret may be sharp-tongued at times, but I have never heard her threaten another student in all the time I have known her."

"About last night. I asked what happened last night."

"It was loud and crowded. It was nearly impossible to hear what anyone was saying inside the clubhouse, even when they were standing next to you."

"Really? Were you with her the entire night?"

Josephine nods.

"Were you and Margaret not together talking with some of the other girls there about a challenge of some sort between the houses?"

"Yes, but—"

"And harsh words were exchanged?"

"No, we were teasing each other, like we always do. It was innocent. It was all in fun."

"But Margaret was angry, yes? She didn't think it was all in fun, did she?"

"Who is saying these things?" she pushes back, recalling the animosity Bettina has felt toward Margaret since their first days at the Seminary. "It is a total misrepresentation of what happened. No one was threatened."

"But I was told Margaret left the Pagoda early, quite angry at the other girl."

"No, she left early because she was feeling ill. The party was crowded and overheated."

"And you went with her when she left the party?"

"Yes."

"And that is it; that is all that happened? A group of girls were teasing each other, all in fun, in your words, and then Margaret was feeling ill and the two of you left."

"Yes, that is what happened."

"Where did the two of you go after you left the party?"

"Back to Senior House, of course."

"The two of you went directly back to your rooms."

"Yes, we went back to the dorm."

"Directly back?"

Josephine nods, suddenly suspicious of the agitated teacher's need to clarify her answer.

Miss Price walks to the office door and closes it. Returning to her desk, she sits and contemplates the reply as Josephine, still standing, feels her body sway, ever so slightly, from side to side.

"You are lying." Miss Price declares matter-of-factly. "And I consider the transgression serious enough to warrant the filing of a formal citation under the student code of ethics."

"Miss Price, this cannot be happening. I am telling you the truth. You must believe me," Josephine pleads, her voice quivering with emotion.

"We have rules in place regulating the conduct of our students for a legitimate purpose. If students willfully ignore them, they place not only themselves in peril but also risk harming the school's reputation. Conduct that jeopardizes the institutional standing of National Park Seminary cannot be tolerated. There have been other girls before you who have flaunted these rules and who, as a result, have been told firmly and irrevocably that there is no longer a place for them here. They have been quietly removed and records of their existence here have been carefully expunged. "

"This is madness!"

"Do not use that tone with me, young lady!" Miss Price fires back, again slamming her hand against the desk top, this time toppling over a picture frame next to an ink blotter. "You are walking on the razor's edge. I would caution you to choose your words carefully and to speak respectfully, if you feel the need to speak at all."

Josephine reins in her emotions as tears pool along her lower eyelids. In a calm but unsteady voice she asks her accuser of the charge.

"Miss Price, I have faithfully adhered to the student code. If someone has said otherwise, please let me know what it is I am alleged to have done that would so anger you."

"Did you meet a man on campus last night after the party, unchaper-oned?"

Expecting to hear that her journey to the boathouse with Margaret and Leah had come to the regent's attention, Josephine feels strangely absolved to hear the regent's charge. Partly relieved and partly aghast by the accusation, she struggles to suppress an awkward smile, which only infuriates Miss Price more.

"Yes. I mean…no. No. I didn't go to meet a man. He found *us*."

"*Us?* Did Margaret participate in this late night meeting too?"

Though she does not want to implicate her friend in the matter, Josephine decides to speak truthfully knowing that Margaret's explanation will corroborate her version of events that the meeting was accidental and not by clandestine design.

"Margaret was with me, yes. We were heading back to Senior House from the party, as I said. And she stopped to spend a moment outside to cool off and help clear her head."

"And where were the two of you?"

"We were standing by 'Oh Lord, I Missed the Train,'" Josephine answers, invoking the colloquial name the girls use for the Grief of Cyporis-sus statue. The distraught figure of the boy beloved by Apollo, cradling the limp body of his tamed stag, slain by a hunter's javelin, his hand pressed to

INCIDENT AT FOREST GLEN *271*

his head in dismay, serves as a reference point of significance for those wanting to catch the train at the station across the glen. The rule of thumb, often tested but never proven wrong, is that if you can see the train at the platform when passing the morbid statue, it is already too late.

"You planned to meet at the gardens there?"

"This is a complete misunderstanding, Miss Price. He came upon us unexpectedly while we were standing there. Margaret will tell you the same story when you talk to her."

"I intend to talk to Margaret as soon as I can, alone."

And at that moment, looking at the Miss Price's contemptuous expression, Josephine's fear over being expelled for a wrongdoing she did not commit dissipates quickly like the air rushing out of a punctured balloon. She has seen the look in Miss Price's eyes before. Recently. Yesterday morning. At the hospital ward. When she came upon Josephine talking to Charles Carter.

The shattered pieces of trust between the teacher and student re-form and produce a shocking picture.

"Perhaps Margaret will be more forthcoming with me. I am tired of your defiance. You are doing yourself no favors, Josephine."

"Why don't you ask *him?*" she replies, turning the tables on her accuser, the secret at the heart of the regent's machinations now deciphered.

"What is that you say?"

"You don't need to speak with Margaret. You would only view her story with suspicion, just like you have cast doubt on mine. Why don't you ask him? He will tell you what happened. He will explain to you that the meeting was purely by chance."

Miss Price pauses, taken aback by the girl's audacity.

"You will first need to tell me who you went to meet last night."

Josephine refuses to play along with the elaborate charade and stares down the regent, realizing that she has gained a decisive advantage in the unpleasant confrontation.

"I believe you know his name, Miss Price."

Josephine turns away, opens the door, and leaves just as the hallway chimes announce the start of the morning classes, taking with her the image of Miss Price's stunned expression.

She walks past her history classroom and heads off to the dormitory, unnerved by the exchange and concerned about Margaret's whereabouts.

Contrary to what Miss Price claimed, she finds the door to Margaret's room open and all of the lights on inside. A long coat of lustrous mink is draped across the reading chair, next to a pair of polished brown boots. She hears the sound of water from the needle bath striking the tile floor behind the closed door down the hall. Josephine leans against the bathroom door and hears a series of low moans intermingled with the splashing of water. A violent, prolonged retching follows that alarms her.

"Margaret? Margaret?" she calls out. "It's Josephine. Are you in there? Are you all right? What is wrong, dear?"

No answer, only the continued splatter of the spraying jets.

"Do you want me to come in?" she tries again, hoping to elicit a response.

After a few seconds, Margaret answers, her voice faint and weak.

"I don't think I will be going to classes today, Jo. I am feeling dreadful. Just like last night. I thought a walk would help—"

Margaret's labored explanation is cut short by a deep, guttural heaving followed by a panicked inhalation of air and a fit of coughing.

"How wonderful," Josephine hears her ailing friend mumble with disgust.

"I am coming in," she says only to find the door locked from the inside.

Behind her, somewhere down the shadowy corridor, a floor board creaks loudly and Josephine turns around quickly only to find that she is alone.

"Open the door, Margaret. Let me in so I can help you. Stop being so obstinate and accept help from others for once."

"Just the stomach flu, dear. Not a pretty sight right now, I am afraid to say. Go back to the room and wait there for me. I need some time to get myself together."

Wanting to protest, Josephine thinks twice and heads back to the room. Along the way, she stops at Leah's door and gently knocks. Remembering that Miss Price said someone had been sent into her room earlier in the morning and found no one there, she turns the knob and slowly enters, not bothering to announce herself.

The room is dark and empty, just as the regent told her. She looks around and sees the bed is made and the room is in order.

Upon closer inspection, however, there are inexplicable signs of an altered state of existence. The window shades are down behind closed curtains and the room is dank and fetid like that of a subterranean gaol. The radiator along the wall is silent and cold. The walls, once decorated with felt pennants and satin ribbons, are stripped bare. Josephine walks across the carpet and feels the slivers of glass under foot a fraction of a second before the crunching sound reaches her ear. Overhead, the shattered globes and misshapen arms of a dislodged lamp dangle precariously from the ceiling by an electrical cord.

As she stands at the center of the room, she searches the ring of darkness around her for some possession or personal effect to show that a seventeen year-old girl lives here, but there are none. In this tomb of suspended night, there are only the wooden legs and arms and slats of the dormitory furniture, bare, skeletal forms pushed together in a messy heap in the far corner, a twisted, haphazardly constructed pyre nearly reaching the ceiling.

Down the hall, compressed streams of hot water pour out with ferocity. The stinging spray strikes the bare back of the curled body seated on the tiled floor and renders the exposed skin running along the sides of her protruding vertebrae a vibrant pink. A cascading torrent encircles her hanging head in a corona of dripping water and runs down the length of her weary arms and legs. Margaret draws deep, replenishing breathes, pulling in traces of water that warm the soft, inner lining of her mouth. Billows of steam rise from the floor and form drops of condensation on the stucco ceiling. She stares at the soothing water circle and escape through the slits of the brass drain cover next to her toes and waits for her strength to return. The walk around campus at dawn had proven an effective, albeit temporary, remedy after a fitful night interrupted by cold sweats and waves of nausea, a cycle of illness that has worsened and grown more debilitating in the past day. Unable to marshal the will to move, Margaret lets the jets punish her listless, slump-shouldered body until a burning sensation spreads slowly from her neck down to her backside.

A miasma of images, both real and dreamt, pulsates and then fades inside her distressed, addled mind. One among them— Bettina Braddock's wicked, self-satisfied look—returns over and over. No matter how hard she tries, she cannot shake the feeling of embarrassment she felt at the party the night before. Why did she let the audacious girl and her childish taunts get the better of her? She detests everything about her. Their mutual animosity began years before when they first met, even before they spoke to one and another. It was instantaneous, as if it was imprinted in their genetics, resident in their bloodlines over generations.

A sharp pain ripples deep inside Margaret's body and her breathing shortens. The sides of her torso beneath the rib cage contract with involuntary spasms, little earthquakes that tense already aching stomach muscles.

Must think more positively, she says to herself, attempting by mental fiat to chase away the fevered remembrances of previous evening. Time to pull yourself together, Meg, she urges, thinking of the concert later in the evening and then the dance, the capstone social events of the semester. She musters an anemic smile as she imagines her date arriving tomorrow only to be directed to the third floor bathroom and told to wait for the pruned body to emerge.

She leans her body back and the relentless downpour against her scalp quells her edginess.

Where would she be without Josephine, she wonders? Who else would line her up a date or put up with her acerbic behavior day in and day out? The very existence of their friendship seems hard to explain. How did two girls, so different in appearance and in temperament, find an enduring bond in this school of privilege? Would any of her other friends, either here or in Fall River, notice when she is not around and come looking for her, as Josephine had? In her vulnerable physical state, Margaret wishes she could express to Josephine how much her unflagging faith means to her, and tell her that surely there was a special place in heaven for a girl who willingly tolerates the opinionated and ungracious.

As she is drawn in by the hypnotic swirl of water before her feet, another stabbing pain twists her insides and the throbbing along the back of her head intensifies. She bites her lower lip and fights the urge to cry out, not wanting to further alarm Josephine waiting down the hall. The storm subsides and her eyes refocus. Around the drain, a thin trace of color taints the translucent stream, steadily growing until the flow of water turns burnt red. She looks down between her bent legs and sighs.

"You must be kidding."

Inside the protective, womblike shell of the Grotto, Leah awakens in a disorienting haze. Outside, the morning sun has yet to reach the creek. Her body is stiff from sleeping against the rocky wall and the moist, clammy air

INCIDENT AT FOREST GLEN 275

of the shallow cave has left her clothes damp. She emerges from the stone niche crawling on her hands and knees, her wounded ankle dead and heavy. She pushes up off the ground, steadies herself on one leg, and surveys the creek.

She shuts her eyes and recreates the frightening specter she escaped hours earlier. Out of her memory, it returns—the slowly turning silhouette of a soulless presence, the fearful creature that chilled her blood and held her heart in its malevolent grip.

Opening her eyes again, she is relieved that whatever she saw out on the rocks then is now gone. The mermaid statue rises from a thin layer of mist hanging over the water, its appearance familiar to any visitor of the Grotto.

Leah hops gingerly to the water's edge and looks downstream of the statue for any sign of the dressed doll, only to find the smooth, undulating contours of water rolling over submerged rocks.

She stands shivering before the sublime grandeur of the expansive glen, unspoiled by human presence or the artificial sounds of modern technology. She feels insignificant and alone, powerless and vulnerable to the crushing enormity before her. The glen, once a peaceful, sylvan refuge to her and the other girls away from the structure and formality of the Seminary, is now more ominous, more foreboding in the weak light. The creek and the thick, arboraceous cloak surrounding it are a unified form, a living entity encompassing both the natural and the unnatural, an organism of frightening duality, one that provides sustenance for life while at the same time cruelly robbing the breath of those who it nurtures. And the statue of the slender girl condemned to an unworldly existence is no longer a whimsical decoration to amuse those who come to the lush alcove. The smooth metallic form struck in a graceful, innocent pose has metamorphosed into a different chimera all together, an avenging one who hides its pernicious designs behind delicate feminine features.

When Mrs. Martin arrives to unlock the door to Miller Library she finds a student waiting outside on a stone bench thoroughly wrapped inside a bulky coat and velvet hat and clutching a book to her chest with both hands as if it is capable of producing warmth. The preoccupied woman offers a wave to the girl as she passes and hurries to open the library. Once inside her office, she pulls back the curtains to a reveal a grim, inhospitable landscape and then turns her attention to cajoling the balky radiator to life.

The bell above the front entryway to the library rings and she assumes that her first student of the day anxious to return the borrowed book has left and gone off to breakfast. She sits down at her desk and pulls from her travel bag a Thermos vacuum bottle, a gift from her husband last Christmas, and pours herself a steaming cup of coffee. The commute by streetcar from her house and the walk from the station has left her cold to the bone.

She takes out a newspaper bought from the corner shop next to her apartment building and unfolds it on the desk top, adjusting her glasses down her nose as she peruses the pages, a daily ritual the cantankerous faculty member carries out to stimulate her thoughts and jump start her day before work begins in earnest. The office gradually warms as the radiator rattles and groans. Outside, the sun slowly rises and labors to pierce the thick cover of clouds. The prefect pours over the stories of the day and draws down, cup by cup, the mahogany liquid inside the glass-lined container, smudges of newsprint coating the tips of her fingers.

On the penultimate page, next to the business announcements section below the fold, she quickly scans over the real estate section, reminded by word association of the prolonged and often unpleasant discussion she has had with her husband over the question of if and when they were going to forgo renting and purchase a home of their own. The financial jargon and transactional terms are foreign to her but a familiar thread jumps out as she is about to turn to the back page. Placing her cup and saucer down, she leans forward to read the minute typeset at the bottom of the page.

Sold on November 19, 1921, by Alfred Ray of Silver Spring, Md., 42.5 acres to Highland Trust of New York, NY.

And then a few entries further down the column:

Sold on November 19, 1921, by Martha A. Keys of Silver Spring, Md., 16.8 acres to Highland Trust of New York, NY.

Followed, in quick succession, by other similar land transactions:

Sold on November 21, 1921, by Thos. B. Cissel and E.G. Cissel of Silver Spring, Md., 35.0 acres to Highland Trust of New York, NY.

Sold on November 27, 1921, by W.J. Baxter of Silver Spring, Md., 12.3 acres to Highland Trust of New York, NY.

The prefect folds the paper repeatedly until the section of interest is isolated and held compactly in her hand. She walks out to the main reading room while still contemplating the significance of the listed real estate transactions, stepping blindly around the desks and chairs, a well-worn path learned in her many years at the school. She heads to the reference book section and looks over the framed prints hung on the wall, taking no notice of the girl on the second floor squatting down to reach a book on the lowest shelf.

Mrs. Martin locates the map she is seeking and presses her nose up close near the dingy, dust-covered glass. Prepared after the turn of the century census, the atlas depicts the physical boundaries as well as the roads, railroad lines, streams and other demarcations of the lower county bordering the District line. Black dots accompanied by property owner names written in cursive populate the map, some crammed together in dense, difficult to read patches of faded indigo ink, and others more sparsely spaced over large tracts of farm land in the sloping piedmont rising north of the Potomac.

Using her fingernail, she follows the crosshatched line showing the railroad in the corner of the atlas through the northwest quadrant of the city and the suburban communities strung across the Maryland line until she reaches the Forest Glen station. Holding her finger against the map, she glances down at the newspaper in her other hand and then looks back. There, in a crescent of adjacent properties bordering the National Park Seminary parcel along the county road, the landowner names appear:

Ray, Keys, Cissel, Baxter.

More than 100 acres of land, sold separately over a period of just over a week to a New York City trust—less than a month before Douglas Stratton arrived from Manhattan with his surprising offer to purchase the school.

At that sobering instance, as the unexpected discovery materializes at her finger tip, Mrs. Martin realizes her mistake.

Her suspicion over the school's sale had been wrongfully directed toward Dean Dawson. She had assumed all along that he had succumbed to Mr. Stratton's overture and was either duped or intentionally enlisted to obfuscate the tycoon's plan to purchase and remake the school in a way that might jeopardize her continued employment and that of the other instructors. When from her office she spied the trolley arrive back from the morning trip to Walter Reed and saw Mr. Stratton's assistant meet with a man outside the Glen Manor Hotel, her suspicions deepened further. It was to be suspected that Dean Dawson would turn to Mr. Geary to be his trusted intermediary in the immediate aftermath of the offer. After all, wasn't it the school bursar who stepped into the breach when she questioned the dean about staff continuity the evening before at the dinner in Vincent Hall and deftly deflected the question, turning it into a fawning acclamation of the headmaster's legacy?

She had gone to Mr. Geary's office yesterday as a ruse. She wanted to catch him off-guard, to fluster him, and to see to what level of duplicity he would sink to keep from admitting his knowledge of the negotiations and his role in them. She caught him leaving the businessman's hotel room and talking with Mr. Carter, a man he had only met for the first time two days prior. Her ambush served its purpose. Mr. Geary's evasiveness and unwillingness to disclose his meeting with the wealthy industrialist only deepened her conviction that the scope and nature of the deal is not what it appears to be. He dismissed her plea that the two of them approach the school's prospective buyer directly as being improper, all the while concealing his own direct involvement in the transaction. Mr. Geary lied to her face, and at that moment she knew he was not to be trusted.

Why he undertook the charade in his office is unclear, however. To advance his own fortunes at the school's expense perhaps. She assumed that self-interest was responsible for his conceit. But to what end? The bursar dared her to take her concerns directly to the dean knowing all along that she wouldn't, a bold gambit on his part that she was unwitting of information that might upset the deal. Mr. Geary banked on the hunch that Mrs. Martin wouldn't approach the man he knew she never fully trusted or particularly respected in the first place.

Dean Porter Dawson. The officious, pompous, platitude-spouting headmaster. Vain-glorious and weak. Easily won over by the slick New York tycoon. Or so she assumed.

What if he is not a duped, co-opted party in the sale of the school after all? Does he know the sale of National Park Seminary is being negotiated on the heels of a front company snatching up available farmland contiguous to the school? No realistic, economically-feasible capital expansion plan would have the campus more than double in size.

The picture of complicity she had constructed in her head begins to disintegrate as she studies the wall hanging further. She shuts her eyes and translates the two dimensional lines before her into recollected images of the named properties:

The Ray property—the simple clapboard home with the rusted hand pump behind the wrought iron fence facing the county road.

The Keys land—with its endless rows of brimming corn in summertime.

The Cissel farm—the prodigious maple tree with the rope swing out front, surrounded by a ocean of shimmering emerald green grass dotted with grazing sheep and goats.

The Baxter tract—its towering red barn, paint peeling and slightly listing to one side, with its white, vented cupola topped with a rooster weather vane.

How could she have been so blind? It was in front of her the entire time.

Each morning she boards the trolley three blocks from her District apartment and rides the six miles to Forest Glen, through congested streets and past dark alleyways. And then the shadows of the tall buildings give way to the spacious, tree-lined streets and porch-encircled homes. Further down the line, away from the heart of the capital, the trolley passes the junction at the state line with its grocery and florist and tailor shops. In a matter of minutes, for those riders who care to look up from their morning fog and break-out of the soothing trance of the streetcar's rhythmic clatter, the telltale signs of progress appear. The powerful engine of commerce at work. The newly excavated foundations dug out of the red earth passing by the car window like rows of oversized graves. The wooden scaffolding and skeletal frames rising from fields that the previous summer grew tender shoots of golden wheat and floppy broad leaves of tobacco. Large painted plywood signs heralding the coming wave of affordable homes.

The transformation of the land north of the District boundary had been inexorable in the years she commuted along the familiar route. It seemed that with the passing of each day, the rising sun revealed some new alteration to the landscape outside her window onto the fast-moving world. Shovels and graders rumbled over the land like mechanized beasts, snorting diesel smoke and growling their discontent to the masters riding atop and directing their

280 ANDY JOHNSON

labor. Lines of broad-shouldered, muscular men pulverizing the ground with pick axes and sledge hammers. Acres of tilled soil buried under rivers of lustrous black cadmium poured from blistering cauldrons that hissed and smelled as if they were purloined from the underworld.

Mrs. Martin hears someone at the checkout desk behind her and turns to find the girl that was waiting outside the library when she arrived bent over and writing down her name and the book she is borrowing.

"You there, what is your name, Miss—"

The girl looks up, startled by the abrupt question.

"King. May King, ma'am. You were my sophomore English teacher when Miss Morrison took a leave of absence."

"Yes, of course, I remember," the prefect lies with a forced, unconvincing smile.

"Are you about to leave now?"

May nods, suddenly worried she has done something that has inadvertently triggered the prefect's ire.

"I was only checking out my book again, Mrs. Martin. It was due today."

"That's fine. Would you mind delivering a note to the headmaster's office, directly to Dean Dawson? It is an urgent matter. My assistant hasn't arrived yet or I'd do it myself."

"Why of course."

"Good, wait here one moment and then I will send you on your way."

May watches the prefect shuffle off and disappear into her office as she slips the slender book into her coat pocket and puts on her gloves.

Josephine sits in her morning elocution class and listens while girls take turns reciting a speech of their choosing in front of the teacher and the other students. The assignment is the culmination of the class work for the semester and the only requirements placed on the girls by their teacher, Mr. Warren, a retired lawyer who held a plum position in the McKinley administration Justice Department, is that the oration be of historical, governmental or literary note, that it be at least three minutes in length, and that it be delivered from memory—no notes allowed. And, most importantly, no Shakespeare. None of his sonnets or soliloquies. No Hamlet or Macbeth or Henry V. Mr. Warren is not an English professor and his tolerance for the familiar servings of the Bard reached its breaking point the first year at the Seminary, requiring the institution of the strict stipulation.

For many of those taking Mr. Warren's class, the assignment is viewed with ponderous dread that festers and builds over time from the first day of class when the course work for the semester is reviewed in meticulous detail.

"You may not want to carry out this requirement," he tells all of his classes. "The mere thought of speaking in public may strike fear in your hearts and turn your stomachs in knots. Whatever misgivings you have about opening your mouth and articulating well-honed thoughts, be they small or large, be they about genuine events or imagined, your fears will be overcome. No girl in the past eight years has left this room without successfully completing the final assignment, and I will not allow any one of you sitting here today to be the first to fail.

"Girls must be taught to speak up for themselves," he intones to the wide-eyed students. "Girls must be taught to be heard," he bellows for effect. "Girls must learn that standing on their own two feet before a group of their fellow humans, alone and unprotected, is not a circumstance to be avoided, but an opportunity to be embraced."

Confidence, he writes across the slate board at the front of the classroom.

Annunciation, he spells out below it.

Persuasion.

"Elocution. The art of expression. Well-formulated thoughts, expertly spoken, are powerful. Much greater than the physical strength of man and machine. They can bring the celestial jewels within arms reach and they can bring down fortress walls. But only if the speaker can move her audience," Mr. Warren cautions, as if revealing a secret potion of boundless potential. "And to do so requires, first off, the courage to speak, to raise one's voice above the level of polite conversation and intimate confidences. I am speaking of the willingness to stand before one's own peers and declare with unassailable convictions your beliefs."

While Josephine waits her turn to stand in judgment before the class, her thoughts are distracted by Margaret's growing lethargy and sudden illness. Though Margaret was initially dismissive of her concerns, Josephine could tell from her lack of color and bloodshot eyes that whatever is ailing Margaret is more serious than originally assumed. Only by promising her that she would dress and go directly to the school infirmary did Josephine

282   ANDY JOHNSON

agree to leave her friend and go to classes. Normally she might be suspicious of Margaret's resolve to carry out her promises when it comes to seeking the help of others, but she could see that the independent-natured girl felt miserable and the symptoms of sickness were too acute to dismiss as being nothing to be worried about.

The speeches continue as the ancient rhetoric of Cicero and Seneca is recited along with the more contemporary contemplations of Hawthorne and Thoreau. Some of the presenters stumble often, while others speak in a monotone delivery devoid of inflection and severed from the meaning of the text. Expressions of relief shown by each girl who finishes provides those who nervously wait with encouragement that the stiff medicine they obsessed about over the past months and desperately hoped to avoid isn't so bitter after all.

The sound of clapping following each recital interrupts Josephine's preparation. She tries studying the familiar sheet of paper on the desk in front of her but to no avail. She continues replaying Miss Price's threat in her mind. She is powerless to stop the teacher's recriminations and expressions of rage from burrowing into her brain. The possibility of expulsion frightens her. The severity of the sanction, a ruinous and indelible mark on her reputation, is beyond comprehension. Miss Price has twisted the innocent interaction between Josephine and the stranger from New York into an elaborate fabrication, a non-existent web of deceit in which she is somehow the victim. Josephine recalls the look of jealousy in the teacher's eyes hours earlier and how it unhinged her normal, even disposition, hardening the pleasant lines of her face and poisoning the tone of her words.

Is that all it takes? Are the vows of her confidant and mentor so ephemeral, so easily torn apart, by the unsolicited affections of a man, a man who has entered both of their lives mere days before? How can the regent turn against her so quickly?

Clarissa Knight, a shy senior from northern Florida, approaches the end of Lincoln's Gettysburg Address, carefully metering her delivery so as to satisfy the minimum time requirement. The plodding recitation of the familiar oratorical chestnut, often chosen by students as a reliable standby, neither too complex nor overly long, elicits polite applause from the girls and a stifled yawn from Mr. Warren. He glances down at the remaining students on the list and calls Josephine to the front of the class.

Expecting her turn to be later, she frantically tries to clear her mind. Miss Price's threat. Margaret's condition. Leah's cold, desolate room. All must be set aside where they are unable to infiltrate her thoughts and disrupt her concentration.

She is aware of her foot steps, the sound of her shoes against the floor, as she passes by the relieved Clarissa on her way back to her desk. The clapping quickly dies away and she turns to face the class, the intimidating, heavily-creased face of her stoic instructor visible out of the corner of her eye.

She pauses and waits to begin. Waits to steady her frayed nerves. Waits to regulate her breathing. Waits in order to live in the moment and look confidently upon familiar faces filled with anticipation. A peaceful feeling calms the storm inside her and in that moment of vulnerability, with the entire class's attention trained on her, she feels unexpectedly content. She looks around the room. After three and a half years of study away from her family, Josephine realizes how much she has come to love her life at the Seminary and the friendships she has made here. No matter what happens, no matter what course she charts next spring, for now this is her home.

"Miss Barnes, do you need more time? Shall we move on to the next student to afford you a few additional minutes?"

"No thank you, Mr. Warren."

She brings her hands together in front her and takes a deep breath. The teacher, bored after a dozen or so pedestrian offerings, searches for reading material on his desk. By the time Josephine finishes the opening lines of her presentation, he removes his glasses and turns to face to his pupil, his attention now undivided.

The isolation of every human soul and the necessity of self-dependence must give each individual the right to choose her own surroundings.

The strongest reason for giving a woman all the opportunities for higher education is the solitude and personal responsibility of her own individual life.

No matter how much women prefer to lean, to be protected and supported, nor how much men desire to have them do so, they must make the voyage of life alone.

Nature having endowed them equally, leaves them to their own skill and judgment in the hour of danger, and, if not equal to the occasion, alike they perish.

To appreciate the importance of fitting every human soul for independent action, think for a moment of the immeasurable solitude of self. We come into the world alone, unlike all who have gone before us; we leave it alone under circumstances peculiar to ourselves.

The great lesson that nature seems to teach us at all ages is self-dependence, self-protection, self-support.

In youth our most bitter disappointments, our brightest hopes and ambitions are known only to otherwise, even our friendship and love we never fully share with another; there is something of every passion in every situation we conceal. Even so in our triumphs and our defeats.

The solitude of the king on his throne and the prisoner in his cell differs in character and degree, but it is solitude nevertheless.

We ask no sympathy from others in the anxiety and agony of a broken friendship or shattered love.

When death sunders our nearest ties, alone we sit in the shadows of our affliction. Alike mid the greatest triumphs and darkest tragedies of life we walk alone.

On the divine heights of human attainments, eulogized land worshiped as a hero or saint, we stand alone.

In ignorance, poverty, and vice, as a pauper or criminal, alone we starve or steal; alone we suffer the sneers and rebuffs of our fellows; alone we are hunted and hounded through dark courts and alleys; alone we stand in the judgment seat; alone in the prison cell we lament our crimes and misfortunes; alone we expiate them on the gallows.

In hours like these we realize the awful solitude of individual life, its pains, its penalties, its responsibilities; hours in which the youngest and most helpless are thrown on their own resources for guidance and consolation.

To throw obstacle in the way of a complete education is like putting out the eyes; to deny the rights of property, like cutting off the hands. To deny political equality is to rob the ostracized of all self-respect; of credit in the market place; of recompense in the world of work; of a voice among those who make and administer the law; a choice in the jury before whom they are tried, and in the judge who decides their punishment.

The girl of sixteen, thrown on the world to support herself, to make her own place in society, to resist the temptations that surround her and maintain a spotless integrity, must do all this by native force or superior education. She does not acquire this power by being trained to trust others and distrust herself. If she wearies of the struggle, finding it hard work to swim upstream, and allow herself to drift with the current, she will find plenty of company, but not one to share her misery in the hour of her deepest humiliation. Young and friendless, she knows the bitter solitude of self.

An uneducated woman, trained to dependence, with no resources in herself must make a failure of any position in life. But society says women do not need a knowledge of the world, the liberal training that experience in public life must give, all the advantages of collegiate education; but when for the lock of all this, the woman's happiness is wrecked, alone she bears her humiliation; and the attitude of the weak and the ignorant in indeed pitiful in the wild chase for the price of life they are ground to powder.

In age, when the pleasures of youth are passed, children grown up, married and gone, the hurry and hustle of life in a measure over, when the hands are weary of active service, when the old armchair and the fireside are the chosen resorts, then men and women alike must fall back on their own resources. If they cannot find companionship in books, if they have no interest in the vital questions of the hour, no interest in watching the consummation of reforms, with which they might have been identified, they soon pass into their dotage.

The chief reason for opening to every soul the doors to the whole round of human duties and pleasures is the individual development thus attained, the resources thus provided under all circumstances to mitigate the solitude that at times must come to everyone. A famous Russian nihilist was once asked how he endured his long years in prison, deprived of books, pen, ink, and paper. "Ah," he said, "I thought out many questions in which I had a deep interest. In the pursuit of an idea I took no note of time. When tired of solving knotty problems I recited all the beautiful passages in prose or verse I have ever learned. I became acquainted with myself and my own resources. I had a world of my own, a vast empire, that no Russian jailor or Czar could invade." Such is the value of liberal thought and broad culture when shut off from all human companionship, bringing comfort and sunshine within even the four walls of a prison cell.

Nothing strengthens the judgment and quickens the conscience like individual responsibility. Nothing adds such dignity to character as the recognition of one's self-sovereignty; the right to an equal place, every where conceded; a place earned by personal merit, not an artificial attainment, by inheritance, wealth, family, and position.

We may have many friends, love, kindness, sympathy and charity to smooth our pathway in everyday life, but in the tragedies and triumphs of human experience each moral stands alone.

You have probably all read in the daily papers of the terrible storm in the Bay of Biscay when a tidal wave such havoc on the shore, wrecking vessels, unroofing houses and carrying destruction everywhere. Among other buildings the woman's prison was *demolished. Those who escaped saw men struggling to reach the shore. They promptly by clasping hands made a chain of themselves and pushed out into the sea, again and again, at the risk of their lives until they had brought six men to shore, carried them to a shelter, and did all in their power for their comfort and protection.*

What special school of training could have prepared these women for this sublime moment of their lives? In times like this humanity rises above all college curriculums and recognizes Nature as the greatest of all teachers in the hour of danger and death. Women are already the equals of men in the whole of ream of thought, in art, science, literature, and government. With telescope vision they explore the starry firmament, and bring back the history of the planetary world. With chart and compass they pilot ships across the mighty deep, and with skillful finger send electric messages around the globe. In galleries of art the beauties of nature and the virtues of humanity are immortalized by them on their canvas and by their inspired touch dull blocks of marble are transformed into angels of light.

We see reason sufficient in the outer conditions of human being for individual liberty and development, but when we consider the self dependence of every human soul we see the need of courage, judgment, and the exercise of every faculty of mind and body, strengthened and developed by use, in woman as well as man.

Whatever may be said of man's protecting power in ordinary conditions, mid all the terrible disasters by land and sea, in the supreme moments of danger, alone, woman must ever meet the horrors of the situation; the Angel of Death even makes no royal pathway for her. Man's love and sympathy enter only into the sunshine of our lives. In that solemn solitude of self, that links us with the immeasurable and the eternal, each soul lives alone forever.

And yet, there is a solitude, which each and every one of us has always carried with him, more inaccessible than the ice-cold mountains, more profound than the midnight sea; the solitude of self. Our inner being, which we call ourself, no eye nor touch of man or angel has ever pierced. It is more hidden than the caves of the gnome; the sacred adytum of the oracle; the hidden chamber of Eleusinian mystery, for to it only omniscience is permitted to enter.

Such is individual life. Who, I ask you, can take, dare take, on himself the rights, the duties, the responsibilities of another human soul?

The class sits in stunned silence, enraptured by the oratorical delight delivered to them, flawlessly and passionately, as if the accolades offered to previous speakers are now grossly insufficient.

"Wonderful, Miss Barnes. Exemplary," the impressed teacher calls out from his desk. "A prodigious accomplishment. Really...I am at a loss for words. But I am not familiar with the author of these powerful words?"

"Elizabeth Cady Stanton, Mr. Warren. She spoke them before a congressional committee, nearly twenty years ago, at the age of seventy-seven."

"And you learned such a lengthy speech verbatim for this class? I am astounded."

The teacher stands up and walks over next to his prized student.

Josephine hesitates before responding.

"I learned it years ago, Mr. Warren. My mother handed me a printed pamphlet of the speech she had received at a women's club meeting when I was thirteen. She told me it was important for me to read it. And when I did, I did not understand much of it, but it affected me. It made me think about things I had never thought of before. I made a promise to myself, a way of challenging myself, that I would memorize the words—the entire pamphlet. And that is what I did. Over the summer and into the fall, I studied it and recited it when I was alone. Bit by bit, line by line, until I committed the entire speech to memory."

"Remarkable indeed. I think we can all agree, can't we class?" Mr. Warren says, leading the room in a loud round of applause.

"I pity the girl who has to follow you," he says just loud enough for Josephine alone to hear before she walks back to her desk.

"All right, let's see. Miss Holston, it is your turn to dazzle the class."

By early afternoon, Mrs. Martin receives a reply to her note: she is to meet at the headmaster's office at four o'clock. Armed with the materials of her accidental sleuthing packed in a leather bag—the newspaper and the county atlas—she makes for Vincent Hall at the appointed time with an attitude of self-satisfaction and a confident stride.

The winds have grown in strength since the morning and the sky is a turbulent, foreboding sea of black peaks and massive swells. Dried out leaves rattle on the branches arching over the walkway leading to the main hall and race across the hardened ground. A group of intrepid girls, huddled for warmth, pass by the prefect on their way to the gymnasium. Off to the left, the first members of the school chorus to arrive hurry up the steps of the

Odeon, buffeted by the chilling gusts, carrying garments bags containing their concert gowns.

Once inside Vincent Hall, Mrs. Martin hangs her coat and hat in the closet outside the dean's office and smoothes down her tousled hair in preparation for her entrance. She opens the door, bag tucked securely under her arm, prepared to reveal Mr. Geary's duplicity to the unsuspecting headmaster.

As she enters, the prefect is surprised to find the dean is not alone. Her note stipulated that she needed to meet with him on an urgent and confidential matter. In fact, Dean Dawson is nowhere to be seen. Seated at the head of the wide, imposing table in the center of the room is Douglas Stratton's young assistant, tapping cigarette ash into a white ceramic tray, with a diffident attitude of a man uncomfortable with the circumstances of the gathering. He glances up at Mrs. Martin and just as quickly returns to sculpting the contours of the gray powder along the side of the dish without saying a word. To his right, seated with his back to the door, is Mr. Geary, his prominent bald head marred with prominent cranial bumps and brown spots. The four regents are seated across the table in silence, aligned as it were in order of class, with Miss Price closest to Mr. Carter. The head of administrative services and the school chaplain also are in attendance.

Mrs. Martin feels someone brush her from behind and grab a hold of the oversized bag holding the framed map.

"Let me help you with this, Mrs. Martin," she hears the familiar voice offer and she turns, not protesting, to see the somber, deflated face of Dean Dawson. "I hope you didn't think you were coming to exchange Christmas gifts," he says with the unconvincing élan of a man headed to the gallows. "Go ahead and take a seat at the table."

He guides her to an open chair and places the unwieldy bag next to her on the floor. She thanks him weakly and looks around the room at the passive expressions before her. As she sits, she glances over at the bursar who is leaning over whispering to the man from New York. She averts her eyes just as Mr. Carter looks up at her while still listening to the private communication.

Dean Dawson unexpectedly takes a seat at the far end of the table, oddly separated from Mr. Geary and the others by a gap of empty chairs. He motions to Mr. Carter at the front of the table, who returns the gesture with a deferential nod.

The dean's announcement is delivered quickly and devoid of emotion.

"The Board of Trustees met this morning and approved the sale of our school. National Park Seminary will soon by under new ownership. I know you were all anxious to hear the outcome of today's meeting and I wanted to personally communicate the news. As I said to you earlier in this very room, I believe we are about to embark on an exciting chapter in our school's history. We should all welcome today's decision as the day when National Park Seminary launched into a new era of growth, prosperity and excellence. The board members have designated Mr. Geary to be their intermediary with Stratton Enterprises in this period of transition. I am in the process of drafting a letter to the rest of the faculty and staff and most importantly to each student's parents announcing the change in ownership and the positive affect it will have on our academic mission moving forward. The alumnae chapters will of course receive copies of this letter. Until such time as my letter is issued, the pending sale and the particulars surrounding it are not to be communicated with anyone else, by strict direction of Mr. Stratton and the Board of Trustees. As I warned before, failure to adhere to this direction will be grounds for dismissal."

The prefect feels the rigid outline inside the bag resting against her leg under the table. Its hidden presence, like that of a smuggled bomb, makes her anxious and jittery. She intended to reveal what she found to the dean privately, where they could speak openly with one another. She never considered that others would be here as well. And now, the explosive evidence sits by her feet and she contemplates the damage, both intended and collateral, it would cause if she were to detonate it now.

After Mr. Geary is sure the headmaster has finished his remarks, he stands up from the table to address the group.

"Thank you, Dean Dawson. One other word, if I may. It is only natural when a business is sold to new owners that its employees feel unsure about what the change means to not only the operation but for them personally. I understand this and I want to do my best to allay any concerns that you and the rest of our accomplished staff may have. I have spoken with Mr. Carter and working closely with Dean Dawson meetings will be scheduled early in the new semester to outline contemplated changes. There is shared appreciation that the competencies of the school's teachers and administrators must be not only maintained moving forward but strengthened."

The bursar turns toward Mr. Stratton's silent deputy expecting him to offer reassurance on this point, but he remains unengaged, slumped in the high-backed chair, pushing mounds of ash from side to side with his nearly extinguished cigarette.

Following the awkward pause, the bursar regains his bearings.

"In the meantime, if I can be of assistance to any of you, I am at your disposal."

When none of the regents speaks up, Dean Dawson takes back the floor.

"All right then, I see no reason to keep you. I will see some of you later tonight at the Christmas concert. For the rest of you, safe travels this evening. We are in for a spell of brutish weather, I am told."

Mrs. Martin looks over at the dean as the others around the table rise, hoping to establish a momentary connection between the two of them, a silent recognition that he received her note and that they had unfinished business to resolve privately. But he consciously avoids her gaze as he pushes away from the table and then walks toward the class regents, taking a moment to speak with each one of them in turn.

While the others in the room mingle about and begin to leave, Mr. Carter remains seated, oddly disconnected from the activity around him, until Dean Dawson, places one hand on his shoulder and the other on Miss Price's. The young regent's mask of placidity is removed at the headmaster's touch.

"Charles, come to the concert later this evening. Mrs. Dawson and I would enjoy it if you and Miss Price could join us in our box. I think it would help us all if we stepped away from the matters of business for a couple of hours and enjoyed the carols of the season. There is a light reception afterward. We expect a strong showing from the community—business leaders, politicians, a few of the board members as well."

Mr. Carter looks up and sees that Miss Price is visibly uncomfortable with the dean's hand resting on her shoulder or the proposition, or possibly both.

"I had a chance to watch the girls practice yesterday and they have perfected their craft. Madame Kaspar, our choral instructor, is remarkable and has prepared them well. Wouldn't you agree, Miss Price?"

The regent nods. "Yes, indeed."

"What do you say then?" the dean presses, ignorant of the distress roiling inside the young man over the secret burden he carries. "Will you be able to carve out time from your schedule and come and celebrate the glory of the Christmas season with us?"

"Of course, Dean Dawson. How could I turn down such a gracious offer?"

Across the table Mrs. Martin watches with amusement as the dean hovers over the two like an elderly village matchmaker determined to broker a union, so captivated by the unfolding scene that she does not notice when Mr. Geary slips into the empty seat next to hers.

"I can only imagine what is going through that brain of yours, Charlotte," he says, narrowing his eyes as if he were viewing a specimen under glass. "What could you be thinking right now? You can be candid with me. After all, you have not been hesitant in the past about expressing yourself."

The prefect remains focused on the drama across the table and does not answer.

"No, not in the talkative mood? What about the others?" he asks looking around the room. "Are they onboard?"

Mrs. Martin continues watching the dean and tries to suppress the contempt she feels for the conniving bursar as he leans in even closer, until his licorice-laced breath caresses her ear.

"Certainly you can appreciate now why I said what I did to you in my office the other day. It was not the time to encourage questions that could not be answered. You know I can read you, Charlotte, even in silence. I can tell when the gears and levers inside your mind are working. While others see only the severe expression of a middle-aged, slightly grumpy woman, I see deeper. So, why don't you tell me what you know and how long you have known it?"

As she considers the bursar's frontal assault, clearly designed to provoke her into a reaction, she feels his leg pressing against the other end of the bag.

"Are you jealous, George?"

"Interesting, Charlotte. Am I jealous, you ask? I will play along. Jealous of what exactly?"

"Not of *what*, of *whom*. Look over there at the two of them," she says tilting her head in the direction of Mr. Carter and Miss Price, who, now that the dean has departed, have left the table and are privately talking at the window next to the fireplace. "You carefully cultivated a mutually beneficial business relationship with our enigmatic visitor and his boss. You held close the cards of the deal until they were ready to be played, and in the process of doing so you betrayed your own employer, the man whose unwavering trust and support have put food on your table."

"Where has this newfound sympathy for the headmaster come from? Have you changed your spots?"

"Such depths of secrecy must draw people closer to one and another. The intimacy of sharing knowledge of what only a few are fully witting of. Is that how it was for you, George?"

"There is much you will never know or appreciate, Charlotte."

"Perhaps, but can you look at the two of them talking and decipher the clues of the mystery between them? For as much as you reveal in your partnership with the young man from Manhattan, he possesses secrets to which you are not privy. Study his mannerisms. Observe the angle and aperture of her eyes. Notice how he avoids looking directly at her. See how their bodies circle around the edges of an invisible barrier between them. Look at how his hands move about as if he doesn't know what to do with them as he speaks. He is a tormented man. He does not wear the crown of self-satisfaction like you. So wipe away that smirk. If you came here to gloat over how well you hid your hand in what has played out and the riches you stand to collect, you can go away."

"You're right, Charlotte. I look at the two of them and do not see what you presume to see. My interests do not lie in the abstract. My job is not to interpret the tea leaves of emotion between a man and a woman."

As Mr. Carter escorts Miss Price into the hallway, the prefect turns to face Mr. Geary.

"What is the Highland Trust?" she whispers.

"I don't know, why don't you tell me what the Highland Trust is?"

"No more games, George. Not now. Not after what just happened. What is it? You owe me that."

Over the narrow separation between the two of them, he is the first to show uncertainty. A crack in the smile. Eyes darting away from her unrelenting stare. A slight twitch along the right cheek.

"I don't know," he acquiesces. "I've never heard of it."

Mrs. Martin takes measure of his sincerity.

"You really don't know, do you? You are telling the truth."

"Have I been branded a pathological liar in your eyes now, Charlotte? Well, tell me, why are you asking about this Highland Trust?"

"Nothing," she answers, reclining back in her chair, and considers the implications of her discovery. "Nothing at all."

Twice a day, except on Sundays, the school mail is retrieved from the post office adjacent to the train station and brought back to a room in the rear of Vincent Hall next to the kitchen and food pantry. There it is carefully sorted and then delivered by freshman girls, enlisted for weekly rotations as a means for familiarizing them with the school's labyrinthine layout, its staff, and their fellow students.

For the Sweets residing in the palatial ballroom apartments, the routine entails an added step specific to their station in the school hierarchy. Letters and packages are handed over to a hired attendant living in a room connected to one of the suites whose job it is to present them personally to the girls during the afternoon ritual of tea on the third floor balcony overlooking the dance floor.

During the weeks leading up to Christmas, the volume of mail increases dramatically as the letters and gifts from family, friends and admirers swamp the post office. The hand-pushed carts used to deliver the daily bounty turn into wheeled cornucopias overflowing with lace-trimmed cards, packages of cured meats and striped candies, velvet-lined jewelry boxes and assorted keepsakes from the finest department stores and curio shops.

In order to cope with this string of uninterrupted abundance, delivery teams of two girls are required to handle the heavy seasonal load. The time it takes to complete the circuit doubles and then triples as the pile of packages on the backroom sorting table grows more mountainous with the approach of the celebrated day. Students wait in their rooms after daily classes are complete and eagerly anticipate the sound of the cart coming down the hallway and then rush to their doors to see what riches wrapped in brown paper await them.

Christmas cards are pinned along door frames and the colorful paper arches are adorned with small ornaments, red-berry sprigs of holly, glistening strips of silver tinsel, and other decorative touches which give the dormitory corridors a festive, carnival appearance.

That a plain envelope bearing no postage could be slipped into the afternoon postal delivery unnoticed is not surprising given the spike in letters and packages received at the Seminary during the holiday season. In this particular case, the envelope's sender is presented with practical limitations that make a normal, more direct communication to its recipient unadvisable.

The success of the National Park Seminary administrators in convincing parents of means from around the country to send their daughter to the school, at considerable cost (for them) and inconvenience (for the young woman), is predicated on an ironclad assurance that the welfare of their daughter while attending the school is assiduously protected at all times. Students are prohibited from leaving the school grounds without notifying a member of the staff and chaperones are provided on trips into Washington and other nearby destinations. All visitors to the school must be registered at the reception desk inside Vincent Hall. And men, single or married, not employed at the school require advance permission to remain on the grounds after sunset. Under no circumstance are visiting men allowed inside the dormitories.

These restrictions are stated prominently in the recruitment literature and repeated to all girls at assemblies held at the beginning of each semester. They are augmented by a canon of unwritten rules regulating the staff interaction with the girls attending National Park Seminary, directed specifically at those of the opposite gender, from the gardeners who toil outside tending to the multitude of floral beds and cutting the acres of lawn to the instructors responsible for cultivating the minds of their charges in academic fields of mathematics and business law and literature. Expectations of propriety and chaste behavior around the girls are pointedly and strenuously spelled out during the staff hiring process, as are the penalties for violations. For an all-girl preparatory school, especially one of established repute as the National Park Seminary, cannot condone any breach in the wall between faculty and student which places at risk the school's integrity and continued viability.

Within these rules of conduct, an additional limitation is carved out concerning interaction between the colored men employed by the school and the students that inhabit it. The parameters of permissible behavior are simple and strictly applied: exchanges with the girls are allowed only in the performance of the employee's duties; communication is permitted only in reply to conversation initiated by a student; and, above all, physical contact is strictly prohibited.

Dining room workers are taught to hold plates and glasses so as to avoid the inadvertent touch of those they are serving. Break areas for the kitchen and laundry staffs are carefully screened in the back of buildings out of sight of the commonly used thoroughfares connecting the classrooms and dormitories. Segregated gardening crews are rotated around the sprawling grounds throughout the day to minimize the likelihood that dark skinned laborers bent over extracting weeds and pruning withered bloom heads will catch sight of the girls passing by.

Eli Raymee had seen a number of men over the years—many of them good, hard workers, others lazy and undisciplined—run afoul of these rules and, no matter how minor the transgression, the end result was the same. He learned early on to avoid the dangerous shoals of working around hundreds of young white women in a job that requires helping students mount and dismount their rides. He always takes the horses outside to the paddock before allowing a girl to hoist up onto the saddle. He holds the harness reins and steadies the mount from the opposite side. If the rider is shorter or needs assistance in pulling up and swinging her leg across the saddle, he keeps a foot stool nearby. Using his interlaced hands and thigh for support to boot-up the leg of a rider—the technique he learned as a young boy and used throughout his life—would necessarily require the brief but forceful physical contact against the rider's leg that would surely get him fired.

The blast of wintry weather that followed on the heels of the heavy rains has curtailed the scheduled riding trips and lightened the work load for Mr. Raymee and his stable boy. The girls stopped coming by after classes and the trial rides to a nearby apple orchard or through the surrounding woods to picnic at Indian Rock, so popular during the fall when the trees in the glen are ablaze with splashy color and the air is crisp and laced with the aroma of burning hickory logs, ceased and gave way to indoor pursuits.

After exercising the pent-up horses and cleaning their stalls in the morning, the man and boy pass the shank of the day playing cards and foraging for downed branches along the county road to keep the wood stove in Mr. Raymee's cramped room fed.

Then, on his way to the outhouse after finishing a lunch of dried beef, hard cheese and bread, the monotony of the shortening days is abruptly brought to an end. Trouble has sought him out and Mr. Raymee is left with no choice. He knows he must make contact even if it means risking the steady if not marginal job he has held for nearly a third of his days.

An unsigned note containing only the most necessary information is given to the stable boy who runs it to the back entrance of the kitchen where it is delivered to a second-cousin of Mr. Raymee's working the lunch shift. She in turn slips the envelope unnoticed into the pile of mail from the post office while bringing the beleaguered sorters cups of cider and freshly baked shortbread crescents from the kitchen.

The old man waits, hoping that she will come, knowing that, of all the girls at the school, she alone will know what to do, she alone will protect him.

By the time Josephine arrives at the stable, the sun has set and plummeting temperatures outside have spread delicate ice crystals across the compacted dirt like a nocturnal contagion. The thick clouds of the day remain and rob the night of any celestial illumination and along the backside of campus the narrow passageways between the service buildings and storage sheds are unlit and treacherous to walk. The pungent stench of garbage and fresh horse dung wafts in the air as she strikes her fist against the darkened doorway.

Mr. Raymee quickly ushers her inside, glancing out into the night for any sign of a witness to her arrival before closing the door. He immediately takes notice of Josephine's clothes and appearance. He is used to seeing her and the other girls in riding jackets and boots, or walking about campus wearing the school-issued uniforms. He has neither reason nor opportunity to see the students in formal clothing. Below the hem of Josephine's coat he glimpses the shimmering electric-blue evening dress. Her soft, blonde curls, typically pulled back and clasped with a decorative barrette, are pinned up, fully revealing her neck line and accentuating her fair features. Stray, wispy tendrils not captured hang down and lightly caress creamy skin adorned with a strand of pearls. The light cast off by the wood stove dances in Josephine's pale blue eyes, eyes that show concern as they meet the stable groom's. In her satin-gloved hand, she holds the white envelope bearing her name and room number.

Mr. Raymee offers her a seat next to the fire as he sits in the green chair with threadbare cushions he has claimed his own since he retrieved it from the school dump years ago. Josephine can sense that he is nervous and waits patiently for him to begin as he rubs his thick, calloused fingers together, over and over.

"Miss Barnes, I hope you don't take offense by me asking, but does anyone else know you have come here?"

Josephine shakes her head, knowing full well why he feels a need to ask her.

"You see, somethin' is going on that's not right. It's all a bit troublin' really and I am not sure what to do about it. I didn't want to bother you. I suppose I could do nothin' but I worry that it may just make things worse still. You see my dilemma?"

Josephine is puzzled but does not lead on. In forging her friendship with the elderly groom and building the tenuous trust that exists between them, she has found it helpful to be affirming in her replies and patient in allowing Mr. Raymee to find his own level of comfort.

"You have a problem, but no good choices on how to deal with it," she interprets.

"Yes, indeed," a modicum of relief comes over his weighted brow. "But I don't want to shift my burdens on to you, you see. It wouldn't be fair if I brought you into my affairs either."

"Are you in trouble, Mr. Raymee?"

"No, Miss Barnes. I keep to my own corner here, and I like it that way."

"In your note to me," Josephine lifts up the card to show him, "you wrote about needing to talk to me about the ride on Tuesday."

"I wrote that so you would know it was from me. Truthfully, it is not about the ride exactly. Well, not entirely, at least."

"Has someone come to speak with you about the ride I and the other two girls went on that morning?"

The man nods with a resigned expression, as if he knew Josephine would get to the heart of the matter quickly. She immediately thinks of Miss Price and the way her interest in Josephine's affairs has become almost obsessive in the past week.

"One of the teachers?"

He shakes his head and holds his tongue, preferring that she guess again and relieve him of the discomfort of explaining why he summoned her.

"One of the other students? Did one of the other girls come to you asking about where we went?"

"No, not exactly. You can see my dilemma now, can't you?"

Josephine consciously suppresses the frustration building inside her. Margaret, still weak from the flu but presentable, is waiting at the Odeon with a few girls from Theta house holding a seat for her.

"I can, Mr. Raymee. The Christmas concert is scheduled to begin ten minutes from now, and I am expected there by my friends," she says gently but purposefully, hoping to spur the reluctant man to be more forthcoming and direct with her.

"Over the years workin' here I have gotten to know folks in the area. You know, folks livin' in the homes and farms around Forest Glen. I see them at the store or sometimes I run into them out on the road out front here. You walk horses around and people naturally come up to you and strike up a conversation. Over time, circumstances come about when I might help them with somethin' and, in turn, they help me out here and there. It's how life is out here. We have our own community where we come to rely on each other."

The meaning of the word *we* is clear to the attentive girl.

"And how does this tie back to the ride?"

As she speaks the words, her naïve tone is belied by the memory of the trying journey after she, Margaret and Leah left the stable before sunrise.

"Today a boy who lives down the road a mile or so showed up here, snuck into the stalls and waited for me to walk past. Scared the livin' daylights out of me. I know the boy, but I didn't expect him to pop out of the shadows like some sort of jack-in-the box. His name is Robert. No more than nine or ten, I think. He lives in the clearing in the woods with the rest of his family. They've been workin' the same miserable piece of land for nearly sixty years, barely able to scratch out an existence. Robert and the other kids run around in rags most of the time. No schoolin'. Just runnin' wild most of the time."

"Why did he come to see you? What did he want?"

"He told me a story. He told me how you and the other two girls— Miss Cleary and Miss Hathaway—showed up on their property and how there were words exchanged between you and Robert's uncle."

Josephine feels the moment has arrived where she can no longer deny her knowledge of what took place.

"Yes, I know Robert. We got turned around in the woods and lost our way during the ride. He helped us find our way back to the county road. He was a life saver. I owe him a debt of gratitude."

"He remembers you. When he came to me he described you as the 'woman who gave my uncle lip.' I had to laugh when he said that. I know what kind of man his uncle is—hard and ornery. And I could think of only one student at this place who wouldn't back down to his blusterin'."

Josephine senses a hint of pride in his words, as if he wished he had been there to witness the standoff by the fire.

"What reason did he have to come to see you, Mr. Raymee?"

"He was scared. Imagine that, he was the one scared and he nearly put me in an early grave jumpin' out at me like he did. That boy Robert can be a real handful."

There is a commotion in the stalls and a horse's whinnying carries down the length of the dim corridor adjacent to the groom's primitive hovel.

"Was it his uncle threatening him? I saw how he spoke to Robert that morning in a menacing way."

"You see, that's the rub. I figured he high-tailed it over here like before. I told him then to stay away, and that he shouldn't be bringing his family business to my stoop. I wasn't his kin and I wasn't his protector when things got rough out there. He needed to fend for his self. When he came out from the stalls today I was ready to lit into the boy, but I could see from his face that somethin' was different and that hothead Zachary hadn't been chasin' him around with a belt again. The boy immediately started bawlin', tears just pourin' from his eyes onto the saw dust. He was genuinely scared. I brought him here and gave him some water and waited for him to calm down. And when he finally stopped sobbin' and got his breath back, he sat where you are sitting and told me what he says he saw last night."

"What was it?"

"He says he was sleepin' in the house when in the middle of the night he heard footsteps outside on the porch. The rest of the family was there in the same room with him, all of them asleep and his uncle in a rocker next to the stove, stone cold still. He said it was late, long after midnight, and he was frightened listenin' to the sound of someone walkin' slowly just outside the door, comin' up close in the dark. And then he says the footsteps on the porch stopped. Then he thought maybe he was dreamin' before he woke and that the noise outside wasn't real but somethin' he was imagining in his head. So the boy says he lays back down on the spot where he made his bed and punches the pillow a few times to stiffen it so it lays higher. And as he turns his head around to go back to sleep, he sees a person's face in the window, bright as day, wide-eyed and looking right at him through the glass. The shock freezes the blood in his veins. When the boy tells me this, I stop him right there, and I tell him he had a nightmare, that's all. He woke up from dreamin' and turned some noise outside into somethin' it ain't."

Mr. Raymee pauses and reaches over and slides a stick between the slats of front stove grate.

"And you should have seen the boy after I said that. He gets all angry and starts tellin' me it was real and that he didn't make it up. So after I listen to him go on for a while, I say to him, how come you are so sure? And he tells, all quiet like, that the white face at the window don't go away. It just stayed there, lookin' at him, eyes wide and such, never movin', never blinkin'. He tells me there was nowhere for him to hide, and being scared to move, he ducks under the blanket and waits in the dark. He's shakin' and when he can't take it anymore he peeks out and catches a look of the face in the window again. Robert says he wanted to cry out and wake the others but he couldn't. The boy starts shakin' some more under the blanket and he's so frightened he doesn't even realize that he is digging his finger tips into the rough floor boards he's laying on top of. He tells me that this goes on for a long while. He isn't sure for how long. He loses track of time and each time he summons the courage to peek out from his blanket, he sees her."

"Her?"

"The face of the watcher on the porch was a girl."

"What happened then?"

"The boy told me he got exhausted and fell asleep again. When he woke, it was morning. The others in the room were already awake and movin' about the room, getting ready for the day's work. And the girl in the window, the bright, white face watchin' over him, was gone."

"What…what a horrible nightmare for the poor boy."

"That's what I thought too," he replies, sliding another branch onto the dying fire. The embers pulsate and the wood crackles. "I thought that was it, that the boy would feel a lot better after tellin' his story to me. Can't imagine anybody under that roof believin' his story or lendin' a sympathetic ear. But the boy just sits there waitin' for me to say somethin' more, like he wanted me to make the memories go away.

Incident at Forest Glen 301

"Then he starts tellin' me about you and the others riding on the property and how at first there was just one girl and then two other girls showed up later and how you gave his uncle some lip. I started to get concerned when I heard him tell me this. You hadn't said anything when you returned that mornin' and I was worried about what Zachary might have said to you. I've heard stories and I don't trust the man. He's shifty and he's a proven liar.

"So, I start getting interested, see, but Robert's not hearin' what I am askin' him. He keeps on talkin' about a girl hiding behind the shed and nonsense like that. The story gets all twisted like and I can't understand what he is sayin', so I get frustrated and start to raise my voice with the ramblin' boy and he shouts out, 'It was her! The girl! The girl in the window was the lost rider!'

"He starts tellin' me about how tall she is and what she looks like and the color of her hair and how the skin on her face was an unnatural white and her eyes were all crazed lookin'—it all pours out him at once. I couldn't get a word in edgewise. 'She came back' he keeps saying, over and over. 'She came back.' When I yell at him he is behavin' like a mad dog, he starts bawlin' again, just like before.

"Then he holds out his hands in front of me and I see the thick splinters of wood pokin' out from under the skin of his finger tips. Like brown needles burrowed into his swollen fingers. They were from last night, when he was trying to hide under his blanket. Seein' that changed my thinkin' about the whole story real quick.

"So I calmed the boy down the best I could. I dug out the splinters with a small pen knife, cleaned the cuts, and then I got him to take a bath in one of the water troughs in the back of the stable. The boy smelled to high-heaven."

"Is he still here?"

"He left a while ago. Gone back home. Didn't want to. But I told him he had to. He couldn't get seen being around here. Get both of us in trouble. I was all right leavin' it at that. Boy sees somethin' at his window at the middle of the night, somewhere inside his fevered brain he thinks of the girl who came riding up on the property a few days ago and thinks it's her. I don't know what to think, but seein' his tiny finger tips all puffed out and red like that made my own skin crawl. But it wasn't any of my business. That's the way I looked at it. The three of you rode out and the three of you rode back. None of you said a thing."

Mr. Raymee pauses and Josephine wonders if this is his way of communicating almost parental disappointment to her that she didn't tell him about the incident and her confrontation with Robert's uncle.

"So I go about my business. I send the boy home a lot better than when he showed up. And I go about my business. I am not going to lie, Miss Barnes, Robert's story bothered me and it made me think a lot. I care for the boy, you see. He's the sort of kid who if he got a break or two could make somethin' of himself. Talks well. Curious. Got a good head on his shoulders. Runs wild too much, sure. But to see him hysterical and cryin' and all that bothered me. I thought about headin' over to the house after he left, maybe bring along a bag of extra feed, just to check out the place and see what's going on. I wouldn't have let on that Robert had come to see me or about what he said to me. That would only bring down a world of hurt on the poor boy. And I was still considerin' it when I was filling up the water buckets in the stalls like I do every afternoon."

The troubled man turns away from Josephine searching for his words.

"Maybe it's easier if I just show you."

Mr. Raymee stands up with some discomfort, battling the painful grip of arthritis in his hips and knees that worsens in winter, and walks over to a work bench and retrieves a kerosene lantern. Even at night, the horses recognize the sound of his steps down the dark stable and arouse from their shallow slumber. He leads Josephine past a series of wood and metal barred stalls until the lantern shines on a familiar leather and brass badge.

The groom reaches above his head and places the lantern handle over a hook covered with ancient cobwebs and then unbolts the door. He walks through and disappears in the shadowy recesses of the stall beyond the light's reach. The unseen horse nickers and then gives off a throaty protest that makes Josephine's heart drop.

Mr. Raymee emerges out of the blackness leading the gray gelding by the neck and mane, whispering softly. The chilling wind outside blows fiercely and the stable's loose side boards and porous roof rattle as if they are about to succumb to the stiff force and separate from their rusted nails. Other horses around the stall move about and exhale deeply as a blast of cold air races through the creaking building.

"What is it, Mr. Raymee? Tell me now, please. Is there something wrong with Sable?"

It is now his turn to calm the alarmed girl.

"Oh, Miss Barnes, don't be worried. This horse of yours is just fine. Strong and fit," he says, patting the horse's broad, muscular neck. The animal's large eyes glimmer in the uneven light and his nostrils flare at the scent of his owner.

"When I went to water Sable, I saw somethin' not right along his hindquarters below the croup. I thought it might be a splash of mud or a streak of blackin'. When I looked closer at his skin, I saw it wasn't anythin' like that at all. It was blood, dried blood that had crusted over. He got cut somehow, real lightly you see, and it had stopped bleedin' and was just startin' to scab over."

"I don't understand, Mr. Raymee. What is wrong with him? Did he accidentally cut himself on a nail in the stall?"

"He's all right, Miss Barnes. You can rest your mind. I cleaned him up real nice and put antiseptic on the cuts and checked him over every which way from Sunday. He's fit. But he didn't cut himself on any nail?"

Josephine grows colder as the raw air bites at her exposed legs and cuts though her coat and the fabric of her dress.

"How can you be sure what happened, Mr. Raymee?"

The groom does not answer but leads Sable around to the side and back into the darkness, now presenting the broad side of the horse to the flickering flame. The sleek mottled skin covering his ribs moves past in the light as he is led by the groom a couple steps further, passing in a fleeting glimpse like a leviathan breaking the ocean surface under a moonlit night. Mr. Raymee steadies his charge and guides him backward until the horse's rear flank is pressed toward the stall entrance.

Josephine gasps at the seeing the illuminated flesh.

"It's all right, Miss Barnes. It's all right," the groom says soothingly, as he approaches the weak light. "It's superficial. Sable's so big and strong he probably didn't feel a thing."

"Oh my God, Mr. Raymee," she says, trying to regain her composure but unable to look away from the wound.

"You can see why I needed you to come here. I needed to tell you. I needed you to see for yourself."

304   ANDY JOHNSON

While gripping the withers with one hand, the groom spreads his other hand wide and with open palm slides it slowly and gently along the contours of the skittish horse's protruding stomach and up along the flank stopping at the crimson lines.

"Shhh," he says to calm Sable and then traces the initial line from the top down the length of the cut and then over to the right, where he picks up the first of two other vertical cuts and follows it lightly until the dark finger rests on a deeper, thicker, more severe perforation running across the flank.

"It will heal real soon. I'll do my best to make sure it heals clean and doesn't leave much of a scar."

The unsettling fear Josephine felt from the moment Mr. Raymee began his story by the wood stove gives way to a growing rage as she looks at the mutilated flesh of her beloved horse. She is transfixed by the crudely carved letters.

L H

"I have seen a lot of flesh wounds in my time and given the condition of the cuts on Sable, I can tell they aren't fresh. Dried but not so far along that they are infected yet. My guess is that they are around a day old."

"I understand what you are saying, Mr. Raymee," Josephine replies, though she finds his implication difficult to accept. The vicious marking of Sable helps confirm the boy's story that Leah had left Senior House and returned to the homestead in the dead of night. It was her face in the window, the ghostly visage that so terrified the boy.

L H

Leah Hathaway.

She had heard Miss Price complain that Leah had gone missing and that she hadn't been seen all night and how she wasn't answering her door. It was true. She confirmed it herself, finding her room empty and the furniture inside strangely rearranged. The broken light. The once brightly decorated room covered inside a black shroud. Her door was shut when Josephine returned from afternoon classes. She was not at dinner and no sign of life was detected inside the room during the evening preparation for the concert. As the hour of the concert approached, Josephine and Margaret speculated about the scene inside the Odeon and what would transpire if the star performer never showed.

Why would Leah do this to her horse? Such a savage, hateful, inexplicable, unforgivable act.

"I know this is a shock and all, but there is somethin' else I need to show you, Miss Barnes."

Mr. Raymee releases his hold on the horse and gently pushes it along to clear the opening to the stall. Josephine watches as the confused beast returns to the lonely corner from which it came, its tail swishing from side to side as it retreats.

The groom reaches over and from a hidden ledge inside the stall pulls out a menacing blade that catches the light and glints as he holds it out for Josephine to see.

She immediately recognizes it as the knife from the boathouse, the one pulled from the canoe she and Margaret dragged out onto the grass.

"Whoever cut Sable used this and left it behind, right on the floor over there. There was blood on it when I found it and I washed it off."

Josephine presses her gloved hands against her face.

"What do you want me to do, Miss Barnes?"

The question goes unanswered as she tries to reconcile all that the groom has told her. Leah's eccentric behavior, previously a troublesome matter for her and Margaret to deal with, is now something graver and more dangerous.

"He's your horse."

Who can I turn to, she asks herself, the stinging accusations from her earlier confrontation with Miss Price still fresh? She must speak with Margaret first. Though she fervently resisted approaching someone in authority about Leah, surely she will think differently when she hears what has happened.

"Do you want me to talk to my supervisor about this?" the groom asks. "I can do that…but I suspect they will want to talk to you and the other two girls about what happened that morning. And once you finish tellin' your stories you can bet that will lead to the police headin' down the road and payin' a visit to Robert's family."

Mr. Raymee bends slightly at the knees in order to look directly into the distraught girl's eyes.

"Is there anything about what took place between you and Zachary that mornin' I need to know, Miss Barnes?"

Josephine shakes her head.

"No. I would prefer that you not tell anyone about this or Robert's story. I think I know what is happening. I don't want either of you caught in the middle, Mr. Raymee. I just need some time to sort it out. I just need you to take care of Sable and let me know if anything else suspicious happens to him."

"Sure. He and I have a relationship. I'll take care of him good."

"I will come by here and see you tomorrow and we can talk more then. I need to go now. I am already late for the concert."

"What should I do with this?" he asks, looking down at the skinning knife in his hand.

"Wrap it inside some cloth and hide it back in the stall. And don't tell anyone about it. We'll figure out what to do with it later."

"Miss Barnes, I don't know what's going on here, but I don't like it. None of it. I didn't like seein' the look in that scared boy's face with his hands all messed up like that. I don't like the idea of his uncle makin' trouble with you girls. I don't like when one of my horses gets hurt, 'specially with this. And I don't like to see you involved with this nastiness."

The groom's words of concern help tamp down the panic inside Josephine and even in the muted light of the stable she sees the emotion in his eyes. She gives him a tender smile and touches him reassuringly on the arm.

"And you as well, Mr. Raymee. I don't know what I would do without your understanding."

The ailing groom secures the stall door and the two figures, so completely different in all respects, walk back to the stable gate side by side, guided by the lantern.

The relentless wind whistles through the loose boards and shakes the tin roof overhead. The intensifying noise highlights the awkward silence that has come between the old man and the young woman.

For a few moments before they part, before Josephine walks out into the harsh night and before Mr. Raymee slowly lowers himself into the worn yet serviceable chair by the stove, they walk in darkness as kindred spirits, undefined by age or color, the differing circumstances in which they were brought into this world rendered meaningless, the trajectory of their futures—one an endless horizon of promise, the other, finite and predictable—now uncertain, entangled together by a threat that neither fully comprehends.

Chapter 9
Denizens of the Pantheon

Good manners are founded upon good morals. A series of talks is given throughout the year upon polite forms and the requirements of good breeding. Individual faults are privately and kindly pointed out. Many a girl, capable, bright and interesting, seriously impairs her usefulness by some unfortunate, obnoxious habit, which her friends are not brave enough to speak of or judicious enough to eradicate. Since personality is one of the strongest forces in the world, surely its perfect development should engage the most earnest attention of the educator. We share the aversion with which the world regards the "woman pedant." Nothing, we believe, has retarded the true progress of women more that the inattention of many so-called finely educated women to those details of person which should be the exponent of their culture, and to those requirements of social life which are, as Emerson says, "our only protection against the vulgarity of the streets." If the higher culture does not render our daughters more charming personally, more attractive socially and more companionable intellectually, then it has failed in attaining its ends. We emphasize the fact that we consider text-book training only part of our work as educators. We shall be satisfied with nothing less that the development of the whole being.

Madame Kaspar waits anxiously behind the heavy stage curtain, closes her eyes, and listens intently. In the distance, the chapel's iron bell tolls seven times, its slow and steady knell reverberating over the abandoned school grounds, into the neighboring homes, and across the black ravine to where the station attendant checks his temperamental pocket watch. When the sound of the last strike dies off, she gives the signal and the audience lights inside the Odeon are switched off, bringing to an end the low rumble of conversations filling the auditorium since students, teachers and guests began arriving a half-hour before.

The foot lights along the front of the stage come to life. Madame steps back and turns to face the choir, still shielded from the view of the audience. Each girl, positioned in their prescribed spots, wears a white, floor-length gown and headband adorned with miniature red roses and baby's breath. Long, angled candelabras, specially made for the occasion by a local welder, are positioned to both sides of the choral risers. The flames atop the ascending lines of ivory candles burn steady and illuminate the faces of the singers in a warm, subdued light. To the right, the school piano teacher, Mr. Bancroft, dressed in formal attire, is seated at the organ, moved with great care and difficulty from the chapel earlier in the day, poised for Madame Kaspar's direction.

In the viewing box overhanging the stage, Dean Dawson slips his fingers into his surprised wife's hand and lets out a prolonged sigh, the day's events unshakeable and weighing heavily on his mind. Perched prominently in the eyes of those assembled, he refuses as a matter of pride and as a demonstration of personal fortitude to give any indication in public of the devastating blow he has sustained this day. His outward appearance remains unaffected and resolute, showing no hint of the turmoil within.

Upon returning from the morning board meeting, he immediately reported the outcome to his partner and confidant of over thirty years. As he expected, her words were encouraging and stressed the optimistic view that their life at National Park Seminary would go forward unchanged and that his authorities would continue unabated.

"Who in their right mind would sack the goose who lays the golden eggs?" was her curious analogy.

Her assurances during difficult times, when he allowed self-doubt to gain a foothold in otherwise confident psyche, had provided him great comfort in the past. He's relied on not only her unfailing support and thoughtful counsel over the years but her steadfast faith that he possessed immeasurable qualities of intellect and resourcefulness that meant he should not yield in the face of adversity and that, in the end, he could not fail. But in the privacy of their Edgewood parlor, as he held her close and felt the strength of her arms pulling him tightly, the wound he felt inside festered. As he listened to the soothing words of love whispered in his ear, he began to see that he had

INCIDENT AT FOREST GLEN *309*

been wrong in insisting that the question of his continued supreme authority be put to the Board of Trustees as a vote of affirmation—a minimal recognition, he believed at the time, of his centrality in the school's success. How he seethed at the board's unkind repudiation. Even when he made great show of his approval of the lavish red and green bows and garland draped inside the concert hall, he stewed in his private discontent. And now, as the Christmas program is about to begin and he shifts in his seat to listen to the seasonal carols that provided him such comfort as a young boy, he cannot ignore the galling reality that his standing in the world he built and carefully tended has been irrevocably diminished. He realized it sitting in the park outside the bank offices earlier in the morning and it was confirmed during the afternoon meeting with Mr. Carter and his senior staff. Though he was the one who spoke of the board's decision, he could tell that the attention of his employees was no longer trained on him. He knew it then. At that very moment. He would continue to be called headmaster, but the title would no longer carry the weight it once did.

There is a new reality in play.

Those were Mr. Geary's words of warning on the park bench.

And now, out of self-preservation, he must bite his tongue and seek out the favor of Mr. Stratton and his assistant with obsequious comments of support and insincere invitations. It is a contemptible game, one that is beneath him. The mere presence of the young man—the assassin's right hand—in the seat next to him is unbearably galling to the dean.

He squeezes his wife's short, plump fingers and lets out another audible exhalation, as if he is releasing pressure from an overheated boiler, and suppresses, for the moment, the urge to cast the smug interloper over the front of the box and into the depths of the deserted orchestra pit below.

As the lights dim, Miss Price takes one last look into the audience. In the middle section, halfway up from the stage, she spots Margaret, the seat next to her still empty. Throughout the day the regent has felt the burden of regret over how she let her emotions compromise her professionalism, repeatedly punishing herself for losing control in front of Josephine. It is not the display of anger that upsets her so, but the provocation. I am not *that type of woman*, she tells herself. I am not the type to let a handsome face and engaging disposition corrupt my judgment and make me weak and susceptible.

It was a painful lesson she learned before—or so she thought at the time. After the drama that preceded her departure from her previous job as principal at Montclair Academy in Maine, she assiduously walled off her interest in men she met while at work. Even the most innocent flirtation could be ruinous, fodder for malicious gossip and trumped-up grounds for dismissal. The experience then was painful and humiliating. But the most troublesome aspect of the ordeal was the feeling of being powerless. Powerless to defend herself against the charge that she had illicit contact with a teacher under her employ. Powerless to challenge the unjust decision. Powerless to sway the opinions of the teachers and parents and students who looked at her and based solely upon her attractive features and assured demeanor found her guilty of the accusation.

"I knew you were that type of woman when I first laid eyes on you," the bitter mother of one of the students spat at her after the termination decision was made years ago.

That type of woman.

Where then was the empathy for Josephine? What blind spot had come over her and made it so she could not see the similar predicament facing the confused girl? She genuinely likes Josephine and sees promise in her spirited approach to life at the Seminary. Her record has been exemplary, her studies accomplished. The girl did not deserve the bitter lash of her jealousy. She is blameless. She had neither the time nor opportunity to invite Mr. Carter's interest. It was thrust upon her through no fault of her own, Miss Price concedes. Her charms and beauty are undeniable; it is only natural that she and the other older girls attract the attention of men they come in contact with, eligible and otherwise.

She witnesses it often accompanying the students on trips outside the school, while walking along the District streets, during guided museum tours, and in the crowded department stores. When she is with them, Miss Price no longer experiences the meaningful glances and the unwanted attention she is use to receiving in different circumstances. It is as if in the eyes of men she and the other chaperones are not even there. Looked past. Unnoticed. Rendered invisible. Eclipsed by the bounty of youth around her.

The overtures are often subtle and clumsily amusing; occasionally they are coarse and cross the line of propriety. But they are more than untoward advances to the protective senior regent. Privately, she views them as troubling reminders that a widening gulf now separates her from the wondrous, carefree days of her past, of cherished memories still vivid and unspoiled by time the avenger. What as a young woman of eighteen she found flattering and heady she now watches with equal parts of contempt and resentment. The way men turn their heads while passing to look at a group of her students walking down the sidewalk. The leering stares from across the street. The inviting smiles and the unsolicited compliments. How men walk past available seats on the streetcar to take the one next to her girls. Strangers brushing against the nubile bodies of unsuspecting students, so briefly and casually, so as to disguise their prurient intent.

She remembers Josephine when she first arrived at National Park Seminary, a thin-faced girl with an easy smile and a bright outlook on the cusp of growing into her body and looking to feed her ravenous intellect. Miss Price was immediately drawn to her then and took a personal interest in cultivating her talents and testing her mettle when she felt the girl was becoming complacent. Eventually the teacher saw her as something of a younger sister or even an earlier incarnation of herself. And now she worries that the trusting bond that existed between the two of them has been irrevocably severed in a matter of seconds by an irrational fit of school girl envy on her part.

The bitterness of her ugly words in the office burn her tongue still as penance for her transgression. She doesn't want Josephine to see her seated next to Mr. Carter, not after their regrettable exchange. She fears it will only further confirm in the girl's mind the source of the regent's green-eyed rant. She wants the opportunity to speak with her so she can tell her that what happened between them wasn't right and to retract her threat about the chance meeting after the party. She desperately needs Josephine to understand that the teacher she saw earlier was not really her, but an aberration. She wants a moment alone, away from the curious ears of the others, so she can apologize and explain that it was all a misunderstanding, and in doing so hopefully find in Josephine's eyes acceptance and forgiveness.

She can't be that type of woman again.

The mechanical pullies above the stage groan and the curtain gathers from the bottom and is levitated behind the proscenium revealing the resplendent chorus. A hush falls over the crowd as the sumptuous, meticulously created portrait in white and red comes to life.

Outside, high above the Seminary grounds, crouched in the shadows between two of the statues lining the Odeon rooftop, Leah awakens from her suspended state and notices a lone traveler approaching along the pathway below. She senses the rage, raw and unrestrained, inside the girl. The familiar swell of music reverberates against the soles of her shoes. The night wind buffets her exposed body causing it to sway over the corner edge revealing a precipitous drop down to the sparkling pavement. Below, the hurried girl ascends the steps and disappears inside the hall.

Leah silently backs away from her overlook and retraces her steps along the soft layer of loose stone and tar toward the interior of the rooftop. She opens a small access door and hears the melodic sound of the organ interlude below. Without hesitation, she turns around and nimbly descends the affixed metal rungs.

She moves around the drafty, lightless attic in silence, carefully avoiding stacks of wooden boxes filled with forgotten treasures of the school drama department. The harmonious voices of the chorus grow stronger as she moves closer to the loosely hinged door and the spiral staircase beyond it leading down the auxiliary room off the balcony parlor. She navigates the tight corners and cramped spaces effortlessly in the dark and rushes down the shallow steps with the agility of falcon plummeting down toward its distant, unsuspecting quarry.

Just as she emerges from the custodial entrance she hears an eruption of applause. The commotion allows her to slip into the balcony level unnoticed. She floats behind the far row, her shoulders grazing the back wall as she steps lightly under the cover of the enthusiastic accolades being offered up. She stops underneath the all-seeing deity hung high on the wall as the clapping trials off. After a brief silence, she hears the opening notes to the familiar piece. She closes her eyes and listens in sweet anticipation for the lyrics to follow. A low rumble inside the cool plaster vibrates along her back and hips. A powerful, magnetic energy ensnares her and reaches inside her torso, pulling against her spine as if it were a rod of steel.

Above her, the serene countenance of the plaster Athenian goddess looks down on the singers assembled to pay her tribute.

Mr. Carter shifts his body from side to side, trying to find a comfortable position in the stiff and pinching antique chair that is causing his legs to go numb. His unsettled behavior draws a quick glance from Miss Price sitting next to him. As he squirms about in search of relief, his thoughts drift away from the concert, thinking of ways he could escape his entrapment in Dean Dawson's private box.

Earlier in the day, he faithfully reported the outcome of the board meeting to his employer by telegraph and received confirmation of its receipt while he was dressing for the concert. Mr. Stratton's reply was brief and concise:

EXCELLENT NEWS STOP AWAIT YOUR RETURN SUNDAY EVENING STOP DS

He was in such a rush, standing half-dressed in the hotel room doorway, that he almost didn't notice the peculiar addendum at the bottom of the flimsy piece of paper:

PS LEFT PACKAGE FOR YOU AT THE FRONT DESK STOP

At Miss Price's recommendation, he spent the rest of the afternoon following the meeting in the dean's office walking through the Villa gardens and touring the curious buildings and statuary spread about the sprawling campus. The hectic pace of obligations since their arrival had kept him from seeing the intriguing architecture up close in the daylight. After the awkward exchange of power, he needed time alone to clear his head and reconcile his conflicted feelings about his role in the sale and the secretive plan now underway to shutter the school. An opportunity to strike out on his own, to feel the pavement under foot and the winter air against his face, was what he desperately needed. The hour spent briskly walking among the eclectic buildings left him thoroughly chilled and gratifyingly exhausted, the perfect remedy for lessening the crushing weight of remorse he carried with him since leaving the dean's office. And when he returned to his room, the idea of attending the evening concert as a guest of the Dawsons was unappealing. He needed distance. Too much had changed since that first night on the balcony overlooking the ballroom floor.

He glances over at Miss Price and recalls the change in her attitude when she approached him after the meeting. Her expression was somber and subdued. Gone were the attentive looks and playful remarks. The obvious interest she had shown in him during the ride to the hospital was gone, as if spirited away in the blustery storm. Her words were now more formal, measured and polite, though spoken without a hint of ill-temper. And when he arrived at the Odeon she greeted him in the parlor with a courteous welcome and offering of her hand as if they were meeting him for the first time, the words "*Mr.* Carter" immediately letting him know that the branch of familiarity they had crawled out on had been sawed off.

What is it that has changed your behavior, Katharine Price, he asks himself? What is it that you now know that you did not know before?

He mulls over Mr. Stratton's admonition about how women act out of self-interest and scrutinizes the regent's impassive gaze, considering the soft lines of her pleasing profile. Were his employer's aphorism to be right, today's confirmation of the school's sale should only heighten her interest in him. And yet, there she sits, attractively dressed in navy blue, cold and withdrawn, an enigmatic woman lost in thought, miles away.

A peculiar scent, pungent and out of place, lingers inside the lavish, carpeted anteroom. A loud clicking sound comes from the far side of the empty space as the latch of the auditorium door catches and the metal handle drops as if guided by an invisible touch. Leah, her senses alert, follows Josephine down the darkened aisle undetected, close enough to reach out and touch the tamed curls in front of her. She slows her gait, careful not to run up on the unsuspecting classmate. Josephine stops and scans the rows of seats, unaware of the presence standing in her shadow. After a few moments of searching, she spots the silhouette of Margaret's elongated neck and curved bob near the front and continues on.

The overpowering chorus to 'Hark the Herald Angels Sing' fills the hall as the singers' voices meld with flawless synchronization into a triumphant crescendo. On stage, Madame Kaspar gesticulates authoritatively with her hands, guiding the group through the progression of notes, immersed in the moment, drunk with emotion.

Josephine carefully slips past two girls at the end of the row and takes the empty seat reserved for her. Margaret shoots her a look of mocking disapproval at her tardiness. The medicine she took earlier in the day has dulled the aches and settled her stomach. For the time being, the illness she's labored under for the past couple of days has abated. Josephine flashes back an apologetic grin, pats her friend's leg, and settles into her seat. Her insistence that Margaret rest in her room for the remainder of the night was summarily dismissed, and though Josephine would never admit it to her impeccably dressed friend, she is glad to see her rebound from the violent bout of nausea, though her normally lustrous complexion remains pale and drawn.

Josephine feels conspicuous and slouches down slightly. The slanted back of her seat pushes forward as another late arriver squeezes past in the row behind her. When she looks up at the radiant chorus standing on the stage, her chest tightens and she becomes anxious. The distress Josephine had temporarily suppressed after leaving the stable returns. Her forehead burns and her skin tingles. The shocking image of Sable's mutilated flesh is fresh in her mind and tears at her heart. She bites her lower lip to stem the rupture of emotion. She knows she cannot last like this for long, certainly not for the entire concert, not after what Mr. Raymee told and showed her.

She struggles to comprehend the idea that Leah, a girl Josephine knows to be generally shy and reserved, is capable of such a viscous act. The knife the groom showed her had been retrieved from the boathouse at great difficulty. And even Mr. Raymee understood that it was she, not the innocent creature he cared for, who was the intended target of the savage attack. But why?

She thinks of who else could be responsible for the cowardly deed and continually comes back to Leah as the culprit for the crudely carved initials. How though did she even know about the knife's existence? She was gone by the time Josephine and Margaret came out of the storage building with the canoe. Unless Margaret mentioned it while the two were alone in Leah's room that morning, how would she know the sharp weapon was left there? And what of young Robert's story? Was the boy's nightmarish vision of the girl in the window to be believed, even though it corroborated the suspicion of Leah's nighttime odyssey?

When Josephine wanted to go to Miss Price with their concerns after they found Leah in her room dazed and behaving oddly, it was Margaret who convinced her that they should leave the troubled girl alone and distance themselves from her. In hindsight, had their inaction contributed to the events of the last two days? Had they acted otherwise and followed her initial wishes, would her beloved Sable's smooth gray skin ever felt the sting of the knife's cold edge? Had she now made the same mistake twice?

She continues to torment herself. *I should have told Mr. Raymee to go to the police and tell them everything that happened. Show them the knife. Regardless of the consequences. Bring the hand of authority down.* She has nothing to hide. There is no one to protect. Not now. Not after she saw the blade baptized with her horse's blood.

Josephine's feeling of alarm spikes further in the confining seat. She feels the eyes of others upon her. She doesn't want to be here, playing the part of the polite and attentive student, as her world falls apart around her, piece by piece. She wrestles mightily to keep her disintegrating emotional state intact until she can get Margaret alone, suppressing the urge to grab the forearm next to her and lead her out of the hall in mid-song. She realizes how much she needs Margaret. She wants nothing more than to hear the dismissive, disapproving tone of her voice. She needs to know that their secret, unauthorized trip to the colored family's dilapidated farm is not worth protecting any longer. Not after what has happened. Not now. They must speak to someone, if not Miss Price than Mrs. Martin, or, if necessary, they will go see the dean directly.

A thin layer of perspiration forms on Josephine's forehead and a prickly sensation nips along the back of her exposed neck.

In the flood of sound coming from the stage, in the melodic marriage of voice and musical accompaniment, she detects a series of off-key notes, a strand of discord that renders the triumphant song imperfect. She looks at the girls seated around her and then at Margaret. She can tell by the uniformity of their rapt stares that they do not hear it. The cadence of arrhythmic notes repeats itself, this time, louder and more noticeable. But still no reaction, not a glimmer of recognition from anyone around her that something is amiss.

Her head swims in confusion. The jarring notes repeat over and over, faster each time, slowly narrowing the breaks that connect the string of dissonant noises. An incredulous smile comes over the mystified girl's face. *Am I mad? Am I the only one who can hear this?*

She turns to Margaret and touches her arm to get her attention. As she leans over to whisper in her ear, the tonal resonance of the recurring sounds abruptly changes. The sharp tones soften and the unharmonious notes, once random and indecipherable, now combined, transform into syllables just as the Josephine's lips lightly pass over her friend's earring.

Who's the problem now?

Josephine pulls away as if struck by the fangs of a viper.

Margaret flinches in reaction.

"What is it, Jo? What's the matter?" she asks, alarmed by the wide-eyed, panicked look on her friend's face.

"Was that you just now?! Was that you speaking to me?!"

A girl seated in the next row turns around and with severe look of disapproval lets out a "sshh" to quiet them.

"Relax, Francine," Margaret fires back at the offended girl, and then continues in a whisper. "What are you talking about? I didn't say anything. This stocking full of Christmas chestnuts and has left me drowsy and speechless."

The perturbed girl turns around again, not intimidated by Margaret's previous verbal dagger.

"Really, have the courtesy to be quiet. The rest of us would like to listen without your rudeness."

"This in none of your business, Francine, so turn your pretty little head back around and pay attention to what is in front of you."

Now a third girl off to the side admonishes both of them to stop talking.

Sandwiched in among the cramped seating and surrounded on all sides by the bodies of other students, Josephine suddenly feels claustrophobic. No matter how hard she tries to focus her thoughts on the performance, she obsesses about the tightness in her wrists and arms and along the back of her legs, a creeping stiffness in the tendons and muscles of her limbs. The space around her shrinks and the sensation of being trapped, of being restrained and unable to move, overwhelms her. With each passing moment, the desire the stand and to feel the unfettered stretch along the length of her body grows more acute.

It's been years since she felt such panic. As a young girl of eight she would wake in the middle of the night in hysterics, thrashing about in the bed sheets and short of breath, the dream fresh, raw and every bit as real as the feel of the moist pillow casing against her cheek. She can still recall, in those first addled, waking moments, the abject fear that her racing heart was about to burst from her chest and the way the light from the hallway streamed into her room as her mother came running to comfort her.

It was always the same. A dream within a dream. Waking in total darkness. The smell of pine in front of her face. The air thin and fetid. Spasmodic convulsions as her fists and feet repeatedly strike against the cramped confines encasing her. The immovable, unyielding weight laid over top of her supine body. The horrifying realization that she cannot move no matter how hard she struggles. Helpless, hysterical sobs of desperation. Entombed. Condemned. Death, prolonged and excruciating. No escape from the unfathomable mental torment of being buried alive.

Who's the problem now?

Out of the corner of her eye, Miss Price notices a commotion in the front section of the audience and sees a girl rushing to the aisle not waiting for the others in the row to make room as she passes. She cannot make out who it is or what exactly is going on in the dim surroundings, only that she is being followed by another student. The chorus is still performing and she wonders if the girl has become suddenly ill and cannot wait for intermission. She watches the pair hurry up the aisle and leave the theater through the set of doors in the rear. Seated in the viewing box makes it impractical for the concerned regent to follow them and offer help, and she is content with letting the disturbance pass until Mr. Carter, uncommunicative towards her most of the night, leans over and under the transparent guise of casually conversation observes, "Isn't that one of your students, the blonde girl who went on the trip to the hospital with us?"

The regent curls the concert program in her hand into a tight, narrow tube and taps it repeatedly against her crossed knee, preferring not to answer out of concern that once she starts she can not trust herself to stop.

Leah stands alone in a summer field, suspended in a state of equipoise. The soil under her feet is soft from a passing shower and oozes between her bare toes. Sharp blades of wild grass graze her insect-bitten legs and nudge inside the hem of her cotton dress. A full day outdoors has turned her naked shoulders berry brown and left splotches of red along her cheeks and on the tip of her nose.

The dying sun has lost its grip on the far reaches of the land and ceded the sky to the master painters of the heavens. Pockets of powdery lilac and sweet honeysuckle hang in the evening air. She feels the earth's prolonged exhale, the deep breath of cleansing air rising up from the ground that leaves its dewy kiss on the incandescent yellow petals of the wild rudbeckia plants.

Lush riches of summer abound. The cooling touch of darkness brings life to the sleepy world in miniature. Hidden crickets herald the arrival of night while hairy, white-winged moths emerge and prepare to launch on their clumsy, circuitous journeys toward the unattainable ascending orb like soused men trying to reach a distant bar lantern.

Green lights pulsate and float about her as fireflies perform their ancient mating ritual. Their abdomens glow bright and then fade to black in a frenetic display. The aerial courtship fascinates the girl and she tracks the intermittent signals as they move about her trying to decipher the mysterious code. The fireflies dip and turn and twinkle like remote ships being tossed about in the turbulent waves of an indigo ocean.

Leah reaches out and carefully pursues the nearest insect with cupped hand and snatches it when the glow reappears. She bends down and with her free hand loosens the lid to the glass jar at her feet. The vibration energizes the captives hanging along the sides and at the bottom of the jar and sets off a chain reaction. She shakes the jar to keep those near the top from escaping and removes the lid, deposits her prize, and then quickly replaces the metal cover.

As Leah straightens up, she is surprised to see phosphorescent viscera smeared along her palm. She rubs the green dollop between her fingers, fascinated by the unexpected discovery. She touches her finger tip to her arm and an incandescent dot appears. A second dot. And then a third. Each smaller than the one before.

She retrieves the jar and reaches inside and scoops up two fireflies. She purposely squeezes the first between her thumb and forefinger until she feels the exoskeleton collapse. While she carries out the cruel deed, the second insect escapes and flies off. She dabs at the pool of lime-colored expectoration and runs her finger beneath her right eye lid and then again under the left. One by one, she plucks the remaining bugs from the jar and crushes their rear sections and paints her cheeks and neck and lips with the magical substance until her fingers are covered with the glowing byproduct of her thoughtless slaughter. She waves her hands about and marvels at the beauty of her morbid creation and the way the luminous finger tips leave illusionary trails as they move across the night sky.

The trill of nature about her is abruptly replaced by a high-pitched ringing deep inside her skull. Leah instinctively grabs the sides of her head and presses against her jaw to arrest the growing intensity that feels like its going to tunnel through her brain. She opens her mouth in a desperate attempt to clear the blockage but the pressure continues to build. The piercing sound produces unbearable wincing pain and she staggers about, eyes squeezed shut, praying for it to end. Then silence.

Her chest heaves as she hungrily devours all the air she can consume. Before her, through teary eyes, she sees the impossible, the fanciful creation of her delirious, tortured mind—a multitude of wild fireflies, motionless, their flickering lights hovering in the air, are now arrayed in perfectly formed lines. A constellation of green stars, brought to Earth and tethered before her.

The ground moves. She sees a hunched-back creature race across the wild field to her right, a twisted figure on all four legs scurrying closer and then suddenly stopping. The dark, malformed body hurries closer and halts again, crouched down behind the high grass as if trying to avoid detection. Motionless, the creature studies her, near enough for Leah to discern its grotesque features. Narrow, lifeless eyes. Curved, yellow talons. A ring of quivering, moist lips, red and open.

"No," Leah cries out, "Stay away!"

The hideous beast, undeterred, slowly advances on the petrified girl until Leah feels its gnarled fingers seize her wrists and its sweet, putrid breath hot along her smooth shoulder.

Leah trembles in horror. The array of pulsating green lights now burn with a fiery brilliance that casts a revealing light on the succubus's form and the parted maw poised alongside Leah's tear-streaked cheek. She closes her eyes and feels the cold flesh press against her face and draw on her skin.

"Please, God. Make it stop," she whimpers. "Please, make it stop!"

She feels the demon's hold release.

The uneven contours of the overgrown field turn flat and hard. The disorienting sounds of the summertime nightmare are consumed in an eruption of cheering and clapping.

"Magnifique, Leah," Madame Kaspar whispers in her ear as she hugs the rigid, speechless girl. "Remember this moment always."

Thunderous applause rains down from the balcony and fills the concert hall. Leah looks over at the other two soloists and sees the faint outline of Madame's ruby lipstick on their faces. The members of the chorus, in their immaculate virginal dresses, bask in the showering adoration of their peers and guests, maintaining the placid expressions Madame insists they wear.

In the headmaster's box, Dean Dawson, smiling widely, shoots up from his chair and enthusiastically praises the chorus, followed by Mrs. Dawson and their guests.

Leah struggles to make sense of the cacophonous sounds and sights about her. And as she scans the familiar dimensions of the Odeon trying to reconcile the fear-inducing images still fresh and vivid in her memory with the appreciative faces and warm accolades, the rope is released and the wooden pullies overhead chirr as the curtain slowly falls toward the stage. With a nod from Madame Kaspar, the girls bow their heads in unison, a genuflection of appreciation to the audience just before the curtain touches the stage.

As the lights come up, Miss Price wears a stern expression and wonders if the accusation could possibly be true, that the heralded soloist with the angelic voice is capable of assaulting her hallmate, even one as trying as May King.

Mrs. Martin watches the concert's triumphant conclusion from the front row along with other teachers and staff. When she sees the dean and his guests stand to leave the hall, she heads for a side exit and walks along to the end of an interior hallway where she can monitor their departure. The group of four split when they reach the back of the auditorium—the regent and Mr. Carter heading for the coat check, Dean Dawson and his wife preferring to station themselves at the front entrance so as to greet the departing students and wish them a joyous Christmas.

The prefect loiters in the auditorium waiting for the crowd to thin out and keeps an eye on the back of hall to make sure the dean does not leave without her noticing. The chorus singers, in their white lace gowns, filter out from behind the curtain and descend the twin set of stairs on both ends of the stage to join their classmates, wearing expressions of relief that the concert is now behind them.

She looks about those remaining to make sure that neither Mr. Geary nor any of his financial office cronies are around. It is a safe bet, she thought in her office earlier in the day, he will not be at the concert tonight. The bursar has never shown an interest in school social events after work hours, preferring to maintain distance between his professional and home lives. She knows he is married and that there are children, but he never volunteers any details about his life to her or the other staff at the Seminary. His work demeanor is buttoned-down and businesslike and he refuses to participate in any conversations which stray into the personal realm. That the two became friendly with one another gradually over the years has more to do with the persistent dissatisfaction with the school's management they share than with favorable attributes each sees in the other. They make no pretense of being likeable around each other, nor do they pull punches out of concern that their comments might be viewed as impolite. Their relationship, if it could be called such, is that of a bickering old married couple who find companionship gnawing on the same bone together.

After the dean speaks to the remaining chorus members and greets guests who waited after the show to pay their respects, he helps his wife with her coat, unaware that Mrs. Martin remains behind with a specific purpose in mind.

"Dean Dawson," she calls out as the retiring couple start for the door, "may I have a minute of your time?"

The headmaster turns around unable to mask his annoyance with being delayed.

"Good evening, Mrs. Dawson," she adds with a smile and a nod.

"Mrs. Martin. It is wonderful of you to come tonight."

"Yes, Dean. The girls were outstanding. I enjoyed the concert tremendously. Madame Kaspar is a miracle worker. It is hard to believe she produced such a wonderful program in only a few weeks time."

"Yes, indeed. She has put our chorus program on the map I would say. Well, good night, Mrs. Martin," he says as he turns to leave.

"Dean, I only need a moment with you. I appreciate that you would prefer to not be bothered with school matters, here and now, while you and your wife are entertaining the gentleman from New York," Mrs. Martin pauses for emphasis, "but I am obliged to raise a matter to your attention without further delay."

"The hour is late, Mrs. Martin."

"It's later than you think," she replies, unable to curb her sarcasm.

"Surely this can wait until Monday."

"I wish that it could, Dean. The last streetcar for downtown leaves the station in thirty minutes."

The impatient man considers the earnestness of her words and though he is tired and anxious to leave he tells his wife to wait for him in the car idling outside to take them to Edgewood. Once she leaves, the dean leans against the back row of seats and folds his arms, his displeasure manifest but for the time being under control.

"Your little ambush shows poor judgment. I am surprised and more than a bit disappointed. We've had our differences in the past, Mrs. Martin, but I do expect a certain amount of decorum from you, especially when Mrs. Dawson is present. I am entitled to your respect both in pubic and in private."

The prefect drops the overly courteous tone now that they are alone.

"I would not be here tonight if I had my way, so perhaps we can dispense with the question of what you want or what I want."

"What is it, Mrs. Martin? Why did you stop me from leaving? You said it was important."

"I never said it was 'important.' I said I was obliged to bring it to your attention."

"Fine. What is '*it*'?"

"I owe you an apology, Dean Dawson."

"I'm sorry. I must have missed something. This is all about an apology."

"In part."

"Well, you may be able to redeem yourself after all," he says with mocking surprise. "But do be quick about it. I don't want my wife to be gassed in the car waiting for me."

"Douglas Stratton came here under false pretenses. He didn't come here just because he wanted to buy a school."

"Wait a minute. Hold it right there. I told you and the others this afternoon that I no longer have a formal role in the sale's implementation. The board decided the matter. If you want to voice your opinion about it, go see Mr. Geary. He's riding herd on seeing the deal through."

"I did already."

Her forceful admission takes the dean by surprise.

"I went to George Geary many days ago when I thought Douglas Stratton was pressuring you and the board into rushing the sale. I told him that the two of us should go see Stratton because you couldn't be trusted—"

"'Couldn't be trusted'! What do you mean? You believed that I was working a sweetheart deal with *that* man?"

"No. Hear me out, Dean. I thought you couldn't be trusted to stand up to *that* man, to stand up for your own interests, to stand up for what was best for the school."

"Mrs. Martin, how could you—"

"I thought you weak. I thought you couldn't be counted on. I thought you wouldn't protect us."

The surprising indictment, even from the prickly woman, wounds the headmaster deeply.

"I now know that my concerns were misplaced. And for that, I apologize to you."

The dean studies his newly shined shoes and the way they reflect and distort the lights hanging above, unsure of what to say.

The cagy prefect, realizing the harm inflicted by her confession, continues on.

"Douglas Stratton did not go through the trouble of taking the train from New York just to buy a school, even one as prestigious as ours. The man owns a company that doesn't know the first thing about running a preparatory school for rich girls. The notion that he would see the school as an investment opportunity that required his personal attention, without taking the time to thoroughly evaluate the accounting books, is preposterous. I felt it at the first meeting in your office, when he presented the purchase offer with all the seriousness of a bid at the bridge table. And when you sat there...and...well...let's just say I was concerned, and others were too."

"You see, there is an important piece of information, Mrs. Martin, a central fact that none of us knew at the time, that we now know, information that explains away the source of your suspicion."

The headmaster walks over, running his fingers along the taut brim of his bowler, and stands next to the agitated woman at the top of the center aisle.

"It's his daughter. Elizabeth Stratton. The oldest one. She died in the war. Three years ago. She volunteered to be a nurse after she graduated here. The transport ship she was on was torpedoed on its way to France."

Mrs. Martin, unprepared by the shocking revelation, looks through the dean as the words sink in, her eyes wide and her mouth open in disbelief.

"Do you remember how he talked about his desire to buy National Park Seminary as a legacy to his daughters? None of us knew then about Elizabeth Stratton's untimely death. I have since made amends to Mr. Stratton, without leading on that we could possibly be ignorant of the fact of his daughter's death until now. Whatever damage there is has been done, and we are taking steps to repair it."

"How do you mean?" Mrs. Martin asks, finding her voice.

"Only a handful of others know what I am about to tell you, but we will be dedicating Senior House in Elizabeth's name next semester. After the sale is finalized. It should go a long way at smoothing over any hard feelings."

"Sentimentality. Is that what you believe explains this away?"

"That's a harsh reaction, even for you, Mrs. Martin. Each of us handles loss differently, in our way. Is it right for us to judge how others express their grief or work to overcome it? Put yourself in Douglas Stratton's place. Left with only memories, how much of your fortune would you spend to see that they do not die as well?"

"Mr. Geary made it seem all so ordinary and plausible as well the day I went to see him."

The tall, paneled entrance door opens and a howling blast of air races through the hall. Both turn as a slender man in a black topcoat wedges his way inside the foyer with some difficulty.

"The car is ready, headmaster. Would you like me to take Mrs. Dawson home and return for you?"

"No, that's not necessary. Give us one more minute and I will be out."

After the driver leaves, Mrs. Martin realizes her opportunity is slipping away.

"This isn't about Douglas Stratton's daughter, but it is certainly about Douglas Stratton. George Geary is working for him."

"The board decided—"

"I'm not talking about what the Board of Trustees decided this morning. George Geary has been working for Douglas Stratton a long time before he pulled into the Forest Glen train station. Don't you understand what I am telling you? The bursar you have been paying all these years has been Stratton's man on the inside. He has been feeding him information about the school's finances, its debt, its holdings, everything. Stratton didn't just know the true value of school. He also knew just how enticing an offer would need to be for you and the rest of the board to accept. George Geary gave Stratton a map to all of your financial pressure points."

"What in the world are you talking about? I opposed the sale!"

"He didn't need your support!" she yells back. "He flattened you like a steam roller. He bought the board. The fix was in before you walked into the meeting this morning. Everyone there knew it. Everyone, except for one person. You. Dean Porter Dawson. They must have been laughing on the inside when you stood up and gave your well-reasoned, rehearsed, impassioned speech, telling them how they needed to stand by you as you stood by them in building all of this."

Dean Dawson feels his weakened state of authority erode even more.

"No. This can't be so."

"Poor old Porter. The great orator of the Chautauqua circuit, trying to convert the bought and sold, the ones who have already cut the line, imploring them to deny the person secretly lining their pockets."

"What proof do you have of all this? If you knew of a conspiracy, how come you were silent? Answer me!"

The dean moves menacingly towards her.

"I didn't know. Not until today," she answers with a hint of regret. "As for proof, I have it. But I want to know what you are going to do about before I hand it to you."

"Are you serious?! You are accusing the members of the Board of Trustees and the school's financial officer of fraudulence and graft. And I am simply supposed to believe the word of a woman who opens up the conversation by telling me how much she doesn't trust *me*."

The front door opens again. The driver doesn't say a word; his hangdog expression tells the dean all he needs to know.

"All right," he yells out in exasperation. "Drive her back to the house. And then you can go home. I'll walk back."

"Are you sure, sir?"

"Yes, go."

"But the weather has turned worse."

"I am not a school boy who will get lost on his way home!" the headmaster snaps, sending the chastised man away.

He turns back to Mrs. Martin and takes a moment to compose himself. She dares not speak. Not now. She can see the volatility in his inflamed eyes.

"The school has been sold, Mrs. Martin. The decision has been made and I can't do anything to change it. And regardless of my opposition to the sale, I will profit personally from the sale whether I like it or not. Those are the facts. What basis do I have to level unproven allegations against the new owner, except that by doing so I will forfeit the one thing I truly want, the one thing I care the most about, the one thing I need more than the windfall of money: the title of headmaster of the National Park Seminary!"

Mrs. Martin rears back from the dean's sputtering rage and steadies herself against a seat at the end of the row. Her intimidation gives way to a wry grin and then the laughter begins. Soft and tentative at first, then louder and uninhibited. A mocking, maniacal crowing that reverberates off the rafters and needles the dean's galloping heart.

She draws her hand over her mouth, suddenly self-conscious about her outburst, but the impudence in her wide brown eyes continues to taunt him.

"What is it? What is wrong with you? Get a grip on yourself, Charlotte."

The prefect staggers about looking for her coat while trying to suppress the uncontrolled outburst. When she finds it, she bites down on the herringbone sleeve, the taste of wool an effective antidote to quell her delirium.

"A man with a title. Headmaster of a dying school. A king who rules nothing."

"Watch your tongue, before you regret it. I am warning you!"

She smiles defiantly at the dean's threat.

"If it's proof you demand, all you need to do is look around you. From where I sit, Katharine Price's true allegiance could not be more obvious. You have surrounded yourself with those who will in the end secure your demise. Mark my word. *You* have been warned."

Mrs. Martin rushes out of the Odeon and heads for the footbridge. The station lights wink in the distance as the stiff wind blows the bare tree limbs of the glen wildly about. She leans into the forceful gale and grimaces as the cold stabs at her exposed skin.

The two girls sit on the floor rug in the dark, shoulder to shoulder, wrapped inside a thick, insulating blanket of goose down, looking out through the balcony door. The ambient light of the night bathes their faces in a soft blue as the wind buffets the window panes and rattles the loose brass decorative handle. The voices of the first girls returning from the Christmas program can be heard outside on the stairs and along the hallway.

Josephine, emotionally exhausted from telling Margaret what took place at the stable, leans her head against her friend's and takes comfort in the moment. The panic attack at the Odeon has subsided and her nerves have settled, and she looks out at the night sky, content to stare off into the fathomless expanse.

Margaret reaches beneath the blanket and extracts a treasure from the concealed stash and pops it into her mouth and savors the explosion of cherry liquid and chocolate. For the time being, the sickness that has taken away her appetite has abated.

"I don't understand why my family sends me these packages," she says in mid-chew. "They know I have no willpower and that I'll end up eating them all at once. What's the point? They are going to see me in a few days time. I think they'd be happier if I was plump when they arrived. I really believe they would prefer me stumpy and corpulent.

"You know how all parents go on about wanting their children to have it better than they did. For my mother and father, plentiful food is their way of showing it. I'm serious. They would continually force food on me and my brother when I was growing up, a weird demonstration of their love, I suppose. No matter how full we were, there was another serving being spooned onto our plates or another slice of pie to be polished off. It was simply awful growing up in my house. After reading the story of Hansel and Gretel as a young girl I was convinced my parents were trying to fatten me up to turn me into a meal."

Josephine laughs and nudges Margaret playfully with her body.

"So what happened? Look at you. Another instance of your rebellious nature?"

"Not at all. I didn't protest. I kept on eating. Seconds, thirds, until I was the last one at the table. I was a good child, I will have you know," she rebukes Josephine with a tap to the end of her nose. "I just didn't gain weight. I grew taller instead."

"With a vengeance."

"True. Mean of you to say, but undeniably true. It is the curse I must bear."

"We like you just the way you are."

"For that, you are to be rewarded."

Margaret retrieves another confectionary treat and feeds it to her friend.

"Perhaps it is not too late to turn you into the daughter my parents never had. Lydia Cleary would simply adore you with another five pounds."

Margaret pulls the heavy blanket around their shoulders tighter as if it will keep away the intensifying noise outside her room.

"What am I going to do, Margaret?" Josephine asks, her voice vulnerable in the dark.

"What are *we* going to do, you mean? *We* are going to finish off this box and with any luck I can keep it down."

"You know what I mean. What should we do about our friend down the hallway? You saw how she behaved tonight at the concert, pretending as if nothing was wrong, acting normal around everyone, like before? Her singing was beautiful. It's like she is a chameleon the way she changes from one moment to the next. Who will believe our story?"

"Nothing can be done tonight. Let's talk about it tomorrow morning. I am bone-tired."

"And Miss Price? We can't sit back and wait for her to expel us from school."

"She is a paper tiger. She can't drop us without putting her own motives to scrutiny. And she knows it. You saw to that. Why would she risk her job to crucify the two of us? Plus, Dean Dawson would never allow such a controversy to become public. The school's image is too dear to him, and he fiercely protects it. Remember the time the housemaid was caught stealing from the pantry and how hush-hush it became when she was sent packing? All the girls knew the poor woman was stealing for months— it was an open secret and no one saw the harm if a few bars of soap and bottles of floor wax went missing. But once the administration found out they contrived a story about why she didn't show up the next day, how she moved with her family down to North Carolina or some God forsaken place like that. A tidy explanation for a messy situation, until a group of us spotted her pushing a cleaning cart at Union Station one afternoon. They just couldn't let the truth be known out of fear that it would reflect poorly on the school's image. They didn't want parents thinking that their innocent defenseless daughters were at the mercy of a predatory band of thieves, having their jewelry pilfered and their belongings rifled through. So, poor Mrs. Sparks just disappeared."

"I suppose your right."

"I know I am right."

"I have an idea. Let's just stay here. We should stay right here on the floor, and let the world go by without us."

Margaret smiles at the thought— so impractical, so unlike Josephine.

"There's an idea. We can wait until the end of the semester, for all the lights to be turned off and the doors to be locked and for everyone to leave for home. We can drag the tree up from downstairs. And gather pillows about us like a fortress. With nothing to subsist on but our bounty of chocolates. We can inhabit the dormitory like ghostly spirits. Walking about in the middle of the night. Knocking over lamps and tilting portraits on the walls. Think of the mischievous fun we could have."

"And during the day we could huddle under the blanket and wait out winter storms, watching the flakes fall outside the balcony."

"An ideal winter break. No overbearing parents force-feeding you."

"No Christmas parties to dress up for."

"No visits to see aunts and uncles and cousins."

"No put-on smiles and forced greetings to every one you meet."

"No endless questions to answer, questions about what's next, asking about marriage prospects, mothers who want you to meet their sons, fathers who imagine your family's fortune tied to theirs."

Margaret presses her shoulder against the warm body next to her.

"My butterfly has become quite the recluse."

Josephine searches the arc of nothingness beyond the corniced window pane and feels a hollow sensation beneath her breast bone, the melancholy ache that comes with the promise of new snow.

Dean Dawson sits on the stairs to Honeysuckle Bridge and leans against the cast iron lion on the pedestal next to him for protection against the updraft pushed along the steep slopes of the ravine. He waits patiently as the streetcar slows and stops at the platform, and when he sees Mrs. Martin board with the other passengers, he stands, brushes off the backside of his coat, and continues along the unlit section of the path leading to the station. As he passes the gas lamp out front of the Glen Manor he sees the first flakes of snow hit along the beveled glass and melt away. He rings a bell at the door and the night clerk ushers him inside with a surprised look.

"I need you to let Mr. Carter know that I am here. He is not expecting me but tell him that I need to see him now without delay."

"I can't do that, Mr...er...Dean Dawson."

"Why not?"

"He's not here presently."

"Are you sure? Shouldn't you go check, man?"

"I'm sure, sir. He is the only guest we have," the clerk explains sheepishly.

"Fine. I will wait in the parlor until he arrives."

"Certainly, sir, let me get that fire going for you. It's been a while since we had reason to use it. I'll do it in a jiff. There's some decent wood out back."

The dean finds a suitable seat in the empty room decorated with floral upholstery and dust covered end tables and waits for the harried clerk to return. Alone with his thoughts, he seethes as he replays the heated exchange with the prefect. He cannot fathom that a plot so foul could be hatched under his nose and that the culprit would have the gall to sit beside him throughout the evening, a guest of his hospitality. Worse yet, could it be possible that Miss Price, a recently close confidante, was guilty of unforgivable complicity in the scheme? Had she used the keen intellect and sharp instincts he so admired and played both sides to her own advantage?

On his walk to Edgewood, he considered all the reasons why Mrs. Martin might lie to him, ran through all the possible explanations, until, unsatisfied, he turned around at the county road and headed back toward the glen. I refuse to play the fool, he declared to himself out loud, as he crossed the span and prepared to tackle the question head on.

The clerk returns carrying a leather sling of split logs and kindling.

"Very well. I see you are comfortable," he observes as he hurries over to the hearth and twists around to open the chimney flue. "I know it is a bit late, but it would be no bother at all to make some tea or coffee for you and Mr. Carter, when he returns that is. Or I could join you if you prefer to not drink alone," the smile accompanying the clerk's failed attempt at humor quickly fades when he sees the headmaster's perturbed reaction.

"The fire will be suitable. Thank you."

The clerk prepares the wood and strikes a match to light a scrap of starter paper when the ringer box on the wall in the other room sounds. Dousing the match, he rushes out of the room and ducks under the flip-top to reach the telephone behind the counter.

The dean drifts off in thought as he prepares the list of questions he wants to ask when Stratton's man returns. Of all of the prefect's insubordinate remarks, it is the mocking epithet that stings the most.

A king who rules nothing.

He recalls how unresponsive the board members were earlier in the day, how their discussion was perfunctory and their actions almost scripted. And how it was Mr. Geary, of all the men in attendance, who sought him out on the park bench to soothe his bruised ego. He was too confused then, too addled by the swift reversal of fortune, to see what was happening about him, and happening *to* him. The ground was pulled out from under him, and by the time he could find his footing again, it was over.

He replays the morning board meeting, breaking it down step by step, minute by minute, but this time through the corrective lens of hindsight. He evaluates what took place through the eyes of a man forewarned of the trap set for him. Every word spoken. Every glance exchanged. Every question left unanswered. What was once a confusing, frustrating, infuriating blur is now a picture of staggering clarity.

The smell of smoke wafts past and the dean shakes off the bitter ordeal at the bank office. He looks over at the pristine grate and sees the stack of logs left by the clerk, unlit. He leaves the parlor to locate the unsteady young man, worried that he might have unintentionally started a blaze elsewhere in the hotel, and finds the reception area abandoned and the door leading outside wide open, swaying in the wind. The acrid aroma is even more noticeable, heightening the dean's alarm. When he starts to close the door, he notices a solitary figure beyond the stone entryway waving wildly. He hears a tinny, muffled voice behind him and turns to find the telephone receiver resting on the counter. Just as he is about to pick it up, the clerk bursts through the doorway, snatches the receiver, and leans his body over the counter to reach the wall transmitter next to the crank.

"I see it," he tells the switchboard operator, trying to catch his breath. "I see it, all right. We can smell the smoke from here. Send the fire department. It's burning strong."

Dean Dawson walks out on the front porch without saying a word and sees a thin blanket of gray smoke roll under the lights along the length of the station platform. Inside the hotel, the clerk knocks over something fragile and expensive as he rushes off to the courtyard in back of the hotel to search of an ax in the gardening shed.

By the time the frantic man reemerges wearing a heavy coat and over-sized leather gloves, the dean has left the porch and reached the gravel road in front of Glen Manor. Now clear of the building's shadow and the surrounding trees, he sees a plume of red glowing across the glen, upstream from the bridge, far enough away to not be any of the campus buildings.

"What's on fire?" he calls out as the ax-wielding clerk runs past.

As the man turns around and slows his stride, he realizes that he has forgotten all about the waiting headmaster in the rush of excitement after receiving the phone call.

"It's the boathouse along the creek. The school's boathouse. Your boathouse. It's on fire."

The dean watches as the intrepid volunteer crosses both set of tracks, cutting a swath through the lightly falling snow, and heads for the bridge to join other firefighters at the county road.

The bend in the creek prevents Dean Dawson from spotting the actual blaze, but the red light grows in intensity, fanned by gusts of wind, and illuminates a dark corner of the woods, revealing a trail of thick white smoke rising above the tree line.

A siren awakens in the distance and quickly ramps up from a low growl to a high-pitched, cycling scream that has residents in the nearby community raising their shades and rushing to their doors. Dormitory windows alight across the glen.

Alarmed by the spectacle playing out before him, Dean Dawson does not notice the man approaching from behind, the burning tip of a cigarette breathing in the brutish night air. Only when the stranger stops and stands next to him to comprehend what is happening does the headmaster recognize the tall build and youthful profile of the man he came to confront.

Chapter 10
Grief of Cyporissus

The object of education being, as we believe, the highest development of human power, we ask you to impress earnestly upon your daughter the truth that her school days must not close until this object is accomplished, so far as school work can contribute to that end. No person (parent or child) has a right to limit demand of each one that she be the most efficient instrument possible for good. No one has the right to enter manhood or womanhood as an inefficient being likely to fail in every relationship of life. Only circumstances absolutely beyond our control can excuse us from the duty of striving for the highest, and such circumstances should be yielded to only the most earnest, protracted and determined struggle against them.

In the faint gray light of a bitter winter's morning, a ravenous wide-eyed creature steps out from the concealing forest spires, drawn into the open by the smoky scent lingering in the air. Its ears pivot and search for the presence of others and detecting none the cautious animal walks into the clearing, its dappled brown coat wet and glistening. The yearling, undersized and thin, paws the ground repeatedly until it uncovers what it seeks buried under the wet, suffocating blanket of snow. Bending down, the deer tastes the blackened soil and shakes its neck and head violently at the bitter taste of ash. Disappointed and driven on by pangs of hunger, the weak beast walks across the smoldering remains of the school boathouse until it reaches the creek's edge and draws from the cooling waters.

On the hillside overlooking the shimmering branch, the black-winged sentinel perches atop Vincent Hall and searches the white horizon for warmth, while inside the still dormitories girls sleep under the heavy spell of the approaching solstice, ensconced in crisp linens and plump comforters stuffed with the finest Chesapeake down.

The daily bakery truck rumbles across the bridge and motors through the heart of the slumbering campus before skirting the circular drive and proceeding to the rear delivery entrance. The solitary bird takes wing enticed by the succulent aroma and circles overhead surveying the pristine domain. Spotting the rooftop of the truck, it flies lower and lands on the chapel water spout, and bobs up and down with excitement, positioned to observe the activity in the alley below.

The delivery man yanks the brake, turns off the engine, and hustles to the back of the truck. He pulls his cap tightly down on his head and throws open the rear door. A tray of fresh loaves is pulled out and he backs through the unlatched entrance and carries it to the kitchen.

The bold crow seizes the opportunity and glides down, flapping its wings as it nears the street, and then hops over to the unguarded racks. Inside the truck, trays laden with crusty breads and glazed pastries await the stealthy thief. The famished bird turns its head from side to side, unsure as to which of the succulent offerings to seize. A bounty too abundant to carry away. The momentary delay is costly. The man bursts through the doorway, head down, swaddled about the neck and face with a wool muffler, nearly striking the bird with his steel-toed boot. Shoed-away so close to its prize, the crow protests loudly in the refuge of a secluded footpath separating the main building from the worship hall. A second tray is retrieved from the truck but this time the delivery man pushes the rear doors closed with his foot before continuing inside.

The deterred scavenger hops along the snow-covered brick, following a different scent coming from the trail of boot marks leading to the chapel. The diminutive imprints are recent and oddly spaced, with the steps on the left deeper and more clearly formed than the companion tracks. The promising smell draws the inquisitive crow further down the dank path separating the two buildings. It scours the ground and explores the fissures in the walk with its probing beak for a morsel but finds none. The persistent search finally pays off when the broad-chested hunter spies a rounded form up ahead, motionless under a thin layer of snow. With a grating, high-pitched caw, the crow takes flight and with three beats of its powerful wings is upon the concealed treasure. The penetrating touch of its claws confirms the soft hair of an animal, cold and lifeless, its body and tail faintly visible under the icy cloak, a victim of a precipitous fall from the slippery shingles along the northern wing of Vincent Hall.

The satisfied bird does not wait to be chased off its spoil again and stabs at the hardened skin repeatedly to puncture the bloated belly in its grip.

Inside the pebble-dash stucco chapel, the anemic morning light bleeds through thick panes of stained glass and casts splashes of color along the interior walls. Leah limps past the rows of empty wooden pews and stands before the alter looking forlornly at the primitive cross suspended overhead from exposed beams of oak.

She gingerly lowers her body down on the alter steps and grimaces with pain when her tender ankle clips the corner stone. The folds of her hooded cape, dusted lightly with a coating of snow flakes, spread over the blocks of gray as the pale, haunted girl lays back, her aching and tormented body finding surprising relief on the hard surface. She closes her eyes. No mortal was meant to feel such torment, she thinks, gradually drifting off, the feel of the cold floor soothing against her skin.

Please God, help me, she prays as the light flickers inside her tortured mind.

Please, help me.

Tell me what you want me to do.

Her plea goes unanswered as she pictures the weighty cross suspended above her body. She keeps her eyes closed, not wanting to disturb the refuge of blackness. Here is where she will wait. Here is where she will find peace.

Leah, the voice calls from the depths of her psyche.

Leah.

She is unable to answer, not now; she's in too deep, paralyzed by the dullness that numbs her body and deadens his senses.

Leah.

Leah, stand up, the commanding voice intones.

But she drifts away, falling freely into the endless tunnel of oblivion. Her fingers twitch spasmodically against the smooth floor and her eyelids flutter above prominent crescents of amethyst.

Her descent is arrested violently. She feels her body separate from the sedative touch of the alter stone and rise up, up toward the wooden cross hanging over her. As she ascends, a painful sensation around her neck grows acute. The sustained pull on her cape brings the hood string tightly against her throat and she gasps for air.

She is released suddenly and falls back to the floor, her hands striking the ground with a loud slap. Her back bows. She convulses and fights to regain her breath. Turning over and away from the altar, she sees Margaret's unsympathetic face towering over her.

"You," she stammers, wiping the saliva from her lower lip.

"*You*," Margaret fires back mockingly, her voice dripping with disdain.

Leah takes a moment to comprehend what is happening and where she is. How did he get to the chapel alter? How long has she been lying here?

"You are a hard person to find these days, Leah. You're gone for hours on end. No one sees you at Senior House or at the dining room any more. After the concert last night, you disappeared without a trace."

"Margaret, you look as bad as I feel," she says with a tone of self-amusement, looking at how Margaret's normally refined facial features have transformed into a sickly mask. The smooth curves of her porcelain cheeks have turned drawn and pallid. The skin along her forehead is blotchy. Her lips, typically thin and pink, are bloodless and cracked.

"We both have had better days in front of the mirror, Leah. Now get up off the floor. I am not going to try pulling you up again."

"Perhaps I want to lie here. What is it to you?"

"Stop acting like a child and stand up."

"I'm the child, am I? What I have seen no child should ever witness."

"And no sane woman throws herself across a church alter like some sort of forsaken, homeless waif. Your flair for the melodramatic is growing tiresome. You've become an irritant to the entire dormitory and it needs to stop. I am here to make sure it stops. Do you understand me?"

Leah sits up and struggles to her feet, never breaking eye contact with her insistent classmate.

"That's not why you followed me here, Margaret, and you know it. You don't even believe your own words. You speak so boldly, with such conviction, just like a girl used to having her way throughout her comfortable life. I am not an irritant to the dormitory, as you say. My presence, my existence, is troubling to *you*. I validate the feelings inside you that you would prefer to dismiss as the fabrications of an overactive imagination."

"This is exactly what I am talking about. This behavior of yours, these wild-eyed rantings, it all must end. The way you went on outside the Mission

INCIDENT AT FOREST GLEN   *339*

and in your room after the ride. The row with Kaspar at chorus practice. The way you are acting here, now. It must end."

"I would if I could. But it's not for you or me to decide."

"You've run out of chances. It ends now. You're not going to take us down with you."

"Oh so like Margaret, the infallible queen of Senior House, to blame others for her own failures. You can admit it; there is no one else to hear you. We are alone. We can be honest with one another, can't we? When I came to the clubhouse that night, you knew I was right, you knew that something had happened. You knew something happened at the creek. Admit it to me now. I could tell Josephine knew in her heart. But she was too much of a rational thinker to even consider the possibility. May felt it for sure. I could see it in her frightened little doe eyes. You, on the other hand, with your confident air of composure and tightly-wrapped emotions, you were more difficult to read. I wasn't sure until I overheard you and Josephine talking in my room. I knew then. I had my confirmation. You were just as scared as I was."

Margaret coughs and feels the bilious churning inside her empty stomach.

"You cannot make me responsible for what you've done. Nothing went wrong at the glen."

Leah steps closer.

"And what about the boathouse? Was the fear you felt there simply a bad case of the nerves?"

Margaret hesitates. .

"It's all your doing, Leah, and now you are out of control."

"What if I told you that I know, with as much certainty as the existence of these walls about us, the truth of what happened at the flood? Would you want to know too? Would you want to know the truth?"

"You speak of truth while hiding behind a curtain of deception."

Leah points up at the suspended cross.

"'*Then you will know the truth, and the truth will set you free.*' A damnable lie! The truth is a curse. It has created an imprisonment for me so hellish I would not wish it on my worst enemy."

"Enough, Leah!

"Soon you will understand. I resisted too in the beginning."

"Why don't you tell me about where you've been these past few days? Because some sickening things have been happening while you've been missing."

Leah approaches Margaret and gently takes a hold of her hands and looks up with beseeching eyes.

"I was looking for her," she says with a tinge of poignancy. "I was looking for her. And I found her."

Margaret shakes off Leah's grip and backs away slowly.

"Did you hear what I said, Margaret? I found *her*."

Leah blinks away a tear.

"I...found...her."

She follows Margaret's retreat through the chapel nave, step for step.

"May told Miss Price you attacked her and now she is looking for you. She's going to throw you out when she finds out everything."

"Don't you understand what I am saying? I found the girl," she implores, quickening her steps to match Margaret's. "I found the girl from the glen."

"And Josephine's horse, how could you be so depraved? We know it was you that cut her horse."

"Damn your false accusations!" Leah lashes out as her fists wildly punch the space between them. "I speak of the miracle of salvation and you answer with petty lies!"

"You've lost your mind. Stay away, Leah. Don't you dare come closer," Margaret warns, just as she feels the door against her back. "Stay away from Josephine and her horse. If you threaten either of them again, you will regret it the rest of your days. I will see to it!"

Margaret turns and rushes out of the chapel door. Fever burns along her forehead and cheeks making her feel lightheaded and weak. The intensity of the storm has picked up and as she shuffles through the fallen snow she quickly glances back toward the chapel to make sure Leah is not following. She is alone in the resplendent winterscape, her progress through the realm of pristine beauty observed by a coterie of Olympian figures and mythical beasts. She heads off to find Josephine carrying with her what she set out to find, proof of Leah's madness.

She reaches the porch just as a group of girls from the first floor open the door to leave.

"Margaret, did you hear? Did you hear what happened last night?" one of them asks, thrilled to be the first to break the news.

"No, what is it?"

"Norma just came back from breakfast, and she overheard the waiters talking about how the boathouse down by Indian Rock burned down in the middle of the night. It's completely gone, they said. The musty old shack and the canoes, everything. Burnt to the ground. And then Mary here starts talking about the fire siren she heard and we put two and two together. Can you believe it?"

Mary, not wanting to be relegated as bit player in the drama, speaks up for herself.

"I knew something was wrong but I couldn't see anything from my balcony because it faces toward the front promenade. I wouldn't be surprised if the fire chief or the police are called in to investigate. It all seems rather suspicious, I mean, a fire in the middle of a snow storm."

After much internal debate, May decides to skip the morning meal. For the past two weeks she has limited her trips to the dining room as part of a conscious effort to lose weight before the winter ball. Unwilling to don the required gymnasium uniform, comprised of a white short-sleeved blouse, pleated navy skirt and knee socks, she has eschewed physical training as a way to drop the desired pounds before the Christmas formal. She has instead concentrated on curbing her appetite as a way of fitting into the coral dress made of silk taffeta and lace trim she couldn't leave the dress shop without buying while home over the summer. Her mother had subtly discouraged the purchase, not because of the steep price tag but out of concern over its fit. Even the store's obsequious saleswoman, a frequent beneficiary of the King family semi-annual shopping trips, cast a skeptical look when the headstrong daughter insisted on the purchase without the benefit of trying on the dress. May told her mother at the time that she was growing tired of dressing and undressing and that she was confident it would fit once they got home. If alterations were required, she added, the family tailor could take care of them later. Her mother, not wanting to wound May's feelings, played along, as she always does.

In truth, May knew she could not possibly fit into the coveted dress. The claim of fatigue was a ploy, part of a game she learned many years before when her classmates grew out of their childish bodies and the onset of pubescence turned their rounded features lean and angular, and hers did not. The promise of physical transformation, coupled with May's eternal hope that she could marshal the willpower to trim her waist and arms and legs, had filled the closet of her Virginia home with a stunning array of expensive, never-worn dresses. With each new purchase, the reminders of her past impulsivity and undisciplined eating habits were pushed down the hanger rod, deeper into the farthest reaches of the closet where they would eventually escape notice.

I will look so pretty wearing it, she told herself with a renewed commitment to discipline as the coral dress was folded by the saleswoman into a bed of tissue and boxed.

When May returned to the Seminary in September she brought the expensive garment with her and kept it on the hook on the inside of the closet door, a prominent, daily exhortation to achieve the goal she had set. On weekend shopping trips to Garfinkel's and Woodward and Lothrop's she would explain to the other girls searching the windows how she had already purchased a formal dress and was only along to look, occasionally taking time to revel in the details of the dress' fashionable design and alluring color.

When the Equinox Soiree approached and the weight she promised herself she would lose remained, she begrudgingly conceded to herself that she had squandered yet another opportunity and selected the same loose fitting cotton dress she had worn the previous spring. The fashion dilemma was so mortifying she considered not going to the dance at all until a few girls in the dormitory cajoled her. The embarrassment of being seen in the same dress twice in a row steeled her resolve to finally change her appearance and to shrink the unfaltering bulges, though, implausible as it might have seemed to May at the time, her faux pas escaped the notice of all in attendance that night. When she returned to her room after the ball, she flipped to the end of the calendar and circled the second Saturday in December, the 9th. The social highlight of the semester. The Christmas Ball. Once again, she looked into the mirror and repeated the promise she had made since the age of twelve.

This time it will be different.

May looks out the window of her room and marvels at how the snow has transformed the grounds overnight. The buildings around the campus are barely visible in the ghostly washout and the branches of the nearby trees bend under the weight of the clinging accumulation. A solitary figure approaches Senior House and she lowers the shade as a precaution.

After she locks the door, May switches off the chandelier leaving only the Tiffany desk lamp in the corner. The subdued light makes her antsy, and by the time she takes the garment bag off the closet door hook and lays it carefully along the bed, her stomach is twisted with anticipation. She unbuttons the bag and smiles at the beauty of the dress, hidden from her sight for more than two months now. The color is radiant, the cut of the fabric gorgeous. Just as she remembered.

Turning her back to the full length dressing mirror, May slips off her robe revealing a tight fitting cotton camisole and pair of mannish drawers. She carefully slides her hands up through the bottom of the dress, straightens her body and feels the cool fabric lining shimmy along the back of her arms and down her back. She searches for the arm openings and pushes her hands through until she feels the smooth woven fibers pull tightly around the abundant flesh of her forearms. The pinched contours of the waistline catch on her shoulders and she wiggles about inside the dress to narrow her upper body and round her back. She pulls one of her arms out and up through the neckline and reaches high towards the ceiling. But the dress does not budge. Her body is wedged firmly inside the straining fabric. She is trapped, encased in a shroud of taffeta and lace that covers her face and restricts her breathing.

Unwilling to give up, May struggles to move the dress down her body but the predicament only worsens. Her face is immersed in her own hot breath and when she tries to withdraw her other arm, her hand becomes entangled as well, as if an underwater sea creature has latched onto her body and is pulling her down. A coating of sweat quickly materializes along her neck and chest, and full-panic ensues. She blindly grabs at the neckline with her free hand and hops about the floor, whimpering, suddenly desperate to remove the suffocating material.

She feels the machine-made lace brush against her finger tips. She seizes it and gathers it into her fist and frantically yanks with all the might she can muster in the awkward position. The inner lining of the dress inches along the moist, over-heated skin of her back and she jerks a second time, this time extending her arm fully, and hears the unmistakable sound of ripping fabric that makes her pounding heart sink.

She cries out, a primal yell of unbridled frustration.

By the time she extracts herself, her face is bright pink and her chest rises and falls rapidly. Her tousled hair is pulled over to one side and standing on end. The cherished coral taffeta dress—the jewel she plucked from the dress shop display—lies in a pile on the floor by her feet, beyond repair, ruined.

May, panting and frazzled by the ordeal, bends over and catches a glimpse of her body in the mirror. Even in the muted light, the image confirms what sadly she already knows. The loose folds of skin sagging off from the back of her arms. The disproportionate girth of dimpled skin above the knee. The pendulous mid-section pressing against the camisole. The weeks of missed meals and declined desserts had made no difference.

Instead of covering herself or stepping away, she straightens up and faces the mirror full on, and unflinchingly considers the imperfections of her form. She is exhausted by the fight and signals her surrender. For once, there is no reaction of self-loathing, only resignation.

This is who you are, May King. This is who you will always be.

She tears at the straps of the camisole until they are replaced by red slashes along her bare shoulders, and the top slides to her hips. Staring unabashedly at her exposed chest, May recalls how the simple act of looking at her undressed body used to fill her with unbearable shame.

She was living at the Villa with the rest of the junior class at the time and the premature arrival of the summer heat had made the waning days of the semester insufferable. The unrelenting sun poured down through cloudless skies day after day, torching the ground. The blooms of spring withered away and the carefully tended lawn developed large patches of brown before the school gardeners sprung into action to combat the early drought. An oppressive swelter settled over the glen turning it into a cauldron and sending students and teachers alike in search for relief. No matter how many windows were opened or how many electric fans were brought out of school storage, the rooms were sweat-inducing ovens and many students took to dragging their mattress onto the lawn at night in order to sleep.

Emergency measures were instituted by the administration. The length of mid-day classes was shortened. Ice cream was served up in chilled silver bowls for breakfast. The gymnasium pool was overwhelmed during the heat spell and kept open until midnight to accommodate the suffering girls. On weekends, groups of students headed for the cooling relief of the downtown movie houses. Others took the trains westward into the Blue Ridge Mountains to escape the soaring temperatures. Most simply endured, and life at the Seminary ground to a torpid pace.

It is Sunday afternoon, she recalls. The view outside her room is still and somnolent. The grounds of the Seminary bake under an inescapable, withering yellow radiance. A long-legged insect crawls along the outside of the window screen, probing for a rip or hole in the tight mesh, any opening to escape the heat. May sits in a cane-backed chair, positioned next to the window for the breeze that never comes. Her eyelids begin to droop as she reads over the same paragraph in her book a third time, and she gives up trying to intercept the reappearing drops running along her temples and down the back of her scalp.

The sudden appearance of Besse McClosky at her open doorway chases away the lethargy creeping over her. The girl is surprisingly cheerful and draped with an oversized towel.

"Great, you're here. Come on. Put on your suit. One of the girls has jimmied the lock to the roof. A bunch of us are going up there to sunbathe. The regent would have a fit if she knew we were going up there, but if we are quiet about it, no one will know."

May does not reply immediately, having difficulty comprehending what the fast-talking girl is proposing.

"The roof? What's on the roof?"

"A few of us left here. Julia next door. Ruthie and Irene down the hall. Josephine Barnes from upstairs. She was the one who figured out how to pop the door off its hinges without having to open the lock. They sent me down to round up some others."

"Won't we get in trouble?"

"That's the beauty; no one can see us. We can do whatever we want. It is a genius idea. It's hot as Hades up there though. I'm going to get a bucket and fill it with water, but I'll need some help carrying it up the stairs, so hurry up and get dressed and make sure you bring along a towel and shoes. The roof is like a frying pan."

The enthusiastic girl from Newark rushes off, reminding May to hurry.

The two girls, towels balanced around their necks, carry an unwieldy metal cistern up the rickety set of attic stairs toward the unhinged panel backlit by glimpses of blue sky. Besse holds the front handle and May struggles from the rear to keep the water level as they ascend to the roof. Miniature waves lurch from one side of the container to the other until the cooling water sloshes over the lip and soaks their arms and splashes against the steps. By the time they push past the open door, laughing and dripping wet, the other girls already on the roof voice their approval at the herculean accomplishment.

May squints hard trying to adjust to the abrupt change in light. The sun's rays reflect against the roof's surface with a blinding brilliance that momentarily pains her eyes. She never knew what was up here.

From the ground, the Villa is an imposing edifice built with red terra cotta shingles in the old world Mediterranean style. She never took time to wonder what if anything was behind the lofty ramparts and decorative turrets lining the dormitory's upper floor. When Besse told her of the plan, she imagined a roof top garden or chairs arranged under an umbrella. The discovery is surprisingly ugly and utilitarian. Long, overlapping sheets of gray tin slope away at a gradual angle from a peak that bisects the middle of the roof like the spine of a fossilized prehistoric beast. Pieces of metal flashing, coated with brush strokes of black sealant, line the edges and corners of the low mortar and brick wall encircling the hidden retreat. Besse was right; there is no way they can be seen up here. Blurry waves of heat rise off the tin beach and May detects an unpleasant odor of smoldering tar in the stultifying air.

Girls are spaced about in languid repose, lying on blankets and towels, the flesh of their legs and arms and backs exposed to the full fury of the sun. Some are still wearing their summer shoes, while others, safely situated on their protective islands, have gone barefoot.

The two girls lower the bucket onto the uneven surface and a small cup-sized portion of the precious water, delivered with great care and toil, splashes over the side and hisses as it touches the metal. May watches the lost water roll away down the sizzling chute of blistering tin and evaporate before it comes close to reaching the wall.

"It takes some getting use to, walking in heels and all, so take my hand," Besse says, slipping her fingers into May's.

The two take unsteady steps across the rooftop and May imagines how excruciating the feel of the burning metal would be on the back of her legs if she slipped and fell. Almost as painful as the embarrassment she would be forced to endure.

They carefully side-step a girl propped up on her stomach reading a thin dime store paperback. Beside her is Ruthie, also from May's floor. She's sitting on her towel, bent over at the waist, her head lolling forward above straightened legs, the curved strands of her shortly-cropped chestnut hair hanging down over her forehead, wet and glistening, beads of perspiration steadily falling onto her sinewy thighs.

"Let's lay over here," Besse decides, pulling May along to an open spot near the center. She unfurls her towel and casts a shadow over the girl next to her resting face down.

"Who is doing *that?*" the girl says sharply, turning her head toward the person eclipsing her sunlight.

"Sorry, Margaret. Just getting comfortable," she answers while smoothing out the towel and lowering herself cautiously on the rectangular patch.

May does the same. But when Besse removes her loosely buttoned blouse to reveal a stylish blue-striped suit with a white cloth belt that hugs her slender form and accentuates the curvature of her bust, May balks.

Margaret shields her eyes and looks over the new arrivals.

"You are forgiven, Besse, now that I have seen that suit of yours. You are going to drive the boys crazy at the shore this summer."

"All I need is some color on this fish-belly white body and I will be the toast of the boardwalk and the penny arcades," she says with a smile, shifting her bare shoulders against the plush towel in an attempt to get comfortable. "A summer of nothing but boys buying me ices and taffy."

"Not in this lifetime," Margaret replies sarcastically.

A prolonged silence comes over the group as insects camouflaged in the nearby trees serenade the sun worshippers. After a few minutes, the direct sun is too severe and May turns on her side and catches Margaret's eyes, brown and sultry, staring up at her from the towel. Slowly they close and May notices the girl's rib cage expand and contract just before a heavy audible sigh is expelled from her slightly parted lips.

On the towel next to Margaret, Josephine lies facing upward, her willowy body stretched out across a surplus green bed covering taken from the hallway linen closet. One leg is bent and the sizeable heel of her shoe digs effortlessly into the puckered fibers, securing her position on the gradual incline. The skirt of her white suit has crept down, revealing creamy, flawlessly sculpted legs, long and toned from years of ballet and riding. The protruding points along her hips accentuate the slight inward curve of her stomach and under the revealing light of the sun as its apex May can make out through the fabric the subtle definition, the lean lines, wrapping along the sides of her upper body and disappearing behind her back, the muscularity that gives Josephine the elegant posture and poised presentation envied by others. The halter top tied around her neck reveals firm, rounded shoulders. Her blond curls, tamed by a piece of pink ribbon, are pulled to one side and rest on the green blanket next to her flushed cheek.

"Don't you think we should be worried about airplanes flying over-head?" Besse asks to no one in particular, unable to endure the lack of con-versation. She sits up, supported on her elbows, and scans the exquisite blue sky overhead.

"I see more and more of them flying over the school. Mr. Anderson told us in history class that they come from an airport over by the univer-sity where the Army tests planes. It seems like a day doesn't go by that one doesn't fly over."

"I've heard about that place," May joins in, anxious to display her broad knowledge. "One of the Wright brothers worked there. The airfield is just a short way past the college. A girl from the first floor grew up not far from it. She said there were all sorts of horrible crashes there before the war."

"Which one?" Margaret asks, face down on her towel.

"I am not sure. I think her name is Maureen."

"Not the girl. The Wright brother," Margaret says, noticeably exasper-ated. "Which Wright brother?"

"I...I'm not positive. I think the dead one."

"Well, which one is the dead one?" she presses further, lifting up her head, her complexion moist and radiant.

"I don't know," May concedes.

"Wilbur," Josephine announces to the group, her eyes still closed and lying face upward. "It is Wilbur."

"What reason would they have to fly over the Seminary?" Besse con-tinues on. "Maybe they are trying to show off for us and get our attention."

Try as hard as she might, Margaret cannot let the girl's mindless musing go.

"So you think we are the targets of aerial flirtation? The Army is sending its fly boys to buzz over our school as part of an elaborate plan to seduce us."

"Hmmm. I hadn't thought of that way, but I like how you put it," Besse answers with a suggestive grin. "I have a soft spot for men in uniform."

"You and Josephine both."

"Be quiet, Margaret," Josephine fires back immediately.

"It's not as far-fetched as you might think."

"You're daft, Besse. And for goodness sake, May, take off that blouse of yours. I can barely stand it out here and looking at you still dressed like that makes me even more uncomfortable."

"I'm afraid of getting burned," she partially lies.

"Men like a bit of color on their woman," Margaret says with leering glance, "that's why dear Josephine here, with her fair complexion, is condemned to go through life permanently handicapped in the pursuit of love. Skin with a slight luster speaks to the primitive nature locked inside the male genetics. I learned about it at last month's biology seminar. It's one of the many useful tidbits my parent's tuition checks have provided me."

Josephine turns on her side and faces May.

"Don't let her boss you around. Only if you want to," she says with a supportive smile, her eyes the color of blue topaz in the reflected sun.

May unbuttons her shirt and quickly removes it, placing it behind her head as she leans back onto her towel. The warming sensation along her arms and shoulder is immediate and pleasing. She closes her eyes and feels the fabric of her bathing suit soften and meld against her body. Many minutes pass and a wave of relaxation sweeps over her supine body as the symphony of cicadas lulls her into a half-conscious state.

Out of the dark, a persistent tormentor. A distant drone approaching, drawing nearer, growing louder.

A fly hovers near her face and she shoos it away, and when it returns again and lands on her nose, May turns on her side suddenly aware of the simmering heat beyond the towel's edge. Through narrow slits she sees Besse standing by the water bucket with two other girls, taking turns scooping out water and pouring it down their backs and over their heads. She takes another half-turn and lies on her stomach. She reaches above her head and searches for the discarded blouse she's been using as a makeshift pillow only to find that it has been pushed off the side of the towel and slid along the metal track and come to rest by her feet. When she sits up to retrieve it, she sees Margaret seated on the back of her legs and bent over Josephine's body, positioned in such a way as to block May's line of sight. Margaret's right arm pulls something away and her statuesque body straightens at the waist. Sleek locks fall against the damp vertebrae running the length of her slender neck. She rolls to her side, crosses her arms, and slides her thumbs under the shoulder straps of her bathing suit, unaware she is being watched. May's view is no longer obstructed and she sees Josephine lying on her stomach, face relaxed and turned toward May, her halter untied and pulled all the way down to the delicate curve just above her hips. The entire length of her back is exposed and her round breasts are bare, pressed softly against the glossy satin of the purloined bedspread.

"Don't look so shocked, May-belle," Margaret says quietly. "It's time to grow up. You see naked women every day. You pass them on pedestals on your way to class. The gardens are nothing but a pagan celebration of well-endowed human flesh. Join in on the fun and be one of the girls."

May wants to desperately turn away but is paralyzed by the girl's taunting, provocative words.

"Can't you hear?" Margaret nods over her shoulder. The steady buzz of airplane engines can be heard fast approaching beyond the tree tops. "Besse's fly boys are on their way. They deserve a show for their trouble, don't you think?"

Margaret pulls her top down off her shoulders and does not stop until her hands reach her waist.

May averts her gaze. She could have cast her eyes to the azure sky in anticipation of the approaching airplanes or watched Besse and the others splash about with amusement. She could have turned her look on the blouse at her feet in danger of slipping away or pretended to search out the mysterious music makers hidden in the thick cover of leaves.

But she doesn't. She turns back and searches out the one person she admires most at the school, the girl she secretly envies and hopes to one day emulate, the embodiment of grace, the unfailing compass of fairness in their often capricious and cruel world. But she does not find her. Josephine is no longer the girl May knew minutes before. She is different now. The innocence is gone from her translucent stare.

There is a knock at the door and May answers meekly. An offer to go to breakfast is made through the door and reluctantly accepted.

"I'll only be a minute," she assures her hallmate.

She bends to pick the ruined dress off the floor and then stops. She can't bring herself to hold the torn remnants of her futility and instead pushes it along the ground with her foot until it is balled up underneath her bed, left to be disposed of later.

Josephine circles the fragrant spruce tree, inspecting the ornaments and trying to occupy her mind until Margaret arrives. She fell asleep in her friend's room the night before and awoke in the morning to find Margaret's folded stationary note, pinned to a lace pillow propped up against the door, instructing her to meet at the Spanish Mission.

As she dressed in her room, she started thinking about Mr. Raymee and the selfless concern he showed her last night. She knows she will need to go see him today as promised, the sooner the better. She owes it to the caring man after he put his job at risk by contacting her and keeping the attack on Sable quiet.

He knew but would never admit to her Leah's culpability in the malicious act. It isn't his nature to put her in the position of having to react to such an accusation. This is the level of unspoken communication the two have established over time. The stable groom had let her know that the next step was hers to take. Contacting the police was a risky act, he warned. He wouldn't force her to do it, but he wouldn't stand in her way either. Above all, he wanted her to relieve him of the burden of deciding their fate. Her dilemma had become his, and she felt a deep obligation to extract him from the consequences of Leah's increasingly unpredictable behavior.

Josephine startles as she looks over the decorated tree.

"This is not possible," she says in amazement, lifting the hand-painted ornament made out of blown glass from a branch and turning it around.

She purposely kept the lights off when she entered the clubhouse, but even in the subdued light coming through the bay window, she is able to make out the fine black markings on the back of the ornament:

J.B. 1918

She made it her first semester at the Seminary, around a crafts table in this very room with other girls of the sorority, most of whom are now gone. Those days seem distant and strangely foreign now. She remembers the cloud of homesickness that followed her around those initial weeks separated from her family. And when the Christmas finery was unpacked and sparkling decorations were hung throughout the school, her young heart ached and she counted down the days on her calendar when she would be allowed to return home and be reunited with the faces and familiar comforts sorely missed during her time away.

She made the ornament to give to her parents that Christmas as a lasting memento of their daughter's first journey on her own, but it had gone missing, either misplaced or broken, she assumed then, in the frenetic activity at the clubhouse before the holiday recess.

She turns the delicate ball in her fingers, watching how the light inside the sphere splits into thin colorful rays, and marvels at its reappearance. Three years gone. Forgotten. She unhooks the metal clasp from the branch causing a few dried needles to drop to floor and carefully slips the lost treasure into the pocket of her uniform.

The loud sound of stomping boots outside breaks the serenity and Josephine rushes across the empty room and reaches the front entrance just as Margaret closes the door and turns to peer back outside through a small, inlaid window. Her coat and hat are covered in white.

"What is it?"

"Wait," Margaret answers brusquely, her back still turned.

Once she is convinced no one has followed her, Margaret turns away from the door and Josephine sees she is panicked.

"Smart of you to keep the lights off."

"You're scaring me. Tell me what it is you were looking for. Where have you been this morning?"

"Do you think it is too early for a drink? I can search the woodpile. I am positive what's left hasn't frozen. Not that stuff."

"I'm serious, Margaret."

"I'm serious as well. I could *really* use a shot of alcohol right now. I am freezing and my hands are shaking."

"Where have you been?" Josephine presses again.

Margaret tosses her hat and coat on the foyer rack and rushes past her waiting friend. Alarmed by Margaret's erratic behavior, Josephine follows the trial of wet foot prints into the sorority's central meeting room.

Margaret throws herself on the sofa positioned against the three-paneled window and crouches down low so that her chin rests along the back upholstery.

"What has you so spooked to make you run about playing hide-and-seek?"

"I went to Senior House to see if you were still there," she begins to explain, keeping her eyes trained on the wintry landscape outside the window.

"I came here as your note told me to do."

"Yes, yes, I know what I wrote. I just didn't want to come here and find that you were still snoozing away in my room. By the way, has any ever told you that you snore? You do, you know. Not really loud. Like babies sometimes sound in their cribs. It's kind of cute, but it kept me up."

"Get to the point, Margaret. Why did you leave before I woke? Where did you go so early in the morning?"

A brisk, sustained wind blows along the lawn of the Spanish Mission and kicks up the snow in a swirling tempest that momentarily obscures the ever-vigilant statue of Peeping Tom. Margaret finally turns away from the bay window. Against the white backdrop, she looks tired to Josephine and her face is drained of color.

"While I was lying awake last night, I heard someone's door on the floor open and close. The noise didn't wake you. You were sound asleep. I went to the door and opened it a crack to see who it was. It was dark and all I could make out was the outline of a person down at the end of the hall. Not moving. Whoever was there was just standing in the hallway, down between Leah's and May's rooms. Then the person started walking. I could hear the muffled footsteps on the hallway rug slowly coming towards me. Even as she approached it was too dark to make out who it was. I closed my door but not all the way. I didn't want the handle to make a noise by shutting it completely. So I used my fingers to hold it against the doorway trying to make sure the door didn't move as the person passed by. As the sound of the steps neared, I tensed my body and felt the current of air in the hall press against the door. The sensation of the cool wood pushing ever so slightly against my fingers from the other side was unnerving and I worried that whoever it was would notice the small crack between the door and the wall."

"And were you seen?" Josephine asks as she sits in the chair across from the couch.

"I don't know. But I don't think so. When I heard the steps pass and then grow fainter down the stairs, I shut the door and quickly dressed."

"You should have woken me."

Margaret shrugs.

"That's when I wrote you the note to meet me here. After all this business about Leah's nighttime walk to the poor family's house and what happened to your horse, I decided to follow her. I didn't want to. I felt like death and I am not exactly the type of girl who enjoys leaving a warm bed to go tramping in the snow in the middle of the night. But I felt I had no choice. I had seen what all this had done to you and me both. There was no time to wake you and explain. The longer I waited I risked losing her and the best chance we had at understanding what she was up to."

"Where did she go?"

"Everywhere. And nowhere."

Margaret rubs her hands along the sides of her face and then runs them through her hair.

"Are you sure we can't take a break and search for that bottle in the woodpile out front?"

"I don't understand. Everywhere and nowhere?"

"It must have taken me a minute or two to dress and write the note and by the time I left you and hurried down the stairs she had a considerable head-start. I stood on the front porch and looked around hoping to find some sign of her but if she brought a lantern with her, I didn't see it anywhere. I couldn't detect any movement at all. It was pitch-black. The only lights were those along the walkways and the globes on the drive bridge. The snow was coming down hard and everything was covered. It was so quiet you could hear the flakes landing on the bushes out front. But I knew she had left Senior House. Her footprints were on the stairs. So I followed them. Into the dark.

"At first it was difficult to see what was in front of me, but my eyes started to adjust and I was able to make out the outline her steps in the snow. I could tell from the tracks that she stopped once she left Senior House. Her footprints on the grass in front were all over the place, stepping over each other and turned around, like she was caught in a moment of indecision and not sure which way she wanted to go. The trail then pointed in the direction of the glen and I thought she might be heading to the Odeon. What business she would have there at such an early hour was beyond me, but it made some sense, or that's what I told myself.

"I wanted to get close enough to see her but not too close. It was brutally cold, but I followed. I made sure to sidestep the circles of light along the pathway and stay in the dark to avoid being seen. But when I reached the Odeon, my suspicion was wrong. She had walked right past it and toward the creek. I assumed she was heading for the bridge and was crossing over the glen. I could tell from the spacing of her footprints that she had started to walk faster or possible even started to run. I hurried up and the tracks turned into the small garden right before the bridge. That's where she stopped."

"You saw Leah there?"

Margaret shakes her head.

"I saw the place where she stopped. I saw the trampled snow where she stood before she continued on. Josephine, it was the very spot you and I stood two nights ago. Remember, when I left the geisha party and you came after me?"

The image of Charles Carter stepping out of the shadows, coat in hand, approaching her distraught friend, flashes before Josephine.

"Are you sure?" she asks.

"Positive. I stood where Leah had been just moments before and looked around half-expecting your New York suitor to magically appear again."

"Don't call him that," she protests at the characterization, feeling a rush of blood to her face as she is reminded of Robert's arrival later in the day.

"Then I lost track of her. She had left the path and walked across the lawn back towards Vincent Hall. The wind started blowing harder and my toes and face started going numb. I thought about ending this foolishness and going back to the room, but I remembered the stone staircase leading down to the creek. Perhaps she was cutting over the ground to reach the walk leading to the Grotto. I doubled back and the followed the lights to where I wanted to go. When I finally reached the stone banister at the top of the stairs, I had to bend down to make sense of what I saw. Two sets of footprints. One heading down to the Grotto and one heading back up the staircase. I couldn't believe what I saw. She was running about like a hare. Going here and going there. Too fast for me to keep up. It was dumb luck that I had crossed her path again given how dark it was and with the blowing snow."

"You poor thing."

"But now I am intrigued and more than a little angry over her antics. No matter how tired and miserable I was of the chase, I wasn't going to give up. She was somewhere behind me now, so I kept on following. Down to the Villa. Along the pergola. All the way past the boiler house and the conservatory and to the gymnasium. Stopping here and there, as she went. No matter how quickly I moved, I never caught up to her. It was like she was doing a loop around the entire campus. Always a few steps ahead of me. I never caught sight of her. I never heard her.

"And then a strange thought dawned on me: What if she was leading me on? Had she seen me at the door in the hallway? Was this just a game to her?

"It was behind Vincent Hall, near the water tower, that I lost the trail again. Her steps doubled back over themselves so often I wasn't sure where she went or in what direction I should head. It was starting to get light by this time and I could see the vague outlines of the buildings around me. I was exhausted and feeling lousy. I had been chasing her for probably close to a half-hour and I couldn't feel my hands or feet. So I began walking back to Senior House. Swearing over and over at the futility of it all.

"And just when I had given up, there she was."

"You found her? Where?"

"The colonnade connecting Aloha and Recitation Hall. The one with the stone arches held up by the heads of the statues all in a row. She was walking along, weaving around each of the pedestals like they were racing pylons, wrapping her arm around the caryatids as she went along, like a playful school girl without a worry in the world. I stood watching her go on like this for awhile. If she saw me there, she didn't let on. It was as if Leah was in her own imaginary world. When she reached the end of the colonnade her attitude changed suddenly. Her carefree expression turned severe and angry. I thought she might have sensed my presence. But she kept on walking."

"What did you do?"

"I followed her, of course. Into the chapel. And I confronted her. I told myself I would if I caught up to her. And I did."

"What do you mean you confronted her? What did you say?"

"I told it she needed to stop acting like a lunatic. And I warned her if she didn't she was going to be expelled from the school. I told her that if she hurt you or threatened you again I would personally make sure that she would regret it."

"I'm not sure it was wise to confront her like that."

"It seemed like the smart move at the time."

Josephine detects a hint of self-doubt in her words.

"That was until a few minutes ago when I found out that the boathouse was set on fire last night and burnt it to the ground."

"What?!"

"We had fallen asleep before it happened. The siren was sounded but we slept through it. By the time they reached the fire, there was nothing left to save. You hadn't heard about it?"

"Oh my God, no! I came directly here."

"You should have heard Leah in the chapel, when I told her we knew what she had done. She didn't claim innocence or profess regret. Just more nonsense about the glen and the dress and the non-existent girl. She was as combative as she was in her room after our ride into the woods. She's dangerous, I tell you. And now that I know she's lighting buildings on fire in her spare time, I am really worried. I think she's insane. That's why I was looking out the door when I came. I left Leah at the chapel less than five minutes ago and I was worried she might follow me here."

"You don't think there is any doubt she is the one who burned down the boathouse?"

"Do you think there is any doubt that she took the knife we found there and carved her initials into your horse?"

Josephine stands up and walks around the room trying to process Margaret's story and the shocking revelation about the overnight fire.

"Then what do we do? I need to speak to Mr. Raymee this morning and tell him something. And you need to rest before tonight. You look bone-tired."

Margaret sighs.

"From you too?"

"Huh?"

"Never mind. I say we go to see Dean Dawson first thing. He won't meet with us unless Miss Price is there too. So one of us needs to go and tell her what we know. Everything. If we don't, Leah will get caught and drag us down with her. Or worse. We need to tell the truth first before her lies cast doubt on our word."

Josephine looks out the window and sees that the snow has started to drift along the side of Peeping Tom's pedestal.

"Not the complete truth," she says. "I am the one who found the knife. I went to Sable's stall this morning to feed him a treat. Let's make it a potato I kept from my dinner plate last night. I saw the knife on the stall floor and I recognized it as the one we saw at the boathouse, so I brought it back with me. And when I heard about the fire, I knew I needed to tell someone in the administration about it. When Miss Price asks you about the knife, look surprised. You don't know anything about my discovery or what happened to Sable in the stall. Neither does Mr. Raymee. I kept it to myself. I'll do the explaining."

"Are you sure?"

"I'm sure. I'm going to see Mr. Raymee now and get the knife."

"Do you want me to go with you?"

Josephine sits on the couch next to Margaret and strokes her cheek lightly.

"I think you've done enough this morning. Are you sure you are up for tonight?" she asks with a concerned look. "I can place a call to Robert and let him know there's been a change in plans and that he has no choice but to dash poor Caleb's hopes for a romantic evening."

"I feel like I am going to die right about now. But I suppose I can rally by the time of the dance. He's the cute one, right? You wouldn't take advantage of me, not in my weakened state," Margaret says as she leans back on the sofa.

"I worry about you, Meg. I just want to put this all behind us and get you healthy. I think you should see the nurse again."

"I still have the medicine she gave me yesterday. She'll want to poke me with long, painful needles if I go see her twice in two days."

Josephine plants a kiss on her forehead and feels the heat against her lips.

"Well, you should take some more of it. You are burning up."

Leah's pushes her hands into the snow until they disappear, and then runs them along the hard ground and quickly raises them with an explosive spray of crystals. Over and over she repeats the act, as if she is mimicking the motion of a whale or dolphin breaching the surface of a foamy white sea. Her heart is euphoric as she frolics in winter's gift, drawing childlike pleasure when a fat flake lands on her nose or sticks to tip of her eyelash. She sits on the cold blanket and draws letters and symbols and numbers in the accumulation around her. Her hair is dusted and pearls of ice cling to the wool scarf around her neck. Her playful hands scoop snow around her feet until her boots are buried. The crude compress cools the lingering ache of her right ankle. She unties the taut laces of her boot and sprinkles snow on the knot of purple and yellow flesh under her sock. The relief seeps slowly down to her skin.

She leans back and feels the hard, flat surface of the chiseled granite. Across the county road, Vincent Hall and the surrounding buildings resemble the distant peaks of a mystical mountain range through the blowing snow.

Turning her head to the crumbling gray sky, she closes her eyes and thrusts out her tongue in a curl of pink. Flakes fall over her face and in her hair and she laughs heartily at the tickling sensation of the girlhood game. She snares one and then another, bobbing her head about blindly to capture the elusive precipitation. The game continues until a dark presence emerges and casts a shadow over Leah from above. She opens her eyes apprehensively. The severe features are familiar and her heart drops. The blissful joy she feels evaporates at the appearance of the stoic warrior looming over her.

Josephine leaves the Spanish Mission and walks along the county road to make faster time reaching the horse stable. The poor footing along the path winding along the rear of Vincent Hall would only delay her in reaching Mr. Raymee. She passes by the colonnade Margaret spoke of shortly after leaving and recreates in her mind's eye the spectacle of Leah dancing among the line of statues. The sheltered walk is empty now and, as it is Saturday, Recitation Hall is dark and shuttered.

Across the road an automobile is parked next to a tall, stone and brick column marking the turn-off to the stable. A large bronze eagle sits atop the column, wings unfurled, a signal post to those travelling the road that they are entering the school property.

As Josephine nears, she sees flames and cinders shooting out of a metal canister out in front of the stable entrance. Two men are huddled around the barrel of fire, one she immediately recognizes as the groom. Hands thrust outward, they watch as thick flakes pass across the red, smoky chasm and melt away.

She reaches the sentinel eagle and heads down the hill pulling her hooded cape tightly around her head. As she passes the car, she sees something unexpected. Affixed to the black Packard, in front of the radiator, just below the sight line of the engine hood, is a weathered brass bell streaked with the lines of melted snow. A cylinder shaped siren is bracketed to the outside of the body next to the windshield and along the side panel of the driver's door she reads the words that give her pause: *County Police.*

Not sure what to do, she continues toward the stable. Mr. Raymee turns away from the fire at the last moment, sees her, and shakes his head while the second man continues to warm himself, his back to the road. Not wanting to draw suspicion by turning around, she walks on, adjusting her path away from the entrance and towards the rear of the gymnasium. She can hear the two men talk as she passes by. Their tone is conversational and friendly, and then a violent clanging sound fills Josephine's ears and she flinches. Though tempted to turn around, she maintains discipline and keeps facing forward. A loud, crisp pop, and then another.

"There you go, Raymee," she hears the policeman shout out behind her, "That's getting her going. Throw another one in."

When she is sure she is out sight, Josephine walks down the drive leading to the colored men's quarters and doubles-back toward the rear of the stable, pressing through heavy brush as she goes. Following the perimeter of the paddock she reaches a hand pump and hose and crouches down behind a waist-high whitewashed fence. A putrid aroma comes from inside the building and she hears the two men beyond the stalls still talking around the blaze.

Josephine scissors her legs over the wood boards and quietly passes the slumbering horses. Reaching Sable's stall, she slides the bar along the latch and a piercing squeak shatters the calm inside the building. She stops and then continues more slowly, the grinding vibrations of the rusted metal running the length of her arm. Quietly opening the door, she slips inside. The stall hasn't been mucked out yet and the smell of urine and feces is nearly overpowering. Her horse is turned face-first toward the far corner of the stall napping and she can hear the cycle of his shallow breathing. Josephine searches the interior ledges of the stall until her fingers graze the cold steel of the knife. When she holds the weighty blade for the first time since its discovery at the boathouse, she is frightened by the width of the cutting edge and the menacing tip.

The sound of a car door shutting in front of the stable breaks the silence and she lifts up her cloak and drops the weapon into her front pocket. The leather-wrapped butt strikes something inside and weighs down the fabric of her uniform. A moment of confusion passes and Josephine realizes that she forgot about the delicate, irreplaceable ornament she took off the Theta house Christmas tree. The jagged, shattered pieces of her reclaimed work press against the flesh of her thigh.

"Damn," she says out loud before she can think twice.

Josephine exits the stall quietly just as the Packard's engine fires up and wakes the dozing horses. She decides to wait inside until the policeman leaves and then go and talk with Mr. Raymee about her plan.

"Hello, Miss."

The unexpected voice from behind startles her. She turns around quickly and sees the stable boy standing next to her, wrapped in a soiled, hand-me-down coat too big for his slight build, and wearing fingerless gloves and a cap with flaps to cover his ears.

"Do you want me to saddle him up for you?"

"I…I am not sure. I am thinking I might, but I don't know," she stammers, realizing after she answers the boy that she isn't dressed to take the horse out for a ride. "I wanted to see how Sable was doing. He's not used to snow."

"He could use a ride, I think. Mr. Raymee's kept him kooked up since the weather turned nasty. All the snow only makes it worse."

"You don't like the snow?"

"Nah. Not me. What's there to like? It just makes a mess of things. Makes it hard to keep the horses clean in the stuff."

"I see. Then you've convinced me. I'll let Sable sit it out this morning."

"It's your choice, ma'am," he says with a nonchalant expression. "I'll be here either way."

"Do me a favor, will you? Let Mr. Raymee know that I came by to see Sable and that I may stop by later on to bring him a treat if that's all right. Can you do that for me?"

The boy nods and then runs off to chase a scruffy calico cat perched atop a nearby stack of bailed straw.

The snow continues unabated throughout the morning and by mid-day many of the roads throughout the area are treacherous to drive. The freight and passenger trains run through the Forest Glen station on time, unaffected by the accumulation, while the trolley lines operating out of Washington struggle to maintain schedule. Overcrowded with passengers seeking shelter from the storm, they plow along over covered streets, slowed by icy rails and poor visibility.

Bettina Braddock and Nellie Danaher board at the F Street stop and squeeze through the tightly-packed bodies bulging out both ends of the streetcar. Dragging ribbon-tied boxes behind them, the two girls press toward the center of the car, ducking under a gauntlet of raised arms until they find a small opening along the center aisle to secure themselves. As expected, every seat is taken. A somber-faced woman holding two squirming children to her chest scowls at them from a nearby row, the man next to her slumped over and slack-jawed, his cheek pressed against the fogged window glass. The conductor yanks down on the bell rope and the car lurches forward sending Nellie against the man next to her. He turns and smiles.

"Are you all right?" he asks.

She nods and continues to look up at the stranger until he feels slightly uncomfortable and returns to his conversation with the man standing beside him. The girls look at each other and share a conspiratorial moment. Bettina casually looks around the packed car and then back at the two men next to them. When she catches the stare of the other man facing her she reaches up and removes her hat and blows out a burst of air that sends her red pageboy curls off her forehead. She loosens the top button of her coat and pulls her lapels away from her neck with a look of exasperation over the stuffiness around her. And then, in a convincing display of feigned absent-mindedness, runs her hand slowly down her waist and along her hips to smooth out the non-existent wrinkles in her coat. Nellie giggles silently at her friend's painfully obvious theatrics.

The men lean closer to each other and begin whispering. When the streetcar reaches its next stop, a family wedged into the row next to the two men stands and forces their way through the compacted wall of humanity.

INCIDENT AT FOREST GLEN   363

The tall man with his back to Nellie follows them for a step or two and then stops. He makes no attempt to leave. By moving slightly to the center, he deftly blocks others on the car or who are about to board from moving to claim the vacated row of seats.

The second man quickly taps Nellie on the shoulder.

"Please, some seats have opened up for you and your friend. But I don't know for how long."

Bettina doesn't have to be offered twice. She picks her packages off the floor and pushes Nellie forward, her boxes swinging wildly and nearly clipping the woman and her two red-faced children. Nellie smiles as she passes the man's open arm directing her to the coveted bench. Behind them an agitated man jostles in the crowded aisle and voices his frustration.

"Step aside, Mack. Are you getting off or not? Make up your mind. You're blocking the way."

Nellie slides over to the window and places her purchases in a pile on her lap. Bettina steps forward and softly touches her right hand against the chest of the gallant man, their bodies separated by only a few inches.

"I'd prefer to stand," she whispers, "but you would be a doll if you could sit next to my friend and keep her company. Her name is Nellie. She's a wonderful conversationalist. I think the two of you will hit it off."

"Uh...are you sure?"

"It would be a tremendous help to me if you could hold these while you are keeping Nellie company."

Befuddled but agreeable, the man sits on the bench and takes the packages and hat box and with some difficulty organizes them on his lap, just as his friend returns from his completed mission.

"What are you doing?" the voice over Bettina's shoulder commands. "Let the young lady sit there. Have you no manners? I apologize, Miss—"

"Bettina," she says, craning her neck around to face the man, his body pressed against hers as the car restarts. "I am Bettina and this is Nellie."

"I offered her the seat," the seated man explains defensively.

"He did," she confirms.

"She insisted that I sit and talk with—uh—"

"Nellie, my name is Nellie."

"She insisted that I sit and talk with Nellie and hold her packages."

"I did. That's true," Bettina says with a hint of apology. "I made him do it. I should be held accountable for the breach in etiquette."

The man standing frowns down at his travelling companion, not persuaded.

Bettina turns fully and faces the man.

"But there is no excuse for your lack of manners. I've told you our names, but you haven't introduced yourselves to us."

"Robert Winslow. It's a pleasure to meet you, Bettina."

"Wait a moment. I do believe we have met somewhere before. Nellie, does this fine gentleman strike you as familiar?"

Nellie looks the man over unconcerned with propriety.

"He does look familiar. Aren't you Josephine Barnes' friend—the one going into the Navy?"

"The two of you are from Forest Glen? You're classmates of Josephine's?"

"She is," Nellie answers, "I'm just a freshman."

"You look much older," the man seated next to her comments in a surprised tone. "By the way, my name is Caleb," he adds, offering his hand to Nellie.

"That is it!" Bettina says in mock surprise. "You are the midshipman from Annapolis. You must be on your way to Forest Glen as well. But the dance isn't for a while yet, you know. You are going to be very, very early."

"It's Caleb's idea. He's worried that the streetcars will stop running and that we wouldn't be able to get to the ball on time."

Bettina wrinkles her brow and puts her index finger against her lower lip.

"And what happens when you get there early and the trolley lines shut down, you are sort of stuck, aren't you?"

"Yes," Robert says with a chuckle, "then we'd probably be hitching back into town. It would be a long night."

"A frightful proposition in these conditions." Bettina glances over at the two laughing together in a private joke on the bench. "So, your friend has a date for the Christmas Ball as well?"

Robert nods.

"I'm sure I know her. Who is she?"

When he tells her, she's pretends to be surprised at the revelation she had figured out long before she asked the question.

"Aren't you girls supposed to have a chaperone with you when you leave the school? That's what I was told."

Bettina smiles at his question.

"Let's just say that there are rules, and then there are rules. Some apply to all the girls. Others are—how should I put it— discretionary."

"You are not concerned about traveling around the city, the two of you alone?"

"Not in the least. A girl just needs to know where to go and where to avoid. It's no fun living in a doll house all the time."

Bettina glances over at the Nellie and Caleb and is taken aback at the level of familiarity and uncontrolled laughter between the two of them.

"Nellie, dear, what in the world has gotten into you? What is making you carry on like this?"

They look at each other, trying to suppress their contagious outburst of silliness.

Caleb looks up at Robert.

"Watch this, Robert. Watch this. You will enjoy this more than anyone. This is rich."

Caleb leans back against the bench so that the two standing can get an obstructed view of Nellie. She looks around, suddenly self-conscious, swallows a giggle and takes a deep breath. She surveys the trolley to make sure she is not being watched by anyone else in the cramped car.

Her motions are almost mechanical, like the gestures of a dead-eyed marionette. She slides her coat off her shoulders revealing the navy blue Seminary uniform and v-shaped kerchief. She turns the brim of her hat upward and pushes it back high on her forehead. She tilts her head slightly to the side and pulls her shoulders back as far as they can go, so that her chest juts out. And then she smiles—the sort of girl next door smile that makes men take notice.

When she speaks, her words are exaggerated and delivered in a slow, breathless, high-pitched voice.

"Gee!!

"I wish I were a man.

"I'd join the Navy."

Caleb bursts out laughing.

"Isn't that a spot-on impersonation?!" he asks, referring to the ubiquitous recruiting posters pasted around town since the war.

Nellie readjusts her hat and pulls back her coat. Relieved that the performance is over, she sinks back against the arm placed around her shoulders.

"Very good. Very good indeed," Robert concedes politely. "It's what convinced me to join the Navy," he says with a half-smirk.

Bettina smiles at the girl's audacity.

"Nellie, don't show off all of your tricks too soon. We have a ways to go before we reach Forest Glen."

"How about you?" Robert asks, as Caleb and Nellie once again start a separate conversation.

"I am afraid I have no tricks to offer you and your friend this afternoon," she answers, suddenly demure as she looks down at her feet.

"No, I meant about the school ball."

"What about it?"

"Are you going? Are the two of you going to the dance tonight?"

"We sort of have to. Our suites are in the ballroom above the dance floor. We couldn't escape it if we wanted to."

"You don't sound very enthusiastic. Don't you like to dance?"

"I love to dance. And I am told by others that I am quite good at it too."

"Is that what your boyfriend says?"

She gives him a long, hard look, as if she is either taken aback by his probing question or wondering why he took so long beating around the bush, or both.

"No boyfriend just now."

"I see." Robert's eyebrows arch, unsure where to take the conversation. "She's a shy one," he chuckles, motioning over to Nellie as she presses her palm against Caleb's in a contest to see whose fingers are longer.

"She's a sweet girl. So many of them are stuck up and prim to the point of having all the personality of a telephone pole."

"What do you mean by 'them'?"

"Rich girls," she answers matter-of-factly, purposely letting her words linger.

"I can't believe she's much of a rarity at a place like National Park."

"Well, there is well-to-do, and then there's rich."

"Oh, that's not a distinction I am familiar with."

"I think it's important to have fun and enjoy oneself. I hate it when girls come to the school and all they care about is pleasing their parents and their teachers and practically everyone else, everyone except for themselves. Slave to conventions, the way I see it."

" 'I went to the woods because I wanted to live deliberatively, I wanted to live deep and suck out all the marrow of life, To put to rout all that was not life and not when I had come to die Discover that I had not lived.'"

"Thoreau. My favorite. Not what I expect from a man who plans to make a career out of wearing a uniform and taking orders."

"One day I dream of more than that."

"Really? And what would that be, Mr. Robert Winslow?"

Bettina presses closer, looking beseechingly up at him, her lips parted and beguiling. He does not retreat or shy away and returns her challenge.

"Someday, I will be the one *giving* the orders."

Bettina smiles and searches his eyes.

"Very droll. Very droll, indeed. Josephine is a fortunate girl. You will make a gorgeous couple when you marry. Now, since no host likes an early arriving guest, let's think about what we are going to do with the two of you for next couple of hours."

After a hurried cup of tea, Josephine leaves the dining room and heads off to speak with Miss Price. She knows it is tradition for all the regents and senior administrators and their spouses to attend the Christmas gala but she wants to speak to her alone beforehand. By doing so she hopes to convince Miss Price of the sincerity of her story and raise enough concern that she will agree to bring the matter directly to the dean. Margaret is right. Leah's behavior has taken a dramatic turn for the worse and they can no longer wish the events of the past week away. After the torching of the boathouse, the crisis has reached a breaking point. She is sure that she will be punished, perhaps severely, for her role in covering up what took place, but her options are few, and she convinces herself that her story stands the best chance of protecting Margaret and Mr. Raymee from similar scrutiny and judgment.

She expects Leah will deny her claims, like Margaret said she did in the chapel, but the evidence of her emotional instability is overwhelming. Her ransacked room will be opened and searched. Madame Kaspar will be interviewed about Leah's outburst at chorus practice. Other students will come forward no doubt and tell stories about her peculiar behavior. It will be her word alone against those of everyone else. But will it even come to that, Josephine wonders? It won't be long once they start asking her questions before she starts acting erratically and talking about the morning of the flood, just as she had at the statue of Peeping Tom and then again the next day after Margaret and Josephine rescued her from the farm, dazed and unable to remember what had taken place.

Who will stand up for Leah after what happened to the boathouse? Josephine feels no animosity now, even after what she did to Sable. The girl needs help, more than she or anyone else at the Seminary can give her. Leah will certainly be expelled for what she's done. As Josephine rationalizes it, expulsion is the price of keeping her safe and protecting the other girls at the school. She is confident everyone will eventually see it that way. Surely Miss Price and the dean will view it as a mitigating factor of leniency in her own punishment.

But what about May? What will May say when she's asked, Josephine worries? She saw how Leah played off the insecure girl's weaknesses when she came by the room after the trip to the boathouse. Or was it the other way around? Had May exploited Leah's friendship at a moment of vulnerability? She hasn't spoken to May since that night. Or seen her, she realizes when she thinks about it. How odd is that? Our rooms are fifty feet apart and it's been days since I laid eyes on her. Why didn't I notice this before?

Miss Price told her there was a confrontation between May and Leah the day of the geisha party. She had forgotten about it after the nastiness that followed between her and the regent over Charles Carter. May clearly had been the one to go and see Miss Price about the altercation—what did she call it, *physical assault*—just as she beaten a bee-line to her the morning of the flood. Whatever happened between the girls must have been serious to send May running to Miss Price's office twice in one week. In any case, she can't imagine May siding with Leah now, not after what happened between the two of them.

Josephine hears her name called out as she passes by the sewing classroom and Jennie comes running out to the hallway wearing a manic expression and a pin cushion around her wrist.

"Josephine. Josephine. There you are! I've was hoping I might see you."

"Whoa, Jennie. What is it?"

"I need your help," the freshman explains breathlessly. "The dress I bought for tonight. The alterations weren't done right. I tried it on this after-

INCIDENT AT FOREST GLEN 369

noon and it was a mess. It's too late to take it back to the dress shop now. Not in this weather."

"Slow down. What wrong with it?"

"The hem and the neckline. And I can't sew a lick."

"I can't help you. I am on my way to see someone about a rather important matter right now. I can't help you fix it. I am sorry. If you saw the way I handled a needle and thread you would be glad."

"It's all right. I have some of the girls helping me out to pull it together. We're inside using the classroom machine to make the fixes. That's not the real important news."

Jennie can hardly contain herself, waiting for Josephine to ask before her enthusiasm boils over.

"What? What is it?"

"I received a telegram yesterday from my father. He said one of the actors under contract with the studio is in Washington on his way to New York. And he asked to come tonight, to be my escort to the ball!"

"That's wonderful, Jennie. What exciting news."

"His name is Marvin Morris. He's not a big star or anything. I've never actually seen him in a movie, but my father says he is an up and coming star, and very handsome."

"I am happy for you."

"You don't think the weather will be a problem for him getting here, do you?"

"The snow will just add to what I am sure will be a memorable night for you."

"But, you see, I am really nervous. I'm not sure how I am going to act when I meet him, you know, what to say."

"You'll do fine. I can't wait to meet him. Imagine, a movie star at our very own school. I do need to go though, Jennie. As I said, I must meet with someone."

As Josephine begins to walk on down the corridor, Jennie reaches her hand out into the space between them.

"Can you be there with me, just in the beginning? I know it's silly of me to ask, but I'm very nervous about tonight. Excited, but really scared."

Josephine sees genuine worry in the freshman's jittery expression, and smiles reassuringly.

"There is no reason to be concerned, Jennie. Once he looks at you, he'll be at your side the entire evening. I know it."

The frantic girl follows alongside Josephine, unconvinced, as she heads to the main stairs near the front of the building.

"I know I have no right to ask you this favor, but, please, just for a few minutes in the beginning. You know how to act around men and I don't. You and Robert can meet him before anyone else."

"Jennie, why not the other girls in your dormitory? How about one of those helping you repair your dress? They would jump at the treat."

"Because they are not you."

Josephine is touched by the desperate girl's plea and stops walking.

"Can we talk about this in a few minutes? I really need to be someplace now. What if I stop by the sewing room on the way back and we can talk about it more then?"

Jennie looks past Josephine and her look of consternation quickly changes to one of surprise.

"Oh my God, why didn't you tell me he was here? I had no idea. Why didn't you tell me you were going to see Robert?"

Josephine turns around sharply and spots a man with black hair and a dark suit down the hall in the front reception sitting uncomfortably on a velvet settee too low to the ground. His knees are up by his chest and his long arms dangle at his side over the edge of the upholstery. She does a double-take. Her first reaction mimics Jennie's: what is Robert doing here now, alone? The man looks up and, seeing that he has been spotted, waves at the two girls.

Josephine's inner thoughts take voice but her lips do not move.

"Wait, that can't be your Robert. That's Miss Price's friend from New York, the one who came with us to the hospital."

"So it seems."

"Why is he waiving to us?"

"I have no idea."

Jennie returns to the sewing room to check on the progress of the tailoring while Josephine approaches the seated man cautiously, not completely convinced that it wouldn't be wiser for her to turn around and head in the opposite direction. As she nears, he starts to stand, and with a discreet wave of her hand she communicates that it's best he keep his seat.

"You've rescued me from my personal purgatory," he jokes with an uneasy grin. "According to the rather strict woman seated at the desk over there, I am not allowed inside the building without written permission or an escort of some kind. She's been staring at me for the past hour secretly hoping that I will give up and go away."

"You've been waiting here for an hour?"

"About that."

"To see the headmaster?"

Mr. Carter shakes his head.

"Miss Price?"

"Nope."

She arches her eyes and frowns in annoyance, a silent signal that she is not interested in playing a guessing game. The time for her to find the regent is dwindling.

"I came here hoping that you might walk by at some point. I sent a note to your room but they said you weren't there. I thought my chances were good, given what's going on outside. So I plopped myself down on this ridiculous piece of furniture and decided to wait."

"I am on my way to a meeting. I don't have time to talk, Mr. Carter."

"I am Charles, and I would really like it if you called me by my name. Perhaps we can step outside on the front porch or over there in the parlor and talk more privately, so we won't be under the withering study of ol' eagle eye at the reception desk. She's really starting to get on my nerves."

"Being seen around with you can get a girl in trouble. I think we should stay as we are. You seated there and me standing here."

Mr. Carter shrugs his acceptance, trying his best to not be distracted by the steady flow of inquisitive students through the reception area.

"I will be leaving tomorrow on a train back to New York city. I realize that the details of my departure may not be of keen interest to you, but I wanted to let you know anyway. No, that's not what I mean," he stops, suddenly flustered. "Let me try again. I came to say goodbye to you."

"Mr. Carter, we hardly know each other. I don't see why you would feel it necessary to come here and waste your remaining time on the off-chance of meeting me."

"I don't consider it a waste of my time. I actually enjoyed sitting here and watching the activity of this place, even with my every scratch and sigh being scrutinized by the school watchdog. I had no idea I had such a menacing look about me."

He summons a forced smile in an attempt to elicit a reaction.

"Your timing is not good. The administration is preparing itself for a wave of guests like you arriving in a few hours. Tonight is the Christmas Ball. And they are extremely strict about visitors signing in and being escorted."

"I see. I thought there might be something like that going on. It seems to be the talk on every girl's lips."

The conversation stalls and Mr. Carter looks around the reception room nervously.

"I should be leaving, Mr. Carter. I apologize but I am expected elsewhere," she lies to the suddenly deflated man.

"The fondest memory of my trip to Forest Glen is our conversation the other day at the hospital. I know that might sound odd to you, and perhaps a bit forward. But you possess a certain quality I have never come across before. There is an aspect to your nature that is very attractive, and to be honest, a bit intimidating. And, in the interest of laying out my cards all at once, I've thought about that brief exchange ever since."

He pauses, aware of the increasing number of curious stares from the girls passing behind Josephine.

"Why do they all look at me like I am here to kidnap you?"

"As much as you flatter me, there is someone who would not be pleased by your presence here. She has already made her views on the subject known to me. And it wasn't pleasant."

No clarification is necessary and Mr. Carter stands up, tired of looking up at the girl from the distressing seat.

"There is nothing to that."

"She seems to feel there is."

"Not on my part."

"Then you aren't the one who is caught in-between."

"She has no sway over me, and shortly she will have none over you."

"You make everything seem so neat and tidy. Clean and simple. That's not the world I live in, Mr. Carter."

"I suppose you are right. I don't know the first thing about you or the world you live in. Everything about this place is unreal and foreign to me. This school is unlike anything I have every seen before—like a page ripped out of some fairy tale book. I know a hefty price is paid to go here, but if I was a student, I think I would go mad. It's like being inside a bubble and outside is the real world. You are fed on expensive china and silver. Maids clean up after you and servants fetch whatever you want. Every need and whim is catered to. It is a house of privileged."

"The Seminary educates women and gives them opportunities they would not otherwise have. It is not fair of you to characterize it as *a house of privilege!*" Josephine protests fervently.

"Opportunities they are born to or opportunities they earn? I was reading through the recruitment book Dean Dawson gave us the other day and I hadn't realized the school has done away with examinations as a prerequisite for graduation. There was this high-minded, progressive explanation in the book about how by avoiding cruel tests of knowledge students will be protected from—what was the phrase—*'disastrous and permanent damage to health.'*"

"You are in no position to pass judgment on this school or how it is run."

Mr. Carter can see the obvious anger in her expression and backs off, unsure why he allowed himself to go on such a rant.

"I have been presumptuous, Miss Barnes. I apologize. Perhaps in time you can see that I meant no harm. My words were poorly chosen."

As he puts on his coat, he is surprised to see her still standing before him, expecting that she would storm off by now. He notices the portly matron behind the reception desk stand up and walk out from behind the counter, watching him carefully as she proceeds. He is on borrowed time.

"I would like to write you when I return to New York. I think I would be better served to write out my thoughts and give it some care. There is an important matter I need to explain to you. May I?"

She listens, shaken by the heated exchange, and nods, looking away as she does, unable to return to businessman's admiring stare.

"There is one other matter before I leave. The official purpose for my visit."

"I don't understand."

"Well, I don't understand either."

Mr. Carter pulls a small rectangular box bearing a card from his coat pocket and extends his arm to Josephine.

"My employer wants to give this to you."

"What...I don't...Who is your employer?"

"He is the older man I was with the other night when...when I saw you the first time. In the ballroom, you were dancing with that other girl, the one you were with by the bridge. What am I saying? We didn't meet until the next morning. You had no reason to notice us there."

"I'm sorry. You have me confused."

"Anyway, I accompanied him to Forest Glen. He returned to Manhattan yesterday and he left this behind with instructions to give it to you before I go."

"Now I am completely confused. Why would a man I never met leave me a package?"

"I wish I knew. But there seems to be a lot being kept from me these days."

"Are you sure this is meant for me?"

"Unless there is another Josephine Barnes here, then it's for you."

The stern voice of the matron interrupts.

"Miss Barnes, will you be signing in the gentleman?"

"No," the defeated man answers for her. "I am leaving and going back to the hotel. Maybe I'll take one last look around the campus before it gets dark. Go ahead and take it," he says, pushing the box closer.

Josephine takes the unexpected gift without a word.

"Goodbye, Miss Barnes, and merry Christmas."

Mr. Carter turns toward the receptionist.

"And thank you, ma'am, for spending the afternoon with me."

Josephine toys with the box in her hands and watches him leave.

Outside, the troubled man surveys the conditions from the expansive veranda stretching the full length of Vincent Hall. Mounds of wind-blown snow have accumulated on the seat cushions of the wicker chairs and crept close to the entrance. He looks out at the journey ahead of him and can barely make out Glen Manor in the distance through the falling snow.

He pulls out a cigarette from his breast pocket and walks over to the wall to shield the match he is about to strike. A boisterous group of two women and a man emerge out of the storm and run past the ornamental fountain in the roundabout. They rush up the stairs and bend over to catch their breath, a considerable amount of snow clinging to the front of their coats. A fourth person, a man wearing a round, military-styled hat, follows close behind. Having found sanctuary from the storm, they laugh heartily at each other's wet, cold, and battered appearance, ignoring Mr. Carter's presence. The two men shake out their coats on the porch while the women use their gloves to brush off one another.

The sound of Mr. Carter striking the match catches the attention of the slighter of the two girls. She smiles, the same mischievous, upturned curl he had seen on the ballroom balcony, a glimmer of recognition in her eyes.

"Hello, Suit. Remember me?"

"How could I forget, Dress," he responds coolly, tossing the match over the front railing before plunging headlong into the teeth of the blizzard.

Leah sits in the middle of the floor laboring away. Her fingers pinch the narrow cold sliver of steel and work furiously in the dark to complete her task. The window shades are closed and the chill in her room pains the joints in her hands and deadens the feeling in the tips of her sewing hand. In her rush to finish, she pricks her thumb and places the purplish swell immediately into her mouth. The distinctive warm taste lingers on her tongue and she savors the miniscule drop, the only sustenance to pass her lips the entire day. She listens as the chapel bell rings a sixth time and then resumes her work at an even quicker pace, hunched like a cloistered monk laboring over the creation of the king's coronation robe. Once the pieces are assembled, and the thread is knotted and clipped, she unfurls the completed work on the floor and admires her creation.

Chapter 11
Justice, the Colossus

For the protection of our patrons, who have a right to expect that we take every precaution to safeguard the companionships of their daughters, we request intending patrons who are unknown to us to forward letters of introduction from their ministers and their daughters' last teachers. Our school is in no sense intended for "difficult cases." We shall promptly return to her home any girl who is, in our judgment, helplessly out of harmony with her surroundings, or whose continued residence with us would, in our opinion, work harm to herself and others. Too much care cannot be exercised in the companionship of young girls away from home. The intimate daily contact of boarding-school life is a powerful weapon for good, if members of the school are safe companions, not otherwise. Nothing so fixes the status of the individual throughout life as the friendships made at school. We endeavor to promote friendships that are lasting, true, valuable and salutary. Often girls of equally good parentage and training do not exert the best influence over each other. Such untoward friendships will be carefully watched, and the co-operation of parents will be solicited to assist in controlling the intimacy.

Robert and Caleb are parked in the Blue Bird room adjacent to the dining room under the watchful eye of a middle-aged man wearing a white serving jacket and boat cap who offers them a choice of chocolate malts, ice cream sodas, fountain sodas and other confectionary delights while they wait. They sidle up to the stools and take a seat at the granite counter. Caleb orders a white cow, which draws a nasty, disapproving look from his friend.

"What? I like 'em. Ever since I was a kid."

Robert orders a coffee and the server excuses himself to go see if a pot has been made in the kitchen.

"Your girl doesn't seem happy we showed up when we did."

"I didn't expect we'd surprise her like that. I assumed she be in her room and not standing right inside the door when we walked in."

"Her look was priceless though. You have to admit. I wasn't sure if she was going take your head off or start crying when we popped through the door."

"If you think that's why she's upset, you're thick-headed. Seeing you walk practically arm in arm with her classmate is what set her off."

"Not a classmate, remember. Nellie's younger," he corrects Robert with a smirk.

"Yes, quite a bit younger, wouldn't you say? You're a piece of work, Caleb. How do you think it looks, for the both us, but especially you? She thinks her friend has got a date with a cad."

"We didn't do anything wrong. We shared a trolley ride with the girls. It was all innocent. It's not like we set it up that way."

The waiter returns with Robert's coffee and starts to make Caleb's milkshake.

"Look at us, cooling our heels in the Blue Bird ice cream shop. I didn't borrow a tuxedo and come all this way to suck on soda straws."

The man behind the counter shoots a glance back at Caleb as he scoops vanilla ice cream into a large metal mixing cup.

"It was your idea to come early, so don't complain."

"And it was your idea that I double with Josephine's friend. I am here as a favor and to have a good time, so show a little gratitude."

"Margaret Cleary is a lovely girl. Very pretty."

"Until she fillets you with her tongue."

"You're too particular. The truth is she's out of your league."

"Really! That's what you think? She's out of my league?"

Robert sips from his cup and sucks back the bitter coffee with a grimace.

"I do. She's too spirited. You don't know how to act around women who actually have their own point of view and aren't afraid to express themselves."

"You're nuts."

"Then why are you bad-mouthing your date even before the night's started? She's too pretty for you and she's too strong-willed. Admit it; she's out of your league. You should be thankful to have the chance at a girl as classy as Margaret. But all you do is gripe about having to drink shakes."

The crisply-dressed soda jerk slides over a parfait glass with the white cow.

"Thanks, pal. Could I bother you for another straw?"

Robert shakes his head at his friend's lack of tact.

"And, in the spirit of being completely honest with you since we are such close friends, she's also too tall for you. You don't do well with the tall ones."

The second straw is tossed into his glass and Caleb draws down the drink hungrily, shaking his hand as he sucks on the twin tubes of striped paper.

"Hahum. Hahum," he grunts during the prolonged taste. When he finally comes up for air, the frothy white treat is half gone.

"I think you are onto something. I don't do well with tall women, do I?"

He wipes the trace of milk shake from his lips.

"I hadn't thought of it, but you might be right. There was that girl from Trenton I took to an embassy reception last month. Once we got there, she treated me like I was her brother. And when I walked her to her apartment building afterward, you know what she did—am I not pulling your leg—do you know what she did?"

"What?"

"Standing on the stoop of her apartment building, no one around, after dinner *and* an embassy reception?"

"Get to the point. Tell me already."

Caleb swings around on his stool and faces Robert.

"I turn to her just like this. And there is a moment of silence. I'm looking at her and she's looking at me. I am just about to lean over and kiss her and then it happens."

"What happens?" Robert says with exasperation.

"She reaches over and pats me on the top of the head. I am dead serious. She pats me on the head just this."

Caleb recreates the offense for effect before Robert pushes his hand away from his slicked-back hair.

"That's embarrassing. Maybe it's your boyish charm."

"Yea, maybe too much of the boyish part. I was expecting her to put a nickel in my hand and send me off to the Bijou."

Caleb catches the attention of the man behind the counter and motions to the nearly empty, streaked glass in front of him.

"You'll have a chance to redeem yourself tonight, if you give Margaret a chance and don't get offended over the smallest thing like last time you were around her."

"I will admit, she is the prettiest *mean* girl I've met."

"Just don't mess it up for me. This is last time I get to see Jo before she travels home for Christmas."

Caleb slaps him on the shoulder.

"After she saw you with the redhead, I don't think I am the one you should be telling to not mess up."

Another man enters the Blue Bird, young and in formal attire, he looks over the cheerful sky blue and yellow décor with bewilderment, before taking a seat at a table by the door.

"It looks like we aren't the only miserable souls stranded on this island," Caleb remarks, before turning back around. "Make that two white cows!" he calls down the counter. "Set up our new friend too."

Josephine begins to worry as she walks down the third floor of Senior House, avoiding the line to the bathroom as she passes. There is no sign of Margaret and her door is closed. She knocks gently, just loud enough for Margaret to hear but not generate suspicions from the other girls walking about. She knocks again, but there is no response from inside. She looks down the far end of the hallway and sees that it is quiet and dark next to Leah's and May's rooms, just as Margaret described it being last night. She turns the door knob and finds that it is locked. Pressing her mouth to the door, Josephine calls out to Margaret, urging that she let her in. A few moments pass and she presses her ear closer. A click of the lock and the door slowly opens.

Light pours through the narrow opening into the black room and Josephine watches the back of Margaret's night gown disappear into the center of the room.

Josephine steps in, but only partially shuts the door behind her so that she can see where she is walking.

"Have you been sleeping the whole time?" she asks with concern. "Margaret?"

"Mostly."

The voice is raspy and does not sound like Margaret's.

"Then I was up for a while and couldn't get back to sleep. But I must have fallen asleep again. How long were you at the door?"

"Just a few moments."

"Are you going to close the door?" she asks sharply, the misery of her condition evident.

Josephine shuts the door and they are immersed in darkness. She can barely make out the outline of the night gown as her friend walks across the room. The ghostly form leans over and Josephine hears the snap just before the floor lamp in the corner of the room illuminates.

Margaret squints, shielding her face with her hand and staggers over to the bed. She falls back onto the mattress and turns on her side facing the wall.

"What time is it?" she mumbles half-heartedly, still feeling the effects of being woken out of a deep sleep.

"It's past six. We should be getting ready for the dance."

"We have time before the guys get here."

Her voice trails off and Josephine worries she is slipping away.

"News flash. They're here already, and have been for some time."

"Ughh. Why are men incapable of following the simplest instructions?"

"And you won't believe who they just happened to showed up with."

"You can fill me in later. Tell me what Price said when you went to see her. Did she lose it?"

"I got sidetracked on my way to her office. It's a long story. Then Robert showed up. By the time I got to her office, she was gone. I asked around, but no one was sure where she went."

"Great," Margaret sighs weakly. "What are we going to do about the madwoman now?"

"I'll talk to Miss Price as soon as I get the opportunity, like we agreed, even if it means talking to her at the dance."

Margaret closes her eyes.

"Are you okay?"

"I will be in a few minutes. There is a water pitcher on the table and a brown bottle next to it. Pour me a glass of water and bring it to me with the pills."

Josephine picks up the small bottle and looks it over. There is no label.

"Is this what the nurse gave you?"

"Yep."

By the time she approaches, Margaret is sitting up, her legs over the side of the bed. Her eyes are half-shut and her hair is hanging over the side of her face, uncombed and matted with moisture.

As she leans over with the water and pills, Josephine is horrified at what she sees—the fabric of Margaret's beige nightgown from her neck to her belly is soaked with sweat and nearly transparent in the light of the floor lamp. Beads of perspiration cover her glistening throat and dot her upper lip and forehead.

"Margaret, oh my God…look what the fever has done to you!"

"Are you sure one of the girls didn't sneak in and toss water on me as a joke while I was sleeping," she deadpans, looking down as she slowly peels the thin, cool cotton off her breasts.

"This is worse than I thought. We have to get someone to call a doctor. I'll go get some cold compresses."

"Slow down, slow down. The fever broke while I was sleeping. I actually feel a lot better than I have for a while. I think the worst is behind me. I won't be eating anything at the dance, but I will survive."

She takes the glass of water and drinks it down and hands it back.

"Would you mind?" she asks, gesturing over to the pitcher.

Margaret takes two of the pills and finishes off the pitcher, one glass after another.

"Stay here and rest," Josephine implores.

"That would suit you wouldn't it, two men to yourself?"

"I insist. You are not well."

"I told you, the fever has broken. I'm just a little weak. And I have no intention sitting here while the rest of the school is over at the ball."

Margaret stands up from the bed, smells her night gown, and makes an exaggerated face of disgust.

"I am going to need more time than usual, so you better tell the boys to kick back and relax."

Mr. Geary is waiting in the parlor of the Glen Manor Hotel when Mr. Carter arrives tousled and red-faced from the intrepid walk across the glen. The hotel clerk, initially taken aback at his guest's disheveled appearance, points to the waiting room as the young man stomps his shoes on the welcome mat. After the previous night's fiasco, the clerk is prepared this time—a fire has been lit and well-tended throughout the bleak and wintry day. A second visitor to Glen Manor in less that a day has the clerk on his toes and he bounces from side to side in nervous energy, as if his modest reception counter has become the eye of the storm raging outside the building's Tudor façade. The increase of bookings is not expected until next week with parents arriving at Forest Glen to retrieve their daughters, but the early flurry of visitors is welcome and breaks up the otherwise monotonous stretches of his daily shift.

The bursar rises from his chair next to the fireplace and greets Mr. Carter with a curt look and a firm handshake.

"If you are here to see Mr. Stratton, Mr. Geary, he left yesterday for New York. I thought you knew that."

"Of course. No, I came to see you, Mr. Carter. I took the chance you might be available. So I rode the trolley to see you. I was told you went to National Park and instead of trying to track you down I thought I would wait here for you to return. Please, can you spend a minute or two?"

Mr. Geary gestures to the arm chair beside his. Mr. Carter removes his coat, hangs it on a metal hook in the fireplace masonry, and sits down trying to divine the reason for the stodgy bursar's visit.

"I left Glen Manor a couple of hours ago, Mr. Geary. How long have you been waiting here for me to come back?"

"Quite awhile, to be honest," he answers with a look of disbelief as he glances at his watch and thinks back to when he arrived. "But not here the entire time. I stretched my legs and walked over to the station and then to the Darby General Store down the road. Have you been there? They have everything you need, very well-stocked, and an impressive display of penny candy jars in case you have a sweet tooth."

"No, I haven't. I will have to walk down there before I leave tomorrow—if I have the opportunity."

Mr. Carter pauses, expecting the man to explain his unexpected call and prolonged wait. But the bursar only looks upon him with a stern expression.

"Mr. Geary, you could not have picked a worse night to leave your home on a hunch. Are you headed to the school for the ball? If you are, I'd advise you based on my own experience to find a ride there."

"No. Let youth be served. Look at me, Mr. Carter. I have no business being there."

"It's not always about business, is it?"

The clerk enters the parlor to see if the two men are in need of coffee or tea and is shooed away brusquely by the school bursar.

"So, what is it then?" Mr. Carter asks pointedly, his bluntness welcome by the older man.

"Our arrangement."

"How do you mean *'our arrangement'*?"

"I see. That is how it is going to be."

Mr. Geary's face twists into that of a disapproving parent mocking the predictable stalling ploys of a child in the process of being chastised.

"I had an arrangement with your employer involving preparations leading up to the purchase of National Park Seminary. These preparations were instrumental, you would objectively acknowledge, in producing the desired result. Our arrangement, as it were, promises to yield considerable benefits to your employer, and, in fairness, is advantageous to me and others. I assume you are privy to this mutually-beneficial relationship."

Mr. Carter nods, not wanting to admit to his own ignorance or to interrupt the now loquacious man.

"Our relationship was predicated on a certain understanding of facts, an explicit and implicit agreement, wherein both of us were fully apprised of the other's desired outcome."

"And, am I to assume you don't feel that this arrangement has been carried out to the letter?"

"I do not."

"And what is the basis for your dissatisfaction? The purchase offer was accepted by the Board of Trustees and you have been appointed to head the execution of the deal. Your stock has risen and risen dramatically."

"But during the establishment of our arrangement, a key fact was not disclosed on your end. Had this fact been properly disclosed so that both parties had full knowledge of what was at stake, I feel the particulars of the deal would have been negotiated differently."

"What '*key fact*' are you claiming was kept from you, if I accurately understand your grievance?"

"The Highland Trust."

"What about the Highland Trust, Mr. Geary?"

"Its very existence. Its disguised purpose. Its activity over the past few months in achieving an outcome wholly different than the one I believed I was a party to. Do I need to go on? Am I making myself clear?"

"Regrettably, you are not. For a man trained in the handling of facts and figures and accustomed for drawing clear distinctions between what is black and what is white, you seem to labor when the need arises to speak concisely. You have sought me out at the most inopportune time imaginable, travelling here in the middle of a snowstorm, and yet you insist on tap dancing around what it is that brought you here. I suggest you come to the point."

Mr. Carter needs to flush out what the bursar knows without admitting the limit of his own understanding. His purposely provocative insult has the desired effect. Mr. Geary squirms in his armchair as color comes rushing to his pallid skin, and Mr. Carter awaits the outburst he sees building inside the man seated across from him. Mr. Geary, however, allows the tempest to pass and leans in, his voice now controlled and his tone soft.

"I don't like the type of person who comes here and thinks he can play people for fools just because he is rich and powerful, the sort of man who sells them a bill of goods and then leaves laughing all the way to the bank."

"Again, you are being evasive, Mr. Geary. Speak bluntly if you must, but enough of the evasiveness."

"Fine, Mr. Carter. If I must. Stratton Enterprises is looking to build houses on the Seminary property and on many of the parcels adjacent to it. You've been using an incorporated entity that goes by the name of the Highland Trust to purchase these properties. I have strong reason to believe this trust is under the sole direction of your employer. Contrary to what I was led to understand, Mr. Stratton intends to turn the school into a large tract of residences he can sell at a substantial profit. Am I the one still being evasive?"

"Who made this claim? Has someone told you specifically that Mr. Stratton plans to do what you say?"

"Do not play games with me, young man. I will not accept it from the likes of you. What I have discovered I found out on my own and despite the careful efforts of Stratton to cover his tracks."

"I am still confused. If you had these concerns, Mr. Geary, why didn't you raise them with Mr. Stratton when he was here? Why wait until now? You and I have never spoken about this matter before—am I correct?—and yet you come to me as if you expect me to address allegations I have no first-hand knowledge of and the validity of which I am in no position to either confirm or deny."

"I do not believe that for one minute. But to answer your question, I only became aware of your employer's true intentions after he left here. No one disclosed them to me. I was told of the trust's existence and followed my nose."

"And you come to me in anger over this perceived deception?"

"I came to be properly compensated!"

The table between the two men shakes as the bursar's words carry down the parlor hallway.

"As I said before, Mr. Geary, your grievance should be directed toward the person with whom you had an arrangement. I will certainly carry forward the message to Mr. Stratton, however, and faithfully report it. But I need you to understand that by doing so I am not lending credence to anything you have claimed here tonight. I am acting only as a messenger. If Mr. Stratton wishes to engage you further on the topic, it is his decision alone to make."

"How do live with yourself, Mr. Carter, with your slick ways and law-yerly talk? You know exactly what is going on here, but you pretend to fly above the slop, not wanting to sully yourself with the mess you had a hand in making."

Mr. Carter takes a moment to consider the bitter salvo launched at him.

"I am sorry that your view of me is so low. As a favor and not out of obligation, I want you to know that Dean Dawson came to see me last night. Had our meeting not been interrupted by the most unfortunate fire, I suppose he would have sat in the same chair you sit in now. And I strongly suspect the reason for his unexpected visit was related to sale of the school. I would have sat and listened to him as I have listened to you tonight. Uneasy questions would have been asked in an attempt by the dean to find out why he was all of the sudden pushed to the side by the board. There would have been claims of unfairness and perhaps even accusations about the way the sale was handled. And as I heard him out, I would have had a hard time not thinking of your name—the dean's very own Judas—and imagine how he would handle the revelation that it was you who sold him out. All for a bag of coins that you now complain you were tricked into accepting."

"Damn you, Mr. Carter. Damn you to hell!"

The bursar's angry departure leaves Mr. Carter alone in the parlor contemplating the warming flames before him, his pulse racing. He has accomplished what he intended and forced the disclosure of details that he was not otherwise privy to about Douglas Stratton's plan for carving up the prized property.

Highland Trust. Surrounding parcels.

The new details, though enlightening, make him feel faintly ill and hollow inside. The enormity of his employer's ruse only grows. He stares unblinkingly at the orange glow inside the stacked wood and is drawn into the simple beauty of how the heat slowly devours the split logs. Fire, the unrepentant destroyer of things, enticing as it is dangerous.

Josephine closes her door and walks toward Margaret's room, dressed and late for the dance. Surprised by Robert's unexpected arrival and anxious to check on Margaret's condition, she completely forgot the wrapped box given to her by Mr. Carter until she began undressing in her room. She fished the gift out of the bunched-up uniform at her feet and was tempted to open it then, but thought twice of it. Am I prepared now to deal with what was inside, she thought looking over the box, given everything else going on? Glancing quickly at the clock, she hid it in the back of the top dresser drawer instead, deciding that it was best to unwrap it later. After the dance. Alone.

The third floor hallway is quiet and abandoned. The rest of the girls have gone to the ballroom and she is not worried about being heard like before when she knocks on Margaret's door.

"Let's go, we are nearly thirty minutes late," she calls out. "Margaret, are you ready?"

"Go on ahead. I need ten more minutes," the voice answers. "I'll meet you there."

Just as Josephine is about to protest, a latch unlocks down the hall and May steps out of her room and slowly closes the door behind her. She looks up and sees Josephine standing outside Margaret's door.

"Hello, May."

388 ANDY JOHNSON

"Hi," she answers meekly and begins walking toward the stairs. She is wearing a soft pink cotton dress, generously cut along the waist and hips, and a white cashmere sweater.

"You look nice," Josephine remarks as the diffident girl passes by, her eyes locked on the rug in front of her feet.

May's reply is mumbled and unintelligible. Josephine hopes she will stop so they can at least exchange more than distant greetings but she continues walking. Even with no one else around, May does not want to spend any more time than is absolutely necessary in Josephine's gravitational pull, not while she is dressed like this.

A few minutes before seven o'clock, the doors to the ballroom open and early arrivals like Robert and Caleb are sprung from their temporary confinement. A sea of elegant dresses and impeccably tailored suits teems outside the ballroom doors waiting to get inside as names are checked against an approved list. Those girls without dates for the evening hover in groups like ants linked together in water to stay afloat while the men, far outnumbered, break away from conversations with their dates now and again, scan the room crowded with fashionably dressed women, and entertain fantasies of what it would be like to live permanently in a world of such disproportionate representation.

Inside the cavernous hall, the twelve-person band strikes up and the melody of the opening tune, distant and haunting, carries through the entryway further exciting the assembled partygoers. The ballroom's interior has been transformed into a luxurious playground for the evening. Rows of silver and gold streamers are suspended from one side to the other creating a patchwork of light and shadow on the dance floor. At the front is the elevated bandstand draped with bunting used in the previous spring's graduation ceremony. At the opposite end of the floor, serving tables are arranged in a large u-shape and covered with trays of finger sandwiches, hot hors d'oeuvres, confectionary treats, and two large silver punch bowls. Large circular tables are positioned around the ambulatory and covered with shimmering red linen, each anchored with an intricate wax centerpiece carved in the shape of a swan and ringed with holly and painted pine cones. Oversized, three-dimensional paper snowflakes hang from the second floor balcony railings and the massive wooden wheel suspended over the center of the ballroom.

Caleb stands on the lip of the dance floor, noshing on a plate of food, and watches the first couples dance under the gently swaying roof of crepe paper. Behind him, Robert sits at a table alone, unconsciously chewing on his thumb nail as he waits for Josephine and Margaret to arrive.

A lissome, diminutive figure in a sleeveless, iridescent beaded gown steps up behind the occupied spectator and gently rubs her body up against Caleb's arm to get his attention. The music is loud and though she struggles to understand what he says, she can tell by his animated expression and the way he looks over the form-fitting cut of the sheer dress that he is pleased to see her. She takes the half-eaten plate of food out of Caleb's hand and places it on a nearby table, and then brazenly slips her arm into his and leads him confidently out on the dance floor, where they disappear into the crowd.

Robert has no opportunity to notice his friend's absence. Within seconds of Nellie's appearance, Bettina settles into the chair next to him and smiles broadly when he turns around.

"You were right," she says, nearly shouting to be heard above the music. Still seated, he turns his chair to face her.

"How's that?"

"On the streetcar this afternoon. You told me I wasn't enthusiastic about tonight. And the more I thought about it, you were right. I needed to dress up and have some fun. So, here I am, ready to dance. What do you think about the dress?"

"Very nice."

"Wait, wait, wait," she says impatiently, tamping her hand on his arm in cadence with her words. "You haven't seen the best part."

Bettina stands before him in mock display, her arms bent at the elbow, palms turned upward in a silent gesture of *'what do you think.'* The silver metallic, crocheted dress glints and reflects like the crystals of a glacial cave. The light, fractured and bent, creates a faint pale aura that highlights the underside of her chin and the tips of the lustrous red curls tucked behind her ears.

Robert nods and pretends to applaud with approval. Not done, she extends her arm and holds out her index finger inches away from his straight, Romanesque nose, and broad forehead. She pirouettes slowly and displays the cowl back to the dress running off her shoulder and dipping down to her waist. She pauses mid-turn and Robert is presented with the toned and sculpted length of bare flesh. The narrow conduit of muscle running the length of her spine is dappled with carmine freckles and disappears under a shimmering curve of fabric at Robert's eye level.

Bettina completes her turn and expects an appreciative response. When Robert instead turns away, she realizes she has been too forward. She sits back down and waits for him to make the next move, forced to play the role she least likes, that of the passive girl.

By the time Josephine arrives, the backup getting into the ballroom is gone and she enters into a hall vibrant with rich, multilayered noises and frenetic movement. Just inside the arched entryway, Jennie leans against the papered wall, looking extremely unsteady in her high-heeled shoes. The anxious look she wears tells Josephine all she needs to know.

"No sign of our celebrity guest."

A hint of relief softens Jennie's face when she turns to find Josephine next to her.

"No. And I told everyone he'd be here too. I'll never live this down if he doesn't show."

"He will. I know it. Your father wouldn't have sent you the telegram if it wasn't going to happen."

"But look at it outside. It's only getting worse. If he's not here now, what chance..." she trails off letting the music swallow up her worry.

Josephine rubs her friend's arm reassuringly.

"This is your first winter formal. You need to enjoy it. You're too pretty to be a wallflower. Let's go dance. And when we are out there, we can rate the talent pool on the floor. The guys won't have a clue we're talking about them. All right?"

Jennie puts up only token resistance as she is led across the ambulatory to the growing mass of jostling couples.

At the front of the ballroom, Dean Dawson slides the chair in for his wife as she takes her seat at the headmaster's table near the bandstand. He surveys the magnificence of the ballroom, pleased with the elegance of the interior decorations. He's pleasantly surprised by the turnout of the guests. Earlier in the afternoon, he stood at his living room window watching the snow fall steadily. The thought of canceling the event crossed his mind but was quickly dismissed. Students and staff alike had worked tirelessly in preparing for the ball. Allowing the inclement weather to spoil the capstone social event of the semester would be a disheartening calamity and only further his slide into despondency.

As is tradition at the Christmas ball, students bring their escorts to the headmaster's table throughout the evening to be formally introduced to the dean and his wife. Most of the greetings are perfunctory—an exchange of names, a handshake, season's wishes. Occasionally, a couple will remain at the table for an extended conversation, usually related to the young man's field of study or profession or hometown.

The Dawsons pride themselves on being gracious hosts and are not the sort of figureheads who make a brief appearance at school socials and then retire for the evening. They want to share in the experiences of the girls they are entrusted to educate and nurture and protect. In doing so, they seek only the small reciprocal demonstrations from their charges that validate the familial bond between teacher and student they strive to create. In his role as father figure to girls who are often living away from home for the first time, the dean wants to be viewed as both benevolent and strict, personable enough that students are comfortable in approaching him, but also viewed as the unquestioned paragon of authority.

Bettina looks about the ambulatory for a sign of Josephine, curious about her absence but not wanting to invoke her name to Robert. She spots Nellie and Caleb dancing near the bandstand and leans over to the sullen-looking man seated next to her.

"It seems your friend is enjoying himself. How about we go join them? It sure beats just sitting here. What do you say?"

"I'm not sure."

"I know what's wrong. I bet you aren't use to having a girl ask you to dance. It's a habit you pick up going to an all-girl school. If it makes you feel better, you ask me to dance."

The song ends before Robert, conflicted and indecisive, can muster a reply, but Bettina can tell by the shiftiness in his eyes that she is best served to not press the point further. A different tact is in order, she decides.

"On second thought," she says without a hint of disappointment or pique over being turned down, "I see some of my friends over by the punch bowl."

As she swings around in her seat, she rests her hand along the sharp crease of Robert's pants leg, feeling the broad width of his muscular thigh.

"Enjoy the dance, if I don't see you again," she half-whispers into his ear before walking slowly over to the crowd ringing the refreshments table. Just as she expects, he watches her leave and wonders whether he was rude to not accept her offer.

By the time Josephine locates their table off the floor, Caleb has rejoined Robert, sweating and red-faced from an uninterrupted stretch of vigorous dancing. The stocky congressional aide is the first to catch a glimpse of her and nudges Robert sharply with his elbow. When the midshipman looks up, he grins and immediately stands out of courtesy.

He's never seen her in an evening dress before and he looks upon her with unabashed delight as she weaves her way through the crowd, a striking figure in a black silk dress trimmed with gold lamé and delicate beadwork. Her lips are a deep red and her hair is parted on the side and unusually blanched, its natural, rich yellowish hue bleached out by the room's lighting. Except for a pair of diamond pendent earrings, she wears no jewelry, the flesh above the scoop neck naked and uncluttered. A pair of t-strapped heels and white stockings adds to the overall appearance of contrast, of the intoxicating interplay between white and black, light and dark, innocence and desire. Her transformed physical appearance is a revelation to Robert. She embodies an air of stylish simplicity that stands apart from the more elaborate and showy dresses around her. She moves across the floor, a woman among girls. Her bare arms, long and sculpted, brush gently against the swaying fabric along her hips as she reaches the table and hugs Robert.

"I thought I'd been stood up. You look absolutely gorgeous."

"Hopefully worth the wait."

He holds her hand loosely in his and the warmth of her smooth skin sends an electric spark along the length of his arm to the base of his brain.

"Ten times over."

He suddenly feels self-conscious speaking intimately in front of Caleb and helps her with her chair.

"Where's Margaret?" he asks, nodding toward his friend.

"Fear not, Caleb, she was born late and will go through life always behind schedule. She is on her way. She apologizes, but she needs a few minutes more. She's excited to see you again."

Caleb returns a cheerful but unconvincing smile.

"But first, Robert, I need you to do me a favor while I keep Caleb company."

Miss Price walks along the ambulatory complementing her students on their dresses and carrying out her chaperone responsibilities as unobtrusively as possible. She spots Josephine at a table across the dance floor. She knows they must talk at some point and resolve the messiness that was left after they last spoke. As much as she would like to dispose of the guilt festering inside her, now is not the time to approach the girl, not in a place so exposed. Perhaps tomorrow. After Mr. Carter has left for New York. After life at the Seminary returns to its normal, predictable pace.

The fire at the boathouse has provided a temporary and worrisome distraction to the pending sale of the school. For the past day, the fate of her position at the school and the future of its very operations were temporarily set aside as the focus turned to the act of arson. That is what the fire marshal calls it—arson—and the police have already scoured the site for clues. The troublesome fact—coincidence or not—that students under her supervision were known to be at the glen on Monday and two had gone missing the night before the fire is hooked in her brain like a burr snagged to wool.

At her meeting with Josephine—that lamentable, reprehensible exchange of transparent jealousy—she saw for the first time a hint of deception in her student's face. Still, the regent can't conjure a realistic scenario for why any of her girls, not to mention the upper echelon of the senior class, would be involved in such a crime. The police surmise that vagrants are the likely culprits and that the fire may have been accidental. An unintended fire or a knocked-over lantern, they suggested. No combustibles were stored at the storage building and it had been secured weeks before. After all, as the police officer explained to Dean Dawson earlier in the morning, what reason would anyone have to set the secluded building on fire in the middle of winter? There have been no similar acts of vandalism in the area and the police found no discernable footprints around the burnt foundation. The snow had taken care of that.

The senior regent ascends the stairs to the second floor and looks over the dance floor. The view is mesmerizing. Looking down, she sees an overheated, vibrant army of young dancers, jostling about for space, brimming against the invisible boundaries of the rectangular wooden floor. Their identities blur, forms without names, as they move about the floor to the rhythm of the music, in tune with the melody, slaves to their partners' touch and guidance.

She imagines the sweet pungent smell of bodies pinballing against each other. The thrill of feeling alive as friends and strangers—men and women both—ricochet against you, press against your back, push along your arm, glance off your hip, the flattening of breasts, the helpless, blissful feeling of turning yourself over to a collective force drawing from the movements of all. Delirious. Succumbing. Irrepressible.

Miss Price remembers the exquisite sensation of being…of being them. She longs for the sensory feeling of being out of control like they are. Excitable again. Not as an observer from above, but at their level. With them. Among them. A part of them. The warm breath of other dancers against her neck. The feel of a stranger's flesh touching upon her own—drawing from her, in a fleeting instance of contact, the succulent nectar of youth. Body against body. Warmth and weight. Pressure and pleasure. Vibrant and alive. The intoxicating drug of anticipation.

She moves along the railing, eyeing the ghostly vestiges of her youth. She looks upon them with envy, longing to return to who she once was, to live within their skin and move as effortlessly as they do. Blithe ballerinas in a wasteland of innocence.

A group of underclass girls passes Miss Price on the way to the dance floor and greet her, their lean and nimble figures adorned with the latest fashion from the upscale dress shops. She nods back as a reflex, but her gesture is a hollow, insincere one.

The contemplative regent turns away from the dance floor and looks out the outside balcony at the ephemeral traces of white moving rapidly past the window pane. The physical arrangement of the moment—her forlorn gaze, the thin, clear glass barrier, the flourishes of winter beyond the separation—pulls her back to a more innocent and vulnerable time in her life, when, at the tender age of thirteen, the daggers of unrequited affection plunged repeatedly into her fresh and unscarred heart.

Life was simpler then. A two-dimensional existence. The trajectories of emotion, steep and easily mapped, but hard to temper. She remembers sitting on the bench next to her bedroom window and looking out on the fields at the relentless snowfall and feeling the tremendous weight of isolation from the life beyond the distant boundaries of her family's farm. Winter had handed down a cruel sentence, depriving her of seeing the boy she met earlier that summer at the fair. A life in unbearable exile.

The particles of her memory swirl about like the flakes beyond the window. She struggles to recreate the contours of his face. Why is it so hard to recall? Is it so meaningless now? She stares out into the black and stormy night and ponders the lost simplicity over the intervening years of her life, and whether she would even recognize the girl sitting on the window sill today. Out of the fog, a picture emerges that brings the painful remembrance into focus.

He was a lanky, freckle-faced boy with the easy smile who wore overalls and always made sure he was around when she came into town. Yes, the loose-limbed, tanned son of the storekeeper who was never far from her thoughts when they were apart. That summer she would replay over and over their brief flirtations while lying in bed in the dark until she committed to memory every word spoken between them as if they were scripted lines of a play. But just when the awkwardness of their meetings began to dissipate, the days of endless sun and freedom grew fewer and then gave way to the demands of harvest. What was so heady and natural and full of adrenaline-soaked promise between them came to an abrupt end, and the oft-repeated and cherished exchanges were replaced by the imaginary sentiments she wished she had spoken to him when she had the chance, and the ones he would surely have spoken in return.

Alone in her room, a prisoner surrounded by the impassable barrier of winter, she could not bear the thought of waiting weeks before their next meeting. If he felt the same, he would send a letter or find a way to reach her, she told herself repeatedly. And with each passing day, she grew more contemptuous of the falling snow, her callous jailer, and would write in her journal how she could not possibly survive the winter apart from him. But she did. As the nights grew longer and fiercer, the entries in her journal grew farther apart and eventually ceased, as did the time spent sitting at the bedroom window sill watching over the curved road that linked their isolated homestead with the outside world.

With the arrival of spring, she emerged from her confinement a different girl than before, emotionally hardened and more mature. The moments of longing she felt the previous summer, while not forgotten, had lost their hold on her and when she reflected upon them or how she pined in her bedroom for a sign from him, she felt deep embarrassment, as if the sloppiness of her emotions were the childish wants of a school girl. It all changed for Katharine Price that pivotal winter. She shed the skin of adolescence and walked forward in life with a tighter rein on her feelings and a more profound awareness of her surroundings and those who populated it. By the time she saw him again weeks later, they barely acknowledged each other. The promising spark of summer romance had been snuffed out in the blowing snows outside her window.

The tempo of the music slows and Robert slides his arms around Josephine's waist and pulls her close against his body. She rests her arm over his shoulder and lets her cheek graze the side of his face as they move slowly about the dance floor.

"You were wonderful to dance with Jennie. She is such a nice girl, but very insecure."

"What choice did I have?"

Josephine taps the back of his head playfully with her hand.

"You did it because you're a nice man, Robert Winslow, not because I asked you to. She needs to stop thinking about her date arriving, and besides, the man most resembling a movie actor here is you. You were the ideal fill-in for the part."

"Ah, you see me as an understudy rather than a leading man!"

The lights in the ballroom go dark for a split second and then turn back on, only to flicker spasmodically before eventually returning to full power. The momentary interruption elicits murmurs of concern and a few laughs from those assembled in the ballroom. Surprised at being cast into brief blackness, Josephine instinctively grips Robert tighter. The band continues playing and she spots two of the dance chaperones rising from their seats at the headmaster's table.

"That was a bit unnerving."

"I think it's exciting. Losing electricity would make the evening sort of romantic, don't you think? The two of us alone in the dark, no peering eyes, dancing together, letting the feel of our hands guide us."

Robert unexpectedly kisses her, and Josephine quickly looks about to see if the transgression has been witnessed by any of the school staff.

"You can't do that. Not here."

"Then let's go someplace where you won't have to worry about being watched."

"I can't. Not now."

"You're to blame, you know."

"What are you talking about?"

"It's the way you're dressed. I can't control myself."

She pats him on the shoulder and looks about for a sign of Margaret. A clarinet solo rises above the music as they move about the dance floor.

"You know I've risked my personal safety to be here tonight and I've had to endure great hardship and expense to see you," Robert continues with a mischievous grin. "We owe it to ourselves to find sometime alone together."

"We are alone, now."

"You know what I mean, Jo. Away from this crowded fishbowl."

"I need to be here now. Margaret hasn't arrived, and I am worried about her. And Jennie, well, she is an absolute mess."

"And what about us? You and me?"

Josephine does not answer, remaining silent in his arms as their bodies sway to the music.

Again, the lights dim and pulsate. This time, two or three seconds pass before the illumination around the dance floor and along the upper floors is restored. A stiff gust rattles the panes of stained glass high overhead and Josephine follows the noise as it reverberates around the ring of niches with the plaster busts looking down upon the assembled. She looks at Robert's handsome features and pleading, endearing eyes.

"All right. We should find a place to go where we can be alone. The next time the band takes a break. Something important has happened I need to tell you. I've been keeping it from you, but there is serious matter we need to talk about."

Employees of the school file into the ballroom carrying unlit lanterns and begin placing them on the tables. During the commotion, the dean confers with an older man dressed in work clothes who Josephine recognizes as the supervisor of the school grounds and buildings. A third interruption in electricity sends many of the dancers back to their tables and Josephine glimpses a flash of green in the blinking light that makes her heart race.

"She's here," she says placing her hand on her confused partner's chest and pulling him off the floor.

Margaret's arrival turns the heads of more than just her friend. Poised just inside the entrance doors, bathed in a corona of white light, she strikes a statuesque pose, resplendent in wispy smooth Nile green chiffon that enticingly reveals the curves of her body. The sheer sleeveless dress is unadorned except for the small grouping of glittering Rhine pebbles in the shape of a flower along the right shoulder. Her face is pale and shows no emotion. A fine, undetectable powder covers the uneven splotches of color along her face and exposed neck line. A shoulder scarf dangles from one hand while the other caresses the straight line of her dress below her narrow hips. Men in the room devour her beauty with their eyes while their dates see her arrival and stationary display as further proof of her manipulative, self-admiring, narcissism.

Josephine slips her hand into Margaret's and leads her to the table where their two dates wait.

"This is not going to be easy," the late arriving goddess says through clenched teeth as they navigate through the crowd.

Caleb's jaw goes slack when he sees Margaret for the first time since they met six months earlier. Momentarily stunned by the sight of her, he shakes out of his stupor and pulls out her chair. Standing next to her, the top of Caleb's head barely clears the height of her shoulder and he shoots a knowing glance toward Robert.

"I practically broke my ankle getting here," Margaret announces to the table, eschewing typical introductory banter around the men. "The electricity kept turning on and off when I was walking here. I tripped on the edge of a rug outside the parlor and nearly toppled a hallway table the last time it happened. You should have seen the faces of the girl and her date walking in front of me when they heard what came out my mouth."

"I'm glad you made it in one piece," Caleb says, "It's good to see you again, Margaret. You are looking very nice tonight."

"Likewise, Caleb," she replies, feeling Josephine's judgmental gaze upon her. "You are looking *nice* as well. A tuxedo can really transform a man."

He glances over at Robert as if to say 'I told you so.'

Robert dodges the look and turns back to Josephine.

"Let's go dance. I think the band is going to break soon."

INCIDENT AT FOREST GLEN *399*

She feels the abruptness of his request, so soon after Margaret's arrival, is rude but she relents, if for no other reason than to allow the two some time alone. As they hastily depart the table, Caleb shifts closer to his date in order to be heard over the music.

"I've been looking forward to tonight. This is really unbelievable. Robert told me about the school, but I never pictured this place as being so incredible. I suppose it's old hat to you though, being here all the time."

"It has it nice points. But I am ready to leave it. I've never really felt comfortable fitting in here."

"Everyone I met so far has been very nice."

"Yes, I heard that you picked up an escort on your way here. A couple of Sweets accidentally bumped into you, or something like that, on the trolley. How fortunate for you."

"What did you call them, *'sweets'*? Is that some nickname of affection you give one and another around the school?"

"You might say that."

"They said they knew you. They were helpful, and a lot of fun to be around."

"I'm sure they were. Don't worry. I suspect they will be coming around to see you again at some point."

"Ah, that's not what I meant."

"Well, I did mean what I said. You see, my understanding of the girls you met is a bit more informed than yours. What you consider to be *helpful* is not as innocent as it sounds. But as you are a man and a couple of years older, I shouldn't have to explain that to you."

"What are we talking about exactly?" he asks, confused over the turn in conversation and more than a little annoyed at Margaret's implication. "When is being helpful a crime?"

"It isn't," she answers dismissively. "Would you mind being *helpful* and fetching me a cup of punch? I can barely catch my breath it's so stuffy in here."

Robert leads Josephine to the dance floor but does not stop until they are clear of the other couples and headed toward the entrance doors. She slows when she realizes where they are going and pulls against his hold on her wrist.

"Wait, Robert, wait."

But he does not heed her protest and continues to lead her past the headmaster's table and the bandstand. The music grows softer as they clear the ambulatory and he pushes open the ballroom doors. Outside, a handful of couples mingle among large potted plants and lean against expensive mahogany tables. Some of the men smoke while others peer intently out at a window near the hallway trying to gauge the snowfall on the ground.

Robert presses on looking for a place of privacy and Josephine does not resist or voice her protest in the presence of others. Down the hallway and through a pair of alabaster columns he finds an empty davenport next to a peculiar antique brass statue of a young girl bent slightly at the waist and holding a lighted globe in end of each of her outstretched arms. A colorful, Mercer tiled fireplace, situated further along the curved hallway leading to the enclosed causeway connecting with Senior House, is dormant and cold, its hearth shelf cluttered with an incongruous collection of decorative keepsakes including a crystal obelisk procured in an Arab bazaar and twin candle holders, gilded and in the shape of the Eifel Tower. As the two sit, Josephine looks about to make sure no one is within earshot.

"Look," he begins, cutting her off just as she is about to speak, "I know we said we'd wait until the break, but I couldn't wait. I want to be alone with you and I wasn't sure what else was going to happen in there. I couldn't wait—"

"All you had to do was give me a minute or two, Robert. Margaret's been ill and I didn't want to leave her alone just yet. And, although you may not understand, I have a responsibility to Jennie, the girl I asked you to dance with—"

"I do understand, but aren't you glad that *I* am here? You seem preoccupied with everyone else's affairs, but your own—and mine."

"That's not true. Of course I am happy you are here. I have missed you terribly since we last saw each other."

"And I have missed you, Jo. And our time apart has only strengthened my love for you."

Josephine is stunned by the unexpected, heartfelt seriousness of his words, unsure what to say next. She smiles warmly but there is some reticence in her reply.

"It doesn't have to be like this—meeting for a few hours once a month."

"I need to speak with you about something very important, Robert."

"At this moment, there is nothing more important than the two of us," he implores her, taking a hold of both her hands, and holding them in the lap of her black silk dress.

"I know you may not think so, but there is. Something has happened and I need to talk to you about it urgently," she says pointedly, hoping to stave off what she senses he is about to say.

"Hear me out first, please, will you, Jo? You are not making this easy."

"Robert, you must listen to me. I need your help. If you would just give me a moment to explain."

"Whatever you are about to say, I want to hear it from the lips of the woman who will be my wife."

"Robert, please don't. Not now."

"Jo, agree to marry me. I can come to meet your family in a week and we can tell them then. I need to be with you. We need each other. I cannot bear the idea of continuing on as we are. Next spring you will be leaving here and I will have one year left at the academy. It's a perfect time for us to be married."

Josephine is powerless to hold back the tears that stream steadily down her cheeks. Robert, initially heartened by her emotional response, waits in anticipation to hear her answer, the one simple word which he replayed over and over in his mind throughout the day. But it does not come, and as her silence continues, the fullness of his love for the woman begins to crumble and slowly turn to bitter dust.

"What is it? Say something, Jo."

The hallway lights begin to fade and the filaments inside the bulbs lower to an orange glow before full power is restored. Shadows consume the soft features before him and then recede.

She shakes her head, and suppresses a sob rising up her throat.

"You don't understand, Robert. That's not what I need. Not now. Not with everything going on."

"What you need? I don't understand. Are you saying you don't feel the same, that you don't love me?"

"That's not what this is about. It's not about you or about us. Something horrible has occurred here and I am not sure how to handle it. And I can't deal with your proposal now."

"So, my proposal is an inconvenience to you." He shakes his head in disbelief. "How can you be so cold?"

"If you only knew the trouble we've been dealing with these past few days, you would understand what I am saying. You caught me off-guard, Robert."

"Then take a moment and collect yourself. This is important. I don't ask for your hand lightly. I have thought it over carefully. I will stay here as long as it takes."

"You don't get it, do you? I need your friendship now. Not an ultimatum. It's not personal."

"It is hard not to take it personally, Jo."

"That's not what I meant, Robert."

"You won't say yes and haven't given me a reason why, other than it is not the right time to talk about it. What am I missing?"

"It's complicated for me to explain. But I want to explain it to you. You just need to be patient with me."

Robert produces a maroon ring box from his front pants pocket.

"I want to spend the rest of our lives together. I am not afraid to say it."

Any number of thoughts could have entered Josephine's mind at that pivotal moment. Does she love the man enough to marry him? Is she prepared to be a military officer's wife and subjected to continual disruptions of moving from station to station? How can she make a lifelong commitment to another when she hasn't decided on her own personal path in life? None of these or other equally pressing questions come to mind however. Instead, she looks down at the cube-shaped box in the palm of his hand and thinks of the sheer absurdity of the gesture and how, twice in only a few hours time, she has been presented with a gift she neither expected nor wanted from men declaring their affections for her.

"Take it. Open it."

"I can't," she answers in a trembling voice, her eyes welling up once again.

"Not just now or never?"

"Oh, God! Don't force me, Robert. Give me a chance to tell what has happened. Then you will understand why I can't."

"I see."

His voice is deflated in sober resignation that, in a moment of desperation, he has pressed too hard for an answer, and he slips the spurned offering back into his pocket.

"What purpose is there to listen to words intended only to soften the blow or obscure your honest feelings. I am past that point now, Jo. You have given me your answer."

"Will you please listen to what I have to say?"

Robert stands and walks back down the corridor toward the ballroom refusing her request, wanting only to create as much physical distance between them as quickly as possible.

"Wait Robert, don't leave. Please don't abandon me. I need you," she cries out in vain and then listens to the rapid steps along the rug fade away.

Her plea goes unanswered, but not unheard, for just around the corner past the tiled hearth, mere feet away from the davenport, a girl remains frozen, carefully controlling her breathing and steadying herself in place, listening to muffled sobs that signal the end to the uncomfortable yet riveting drama she has overheard.

Caleb successfully coaxes Margaret to the dance floor, and by the time Josephine returns to the ballroom after a trip to the ladies' room to tend to the red puffiness around her eyes she finds that their table has been abandoned and taken over by new arrivals. A few of the girls are huddled about the chair where Josephine sat before being led away by her boyfriend. Without demonstrating any overt concern, she surveys the room for Robert, now and again interrupted by other students complementing her dress or asking about her date's whereabouts. When she approaches the table looking for a sign that he may have returned there, Marion Kittle sees her and tracks her down wearing an exuberant grin that wrinkles her nose and turns her eyes into narrow slits. Josephine expects a resumption of the friendly ribbing that took place at the geisha party when Marion and her fellow Beta sorority sister, Audrey, challenged her and Margaret and the other girls to a bowling tournament, before Bettina arrived and sent the whole friendly wager into a tale spin. Distracted and emotional from what just transpired with Robert, she is in no mood to engage Marion further on the trifling subject. She is trapped, however, in a tight gauntlet of chairs that prevents her from tactfully avoiding the jovial seeker.

Marion rushes up to her and grips her by the arms.

"What a wild night, right? First the snow and then the lights going on and off again."

Josephine returns a halfhearted smile, preparing to think up a white lie to shed her talkative classmate.

"But what in the world did you bring with you to the dance, Josephine?"

"I'm sorry. What do you say? *Who* did I bring to the dance?"

"No, no, we've been looking over your date all night. Very nice. Very nice, indeed. I'm talking about that thing you brought with you to the table over there."

"Marion, I don't know what you are talking about. I am trying to find Robert right now."

"Sure you do. We saw the two of you sitting at your table, and when you left to go dancing with your beau and then didn't come back, one of the girls noticed you left something on the chair. She thought is was a wrap or scarf or something."

Josephine looks over at the table and now notices that three girls are congregating around her chair, just as Marion had said.

"I'm guessing you were going to give it to Margaret or one of the girls as a practical joke or something like that. If you are, that's one nasty looking piece of work."

As Josephine snakes her way through the closely bunched tables, the electricity begins to fail again, but this time, instead of a pulsating ebb and flow of current, there is a bright lightening flash that shatters half of the bulbs in a quick burst of popping sounds, like that of a cannonade barrage, and peppers partygoers throughout the hall with shards of thin glass. The lights remaining intact burn brighter than normal as if the energy from the overloaded bulbs has been diverted and is now surging into the surviving sockets. The band stops immediately in mid-song and the first scream is quickly followed by other girls unnerved by the shocking, but harmless, explosions.

Josephine continues toward the chair, fighting against a tide of bodies moving away from dance floor and the walls along the ambulatory. But there is still plenty of light in the hall and the panic is only temporary as nervous laughter replaces the smattering of shrieks from the more excitable students.

The girls remaining at her table are too distracted by the pyrotechnics to notice Josephine as she steps closer and looks down at the brown and gray pile on top of the seat cushion. Without trepidation she reaches down and touches the coarse fur with the tips of her fingers. She carefully pinches one end of the cumbersome skin and pulls it off the chair and lays it on the red table linen. She smoothes out the folds of the macabre cloak and sees the crude stitching holding all the pieces together. Stepping back from the table, she sees that it is not one skin but no fewer than five different ones sewn together to fashion a composite pelt of field animals. The furs have been expertly removed and are intact, making the identity of each skinned creature recognizable, even in a flattened and splayed form.

Marion catches up to her at the table.

"Oh my God, was that the wildest thing you have seen? It's like the whole building was about to explode."

She immediately notices the unfurled patchwork of fur in front of Josephine.

"So where did you find this monstrosity? I mean, what is it—a vest or a type of hunting disguise? Have you become friends with one of the local woodsmen?" she laughs nervously.

"I've never seen these ugly furs before in my life," Josephine lies convincingly. "I think someone is playing a joke on the both of us."

Bill Weller, the grounds and buildings supervisor, fumbles with a ring of keys on his belt looking for the one that will open the lock to the power plant station while his assistant holding a lantern presses close trying to shield him from the stinging wind. Minutes earlier, after the initial outages, the dean had instructed the supervisor to inspect the cinder block building for any indication that the power switches were malfunctioning and causing the hiccups in the flow of electricity to Vincent Hall.

"Pull the light closer, boy" the ruddy-faced man spits into the wind. His hair blows about wildly as thick sausage-shaped fingers, aching and stiff from the prolonged exposure to the cold, sort through the collection of skeleton keys. One key after another is placed into the padlock until on the sixth try the frozen tumblers fall in place and the gray u-bolt pops up, prompting his assistant to dance an impromptu jig. The thrashing of boot heels against the ground uncovers something buried under a shallow coating of snow as the supervisor fumbles about trying to muscle the bulky lock from its latch.

"What's this?" the assistant mumbles looking down at his feet, his question followed by a string of vile expletives spewing forth from his supervisor's mouth after the man's grip on the lock slips and his knuckles graze the steely surface.

He pushes the dark object along the ground with the toe of his boot. It's hard and oddly shaped. He crouches down and places the lantern on the ground. A thin, bent hook of some kind protrudes out of the snow.

The supervisor's reaction is immediate, angry, and predictable.

"What the hell are you doing?! Bring that light back up here."

The assistant brushes the ice crystals off of his discovery with his glove and reveals a cloudy, lifeless eye. He picks up the stiff form and is amazed at how light it feels in his palm.

"What the hell is that?" the supervisor demands. As the young man pulls the corpse close to the protected flame, a broken wing hangs limply to the side.

"Poor bugger. It must have smacked into the side of the building during the storm and froze to death out here."

"Yeah, just like us unless you help me get this lock off. Get rid of that thing and lend a hand before I clock you upside the head."

With a half-turn, the assistant flings the ebony-feathered bird into the night and loses sight of it as it is swallowed up in the ferocious storm.

A solitary figure walks quickly through the blowing snow and ice and reaches the partially obscured statue of Cyporissus just as the glowing lights of the arriving streetcar pulls into the distant station house. Breaking into full stride, the man runs along the remaining stretch of pavement winding through mounds of buried shrubbery and onto the straightaway of the bridge spanning the dark chasm. The wood planks are slippery and his smooth-soled shoes twist and slide through the slush, his progress steadied by hands skating over the cold railings for balance. Once he reaches the far end of the bridge he yells out to the conductor backlit inside the glass booth and continues running up the considerable rise to the station. The driver does not acknowledge his flailing arms or frantic calls but instead steps out of the car and rushes inside the station. Relieved that he won't miss the car returning downtown, the harried man slows and begins walking toward the vacant platform, panting heavily.

When he enters the station he sloughs off the snow from his shoulders and surveys the well-lit interior waiting room decorated with butterscotch stained benches and dirty speckle tile flooring. Oddly, his appearance out of the storm does not garner the attention of any of the few people remaining inside. The station agent is offering the conductor a short cup of coffee from his Thermos while a third man in a thick wool coat with a fur collar, the sole traveler on the arriving streetcar, stands by the window looking curiously out at the glittering lights of the school in the distance.

"When are you turning around?" Robert asks the trolley conductor warming his hands around the steaming brown liquid.

"Not more trips tonight, son. The line is closed."

"I just saw you pull up a couple of minutes ago."

The man by the window turns to listen in on the conversation.

"Aren't you scheduled to return back to Washington?"

"Sure am, but the snow's too heavy and it's knocking down power lines all around the city, even some feeder trunks. Headquarters has sent out the word that we are to stop once we reach the terminus. They don't want cars losing power and getting stuck on the tracks."

"Unbelievable," Robert sighs.

The station agent speaks up.

"You're not out of luck, young man. A cargo locomotive is expected by here in about an hour, eastbound, headed to the city. We are sending signals to the driver to stop and pick up Charley here and take him back to Union Station. I can't see how it would be a problem if you tagged along."

"Thanks," the stranded traveler says with relief, removing his coat, preparing to find a comfortable place to sit. "That would do just fine. It's kind of you to offer. I'm kind of stuck in a bind."

"You are not alone. This storm took a whole lot of people by surprise. Before it's over, a lot of folks will be sleeping in strange beds."

The man by the window purses his lips and approaches the group with a quizzical look on his toned and tanned face. His thin, coal-black hair is slicked back in a wave of pomade and separated into clumped rows of sodden excess running the length of his scalp.

"Pardon me, gentlemen. Is that the—" he pauses and pulls out a folded piece of paper from his breast pocket. "—is that the National Park Seminary for Young Women?"

"You found it," the station attendant says in an overly enthusiastic tone.

"Any chance that there is a car service running from here to there?" he asks, pointing toward the school across the glen.

"Nope, not unless you've made arrangements with folks at the school. But in this weather I wouldn't trust a car to make the trip."

"Not a taxi either then. I suppose?"

"Not in good weather or bad. This ain't the city, mister."

"I see. Thank you so much," he adds with a polite smile and then returns to his place by the window.

Robert lays his coat over the back of one of the benches and sits with his legs splayed and buries his head into his hands, rubbing them back and forth over his face trying to make sense over what was said between him and Josephine. When he pulls them away he sees that the hesitant, well-dressed man is standing before him.

"Sorry to bother you. You looked deep in thought. I don't mean to disturb you."

"That's fine. What is it?"

"You were talking to the conductor just now about a train that's going to stop here and take you back to Washington."

"That's what he said. You know all that I know. It's supposed to come by here in an hour. I'm just waiting."

"Do you think it is possible that I could join you in heading back?"

"It's not my train."

The man smiles at his presumptive question.

"Of course. You see, I've gotten myself into sort of a pickle. I am stranded here for the time being."

"You and me both."

"Do you mind if I join you?"

Robert pushes his coat further along the back of the bench and slides down, gesturing silently with his hand to the open space he's created.

The two men sit in silence, side by side, looking out on the station platform and watching the snow fall while the conductor and the station agent continue their conversation by the ticket window.

INCIDENT AT FOREST GLEN   *409*

Robert wants to be alone and is in no mood to pass the time talking with a stranger he now has the misfortune of being stuck with for the next hour, so he closes his tired eyes and feels the instant relief of shutting out the glaring lights. He suspects the man next to him is a talker, just by the look of him. The way he asked him and not the other men about the train leads Robert to believe the stranger would like nothing better than to kill time lamenting their predicament. And yet, surprisingly, the man says not a word, content to share the bench with Robert in silence. The only sound confirming his continual presence is an occasional prolonged sigh, like air being slowly leaked from a tire.

A few minutes pass and Robert feels the weight of fatigue deaden his arms and legs and loosen the tightness in his jaw muscles. The clock in the waiting area chimes. And then just as he is about to slip away, it chimes again, the pitch different this time and oddly irregular. Robert opens his eyes and sees that the man next to him is reading a folded newspaper left from the day before. Above the door leading outside to the platform, a brass bell on a coiled metal bracket bobs up and down slightly, recently silenced. Traces of snow leading to the ticket window are melting on the floor. The station agent leaves his coffee and steps over to the bench, holding something in his hand.

"Okay which one of you lucky gentlemen is Robert Winslow?"

Robert raises his hand off his lap.

"That's me."

The agent hands him an envelope bearing his name written in narrow, elegant script, along with a simple instruction, 'Eyes Only.'

"This was just delivered for you."

The man seated next to him leans over subtly just in time to read the inscription and when Robert turns the envelope over to open it he spots the school's embossed initials on the flap.

"NPS, isn't that the school?" he blurts out, not the least bit embarrassed in revealing his snooping. "You're from there? You came from there?"

"No...I mean, yes. Excuse me."

Robert leaves the bench annoyed with the stranger's intrusive questions and walks under the light next to the doorway, sidestepping the small puddles of melting snow.

He opens the envelope and reads the note card inside.

My Dearest R—

If you are at the station I pray that this note has reached you in time. You left in anger and without saying goodbye. I was confused and regret what I said to you. I do love you and I want to be given a second chance to reply to your proposal as my heart would have me do. Come back now. I will wait for you under the covered walkway next to Vincent Hall. Please forgive me.

J—

Robert, stunned by the unexpected reversal in Josephine's wishes, closes the note and looks across the glen.

"Bad news, boys," the station agent announces. "The locomotive is slowed by frozen signals. He's moving at only fifteen. Your wait is going to be a lot longer, so you might as well get as comfortable as you can."

Robert turns around and sees that his companion in purgatory is now wearing a crestfallen expression.

"Wait. I know you," he says, catching the stranded traveler in the fur trimmed coat by surprise. "I know you."

The man is all of the sudden pleased to be recognized and grins with false modesty.

"I'd be lying if I said this hasn't happened before."

"I know who you are."

"Yes, I'm in pictures. Marvin Morris."

He extends his hand toward Robert and flashes twin rows of prodigious white teeth.

"And you are here to see a girl named Jennie," Robert completes the circle, grabbing his hand firmly.

"You know her! Imagine that. You were at the dance then. I wish there is some way for me to explain to her why I was late getting here. And now with all this. I just hate to disappoint the poor girl. But I can't get stuck here in…where are we?"

"Forest Glen."

"That's right. Sorry. You see, I have to be in New York in two days. The producer will have my hide if I am not there on time. With the storm and everything, I'm a bit worried I'm not going to make it."

"When I left the school, Jennie was pretty busted up that you hadn't come. As chance would have it, I'm going back there now. We can go together. I'll show you the way. The walk isn't as far as it seems. We'll take the motor bridge over there. You see those two lines of dotted lights. The footing will be better."

The wayward actor looks skeptical as he considers the proposition.

"We can be there in five minutes. You still have plenty of time to make an appearance and have a dance or two with Jennie. You heard him say the train won't be here for a while. It would make her night. She's all worked up about you coming. What do you say?"

As Caleb spins Margaret around the dance floor she grows disoriented and nearly succumbs to the creeping nausea she has felt since entering the overheated ballroom. Her skin is burning up and she would like nothing better than to rip the pale green dress off her body and run out onto the ballroom terrace and lie down in a bed of soothing cold snow.

She hesitates in following his lead and lowers her head trying to focus her blurred vision on the lines separating the floor boards. Unable to get her bearings, she stops moving, but Caleb does not recognize her faltering state and continues to pull at her arms until Margaret begins to lose her balance. She pulls back violently nearly lifting him off the floor, and he finally slows, astounded by the willowy girl's remarkable strength. She places her hands against the front of his jacket for support and closes her eyes. The two stand still as the rest of the dancers moved about them in a cyclonic whirl of arms and legs.

"I'm sorry," she mumbles through parched, ashen lips. "I need to go."

"Wait. What's the matter?"

"I need to go. Now."

Margaret does not wait for him to protest further and rushes off the dance floor, leaving her date standing alone, abandoned for all the others about him to see. She runs out of the ballroom, her legs weak and wobbly, and barely reaches the restroom stall in time. Her sweat-covered forehead pounds after the painful, exhausting retching and she leans against the wall and feels the bracing sensation of the cool tile through the diaphanous fabric of her dress. Veins protrude from her slender forearms and her trembling fingers hang at her side. She hasn't the strength to move. She considers just sliding down the wall and spending the rest of the night curled up on the floor. All she wants is for the persistent nausea to cease. Her lungs burn as her breathing grows shallow.

About to succumb to the debilitating fever, she hears the door open and close behind her but cannot marshal the energy to turn around. She stares at the sink across the room and imagines the rapturous feel of cold water splashing over her face. The footsteps behind her stop and she looks into the mirror above the sink and immediately recognizes the angled two-dimensional image it holds.

"There you are."

As Robert leads the missing celebrity over the vacant bridge, he turns his head to the side and away from the brunt of the wind and sees the Odeon and the Senior House prominently positioned across the great white divide. The looming tower of Vincent Hall is up ahead and as the two men fight the wind, the lights along the bridge are abruptly doused and a ghostly shape, previously concealed in the glare, appears on the lawn in Robert's line of sight. The image, that of a gigantic figure, seated in profile, looking out onto the glen, is jarring and he squints to make sure it is not an illusion formed by the storm. The statue's shoulders and legs and head are covered with snow, but the contours of its chiseled features and brandished sword are clearly visible against the spectral backdrop. The globe lights on both sides of the bridge come back to life and the ominous vision is gone as quickly as it appeared.

The two men continue on in silence, one behind the other, their steps striking deeply into the rising accumulation. Like travelers sucked into a vortex transporting them back in time, they walk past the medieval castle and then the slowly turning masts of the Swiss cottage. To their right, the Italian renaissance fountain is still, the spouts along its multiple tiers choked with ice.

When they reach the light on the veranda, Robert gives instructions to the rosy-cheeked actor on how to reach the ballroom in the rear of the building.

"Aren't you coming in too?" the grateful man asks, perplexed at their parting.

"I might see you later inside. Most likely, we'll catch up back at the station. What you are doing is a good thing, Marvin. She's a nice girl. Let her know you wouldn't be kept away from seeing her. She'll want to hear that, I think."

The men shake hands and the actor brushes the snow from his coat collar and lapels before going inside. Robert hears the faint strains of music seep out through the opened door for a brief moment, and then all that is left is the sound of the howling wind. He folds his hands under his arms and searches the night for Josephine. He feels the corner of her note inside his coat press against his chest. The harsh blizzard has robbed the eerie landscape of any sign of life. He abandons the temporary shelter of the veranda and heads back into the storm in the direction of the tangle of wrist-thick vines wrapped around the black pergola.

The band leader approaches the edge of the stage and looks out on the vacated dance floor. He grips the microphone stand and pulls it close. The electrical surge has disrupted the dance and siphoned off the exhilaration in the room, sending many of the couples to their tables and the windows to fret over the storm. He speaks sharply to be heard over the buzz around him.

"All right then. Before we start our next musical offering, I have the privilege of making an important announcement. So if I can ask each gentleman and lady to suspend their conversations and give me their undivided attention. Would those of you at the tables in the back please come forward and gather on the dance floor with the others for one minute? I will wait a moment to give those of you seated farther a way a bit more time."

Dean Dawson leans over the headmaster's table.

"What is this all about, Miss Price? What is this about 'an important announcement'?"

She shrugs her shoulders, having grown weary of his incessant questioning throughout the evening.

"Very nice. Thank you," the band leader encourages the guests. "Would the group of young ladies over by the window be good enough to join us front and center? Yes. Thank you."

The band percussionist begins tapping a slow beat on the snare drum and is joined by the clarinet player who plays a languid melody, mystical and hypnotic, like that of a snake charmer. The interest of the assembled now piqued, the band leader smiles with a glint in his eye and presses the microphone to his lips, his voice low and seductive.

"We promised you a special treat at tonight's Christmas Ball and without further delay I present to you directly from Haa—lee—wood Caa—lee—for—nee–yaa, from the studio of Chaplin and Fairbanks and Pickford, a rising star of stage and screen, that's right, United Artists' own Marvin Morris!"

The actor steps out from behind the curtain and jogs out to the front of the stage as the band leader joins others on stage in applauding. The crowd presses closer to the stage as if on cue, many of the girls visibly giddy with excitement over the unknown actor's appearance.

"Thank you. Thank you all for such a warm greeting on such a cold night. You sure know how to make a westerner like myself welcome. Although, I have to say, I could do without all this white stuff. I know it will be Christmas soon, but where I live we're just starting to put on long pants during the day."

The crowd laughs at the cornball greeting, won over by actor's infectious smile and breezy manner.

"Now that I am looking at all the pretty girls here tonight, I'm kicking myself for showing up late. I have to be honest, when I walked in here I thought for a second I was at a studio party, what with all the gorgeous faces and how every one is dressed up. But the truth is I am here as one girl's date for the evening. So, Jennie Milburn, if you would join me on the dance floor, I think we have some catching up to do."

The actor bends down, places his hand on the bandstand, and with acrobatic flourish jumps down to the dance floor, landing in the midst of a group of smiling students. The crowd parts and he walks to middle, patted on the shoulders as he passes by. He can tell from the reaction along the rear of the crowd that his heretofore unseen date is about to emerge. When she does, the actor throws his arm out in her direction which prompts a thunderous round of applause from her envious peers and their suddenly diminished dates. An impromptu circle is carved out and the man with the striking jaw line and wide, endearing eyes gently takes the euphoric girl's hand as the band strikes up a slow tune.

As Jennie sways in his arms she can't stop grinning. He places his cheek close to hers and then guides her around wall of spectators, making sure that they get a nice long look of the two of them dancing together. He feels the jittery movement of her fingers against his.

"You know, Jennie," he whispers softly in her ear, "I think you are the sensation of the ball. And right now, there a lot of folks who would love to trade places with you and me both. Merry Christmas girl."

She buries her head on his shoulder to hide the emotion welling up inside her and the few of her on-looking classmates let out what can best be described as a cooing sound.

The band leader reclaims the microphone stand.

"Everyone please join our special guest, Marvin Morris and his date, Jennie Milburn, on the dance floor in joyous celebration of the approaching holidays!"

And the space around the couple quickly closes and disappears.

As he holds onto the wood post at the entrance to the pergola, Robert is aware of two things: how completely and utterly dark the covered walkway before him is, and the hammering of his heart against his sternum. He assumes that the excitement over Josephine's note and the exertion of trudging through the snow back to the school are the causes of his racing heart, but the physical sensation is nevertheless disconcerting. He enters the protective tunnel and starts thinking about how dreary the plight of a coal miner must be working in cramped, stifling, lightless confines for hours on end. He catches glimpses of white ground through the tight weave of dormant vines running along both sides of the trellised arbor but the weak illumination is not enough to penetrate the cold, fathomless corridor.

A pin-prick of light appears far down the walk and then wanes. He narrows his eyes and the dwindling point grows into a flame that is quickly covered by a lamp glass. In the projected light, he discerns a woman's hand and arm.

The whispery, disembodied voice travels down the lengthy passage and reaches him as words on a wing:

"Robert, follow me. I know where we can be alone."

The light grows smaller as it is carried away down the pergola toward the Villa. Robert continues on, his steps still uneasy and tentative in the pitch-black.

"Wait," he calls out, "Jo, wait. Let's walk together."

But the light continues to drift away from him down the tunnel, moving faster than he is walking. He quickens his pace and gradually he makes up ground until he can see Josephine's coat in the halo cast off by the flickering lamp.

"Would you wait up, please?" he yells out, his voice echoing down the drafty walkway, not nearly concerned as she is about being detected.

And then the light goes out. He walks faster still, calling out her name, and then breaks into a jog, unsure if the wind has extinguished the lamp flame or possibly that it was part of her game to confuse and test him.

"Jo!"

He slows down to a walk as he reaches the approximate spot where he saw the light last.

"No more games, girl," he calls out. His breathing is shallow and produces sprays of dense vapor. "It's really cold."

As Robert searches about for a sign of Josephine's presence, he notices a break in the pergola up ahead where another path crosses under the trellis roof. Thinking that the opening may take him back to the main building, he continues on and is disappointed to find that the egress point leads to the automobile bridge on one side and to a murky wooded grove on the other. Heavy, wet flakes of snow are falling faster than before obscuring what's beyond the protective arbor and Robert debates which way she has headed.

"Over here," Josephine cries out and he heads off in the direction of the nearby trees.

With little in the way of markers to guide him, and no sign of Josephine's lamp, Robert shuffles across the uneven ground and makes for the wide, slanted trunk of a sycamore.

"Yes, my dear, I am following, but my patience is growing thin," he shouts back.

Exposure to the extreme weather is immediately debilitating. Wind-blown pellets lash his face and neck. His cheeks sting from the biting cold and the rims of his pants legs are hardened icy white. Squinting through the poor visibility he reaches the tree and leans back against the trunk, positioning his body in such a way as to minimize the brunt of the chilling blast. He looks back and is surprised at the distance he has covered in a short time. In the opaque conditions, the long, vine-covered walkway spreads over the pale ground like a mummified carcass of a tremendous snake. He pushes his aching hands into his pockets for protection and warmth.

"Jo, let's go back inside. It's ridiculous to be out here."

"There's a cottage in the woods just ahead," she calls back. When he turns toward her voice, he sees her standing up ahead in front of a copse of trees.

"Thank God," he exclaims as he shuffles off to her, desperate to find shelter of some kind.

In his haste, he clips the toe of his shoe on a buried root and falls, hands still inside his pockets. Only by instinctively turning his shoulder at the last moment does he avoid hitting his face flush against the ground. The impact leaves him dazed. A sharp pain shoots along the side of his neck and down the length of his arm. He hurries to his feet, shaken by the fall and slightly embarrassed, the side of his face encrusted with packed snow. Robert's entire body throbs as he brushes himself off. He looks up and now sees his error. The figure he believed to be Josephine is only a statue of a Greek women hidden on the edge of the woods. The oversized cast looks down upon him, her expression cold and judgmental.

"Jo, I'm heading back to the school," he calls into the black recesses before him.

The lost lamp reappears, farther off now, casting a compressed beam of light along the tawny bark of a tree stand.

"It's here. Follow my light. Come to me," the voice beckons.

"Damn it. Damn it," he swears into his upturned collar.

The path to the orange-red flame is flat and unobstructed. As he makes the final leg of the arduous journey, Robert savors the thought of Josephine's warm body welcoming his and the comforting feel of her breathing, in tune with his own, when he wraps his arms tightly around her, the caress of her soft curls against the back of his covetous hands. The thought of being reunited sends a surge of excitement through his chilled veins and he quickens his pace toward the radiating lantern, cutting though the blowing snow and ice with renewed resolve. The promise of their future together lies ahead, across a hundred feet of open, wind-swept ground. A wellspring of heady optimism overflows inside him. They will walk together into a world without limits, sustained by an enduring bond of devotion.

The light pulsates in the blustery night. With each step, he draws closer to the woods and the woman with the seductive blue eyes waiting for him.

418   ANDY JOHNSON

High above the forest floor a barred owl, round-faced and alert, perches on the limb of a lightning-scarred oak, a stealthy hunter surveying the arboreal maze for nocturnal prey. A loud crack shatters the silence and the owl's head swivels around and then upward. The upper boughs of nearby cedars are strained by the weight of the wet, fallen snow and bowed. The bird smells the air for the fresh aroma of a split or severed limb but detects none. Sensing the presence of another close by, it takes flight, its sudden departure sending a powdery white spray into the air.

The majestic forest dweller glides low through the dense growth in silence, emerges over an open field, and then beats its powerful wings repeatedly to gain height. The telltale signs are now all about. Particles of burning kerosene are swept up by nostril slits. Acute ears locate a large, clumsy creature moving across the snowy terrain below, its movements halting and unsteady. As the bird continues its flight, dilated irises focus on a trail leading toward the woods, a shallow trench cut through the snow that goes halfway across the ice-covered pond and then ends.

The owl circles.

A slight whiff rises up from the disturbance below and is instantly recognized—the smell of moist decay, brackish and putrid.

Yellow warmth emanates from distant windows. The eyes of the scattered buildings burn bright in the moonless, starless night, holding the encroaching blackness at bay. As the owl heads toward the constellation of lights, searching the ground for field mice, the electrical line powering Forest Glen, under attack by the storm the entire evening, finally succumbs, severed by the weight of a falling tree weakened by a disease that secretly hollowed out its interior, ring by ring, over many years.

Darkness, malevolent and absolute, settles over the National Park Seminary for Young Women.

The outage hits just after the building supervisor reports back to Dean Dawson that the campus transfer station is operating as it should and that the electric company is reporting widespread loss of power throughout the metropolitan area due to downed lines. The kerosene lamps positioned around the ballroom earlier are lit and students and guests alike are told to wait until more details can be learned about the duration of the outage. Men in formal attire huddle in groups discussing options for returning to their homes. Some have driven or been driven to Forest Glen while others who took the streetcar to get to the ball speculate about whether the electrified tracks are down as well. Though none of the lights across the glen are visible from the ballroom, some argue that the trolley line runs on a separate line.

After ten minutes of confusion and rampant speculation, the visiting Hollywood celebrity takes to the bandstand again and announces that the trolley line was, in fact, taken out of operation even before the loss of electricity, but that an eastbound freight train coming from Cumberland, the last of the night, will be stopping at the station shortly. His command over the crowd is further solidified as he imparts the news and offers the lifeline to the despairing guests, and then follows it by matter-of-factly declaring that, "Speaking for myself, I am going to be on that train."

The dean takes to the stage after the actor and explains to those who don't feel they can safely make the trip home in the storm or who are otherwise stranded that a limited number of cots and blankets will be brought into the ballroom so they can stay until morning. As he continues to speak, a contingent of the invited guests, after saying hasty farewells to their dates, gather around Marvin Morris, his coat already on, and Jennie near the main entrance.

In the corner of the ambulatory Caleb sits with Nellie at a table abandoned by other couples heading to the front of the hall.

"I'd better go find Robert so we can catch that train. I have no clue where he and Josephine went. They got up to dance and then just disappeared. Have you seen them around?"

Nellie shakes her head and pushes her hand under the table until she finds Caleb's.

"Maybe the two of them went off to find a quiet spot to be alone. And one thing led to another."

"Not something Robert would likely do. Definitely don't see that in his girl either. Your headmaster and his crew have a tight lid on this place."

Nellie squeezes his hand and runs the smooth skin of her thumb over the top of his, back and forth until the wrinkled lines along his mouth and at the corners of his eyes go soft and smooth and his lips droop slightly.

"I suppose they are in love and they feel a need to act on it. I saw the way he looked at Josephine when we walked into Vincent Hall together.

Especially now, with it being dark and all. I think it is primal and romantic. It's what I've dreamed of since I was a girl. The chaos around us is exhilarating. You know, it's all very Gothic. Maybe it was too much for the two of them to handle."

"Naw. I see what you are saying and all, but I can't see Robert going off like that and leaving me here stranded. Everything is shutting down and he just slips away? Not like him."

Nellie glances back and makes sure she is not being watched and takes her other hand and rubs it along the length of Caleb's shoulder. When she reaches the starched collar of his shirt, she hooks her manicured finger on the inside and traces the smooth, cool surface of the red nail along the back of his neck, summoning the short clipped hairs that rise up and meet her touch.

"You're warm," she purrs, blowing lightly against the moist flesh.

Caleb laughs nervously.

"You are making this difficult for me to do what I need to do."

"And what's that?" she sighs.

"To leave. If I don't get up and leave I won't find Robert and we're going to be stuck here."

"That wouldn't be so bad, now would it? Didn't you hear the dean? You can stay here tonight. And I would be right up there." Nellie's doe eyes glance upward. "Just a few feet away."

She leans closer.

"Your friend probably found a way home already. Why leave me and chase after someone who isn't even here? Not to mention that long walk in the storm."

The dark outline of a person approaches the table and is upon them before Nellie can retract her hold.

"Caleb," the urgent voice commands.

"Josephine, is that you?" he sputters, the table lantern too weak to reveal her face.

"Where's Margaret?"

"Hey, Josephine," Nellie adds in a friendly tone, flashing a seductive smile, conscious that they are blind but can be seen.

"She got sick while we were dancing. And then she just ran off the floor without a word. She never came back, not even to say goodbye. She didn't

INCIDENT AT FOREST GLEN *421*

look good at all. It looked like she was really hurting. I was really worried when she ran off."

"I can see that," her voice pointed and unforgiving.

Caleb gently pushes Nellie away.

"How long ago did she leave?"

"I don't know. Maybe a half hour. Is Robert with you?"

But his question goes unanswered as Josephine grabs the lamp off the table and hurriedly heads to Senior House, leaving Caleb and his siren in the darkness.

Josephine's rush to the exit catches Miss Price's attention and she steps away from a table of concerned students she's been calming to intercept the girl before she leaves. She can see the distressed look on the girl's face as she draws near. The regent reaches the doors and thrusts her arm out just as Josephine, unaware that she is being pursued, moves to open the door. The frantic girl turns wildly to see who is barring her from leaving.

"Where are you going, Josephine?

"I need to leave," she responds flatly.

"I want you to stay here until everything gets sorted out. It will give us a chance to sort out some things between us as well. I've wanted a moment to speak with you since we had our last exchange."

The girl is unresponsive to her entreaty and Miss Price reaches over and pulls gently on her arm.

"Did you hear what I said? We need to talk."

Josephine turns to face the regent, her face under-lit in the darkness by the lamp dangling by her side.

"Please, Miss Price," her voice quivers, "I don't think I can take it. Not now. Please."

"What is it? What's bothering you?"

"I just need to leave this place."

She moves away but the regent does not relinquish her hold.

"You need to get control of yourself, Josephine. Let's go over here and sit down. Just the two of us."

Now it is Josephine's turn to resist.

"No. I won't."

"I insist. I am not asking, young lady."

Josephine's eyes grow glassy and the emotional storm within her subsides for a moment.

"If it's about the expulsion—"

"Let's sit down and we can talk it through, everything. I need to get something off my chest."

Dean Dawson, exercised over the regent's absence during such a critical time in organizing the arrangements for the remaining guests, spots her by the doorway talking to a student.

"Miss Price, I need you over here immediately!"

"Coming, Dean," she answers back and lowers her head in exasperation.

She searches Josephine's face for some indication of what is causing her panic but finds only pain and confusion.

"Tomorrow morning then. Nine o'clock. My office. Be there. No excuses."

She releases the girl's bare arm and watches her escape through the dim portal. Her heart sinks over letting the troubled soul leave.

Josephine runs through the darkened corridors alone, confined by her dress and hindered by heeled shoes. She sees no one. The unlit causeway leading to the dormitory is empty, except for the framed portraits on the walls witnessing her passage. Guilt drives her arms and legs faster. How could I have left her alone like that? The jarring image of the animal skins taken from the stranger's canoe and left on her chair only confirms Leah's descent into madness. She had gone back there. The story the frightened boy told Mr. Raymee is true. The crude patchwork of pelts. The knife left at the stable. The boathouse fire. All meant to... to what exactly? To frighten them? Or worse. Leah mental state is more dangerous than even they had imagined. As she reaches the first floor of Senior House, pangs of remorse rack her frenzied mind. Why didn't I tell Miss Price just now when I had the chance? I had decided to do so, after all. The opportunity presented itself. And I pushed her away. I wasn't thinking clearly in the rush to find Margaret.

Josephine hikes up her dress and takes the stair steps two at a time until she reaches the third floor, breathless and staring down the quiet hallway. Deprived of light, the corridor is bleak and sinister looking. Leah's doorway at the end of the hall is concealed in blackness. Josephine walks slowly to Margaret's room, never taking her eyes off the frightening emptiness. She listens intently for some sign of Leah's presence, but hears only the sound of her own shoes against the hall rug. The air inside the dormitory is cold and laced with a peculiar sour aroma.

She reaches Margaret's room and rattles the locked door handle.

"Margaret, open up. Are you in there? Say something. Are you there?"

Josephine hears movement beyond the door, a rustling sound in the direction of where Margaret's bed is positioned.

"Open the door, Margaret, now. I need to see you," she commands and then looks back in the direction of Leah's room.

"You woke me up."

The voice is faint and unsure.

"Fine. Now get up and unlock the door."

"Sleeping."

"Not anymore. I must see you."

No reply, only silence.

Josephine presses her ear to the door trying to hear if Margaret has left her bed.

From the other side of the thick, varnished wooden divide, Josephine's voice is stripped of its urgency. Her words carry through the rank cloud of pestilence that permeates the room and reach Margaret's ears muffled and dreamlike. She lays on her bed, drenched with hot beads of moisture, a cool hand towel neatly placed across her feverish forehead.

"In the morning," a voice tenderly whispers into her ear.

"In the morning," Margaret repeats.

"It can't wait," Josephine insists through the door.

"I need sleep," she's told to say, the feel of exhalation across her neck providing perverse relief to her enflamed skin.

"I need sleep."

"Please, Margaret." Josephine's voice grows more desperate. "Open the door."

"Go away. Leave me alone," the body lying next to Margaret commands her to say. But she hesitates, and the words are repeated into her ear. Again she balks, hovering just above the wavering line of lucidity.

"Jo, don't worry. Everything will be all right. I'll come and see you in the morning. I love you."

Her friend slowly backs away and covers her mouth to stifle her sobbing as she retreats back down the corridor to her room, overwhelmed by the oppressive sadness that crashes over her like a black wave.

"That's sweet," the voice whispers into Margaret's ear.

Margaret, her lips parched and her lungs searing in pain, feels her body rise toward the ceiling ever so slightly as the mattress lightens. Leah stands before her, wringing out a cloth in a porcelain bowl filled with cool water.

"But I am the one taking care of you. Josephine, on the other hand, was off with her man without a care for what might happen to you. You are lucky I was there."

Leah kneels down next the bed, and peels the old compress from Margaret's burning skin and replaces it with the new one.

"I won't leave you, Margaret," she says, staring intently into the sickly girl's listless eyes.

She caringly pulls away wet strands of hair from her neck.

"Our time is short. Just as you comforted me after the boathouse, I will see you through this difficult passage."

"Get a doctor," Margaret pleads softly. "I need a doctor."

"What do they know, right? You have all you need now that I am here."

Margaret closes her eyes slowly, her breathing rapid and shallow. Leah smiles.

"Rest, my dear," she says, stroking her patient's cheek.

She stands back up and walks across the dark room and retrieves something from the dresser top and brings it over to the bed. She unfurls the carefully folded fabric and places it up against her body. Leah's white, pristine chorus gown sends off a ghostly glow.

"It will be short on you, but I think it's time we get you into it."

The brilliance of the morning sun streams through the window of Josephine's room, and warms the bed linen. The infusion of light through the open drapes rouses Josephine from her sluggish state. As she sits up in her bed, she struggles to recall how she came to be like this, lying in bed still wearing her formal dress. She looks over at the desk clock and, seeing the lateness of the hour, untangles the twisted sheets around her body and rolls off the mattress. She must go and see Margaret. She pushes the straps off her shoulders and the silk dress drops to the floor at her feet.

As she undresses, another memory emerges from the haziness in her brain, the words of Miss Price just before she fled the ballroom:

Nine o'clock. My office. Be there. No excuses.

A bolt of panic strikes Josephine as she realizes she's stood up the already upset regent.

While she puts on her uniform, she sees that a brown envelope has been slid under her door.

She bends down and picks the envelope off the floor, still shocked by how exhausted she must have been to sleep past ten. The telegram is addressed to "Miss Josephine Barnes" and sent from a District address.

WAS TO MEET RW AFTER DANCE BUT HE NEVER SHOWED AT STATION OR AT MY APARTMENT STOP PLEASE SEND CONFIRMATION THAT HE IS AT FG STOP CALEB

Josephine drops the message on the floor and fastens the back of her uniform as she heads out of her room to go see Margaret. The hallway is curiously empty for a Sunday morning. Church service is over by now and there should be plenty of girls walking and talking about. As she turns the slight bend in the corridor, she is stunned to find Dean Dawson standing before her, arms folded and head down, as if in deep reflection. Next to him, speaking in hushed tones is Miss Price. Their eyes meet and the regent can see the surprise registered on Josephine's face.

"Miss Barnes, we need to speak with you," her tone formal, severe, and directive.

Is the stern tone for the benefit of the dean or is the anger genuine, Josephine wonders?

"Please return to your room and we will join you there."

Josephine steps away, looking at the closed door to Margaret's room just beyond where the two are standing. She retreats to her room, hurriedly picking up the telegram and dress off the floor and tossing them in the closet before they enter behind her.

Miss Price is the first to walk in, followed by the dean, who closes the door after him.

"Why don't you sit down, Miss Barnes," she says, pointing to the reading chair in the middle of the room. Josephine does as she is told.

"For the record and the benefit of Dean Dawson, I want your concurrence that you and I have spoken a number of times in the past week about your recent conduct and your adherence to the letter and intent of the rules and expectations at National Park. Is this not so?"

Josephine nods and can feel the dean's uncomfortable, judgmental stare of disapproval from across the room.

"And during these consultations did I not instruct you of your obligation to inform me of any and all matters in which these requirements concerning student behavior were in question?"

Josephine nods again.

"Speak up. You have a voice."

"Yes."

"Were you not aware that your senior classmate, Margaret Cleary, was ill, in fact, seriously ill?"

"Yes, I—"

"Did you at any point in time communicate this to me or any member of the school administration?"

"I didn't need to. Margaret went to the nurse herself and the nurse treated her, and she gave her medicine to take. I saw her take the medicine."

"You went with her to the nurse?"

"No, but I saw the medicine she was given. You can ask Margaret. She can tell you."

"I've spoken to the nurse. She never saw Miss Cleary. And there is no record that she ever stopped by the school infirmary. If she was taking medicine for her illness, she didn't get it from the infirmary."

"I don't understand," she says, thinking back to the brown apothecary bottle without the label in Margaret's room.

"There is much I don't understand, Miss Barnes, despite repeated attempts on my part to impress upon you the need to present critical matters concerning the welfare of students to me without delay. To be direct, two nights ago I came to see you after the completion of the concert. You were not in your room that night. Where were you?"

"After the concert, I came back here to Senior House. I spent the night in Margaret's room."

"I see. Why would you spend the night in your sick friend's room?"

"We were talking."

"About what?"

Josephine pauses, wanting to slow down the interrogation, so she can make sense of the dean and regent's unexpected appearance in her room.

"We talked about what to do about Leah."

"What about Miss Hathaway?"

"She's been acting very strangely.

"She's not the only one," Miss Price shoots back.

"Leah was acting oddly, leaving campus alone in the middle of the night, threatening other girls, and even Mrs. Kaspar."

"Wait," the dean finally speaks, more to the regent than Josephine. "Are we talking about the girl in the chorus, one of the soloists?"

"Yes, Dean," Miss Price answers, "she lives on this floor, just down the hall. She is one of the four girls I told you about who went to the glen Monday morning during the flood. Miss Barnes, if you were so worried, why did you not bring your concerns about Miss Hathaway to my attention as you should have felt obliged to do?"

"We—Margaret and I—agreed that I would talk to you yesterday and tell you all that she had done and show you the—"

"The what, Miss Barnes?"

"What Leah had been doing."

"But you didn't come to see me, did you?"

Josephine shakes her head.

"Again, why not?"

"Everything happened all at once. Jennie, the freshman girl I mentor, stopped me in Vincent Hall in the midst of a personal crisis and then my... my date for the dance arrived early. I was on my way to see you and tell you about what happened, honestly. I came to see you, but you were gone by the time I got to your office. I needed to show you the—"

Josephine pauses again, unsure of how much detail she should confide and still protect Margaret and Mr. Raymee in the face of the regent's insistence for a full-accounting.

"Show me the what, Miss Barnes?"

"I need a moment, Miss Price."

The defiant regent steps into the hallway and returns holding the crude quilt of animal skins left on her chair at last night's ball.

"Perhaps this? The girls I spoke with said you brought this last night."

She tosses it on the floor in front of Josephine.

"Explain it to me."

"That's not mine, Miss Price! That's Leah's doing! She placed it on my chair when I got up to leave the dance. It's all part of her sick, vulgar game."

Josephine stands up, light-headed, her face flush with anger. The air in the room, baked by the strong rays of the morning sun streaming in through the curtain, is thin and suffocating. She walks over to the window and unlocks the latch and pushes opens the glass, feeling the dean's withering stare against her back. She draws the cold air, pure and refreshing, into her lungs over and over, trying to clear her head. She closes her eyes and feels the coating of perspiration along her forehead tingle as the crisp touch of winter washes over her.

"Miss Barnes," the voice calls her back.

Josephine opens her eyes and looks upon the brilliant white landscape, smooth and virginal, a blinding field of twinkling diamonds, like a bountiful gift bestowed upon the Earth overnight by benevolent gods.

"Miss Barnes."

She ignores the regent, content to stare across the magnificence before her.

"What is this?"

How do I explain the pelts to her, Josephine thinks, so that she will understand what has happened? How can I make her understand Leah's disintegrating mental state? I must make her see that the girl she should be subjecting to questions is down the hall.

"What is this?" the impatient woman repeats with greater urgency. "Is this blood?"

"Oh my Lord," the dean cries out with alarm.

Josephine turns around from the window. Miss Price, her face in abject horror, holds a cloth satchel and Josephine gasps at seeing the silvery blade and looks over quickly at the nearby desktop where she left the purloined dagger the night before.

"Weapons are strictly prohibited anywhere on campus, Miss Barnes," Miss Price declares, "and most definitely not allowed in dormitory rooms."

"That's the knife Leah used to cut my horse. I found it in the stable stall. That's what I am trying to tell you. She's a menace!"

"Oh my Lord," the dean repeats. "This nightmare only gets worse."

"What are you saying, Miss Barnes, Leah Hathaway used this knife against a horse, your horse?"

"That why we wanted to meet with you. She's gone mad, Miss Price. She's mad and she's dangerous. She must be stopped before she hurts anyone else."

Miss Price steps away, her condemning eyes locked on Josephine as she moves to the door.

"Dean Dawson, please stay here while I go find Miss Hathaway," she stammers, taking the cloth sack with her as she backs out of the room.

The dean shakes his head in disbelief, suddenly unable to look upon the scandalous girl.

"Dean, you must understand—"

The dean cuts her off with a violent, dismissive sweep of his hand and staggers away from the protesting girl until his back finds the wall by the doorway.

She turns around to the cracked window as a gentle breeze of chilled air inflates the lace curtains and sends them dancing along the sill. She hears the hollow sound down the hall of Miss Price pounding loudly against the Leah's door. Her thoughts fixate on her ill friend. She thinks about Margaret and the school nurse and tries to come up with an explanation for her ruse about the medicine. Why would she lie to me? Whatever the reason was, at least now she is being cared for properly.

Another round of fist pounding echoes down the vacant hall, followed by the rustle of keys.

Once Miss Price sees the condition of Leah's room, she will understand what I was saying, Josephine tells herself. The image in her mind's eye of the three of them—her, Margaret and Leah—together, finally coming clean before both the dean and Miss Price brings about an anticipatory feeling of relief, as if the crushing burden of the past week is about to be levitated off of her, allowing her to once again breathe without feeling the tightness across her chest and the compression along the length of her body.

A long, unbearable silence follows the disturbance down the hallway, and Josephine goes to shutter the window looking out on the pristine grounds, steeling her resolve for when she faces Leah and spells out the truth of her classmate's erratic, sadistic behavior.

A small black dot, perhaps a trick of the eye, appears against the whitewash of snow outside Josephine's opening to the reborn world. She raises her hand to her forehead to filter the penetrating glare. The lone smudge, a discordant mark against a field of almost heavenly purity, moves about her field of vision, distant but clearly identifiable in the sun's all-revealing brilliance. She hears words, urgent and fractured, from down the hall, their import registering on the dean's somber face. But she remains focused and watches from the third floor window as the animated figure disappears and then reappears repeatedly across the coated lawn.

Then, as if rendered on a miniature canvas, Leah's sharp, dark features come into focus. Miss Price has gone to retrieve a girl who is no longer in her room. There she is, in spirit or in flesh, or the embodiment of both, moving around the imposing statue in the field, the implacable warrior of righteousness. Her movements are like those of a pagan woman dancing about a ceremonial totem.

Josephine steps away from the window, her emotions buoyed by her discovery of Leah's whereabouts. She notices immediately that the dean has moved from his previous spot leaning against the wall and positioned himself to block the open doorway. A voice—Miss Price's voice—rings in her ears; she is angry, she is scared, she is panicked. The voice grows louder, but no less convoluted.

Dean Dawson turns around slightly to glimpse how far away the regent is from returning, and a capricious force propels the captive girl forward across the room and through the token physical resistance she meets. Josephine heads in the direction of the stairs, the clamor in her wake of no concern. She slows as she reaches Margaret's room. The door is slightly ajar and gives her hope that Margaret has returned from the infirmary and is resting. She presses her fingers against the door, just as the plea, no longer formal and detached, reaches her ears.

"Josephine, stay where you are!"

But the warning is too late, and even if it were not, the regent's words would not have stood a chance in holding back the desire Josephine felt in her heart at that hopeful, dream-like moment.

The balding middle-aged man, slight and dour, sitting on the chair is a stranger to her, and his delayed reaction to her sudden appearance and stilted physical response resemble those of an automaton. He looks up at the girl in the doorway with dull eyes and says nothing. He does not smile or scowl. He is emotionless. He is dressed in a simple black suit, his groomed and spotless hat resting in hands marred with brown age spots and prominent green veins. He is a protector, an overseer, one who shepherds those to their next place.

Beside him, a white sheet, imprinted with the block letters of the school monogram, covers a still, slender form lying on Margaret's bed. Under the peaks and folds of the shroud, the vague outline of human features is discernable, dissembled into fractured protrusions of flesh and bone and hair.

Josephine turns to stone. The incomprehensible appearance of her friend's body renders her speechless, breathless and paralyzed.

The image is so simple and elegant that Josephine momentarily admires the perverse beauty of the figure resting before her in the soft light, just before the hammer blow catches her squarely against the base of her skull.

A different voice—the third incarnation of Miss Price—speaks now. It is not that of officious inquisitor or hysterical alarmist. This voice is naked and vulnerable, stripped bare of any pretense. She is no longer the woman manning the breastworks of an institution in crisis. She is unconcerned by Dean Dawson authoritative presence. Her words are maternal, conciliatory and compassionate.

"I was going to tell you when the moment was right. I am so very sorry. It's an unfathomable tragedy. She was found in her bed a little while ago. She was not breathing. We're keeping the others away until the police and the coroner arrive."

Josephine feels Miss Price's hand rub her shoulder lightly.

"I want you to come back to your room until they get here. I will stay with you."

"Take the sheet off of her."

The seated man, a local doctor called once Margaret was found, looks over at the regent.

"Now is not the time, dear. Come back to your room. We can talk there."

"Take the sheet off of her. I want to see that it is Margaret. I don't believe you. Any of you. I want to see her face."

She struggles to remain composed but the notion that Margaret's dead body lays just feet away rips at her heart.

"You are in shock. We are all in shock. But I need you to focus on what I am saying. Come back to the room with me. The headmaster...I need to understand what happened last night."

"If you don't take the God damn sheet off of her face, I will do it myself!" she gnashes at the man as her vision goes blurry.

She wipes her eyes and lunges toward the bed only to be grabbed from behind by Miss Price and pulled backwards. The struggle is brief but intense and the teacher is thrown to the floor. Josephine staggers off to the side and regains her footing near the bed post. The shocked doctor slides his chair away from the two and refuses to prevent the girl's advance.

She wants to throw herself on the placid shape and rip at the oversized sheet with her hands until it lay in shreds on the floor about her. Her path to Margaret's bed now unimpeded, she hesitates though. Something about the outline of the covered body on the mattress is hauntingly familiar.

The slight turn-out of her feet, the protruding curve of her thighs, the rounded points of her hips, the board-flat run along her stomach.

This is how Josephine found her sleeping at first light nearly a week ago, when she snuck into her room and playfully pounced on her unsuspecting friend, the day the great flood lapped at the foundation of the Seminary.

The tenderness of the memory smoothes out the sharp edges of Josephine's mania and by the time she grips the sheet at the foot of the bed, she half-expects Margaret to react to her touch, as she did that fateful morning.

Miss Price rises up off the floor just as Josephine pulls back the bed linen and reveals the lower half of the body.

Josephine turns around, her face ecstatic, looking back and forth between the cowed physician and flushed regent.

"Whose dress is this?! This is not Margaret's! She abhorred white. Never wore it. She always said she wouldn't be caught—"

She cuts herself off, aware of the wickedness of the words that nearly escaped her lips.

"Margaret doesn't own a white dress. I am a hundred percent positive, Miss Price!"

The sheepish doctor finally speaks up, his droning, nasally voice devoid of warmth.

"Miss, it is for your own protection and out of an abundance of caution that I ask that you not touch the deceased and step away from the bed. The cause of death may have been a communicable virus and we cannot compound this tragedy by propagating it."

"Miss Price, do you understand what I am telling you? This is not Margaret! I know every dress in her closet. This is not our Margaret!"

The regent does not need to be told again. From the moment Josephine pulled back the sheet, she hasn't taken her eyes off the distinctive formal dress, the one she and hundreds of others had seen the chorus wear two nights before. Her composure shatters and the bricks of her resolute façade begin to crumble away, unleashing the hysteria held at bay.

"Miss, please step away from the body," the doctor warns a second time.

Josephine takes Miss Price's emotional collapse as a sure sign that she has uncovered a flaw that has done the impossible and miraculously reversed, in Dean Dawson's words, the nightmare.

Margaret cannot be dead. She has proven it not so.

"Don't you see, sweet girl," Miss Price manages through a filter of fingers closely pressed against her mouth. "That's not her dress. But that *is* Margaret."

Josephine, headstrong and unpersuaded, knows what she must do to convince her. She pulls the sheet back revealing fully the dress and the familiar form within it.

"That is enough, Miss! I must insist that you not disturb her!"

The doctor leaps forward and grabs the sheet from Josephine's hands and hurriedly places it over the peacefully posed corpse.

"Please, will you escort the young lady out of the room? She needs to be someplace other than here now."

As Miss Price tries to pull herself together enough to answer the irate man, Josephine stares down at the bed.

"What have I done?"

"You poor girl. Come with me, Josephine. Please. There is nothing you can do now. She's gone."

"What have I done?"

Josephine begins to feel the walls closing in around her. A suffocating veil falls over the room and extinguishes the morning light. The burden of existence is agonizing as she stands before the stilled heart and pale, lifeless flesh of her closest friend. The confines of the room continue to shrink until it is just her and Margaret. Nothing penetrates the walls of their entombment. They are now alone. She feels the crushing force—first against her back and then along her shoulders—that propels her forward toward the bed. She leans over and touches the space on the bed next to Margaret. The bed sheet is cold and the air around them turns spare and stifling. Gently she takes her place next to her friend, not wanting to disturb the beautiful creature in repose. As she leans her back slowly down on the mattress, she feels the weight of Margaret's body next to her. Above her, only blackness. The cover has been placed over them and secured. Josephine closes her eyes and exhales and feels the warmth of her breath pushed back along her nose and cheeks and mouth.

She remembers the wish she made to Margaret when they last sat in this room shoulder to shoulder the night of the concert.

Let's just stay here. Let the world go by without us.

Shadows of shadows awaken.

Josephine opens her eyes and sees the distraught face of Miss Price standing next to the bed, hand extended toward her.

"Come with me, sweet Josephine. Let me comfort you. We need each other now."

Dean Dawson motions to the doctor as Miss Price guides the stunned girl away from the bed.

"Who will take care of her, Miss Price? I can't leave now."

The doctor thoughtlessly answers for the regent.

"She will be taken care of, Miss. That's not your problem now."

That's not your problem now.

Not your problem now.

Whose problem is it now?

Who is the problem now?!

Josephine breaks away from the regent's comforting hold and dashes out the room, clipping the stunned headmaster and sending him hard against the wall.

"Miss Barnes, you are to remain in your room," his words follow her down the hallway as she sprints for the stairway, the strength in her legs returning with each stride.

By the time Miss Price recovers and follows her, the manic girl has reached the stairs and is hurtling down them recklessly.

"Let the police handle it, Katharine," the dean calls out as the regent pursues her, the last words Josephine hears before she reaches the empty dormitory lobby.

She bursts through the front door and descends the perilous, snow-encrusted steps, dressed only in her school uniform, heading across the unmarred, horizonless, white expanse stretching before her. Her movements are that of a sleek predator flying across an open field. Her long strides dig into the snow just long enough to gain traction and then release and repeat over again, her arms synchronized and pumping furiously, propelling her body forward, her head centered and nearly motionless, despite the frenetic strain of muscle and tendons on the bones throughout her body. Her body slices through the cold air, lifting her untied hair off her shoulders. The roughness of a million cutting crystals quickly produces red abrasions along her exposed shins and ankles. Warm adrenaline courses through her body pushing her past the pain. The cadence of her breathing—three short draws in, one long push out—fills her ears and blocks out all other sounds around her.

Halfway across, the lawn begins its gradual slope and as the ground yields, Josephine's destination comes into sight. Her furious pace quickens. She wants to cry out from the stabbing pain in her lungs.

Why does she not see me? Why does she not hear me coming?

Leah dances alone before the imposing Statue of Justice, the divine beauty seated with its broad sword raised toward the heavens. She smiles as she moves with a carefree, childlike, looseness about the trampled snow in front of the gargantuan statue. Soft words of approval drift down and fill her ears, rapturous notes sweeter than any every sung from the stage of the Odeon. She turns and looks up at the benevolent guardian towering over her, her cheeks and nose ruby red from the morning chill.

It is this portrait of contentment—Leah's smiling, rosy face, her eyes upturned, her lips parted—that brings Josephine's rage to an uncontrollable boil.

Leah speaks in a peaceful voice and declares her place among the deities.

"Deliverance."

It is the last sound before the avenging angel swoops down upon the unsuspecting girl.

The first blow catches Leah flush on the cheek and produces a sickening crack of shattered bone. Josephine throws the weight of her body against Leah and drives her into the frozen ground with tremendous force. Stunned by the vicious attack, Leah relents and does not struggle when Josephine turns her on her back. Both left and right fists target the pinioned girl's head, not with undisciplined punches launched wildly from the side but direct, efficient jabs that fire from the shoulder, like powerful pistons, and pummel their target over and over until the impact of fist to flesh grows viscous and slippery and a halo of crimson forms in the snow around Leah's splayed brown hair. The punishing blows slow and Josephine, uncaring of Leah's pain, sees the smiling girl's eyes fluttering on the edge of consciousness. Her arms heavy with fatigue and her knuckles aching and covered with the slick warmth of flowing blood, she rolls off her tormentor, gasping for breath.

"You killed her, you horrible beast!"

Leah rises up from the ground and staggers to her feet, streaks of bright red running down her chin and neck and dripping along the front of her coat. One eye is already swollen shut and the misshapen cheek gives her a ghoulish appearance. She looks down with pity upon her attacker panting in the snow.

"Her death was not by my hand," she answers calmly, smearing the blood from her upper lip with a draw of her hand. "I was the one who kept her comfortable and prepared her to accept the end. I was there for Margaret when you weren't. If it wasn't for me, she would have left us, alone and confused and scared. I stayed with her the entire night until they took her away and relieved her of her pain."

"Murderer!!"

"She was marked for death. There was nothing I could do to stop it."

"What made you into this monster!?" Josephine forces out, exhausted, half-crazed and still in shock over finding Margaret's lifeless body.

"Then I am God's monster. The hand of Nature is neither indiscriminate nor cruel. Curse if you must, but I see order and meaning in the chaos around us."

"You will burn in hell for what you've done."

"Josephine, you still don't see, do you? I was there when Margaret needed someone to help guide her in those final, difficult hours. And when she was faced with her own mortality, just as the sun rose, when her remaining breathes were few, she knew she could no longer control her fate, any more so than you or I can decide to break away from their hold.

"You speak as if Margaret's life was nothing! Don't you even care that our friend is dead?! Her poor parents…"

Josephine succumbs and lets out a prolonged wail of inconsolable grief.

"It was Margaret's time to go."

"Stop saying that!!" Josephine snarls. "Tell me why I shouldn't come over right now and grab you by the hair and dash your brains against the stone?"

"Because *they* won't allow it."

"Do you think I care what they think after what you've done to Margaret? The dean's called the police. By the time they get here, it will be too late for you."

Leah lets out a mocking laugh over swollen, bloodied lips that further enrages the frenzied girl.

"I'm not talking about the police or the dean or Miss Price or any of the other ants that walk about this place."

"Tell me what you did to her. So help me God, tell me now, Leah, or I will make you tell me. I don't care anymore what happens to me."

"There is a greater power here, and we glimpsed its face in the waters the morning they took the young girl. We are weak in the glow of their magnificence. They decide who stays and who goes, who lives and who dies. You scorned me when I came to you for help in the beginning, but I don't blame you. We were all meek and obedient; we had no reason to question the reality of our surroundings. After the storm, even I didn't understand how the four of us being there, touching the waters, blessed us and gave us purpose. From that moment forward, our lives were changed. We no longer controlled our destiny. All of us were anointed—even you—we just didn't know it at the time. Our existence has new meaning now."

"No one drowned. You know that. There is no missing girl. I am talking about poor dear Margaret! She'd dead and all you can do is laugh and dance about like a madwoman!"

"Pity the one whose life is touched, no matter how brief, by the hand of God—how can I? We are the lucky ones. The proof of the miracle is all around us. Flesh is temporal. But they endure. Does the voice speak to you? I know you hear them too. You are too frightened to admit it. Accept them, Josephine. They speak to you, just like they speak to me. They tell me so."

Josephine looks up from the ground at the disfigured girl. Her arm is pointed up at the stone colossus.

"What are you saying?"

"I know. Isn't it amazing how their voices guide us? The others walk about them oblivious, clueless of their omnipotence. They're all about us. Sacred guardians. Watching over the Odeon stage. At the Grotto. In front of the Mission. We pass them everyday. Along the gymnasium walk. By the Senior House steps. But they chose us—out of all the girls here—they chose us. They have given us the gift of enlightenment, and they will guide us in our journey."

A sickening thought, overlooked in the hysteria she woke to, crosses Josephine's mind and brings forth a wave of physical revulsion. The black letters of the telegram slipped under her door scroll across her mind's eye.

"What do *they* say about Robert, my boyfriend?"

Leah, one-eyed and gruesome from the unabated flow of blood from her nose, walks slowly over and squats down next to Josephine.

"He is gone. He would only have brought you heartache. His love was not true and pure, like theirs. Stop resisting, Josephine. Do as I have and allow them in, and then you will see what it is to be loved eternally."

"Oh dear God, no! This can't be happening! What have you done?!!"

"I saw it on Margaret's face just before her heart was halted. When she stopped resisting. The pain of existence had left her. It was spiritual."

Leah drops to her knees and wraps her arms around Josephine's slumped shoulders and burrows her mangled face against the panting, unresisting girl's neck.

Through a curtain of matted brown hair, Josephine sees four figures approaching down the hill. Leah's breath is hot against her exposed skin.

"Wait for it," the voice whispers into her ear.

Josephine's cold, trembling fingers slide inside Leah's open coat and move hesitantly along both sides of her rib cage and feel the vertical stalk of bones protruding from under the deranged girl's dress. She pulls Leah close against her body and feels the reciprocal tug along her shoulders.

"Wait for it," she hears repeated softly.

The figures draw nearer and she recognizes Miss Price and Dean Dawson through the dark veil. The other two men, larger and wearing uniforms, catch sight of the blood-stained snow and begin to run towards them.

Josephine's numb, jittery hands intertwine and pull Leah closer still. Her eyes squeeze shut and she draws a deep breath and holds it, waiting for Leah to exhale first. When she does, Josephine clamps her palms against the middle of the girl's back violently and tightens her grasp with all her might. The effect is immediate and debilitating as Leah struggles to escape, unable to draw another breath. Her hands clench and spasm, clawing frantically at the fabric of her captor's uniform. But Josephine does not relinquish her hold and continues to compress Leah's squirming body as the remaining air is pushed out of the weakening girl's lungs. Bright lines cascade down inside Josephine's eyelids like stars plummeting from the sky as the resistance in the constricted flesh slowly drains away. She feels Leah's mouth gasp and sputter against her neck.

Only they will save you now.

Chapter 12
Phoenix Reborn

National Park College
Successor To National Park Seminary
Forest Glen, Maryland
Suburb of Washington, D.C.

September 22, 1942

To Alumnae and Former Students of National Park College:

When a nation is fighting for its very existence, it is necessary for its Government to draft institutions as well as individuals for war emergency purposes. In the crisis that now confronts our Nation, men and women have been called from practically every home in the land to serve their country. Educational institutions have also been called to serve their country.

I deeply regret to inform you that the United States Government has found it necessary to take title by condemnation proceedings in the Federal Court to our entire National Park College property, for use of the United States Army as a hospital. The fact that the campus and buildings are near Walter Reed Hospital Army Medical Centre makes them desirable and necessary for the use of the Government in the war emergency.

Under the circumstance there is nothing we can do but accept the Government's decision and make this sacrifice for the welfare of our country. I know that this will come as a shock to you, as it has to us, but I hope that you will feel that the sacrifice is not too great when you realize that the College will house the sick and wounded who are fighting for democracy.

Since the Government has taken title to the property, it is not possible to make any plans for the future. However, I know that those who lived at and loved National Park will treasure memories of the days they spent here. I hope that the ideals and traditions of National Park were developed and maintained by administrative officers, faculty and students during its long and useful service as an educational institution will guide and strengthen all of us in these trying times.

I shall find a place to safeguard the College records and make them available to those who may need transcripts of their grades in future years. I hope that the alumnae clubs will continue to maintain their organizations.

I am
    Yours very sincerely,

    Roy Tasco Davis

The procession of cars and hauling trucks begin arriving before ten in the morning. When all the spaces in the rear of Vincent Hall are taken, the overflow of vehicles crowds the curbed roads of the adjacent residential neighborhood. It is a balmy fall day and the immature street trees parched by a dry, scorching summer have already dropped their color. A toddler plays in his front yard under the watchful gaze of an elderly woman while a black terrier races back and forth along a perimeter fence challenging cars and mothers pushing carriages down a smooth, unstained concrete sidewalk.

Rumors about the National Park Seminary's closure have been circulating for two decades. After the property's sale to Stratton Enterprises in the early twenties, a development plan to combine the central campus with bordering, undeveloped parcels into a new incorporated township served by public transit lines was shelved. Business soothsayers speculated at the time that the softness of the real estate market was responsible for the grandiose project's demise. While the school was saved from the chopping block for the time being, modestly-sized neighborhoods were built on the newly purchased farmland, bringing the wave of development to the boundary line of the encircled school. Trolley service to Forest Glen ended a few years later and was replaced by diesel engine buses that could better and more cheaply serve the expansion of residential construction into the wedges of verdant piedmont once served by colonial carriage routes.

When school enrollment withered during the Great Depression, a few desirable tracts along the edges of campus, such as the tennis courts and the riding paddock south of the county road, were sliced off and sold to help pay the crushing debt coming due for the aggressive capital investment of the previous decade. Soon after, Edgewood, dilapidated from neglect and no longer suitable as the headmaster's residence, was shuttered and eventually fell victim to an arsonist's match. The ancient trees on the antebellum property were cut down and the land was subdivided to be marketed as individual lots served by a pipestem drive under the billboard name of Edgewood Estates. Douglas Stratton's death in 1933 from pneumonia put this development scheme and many other financial propositions on hold as the extent of his corporate and personal holdings and the true value of his once-considerable wealth were put under the microscope of probate court and the scrutiny of a cadre of litigators hired by his descendants, some of whom claimed the widower's will to be *"ambiguous as to intent"* and *"built upon a foundation of factual errors and willful misrepresentations."*

With the school's viability in doubt and its main benefactor dead, National Park Seminary seemed destined for quick closure. But the property was sold at a bargain price to a wealthy financier highly influential in Republican circles who was enamored with the sleepy, bucolic setting but found the concept of a high-priced finishing school for rich girls to be a quaint yet antiquated and unsustainable concept in such dire economic times. He renamed the venerable institution National Park College, liberated its students from many of the dusty traditions such as uniforms and chaperones, and successfully pursued a junior college charter.

As the nation emerged from the lost decade, efforts to bring modern changes to National Park and fashion a curriculum less elitist and more conducive to equipping young women for the twentieth century workplace paid dividends. Enrollment steadily rose and the school was on the road to recovery as it approached its golden anniversary as a preeminent educational institution, generously supported by distinguished alumnae occupying the highest rungs of the societal ladder afforded to women. The advent of a second cataclysmic war snuffed out this restoration, however, when the government laid claim to the sprawling campus as an annex to its central Walter Reed hospital operations a short distance away. The Seminary's eclectic buildings

442 ANDY JOHNSON

and tranquil grounds would be saved, but now dedicated to the rehabilitation of soldiers with disfiguring and debilitating war wounds and prolonged mental trauma. The peaceful setting would be an ideal recuperative hospital, military planners decided, for those struggling with the horrors of combat.

An employee of Wechsler's Auction House stands at the wrought iron gate handing those who enter a flier directing them to the front of Elizabeth Stratton Hall where the liquidation sale will be held. Representatives from area hotels and schools mingle with private buyers and curious locals along the path winding through the quiet, overgrown grounds, marveling at the aging architectural flourishes and oddities around them. On the central roundabout in front of Vincent Hall, a large crater of recently excavated ground is cordoned off with rope to prevent those entranced by the exotic buildings from inadvertently stepping into the steep hole where the garish Italian fountain once was. It, along with other large pieces of metal around the campus, such as the Amazon warrior statue in the senior dormitory lobby and the Mermaid of the Glen, were taken for scrap earlier in the year to feed the war mobilization effort.

Much of the school's remaining contents are segregated onto two dozen of so large pallets under a massive, triple-peaked tent pitched on the lawn. A vast assortment of tables and chairs, lamps and paintings, rugs and pianos are on display under the sheltering tarp. Smaller items, such as dishes, linens, clocks, and books are packed in a multitude of reinforced boxes and surplus crates stacked on the sagging wood slats. Prospective buyers circulate about inspecting the lots for sale, scrutinizing the appearance and condition of the discarded surplus with the trained eye of an art connoisseur evaluating the hung works of a deceased master artist. But the sheer enormity of the items up for auction and the approaching time for the starting gavel makes a thorough inspection impractical. Buyers look about, size up their competition, and realize that bargains will be had at today's auction, even if it means buying lots with some containers of ultimately useless or unsellable possessions.

A middle-aged man stands before Lot 27 drawing on a Chesterfield and admiring the pair of ebony nymphets holding glass globes above their heads and wonders whether the sleek statues would be too risqué for his corner Mediterranean restaurant. He considers the frayed carpet rolled and propped against a tower of boxes as a worthy addition to the back dining room, but debates the wisdom of purchasing the provocative twins, despite his fascination with their smooth nubile forms.

He begins rummaging through opened boxes situated along the ground looking for other fixtures or kitchen utensils that will tip the scales of his indecision. Many of them are filled with administration records and papers of no interest to him. He walks among the detritus of the school's storied past searching for useful items, pushing aside books and binders as he tries to unearth hidden treasure.

As he shoves one of the stacked crates to the side to reach a large container in the back, it topples over, sending the contents of an overstuffed folder across the pallet. He looks around and, seeing that the accidental dumping was witnessed by others nearby, sighs, places the Chesterfield between his lips, and bends down to refill the crate. A light blue pamphlet, faded around the edges by sun exposure, attracts his attention and he reads the front cover through a haze of white smoke before tossing it back into the box, failing to notice the card protruding from inside the publication.

Had the annoyed restaurant owner not been in such a rush and possessed a sense of curiosity broader than the search for cooking pots, serving plates, and the like, he may have been intrigued by the booklet's title and thought it worthwhile to investigate further. The embossed marker, bearing the name and title of *Mrs. Charlotte Martin, Prefect of Studies*, was left to guide the reader past the report's dry recitation of empirical data and geological surveys and clinical epidemiology to the most sensationalistic and enduring chapter of the school's lore.

Treasury Department
United States Public Health Service
Public Health Bulletin No. 65
May, 1922
Typhoid Fever In Forest Glen, MD
Report Of An Outbreak Caused By
An Infected Water Supply
From A Deep Well

By
W.W. Kuhns
Surgeon, United States Pubic Health Service

Summary of Conclusions
On the request of the State Board of Health of Maryland, the writer
was detailed on January 20, by the Surgeon General of the Public Health

Service, to make an investigation of an outbreak of typhoid fever in Forest Glen, Md.

Flowing though a meadow about 400 feet north of and slightly downhill toward the Rock Creek tributary is a small stream, known by locals as Monkey Run. The bed of the stream is said to be usually dry in the summer, but in times of heavy rains the stream frequently overflows its banks and helps to hold back a considerable stand of water in the low ground to the west.

The residence nearest Monkey Run is approximately 100 feet away, on the north side of the county road. This residence consists of five persons. The privy in use is not provided with a receptacle under the seat and is of the open back, surface variety. Passing within about 10 feet of, and downhill from, the privy is a spring branch which has its origin in the yard back of the house. The dejecta under the privy drain into this open branch, and in times of heavy rains must be washed into it. The spring stream flows across the meadow for the first 40 or 50 feet on the surface and for the rest of the way through a perforated tile drain placed about 2 feet below the ground surface, and discharges into Monkey Run. At the nearest point this "secret ditch" is only about 80 feet from the Rock Creek tributary.

In November, 1921, a man and a girl, the whereabouts of both currently unknown, visited this house. The man took to bed with typhoid fever about November 27 and was subsequently moved from the house to a nearby boat storage facility on the banks of Rock Creek. For the two weeks of the visitor's stay, the illness was not diagnosed by a physician and was not treated as such by those in the residence. The man, however, continued to use the family privy and the individual's excreta was neither treated nor segregated. On or about December 6 the visiting man and the girl departed the area for an undisclosed destination.

The chronology of the outbreak indicated that the period of causation had its beginning in this early December time frame. It is of interest to note that heavy rains occurred at Forest Glen about the time of the beginning of the causation period. The precipitation observed during November and December, 1921 at Great Falls, Md., and Yarrow, Md., the two United States Weather Bureau stations nearest Forest Glen, is detailed in this Bulletin's appendix.

The dangerous pollution of the ground in the neighborhood of the residence, the time of occurrence of heavy rains, and the results of the bacteriological examinations of water along Monkey Run, all support the epidemiological findings pointing to consumption from the water supply as the vector of infection which caused the outbreak. The result of a uranine demonstration test proved that there was a fairly rapid communication between the secret ditch draining the privy and ground in which the dejecta from the typhoid-fever patient had been deposited in November and December, 1921.

In the course of the investigation, school and police records were reviewed and indicate that the first casualty infected in the outbreak, a resident student at the nearby National Park Seminary for Young Women, was in the vicinity of Monkey Run on December 6 on a trail ride with a fellow rider and while dismounted consumed water from a pool of standing water adjacent to the branch, which had recently overflowed from the heavy precipitation of the preceding week. The other rider present did not consume water from the typhoid-tainted stream and was not infected by the outbreak. Close contact between the first casualty, a woman of eighteen years of age, and a third student at the school, resulted in transmission of the contracted typhoid fever. This second casualty was treated and subsequently cured of the illness. The first casualty, however, undiagnosed and untreated for typhoid fever, died on December 11, 1921. No other cases of infection were identified at the school, at the nearby private residence, or in the general Forest Glen vicinity.

Prophylactic measures, including hypochlorite treatment of the water supply, have been instituted and the secret ditch draining into Monkey Run has been plugged.

A brass bell rings from the steps of Elizabeth Stratton Hall and prospective buyers circulating about the pallets under the tent begin to make their way to the auction podium, chasing the season's remaining grasshoppers lurking in the dry lawn as they go.

The restaurant owner shovels the spilled documents and newspaper clippings back into the box without care, grinds his cigarette into the pine floor board, and takes one last survey of the lot for sale. He decides he will bid on it, though he will probably have to incinerate much of it after he hauls it away and sorts through the remaining uninspected boxes.

As the man jogs over to join the other bidders congregating in front of the erstwhile dormitory, a welcome breeze stirs the treetops in the distance and sweeps down along the shaded contours of the glen and across the rusting pedestrian bridge. When the gust reaches the horseshoe of vacant and bordered buildings, it swirls about and ripples the tethered canvas covering the items for sale. The discarded papers returned haphazardly to the open box rustle in the wind and some are blown out and land unnoticed across the lawn.

Among the litter of forms and papers strewn about is a clipped article, brown and fragile, reporting the unsolved disappearance of a U.S. Navy midshipman who went missing in a snowstorm after he left the annual Christmas gala. Despite a coordinated investigation involving the Montgomery County and District of Columbia police forces and Naval Academy criminal investigators, the case never produces a credible lead as to Robert Winslow's whereabouts or a motive explaining his disappearance.

Leah's indirect culpability in Margaret's death and her unraveled mental capacity make her the primary focus of the investigation. Once her violent behavior toward Josephine and May over the preceding days is revealed, the court of common opinion among shocked and grieving students and staff condemns the unhinged musical prodigy for Robert's disappearance as well. But when investigators reconstruct the timeline of events on the night in question, they are unable to place her with the missing man at anytime after his arrival. Her alibi that she was in Margaret's room before the time the midshipman was last seen holds tight. During many hours of repeated police questioning, she tantalizingly offers only that "I am told he is gone," but refuses to explain further who told her this or where he went. A year will pass before the investigation is closed over the strenuous objections from his grieving parents and family members who steadfastly argue a man of Robert's character and promise could not simply vanish from the face of the Earth without a trace.

Josephine is hastily withdrawn from the Seminary by her parents immediately after the inquiry into Margaret's death is completed and never returns to Forest Glen. Her personal belongings are packed and shipped to her family's home on Christmas Eve. Prohibited by her parents from attending her closest friend's funeral, she sends a lengthy letter to Margaret's family recounting the many stories and remembrances she has of their years together at the Seminary. But she never receives a reply.

Robert's mother and father, on the other hand, carry on a steady correspondence with Josephine in the months that follow in the hopes that the girl they never met, the one Robert had confided to them he loved, might remember some detail which would shed light on his fate. The letters are heartfelt and painful and Josephine answers them dutifully, always reminding them that she too has not given up hope he will one day be found. Something important is withheld from these emotionally raw communications however, a gnawing secret she refuses to reveal to the worried, angry, grieving parents or anyone else in the aftermath of the tragedy: Robert's spurned proposal of marriage. The possibility that her devastating rejection could have played a role in his disappearance is too much for her to bear. She carries the weight of what might have been in solitude, forever wondering how the course of events would have been altered had she not let him walk away down the empty corridor that fateful night. In time, the letters from the Winslows become more infrequent and one day stop arriving all together, just as the scar tissue around Josephine's heart grows thick and calloused.

The auctioneer's gavel strikes hard and another lot is sold. By mid-afternoon, over half of the items for sale have been bought. Hand carts and dollies are busy transporting furniture and other cumbersome purchases to waiting trucks in the rear of Vincent Hall as the crowd begins to thin out.

A man walks about the remaining pallets searching for bedroom furniture holding the hand of his young daughter who strains and begs to break free and hide among the enticing clutter of statues and lamps and mountains of stained wood. A honey brown chest of drawers with brass handles catches his eye and he releases his pleading daughter so he can better inspect the piece. The curved drawers are dovetail jointed and slide open smoothly as he tests each one. The top drawer balks, catches on something inside, and dislodges from its runner. He tries unsuccessfully to straighten it and is forced to pull the drawer all the way out in order to fit it back in properly. When he does, he locates the obstruction, a slender rectangular box wrapped in thin paper, jammed against the back of the compartment. He takes it out and shakes it and a note card held in place by a twisted ribbon falls on the dresser top. His mischievous daughter returns and snatches the intriguing package from his hand before he can react and sits on the ground nearby. The curious man opens the card and reads the cursive script of an unsteady hand.

Dear Miss Barnes, we are warned not to accept gifts from strangers. However, I have been carrying this with me for quite a while waiting for the opportunity when I can share its meaning with someone who can truly appreciate it. Her name was Elizabeth Stratton. She was my daughter. And I loved her more than she ever knew. Her compassion for others made a mockery of my own self-indulgence. I am told you possess the best of my dear Elizabeth's nature and are a worthy caretaker of her legacy. Please take this and remember the girl who also heard the cries of others and had the courage to answer them.

Respectfully, Douglas Stratton

"Daddy, look. I am a soldier. Daddy, look!"

The man turns around and sees the shredded paper and the empty box lying at his daughter's feet. In her hand is a pristine war ribbon of imperial blue and red affixed to a gold cross. She presses it to her chest and smiles with delight.

"Can I have it, so I can show all the kids at school?"

The auction grinds on throughout the day and by the time the sun sets and a few lots remain to be sold, pole lights are brought out of storage and hooked up to gas generators and the sell-off continues until all that remains are the boxed and catalogued holdings of Miller Library. A spirited bidding war among three buyers representing local preparatory schools breaks out over the wall of stacked boxes and prolongs the marathon sale. The exhausted, raspy-voiced auctioneer is revitalized however, finding the evening competition between the only remaining buyers peculiarly humorous. When the prevailing bid is gaveled down, the auction house workers congratulate each other on their endurance and begin to break down the podium and collapse the empty rows of folding metal chairs. The winning bidder works the dolly under the first stack of three boxes and shakes his head ruefully at the mountain behind it ready to be carted away.

It will take many days before the librarian at the recipient school sorts through the hard-won prize and inspects and triages those books to be stacked, those to be donated, and those to be destroyed. The valuable first editions and printed rarities are culled from the thousands of tomes and the remaining collection is then grouped by subject and author. The library is well-preserved as a whole and only a handful is deemed unworthy of being added to the school's library expansion due to inferior condition or irreparable damage. Among this small group of rejects is a sadly vandalized early printing of the *Poetic Works of Edgar Allan Poe.*

The book's cover is immaculate. The gold embossing is unmarred and shiny, and the binding is strong. The edition is intact and the edges are sharp with no rips or creases. Its defilement is evident, however, when the librarian opens it for a cursory examination of the crisp pages. A thick black line—the mark of a grease pencil or wax crayon—has been drawn down the center of each page, both front and back. The librarian flips through the book stunned by the extent of the defacement. Whoever ruined the nearly two hundred pages spent a considerable amount of time and took perverse care in doing so.

INCIDENT AT FOREST GLEN 449

Each vertical line is identical in length and so uniformly straight that a ruler or edge of some sort must have been used to draw them.

The waste of a good book, the librarian thinks to herself. As she thumbs through the volume of poetry she catches a fleeting glimpse of a broken pattern. She stops and turns back five or six pages until she finds it again. There. The only page in the entire compilation not defaced with the vile slash. The librarian adjusts her reading glasses on the bridge of her nose and reads the curiously spared and therefore highlighted verse.

THE VALLEY OF UNREST

Once it smiled a silent dell
Where the people did not dwell;
They had gone unto the wars,
Trusting to the mild-eyed stars,
Nightly from their azure towers,
To keep watch above the flowers,
In the midst of which all day
The red sunlight lazily lay.
Now each visitor shall confess
The sad valley's restlessness.
Nothing there is motionless—
Nothing save the airs that brood
Over the magic solitude.
Ah, by no wind are stirred those trees
That palpitate like the chill seas
Around the misty Hebrides!
Ah, by no wind those clouds are driven
That rustle through the unquiet Heaven
Uneasily, from morn till even,
Over the violets there that lie
In myriad types of the human eye—
Over the lilies there that wave
And weep above a nameless grave!
They wave: —from out their fragrant tops
Eternal dews come down in drops.
They weep: —from their delicate stems
Perennial tears descend like gems.

She turns to the inside of the book's back cover and pulls the borrower's card from the affixed envelope. Cramped rows of names fill the front and back. The writing in the compact log is faded and difficult to read. The last name on the card stands out however, not because it is familiar but because it is repeated three times—the name of the culprit responsible for the damage is memorialized in the delicate signature of *M. King.*

The librarian shakes her head and tosses the collection of poems into the wheeled laundry bin where, at end of her lonely shift, it, along with the other ruined books, will be pushed to the basement and burned in the furnace with the rest of the school refuse.

On a bluff overlooking the city, in an Italian Gothic Revival building along the Anacostia River, a woman walks alone down a parquet-tiled hallway, waxed and buffed to a high sheen earlier during the dinner hour. The door at the end of the corridor is locked and when she reaches it, a man stares down at her from the other side. In a subservient whisper, she asks the man for permission to pass.

"Not yet," he tells the hopeful woman through the glass pane reinforced with wire.

Her hair is fully gray and crudely cropped close to the scalp. She smiles, turns around without saying a word, and walks back the way she came. She passes other patients of St. Elizabeths Hospital along the corridor as she sets out on her nightly ritual, pacing back and forth repeatedly, like a caged animal continually testing the unchanging confines of her imprisonment. Her demeanor is calm however, almost reflective, as she moves about the narrow ward.

When she reaches the door at the far end of the hallway, a second orderly, not possessing the patience of the first, doesn't wait for her to speak. Why would she? After all, the question is always the same. It has been for years now, day after day, week after week, month after month. Always the same.

"Go ask him," she says in an uncharitable voice.

The compliant woman turns without protest and begins walking dutifully back along the shimmering floor. As she moves, the loose white gown flows around her thin, wasted body. Her skin is tightly drawn over her cheeks and skull but sags along her atrophied arms and spindly legs, giving her the appearance of a woman twenty years her senior.

She smiles warmly at the other patients as she passes, though her friendly overture is usually ignored or goes unnoticed. They too walk about wearing the cloaks of the demigods, overseeing their respective realms. They followed her here. Or was it the other way around? Had she been the one accepted into their fold? Either way, she walks among them now and talks with them when it is allowed. They are a mercurial lot, temperamental and prone to rage. And is it not to be expected, stuck here in this infernal purgatory?

Again she reaches her destination. "Can I enter now?" she asks the stoic face looking down at her.

"Not yet," the soothing voice repeats.

And the journey to nowhere continues into the night.

Epilogue
Asclepius' Rod

You feel the train begin to lose life and instead of the brisk forward motion and the constant rush of wind outside the window the car rocks from side to side as it decelerates. You are now aware of the clatter of each intersection of track and how the repetitious sound is growing further apart. You busy yourself by looking out the coach window for recognizable landmarks to take your mind off of the nervousness growing inside you, but the landscape of the approaching railyard is grim and unappealing in the weak light of dusk. A quarter-mile out from the station platform, soot-covered observation towers and controller buildings rise out of a vast mechanized field, where scores of rails divide the land like plowed rows of steel. A newly built humpbacked armory rises up on the left, its enormous curved roof dwarfing the nearby red brick buildings. The train lurches violently to the side as it switches tracks and you instinctively grab a hold of the suitcase resting against your legs.

A man with an ill-fitting cap and ticket punch clipped to his belt walks down the corridor announcing in a baritone voice that the train's final destination—Union Station, Washington, D.C.—has been reached. The words heighten the anxiety you feel and you watch the other travelers retrieve their belongings and jockey for position in the congested car. They are in a rush to disembark; you are not. Though this is what you wanted, and the decision you insisted on making, the moment has arrived, the point of no return, and it frightens you like nothing else ever has before. Was it a mistake after all, you ask yourself? What have I gotten myself into? Is it really too late?

The train slows to a crawl and the concrete platform and protective awnings come into view. It is already crowded, a sea of travelers, many in uniforms and carrying duffel bags over their shoulders. You are used to crowds, around them and in them all of your life, but this one is different. These are not the people of your city and you are alone.

You wanted it this way. A clean break. Farewells and hugs and tears before you departed, and then the hours by yourself, a chance to think and to ponder the enormity of what awaits you. You knew the initial feeling of

454   ANDY JOHNSON

excitement would turn at some point, but the distress that makes your heart beat faster and starts your skin tingling is more powerful than you expect.

The collective pull of the departing passengers is powerful too. You feel the vortex of motion pick you up from your seat and draw you towards the stairs at the end of the car. Looking at the calm faces surrounding you is reassuring and tamps down the panic you feel waiting for the train to unload. They stand patiently in formation, somber and reflective, and then the doors open noisily, one by one. You join them, emboldened that the first step is the hardest but that once you are embraced into the fold your instincts will take over.

The conductor holds your hand and helps you off the stairs onto a metal step stool while you balance your suitcase at your side. He says something to you in a polite voice but you are not really sure what as your senses focus on the boisterous crush of bodies on the platform. You find a small opening and are carried off by the current of humanity, not as much walking on your own as allowing yourself to be pushed along. There is no turning back now, even if you wanted to. The confluence of arrivals from different platforms slows your progress through the doors leading inside of the station. Bodies pressed against bodies. You can see nothing and there is nothing to see, other than a migration of men and women jostling to get ahead and waiting for their passage through the tunnel gates.

Once you make it through, the tight, claustrophobic world of the past few minutes immediately opens up. The grand visitors hall is cavernous and everyone moves about freely, some heading to hail a cab, others embracing family and friends, while many huddle around ticket booths or wait on long wooden benches. You marvel at the ornate, neo-classical and Beaux Arts design and the abundant columns and statuary encircling the mezzanine above the hall. Inside this Romanesque temple of marble and gold leaf, a cloth poster of gigantic proportions hangs from the vaulted ceiling above the entrance to the station's north wing. Its patriotic depiction is captivating: a row of GIs marching in lockstep under an ominous gray sky looking over at the ghosts of colonial freedom fighters holding the standard of a new nation.

1778 1943

AMERICANS
will always fight for liberty

Below the imposing banner you see a square-shaped arrangement of tables decorated with red, white and blue bunting on all sides. Those congregating around the induction station are mostly young women like you, and now you realize that the moment you have often imagined has finally arrived.

You do not say a word as you approach tentatively, but the woman behind the table can tell why you are here. She smiles and beckons you over. She recognizes the look on your face having seen it in so many other women who have made the same walk to the makeshift booth. Behind the barrier of tables you see nurses dressed in white and wearing caps bearing a red cross greeting and mingling with others who have just arrived.

You tell her who you are and she looks over a sheet of paper and finds the name *Carter* near the top of the list. The noise inside the station is overwhelming and reverberates around the lofty ceiling, and when the woman speaks, her words are lost in the din of hundreds of other conversations. She repeats herself and extends her arm, ready to take your suitcase behind the desk for safe keeping so that you can join the rest. When you hand over the new brown luggage, a sharp pain of separation comes over you, as if something is being severed. The simple act produces a feeling of finality, that the course of events about to unfold has now been set in motion and is irreversible.

The woman takes the suitcase from your hand and glances at the softened, well-worn leather tag attached to the handle engraved with the letters *M.C.*

Your mother gave it to you many years ago when you were a young girl, the cherished belonging of a lost friend, the namesake you never met.

Acknowledgments

While the characters and events in *Incident at Forest Glen* are fictional, the National Park Seminary for Young Women did exist and has a fascinating and storied past. The descriptions of the school's layout and its eccentric architecture are faithfully depicted in the novel. A significant number of the buildings described in the book were preserved over time and recently redeveloped as a residential housing complex. The Seminary campus, including remnants of the original statuary, can still be toured today. Sadly, many of the school's physical treasures were lost, stolen or destroyed during the over fifty years of Army ownership.

The passages used to introduce each chapter are excerpted with minor editing and additions from a 1912 school annual entitled, *A School for Girls*. The letter opening Chapter Twelve describing the federal government's takeover of the school in 1942 to aid the war effort is genuine and printed verbatim. The public health bulletin also depicted in the chapter is fashioned after a similar U.S. Public Health Service study published in 1919 detailing a typhoid outbreak in the city of Rockville, Maryland, located a few miles west of Forest Glen.

Comments, opinions and questions about *Incident at Forest Glen* are welcome and can be sent directly to the author's attention at forestglen1921@ gmail.com.

Made in the USA
Middletown, DE
06 November 2018